Praise for Sharyn McCrumb's
bestselling novels

Ghost Riders

"Another tribute to the artful power McCrumb wields when she writes her Appalachian tales . . . as vivid as a campfire and every bit as inviting." —*Houston Chronicle*

"McCrumb is the true reenactor, re-creating a little known and fascinating part of the Civil War."
—*The New Orleans Times-Picayune*

"McCrumb's tapestry of voices is admirable . . . a notable addition to an oeuvre that explores her colorful Southern heritage." —*Rocky Mountain News*

"This novel . . . is enough to convert anyone into a Civil War buff . . . an absolutely fantastic novel that slips readers a serious historical mickey." —*The Tampa Tribune*

"Another epic ballad of a novel, a multitiered Civil War story that links past and present with an otherworldly twist. McCrumb writes high-spirited historical fiction, her lush, dense narratives shored up by thorough research and convincing period detail. Her latest is another harmonious, folksy blend of history and backwoods lore." —*Publishers Weekly*

"A compelling Civil War tale with a chilling twist. McCrumb proves once again to be an especially fine storyteller, and her characters' observations about war in general—and this war in particular—resonate. As well researched as it is told, this will appeal to Civil War buffs in addition to McCrumb's fans." —*Library Journal*

"Sprawling, multilayered . . . McCrumb brings alive a time in which nearly every family had relatives fighting on both Union and Confederate sides and peoples it with figures drawn from history." —*Kirkus Reviews*

"One of those books that makes you go back and reread passages just to soak in the power and the beauty of the words." —*The Florida Times-Union*

continued . . .

The Ballad of Frankie Silver

"Some stories wait more than a hundred years for the right teller to come along. . . . McCrumb shifts easily back and forth in time, combining police procedural with an old-fashioned historical narrative worthy of Dickens or Jane Austen." —*Asheville Citizen-Times*

"*The Ballad of Frankie Silver* . . . invites us to pull up a quilt and turn our faces to the fire . . . dense and lovely."
—*The New York Times Book Review*

The Rosewood Casket

"A tale artfully crafted, a novel written as folk art. With fluid writing and sensitive telling, McCrumb presents her Appalachian series as perfectly as dogwood in the spring."
—*Houston Chronicle*

"Suspenseful . . . spellbinding." —*The Washington Post*

She Walks These Hills

"Eloquent prose . . . a richly detailed novel. . . . In a triumph of plot construction, several lines converge in a remarkably dramatic final confrontation. . . . The reader can't wait to see how it all comes out, but is at the same time reluctant for the book to end." —*Los Angeles Times*

"Mesmerizes with haunting beauty."—*Chicago Sun-Times*

The Hangman's Beautiful Daughter

"Elegiac. . . . Ms. McCrumb writes with quiet fire and maybe a little mountain magic. . . . Like Nora, she plucks the mysteries from people's lives and works these dark narrative threads into Appalachian legends older than the hills. Like every true storyteller, she has the Sight."
—*The New York Times Book Review*

"A haunting novel . . . rich, complex . . . a major book by a major talent in the field." —*The Denver Post*

GHOST RIDERS

A NOVEL

Sharyn McCrumb

A SIGNET BOOK

SIGNET
Published by New American Library, a division of
Penguin Group (USA) Inc., 375 Hudson Street, New York, New York 10014, U.S.A.
Penguin Books Ltd, 80 Strand, London WC2R 0RL, England
Penguin Books Australia Ltd, 250 Camberwell Road,
Camberwell, Victoria 3124, Australia
Penguin Books Canada Ltd, 10 Alcorn Avenue, Toronto, Ontario, Canada M4V 3B2
Penguin Books (N.Z.) Ltd, Cnr Rosedale and Airborne Roads,
Albany, Auckland 1310, New Zealand

Penguin Books Ltd, Registered Offices:
80 Strand, London WC2R 0RL, England

Published by Signet, an imprint of New American Library, a division of Penguin
Group (USA) Inc. Previously published in a Dutton edition.

First Signet Printing, May 2004
10 9 8 7 6 5 4 3 2 1

Grateful acknowledgment is made for permission to reprint the following: An
excerpt from "When the Towers Fell" by Galway Kinnell, originally published
in *The New Yorker*.

Ⓟ REGISTERED TRADEMARK—MARCA REGISTRADA

Printed in the United States of America

To David K.

*Is there a mechanism of death
that so mutilates existence no one
gets over it not even the dead?*

—Galway Kinnell

Zebulon Baird Vance at twenty-eight years of age.
Clement Dowd, Life of Zebulon B. Vance, *Charlotte, 1897*

Malinda "Sam" Blalock in a photo taken some
twenty years after the Civil War.
*Southern Historical Collection, Wilson Library,
University of North Carolina at Chapel Hill*

Prologue: Rattler

The boy stood still in the moonlight watching the riders approach. The chill of the night air had shaken the last bit of sleep-stupor from him, and he shivered, feeling the wind on his legs and the sensation of his bare feet touching the rough boards of the porch, and knowing that he was not dreaming. He had stumbled outside to make his way to the privy, but now something—not a sound, more like a feeling—made him stop a few feet from the door, and for long minutes as he stood there he would forget the push in his bladder that had sent him out into the cold darkness of an October night.

Night riders.

Horses were not an everyday sight in the mountains nowadays, as they had been in his daddy's time. Now that the Great War had ended in Europe, the world had changed. People talked about aeroplanes and automobiles and store-bought clothes. Every year brought more Model A's into the county, and those folks that didn't run an automobile could take the train into Johnson City or Asheville if they needed to go. You sent money to the mail-order catalogue, and the postman would bring you the goods, all parceled up in brown paper, whatever you'd asked for. They called it "the wish book." But nobody ever wished for the old days, not in these mountains. They all wanted the future to get here double quick.

But tonight was an echo of the old days . . . there were horsemen at the edge of the woods.

The boy wondered who these riders were, out on the ridge past midnight, far from a road and miles from the next farm. He could make out three of them just this side of the trees beyond the smokehouse, but in the faint light of the crescent moon their features were indistinguishable. They carried no lantern, and they rode in silence. It took the boy three heartbeats longer to register the fact that the horses made no sound either. He heard no rustle of grass, no snapping of twigs beneath their hoofs.

One of the riders detached himself from the group by the woods and trotted toward the porch where the boy stood. He was a tall, gaunt man in a long greatcoat and scuffed leather boots, and he had a calculating way of looking through narrowed eyes that froze the boy to the spot like a snake-charmed bird. The rider looked to be in his twenties, with dark hair and black whiskers outlining his chin, as if he were growing a beard by default and not by design. The boy stared at the face, a pale oval in the moonlight, and he forgot to move or cry out.

The man smiled down at him as if he had trouble remembering how. "Evenin', boy," he said in a soft mountain drawl. "What's your name then?"

"Rat—they called me Rattler, mister." It took him two tries to get the sound to come out of his throat.

The rider grinned. "Rattler, huh? Mean as a snake, are you, boy?"

The boy lifted his chin. Even if he was shivering in his nightshirt, he was on his own porch and he would not cower before a stranger. "I don't reckon I'm mean," he said. "But I give salt for salt."

"Fair enough." The dark man looked amused. "I guess I do the same." He glanced back at the woods where his companions waited, motionless, shadows in moonlight. "And you'd be—what? About twelve?"

"About," said the boy. He would be eleven in January.

"Well, snake-boy, what do you say? You want to ride with us?"

The boy shrugged. "Got no horse."

"Reckon we could rustle you up one." The smile again, cold as a moonbeam.

The boy hesitated. "You never said who you are, mister."

"I figured you knew. You've got good eyes on you, boy. And you don't scare easy, do you? So, what do you say? About riding with us, I mean."

"I—" The boy took a step backward until he stood in the doorway, under the iron horseshoe his grandaddy had nailed up over the front door. "Mister, I reckon my momma would skin me alive if I was to go off at night without telling somebody. And if I was to ask, I reckon the answer'd be no, anyhow."

"Well, women are mostly like that," said the rider, smiling again. He looked over his shoulder again at the shadows beyond the smokehouse. "Not all of them are, though. But most. Good evening to you, boy." With that he turned his horse and trotted back to the edge of the woods.

The boy could hear the oak branches scraping against the tin roof of the house, and he heard the rustle of the wind in the bushes that flanked the porch, but even though he stood stock still and strained to listen, he did not hear the sound of hoofbeats in the dirt. A moment later, the mewing of his mother's cat startled him, and he turned to see where it was. The cat hissed at him and puffed up its fur until it looked like a dandelion. When he looked out again across the yard the riders were gone.

He told no one about this midnight encounter, and it was years before he realized who he had seen on that October night. He started keeping a mason jar beside his bed so he wouldn't have to go outside to the privy during the night.

You would have thought that losing the war one time would be enough for them. You certainly would have thought that, wouldn't you?

As much sorrow and ruin and hatred among neighbors as was brought to these here hills by that sorry war, you would have thought they'd all be glad they missed out on it by being born a hundred years or so after the fact. They ought to be shut of it by now, ready to let the past bury its dead, and get on with the business of making a less terrible future. But no.

Oh, no.

They will not turn loose of that war.

Nearly every sunny weekend that God sends will find these hills swarming with summer soldiers and sunshine patriots ready to take up arms and take aim at some other tomfool lunatic on account of his uniform being a different color from theirs. They're shootin' blanks this time, of course. I reckon that's an improvement.

When the weather gets warm, there's usually a crowd of reenactors up to something in my neck of the woods. They drive up in their Chevy pickups or their fancy SUVs, stash their cell phones under the driver's seat, and haul out their bedrolls and pitch their tents to make camp so that they can spend the weekend shooting their Springfield rifles at defenseless trees.

I go out there right often to pass the time with the fellows camping out, if I don't have anything better to do. I don't participate in the hostilities, you understand. I just go for the company. I've been living out in these woods for many long years now, and every now and again I get a craving to be sociable. I get right much company, you understand, but that's more work than visiting.

People around here know that I have the Sight, and that I know a thing or two about healing on account of my Cherokee blood, so they come to me right along for poultices and tonics, or advice—with young people it's love and with older folks it's money. I even get folks from as far away as Asheville and Knoxville these days. Earth-shoe people, I call 'em. They want to know if my potions are macrobiotic or holistic or whatever the new buzzword is at the time. I just smile. City people used to look down on the old ways, putting all their faith in the doctoring tribe at the medical center, but lately they've begun to wonder what we know that doctors don't, and they come. One of 'em told me that living in a shack with no indoor plumbing "added to my rustic charm." That fellow didn't need a laxative, but I gave him one anyhow.

Helping people in trouble is my calling, but by and large troubled folk are not good company, so every now and again I go sit a spell with regular folks just for the novelty of society. Most of the time I prefer the deer and the possums who are my neighbors, but a change is as good as a rest, they say, and I give it a try every now and again. When the reenactors take to the woods come spring, I go and visit them of an evening.

I generally know when they are coming, and as much noise as those jokers make, it would be hard for me not to know when they had arrived.

We sit and chew the fat for a spell about the current events as of eighteen sixty-something, which they call "getting into character." I don't generally say much since I haven't studied up on the fine print of history like they have, but they're all too busy showing off to notice. I reckon an audience is just as important as an actor, anyhow.

When dinnertime rolls around, they put my name in the pot, and I accept the invitation to sit supper, because I am not one to turn down a free meal as long as it's offered as hospitality and not for charity. Sometimes I bring along a sack of mushrooms or some field greens and ramps so as not to feel too beholden to them. That always delights them more than the food they spent good money for. They claim my wild plants put them in the spirit of the old days, because it is just the sort of food that the real soldiers would have eaten. Their own grub isn't too bad, on account of they can afford to buy good cuts of meat to start with, which is more than I can say, but at least I don't spend my weekends *pretending* to be poor and dirty. And I am not fool enough to tell them that if they want the flavor of soldiers' rations there ought to be maggots in the meat. No, I'm just as happy with Grade-A fresh beef, thank you all the same. Well, the reenactors like me. They say I am au-then-tic.

"Rattler, it might as well be 1862 for you," one of the pretend officers told me once. "You live out in the woods in a—uh—"

"Shack," I said. "I know it's a shack, boy. But it's paid for."

He winced at that. He's a lawyer. I reckon his house payments would make your nose bleed. "Well, a shack, then," he said. "You have no electricity or running water anyhow. It's no stretch at all for you to get into character as a citizen of the nineteenth century. You're practically there already."

I just smiled at him to let him know he hadn't hurt my feelings, but I did not tell him how right he was. And how sometimes for me that war is a lot closer than those play-actors think. They got a glimpse of it once, though. One time they did.

*   *   *

He was the most authentic-looking reenactor those fools had ever seen. All of them agreed on that. He showed up around dusk on the first day of the encampment for the Battle of Zollicoffer.

In the real war Zollicoffer hadn't amounted to much. They fought it here in east Tennessee in 1862 and managed to have a Confederate general present, but hardly anybody has ever heard of him. General Zollicoffer, as a matter of fact. See? I told you.

The battle—scholars seldom bother to mention it— hardly rates a sentence in a general account of the Civil War, they tell me, but since there hadn't been many battles fought in Appalachia, and since this one had been the first real Union victory of the war, the local reenactors seized upon it as an excuse to stage a sham battle in east Tennessee. They didn't have many other options, because "the mountainous terrain was not conducive to large-scale warfare," as one of 'em told me.

It was, however, conducive to ambushes and guerrilla warfare. Nobody had to tell me that. The bad feelings lingered on right up through my childhood, so I knew about that part, all right. In the Civil War the armies of both sides stayed out of these mountains as much as they could, leaving the latter-day reenactors only a few skirmishes to choose from to display their skills in simulated warfare. Maybe a battle wasn't really representative of how the war played out in the mountain South, but it was what people expected to see and it's what reenactors do. If you reenacted what really happened in the Smoky Mountains during the Civil War, I expect they'd call you a terrorist.

Plenty of the folks around these parts perished in the war, but either they got conscripted and marched off to Virginia to do their dying, or else they stayed home on small farms and starved in private. Some of them died close to home in an ambush or a shoot-out, but those battles were so personal and parochial that it's hard to tell if the potentates on either side ever knew or cared what transpired. The local people knew, of course, about the war as an excuse for murder and the feuds that grew out of such goings-on. It took most of a hundred years for folks around here to forget it. Nobody would thank the reenactors for reopening those old wounds. People want their wars and their history clean and neat, like it is in the movies. So they do little battles—not feuds and ambushes.

Every year as a way to celebrate—and simplify— local history, some of the local war-gamers refought the Battle of Zollicoffer in a well-choreographed and widely publicized weekend event, preceded by an exhibition encampment popular with local school groups. The real battle took place in January 1862, but winter is hardly the time for pageantry. Few spectators and no tourists would be there to observe the ritual, and so, for everyone's convenience, they elected to reschedule the battle in a more temperate month. Later on in the summer, a couple of the more dedicated and affluent local reenactors would make the long drive up I-81 through Virginia to join the uniformed hordes at Antietam and Gettysburg, and perhaps even appear as extras in a movie, but this little local set-to was a yearly tradition, the season-opener for the sunshine soldiers.

Several thousand troops had participated in the real battle—the Second Minnesota, the Fifteenth Mississippi, and a host of local Tennesseans defending home turf—but the twenty-first-century version of the engagement was carried out by fewer than one hundred men, roughly divided between Union and Confederate forces. If the sides were too unbalanced, some reenactors had to change sides to even things up. Many a soldier kept an extra uniform in the trunk of his car just in case he had to change sides for the weekend. (Now *that's* close to an authentic representation of the war in these mountains.) The Union army had won the original battle, which was a good thing these days, since political correctness has replaced witch trials and communist hearings as the preferred way to torment our fellow countrymen.

The opposing forces pitched their tents about a mile from one another along a winding dirt road that alternated between fields and forest. I was visiting on the Confederate side that weekend, mainly because Jeff McCullough was a better cook than his Union counterpart at the other camp. Sometimes Jeff is a Yankee. He says he doesn't much care which army he's assigned to, because he had ancestors on both sides, same as I did.

"By reenacting I'm not trying to get even or to change the outcome of that far-off war," he told me once. "I just want to understand it from the inside out. I think that by sweating in a wool jacket of butternut-gray and firing a muzzle-loader until the barrel burns my hand, I can somehow crawl inside the skin of a long-lost soldier so that his thoughts will somehow become mine."

"Well," I said, "you're a newspaper man by trade, so perhaps you have a longing to experience something instead of always being the observer."

He thought it over. "Could be," he said. "Or maybe it's just that I missed my war—missed any war—and so I'm left with some sort of genetic longing to experience battle to validate my manhood. Combat is our childbirth."

"This isn't the same as a real war, Jeff," I told him. "Not childbirth—just adoption."

He smiled. "I know that. The enemy is firing blanks at me, and my comrades are not my brothers until death releases us, but only until the end of the weekend, when we will all go home to our central air conditioning and cable television. My battles are scripted. I have seen Blaine Kerry's leg blown off a dozen times in mock battles, and I barely hear the spectators' screams anymore when it happens. I know he lost that leg in a tractor accident as a teenager, and he detaches the prosthesis for dramatic effect in midbattle. The sight no longer moves me to fear or horror or pity. And yet . . . And yet . . ." He shrugged his skinny shoulders. "You probably think it's silly of us to even try."

"Not silly," I said. *Dangerous, maybe,* I was thinking, but I didn't say so out loud.

At dusk on Saturday, the troops had settled in for the evening. The sightseers had left for the day, and the boys were relaxing after a blistering afternoon in which they had sweltered in wool uniforms and carried around fifty pounds of equipment in the hot sun. Now they could relax, although most of them elected to stay in character as nineteenth-century soldiers, because that was the whole point of the exercise, wasn't it? I played along with them, a small price to pay for a good dinner and a couple of home-brewed beers.

At the Confederate tent nearest the dirt road, McCullough had set a kettle of Irish stew on the campfire to simmer, and half a dozen of us were sitting around it. The rest were doing the little chores that soldiers had to do in the field: polishing brass belt buckles, cleaning weapons. If they had been real soldiers they might have been picking lice out of their hair as well, but since I was their guest for supper, I decided to hold my peace about these little inaccuracies of theirs. It's not like I wanted them to have lice, and I was afraid that if I brought up the subject some over-zealous fool might take me up on the suggestion.

McCullough had his reporter's notebook out, and he was fooling around with the lead of the feature story he was fixing to write about the event.

None of us ever remembered seeing the stranger approach the campfire, but then we hadn't been paying any particular attention to the road. No sentries stood guard for the evening, because the spectators had all gone home, and the war was not scheduled to begin again until midmorning tomorrow.

"Evenin', boys," he said to us. His voice sounded gruff and shy—just right for an east Tennessean, and so was his accent.

Jeff McCullough glanced up at the new soldier a little annoyed, probably wondering if he had come to cadge some of our stew, but the sight of him faded the frown right off his face. This fellow could have walked straight out of a movie, he was so au-then-tic. Short and fish-belly pale, he looked to be in his twenties, as most of the real soldiers would have been, while our present-day reenactors have infantry men older than the generals were in the real war. Brigadier General Jeb Stuart never reached thirty. Fact. Contemplating that home truth spoiled many a birthday of mine, but as time went on and I outlived Lee, Grant, and Lincoln to boot without too awful much to show for it, I stopped minding so much.

Whoever this runty young fellow was, he was good. His uniform was as dirty and ragged, its material and cut as real as any you'd see in a museum display. It probably *was* real, they were all thinking. Raving hell-bent collectors can get hold of vintage clothing, and sometimes they're reckless enough to wear it to the reenactments. The wonder of it was that the uniform fit him. That was rare. Mostly you see hats and belt buckles that are real—but a uniform? This fellow couldn't have been taller than five feet five inches and he was so skinny that it hurt to look at him. His cheekbones stuck out of pale skin and his eyes were sunk in shadows.

"I felt like giving him my dinner, he was so gaunt," Jeff said later. "I had to admire anybody that perfectly kitted out. I was even thinking the fellow might rate a couple of paragraphs in my feature story."

"Great outfit!" one of the new recruits called out to the stranger.

He didn't react, which was absolutely right, because the comment had been an anachronism. (I picked up on that word after the first two dozen or so mistakes I made in conversation, but now I can talk old-fashioned with the best of them.) A real soldier should have been bewildered by such a remark, and this boy played his part to perfection. He looked at the stew pot for a couple of seconds and licked his lips, but then he kind of shook his head, and he said, "Boys, can you tell me where I might find Colonel Walthall's camp?"

McCullough nodded. "Fifteenth Mississippi." There were about twenty guys from Johnson City who opted to portray that regiment just for this event. It would make sense that he was with them. They have a fair number of students from the college in their outfit. This was probably one of them vegetarian joggers from East Tennessee State, they were thinking.

Everybody had stopped what they were doing and were staring at the authentic-looking soldier. Nobody went over to him, though, because they were all settled by the fire and dead tired to boot. They just muttered hellos and kept gawking.

Me, I didn't say word one to him.

"Yeah," McCullough was saying, "the Fifteenth. You're on the right track, buddy, but you've still got a ways to go. They're encamped along this road, around the bend, and then about another quarter of a mile. Over by the creek at the edge of the woods. You can't miss it."

McCullough stood up and pointed the way down the road, a pale ribbon in the twilight. In another moment he might have offered to show him the way, just for an excuse to talk to him, but the stranger touched his hand to his cap with a nod of thanks and trudged away alone. I wasn't sorry to see him go.

McCullough settled back on the log next to the stew pot, which cheered me up, because I don't like the thought of my dinner being burned on account of a newspaperman's curiosity.

"Damn, that guy was good," said Wade Jessup. "I can look as dirty as that, but damn if I can look that skinny."

I didn't say anything. *Just let it go,* I thought.

"McCullough, you ought to put that fella's picture in the newspaper," somebody else said.

Jeff nodded. "Maybe I will. I'll hunt him up tomorrow sometime. Now, does anybody want to taste this stew before I dish it up?"

Another couple of minutes went by while we argued about whether or not the potatoes were done enough, and then we saw another figure heading up the road in the opposite direction—toward the parking lot. Even in twilight it was easy to recognize Jim Roberts's paunch, and we knew he was on his way to his pickup truck for more beer. There wouldn't be any catcalls about that, though. Everybody took it easy on old Jim, because we knew he came out here and played war to get away from the real battles at home. He kept his beer and his troubles to himself.

Old Jim gave us a wobbly salute and started to walk on by, when Bill Shull hailed him. "Roberts, get over here, you sorry excuse for a Yankee sergeant!"

Roberts ambled over, took a whiff of our dinner pot and shook his head. "We got macaroni and cheese over the way. It's not authentic, but it sticks to the ribs."

"Hey, Jim," Wade said, "speaking of authentic, when you came up the road there, did you notice whether that guy you passed made it back to the Fifteenth Mississippi?"

"Just now?" Roberts shook his head. "Didn't see anybody on the road," he said.

"It's not that dark."

"No. I could see fine. There just wasn't anybody there, that's all."

"You had to have passed this guy," McCullough said. "He was heading in the direction you just came from. And you had to have noticed him. Best-looking soldier you ever saw—clothes, build, everything. The real McCoy . . ."

"The real Hatfield, you mean, Jeff. He was Confederate." That was a good one, and they all had a laugh about it.

Roberts shrugged, wondering if the Rebels were putting him on. "There was nobody on that road, boys. Now I'm going for my beer."

He trudged on up the road toward his truck, and everybody just sat there and watched him go. Nobody said a word for five minutes after that. I don't think anybody wanted to be the first to say what they were all thinking. Then they looked over at me, because word has got around that I have the Sight, not that anybody cares to mention it much on social occasions.

"Well?" said Jessup, peering at me in the twilight.

"Well, what?" I said, taking a mouthful of stew and chewing it slow as I could.

"Well, why didn't Jim Roberts see that soldier on the road, Rattler? *You* saw him, didn't you?"

I chewed as long as I could, but they kept on looking at me, so finally I said, "Yeah. I seen him all right. I didn't speak to him, though."

"Why not?"

" 'Cause I don't hold with talking to dead people," I said.

After that they got all quiet.

Jeff McCullough didn't put that incident in the article he wrote, because he figured he'd never live it down if he did. But I always wondered if that poor lost soldier ever found the Fifteenth Mississippi. The real one.

In all the stories our local reenactors told around the campfire, they never said another word about that lost soldier on the road, and I wasn't about to bring it up, but I've always known that the war's not over.

I never did tell them what else I see. About the

evenings when I stand in the doorway of my cabin, looking out at the woods graying into mist, and out of the shadows in the distance I see them ride by.

They stopped for me one time when I was a young'un, but I was a-skeered to go. I wonder what I would say if they was to ask me now?

The big fellow in the greatcoat comes first with the rifle at his side, followed by one or two of his men—and then—last of all—*her*. She's so little her legs barely reach below her horse's belly, and the pistol on her hip looks too big for her to have lifted, but I know it wasn't. She wears a thick coat, high leather boots, and breeches just like a man, but there's no mistaking her—those eyes, the sharp cheekbones, and her little girl hands on the reins. Her dark hair has come loose under a man's hat. It streams out behind her as she rides, and her pale face glows in the moonlight. For nights on end I'll stand in the dark yard, just waiting, but they don't always come. I've never worked out the pattern of it. Sometimes they come, but mostly they don't. And they never take any notice of me watching. I tried hiding a time or two to see if they'd come or if they might stop, but that never seemed to make any difference.

I don't hold with talking to dead people, but still and all I would give anything to exchange words with *her*. To see her draw rein and turn around so that I could look into those eyes. I'd ask her where it is they're riding to, or maybe I'd just wish her well or ask if she's content with this endless ride or if she wants me to try to help her. I want to say, *You lived through the war, hon. It's over. Don't you remember?*

She never stops, though. She rides on by, looking straight ahead, as if I was the ghost instead of her. And when I try to hail her, the words freeze in my throat so that I can only stand there in the darkness and watch until they disappear into the woods.

I never said anything about the night riders to my

reenactor friends at the encampment. It isn't that I was afeered they wouldn't believe me. I was more a-scairt that they would. Bad enough that the war is not over for them that fought it without having these toy soldiers out there a-trying to hunt up the real ones.

Zebulon Vance

What was I supposed to do? Shoot them? I confess that the thought never even occurred to me until later. When I saw her standing there at attention before me with her shirt hitched up to her chin and those little bird's-egg breasts pointing up at me, it was all I could do to keep from roaring like a muleskinner until tears of laughter wet my cheeks. Now after that, I could hardly have assumed a commanderly pose of rage and ordered the pair of them to their deaths, could I? Why, I would have felt a fool and a hypocrite to do such a thing. So I sent them along home, him for his skin rash, which I do not doubt was contracted on purpose to get him out of the army, and her for the more permanent infirmity of being a woman.

So I spared their lives. Later the army shot people for less, but those two ran afoul of the bureaucracy early in the war, before desperation had made us cruel, and so they escaped the worst that was to come. By the time the war became a nightmare, I had resigned my command for the greater comfort of public office, but with even more onerous duties to perform, and still more young lives charged on my scroll. And what became of those two young fools? They went back to the mountains, as far as I know, and probably never amounted to much, but still I never quite forgot them. They weren't much more than children by the look of them in '62, so small and brave, and since they hailed from the Carolina backcountry as I did, you could bounce rocks off their pride.

The truth is, they reminded me of me, before I got bit with the bug of civilization.

Five years after that incident I'd meet another backcountry soldier who seemed to mirror my younger self, and a path I might have taken in my wilder youth. I could not save him, though, and in my heart of hearts I did not believe him worth saving, but I hope I did my best for him.

Over the years I grew accustomed to the idea of people dying, sometimes on account of my orders or my inadequacies, perhaps, but I did spare those two, for not all the military regulations in the world could persuade me that they deserved to die.

I have come a long way from my birthplace in that log cabin on Reems Creek, the loveliest of all the valleys that I have ever beheld. I suppose my sojourn in the little mountain resort of Warm Springs was the making of me—or the ruination, some folks might say. Anyhow it took me far beyond the shallows of that frontier life I had been born to, and sent me out into the flatlands and onto the flood of political prosperity—and on to a sea of troubles as well.

Picture me in the summer of 1848, standing there before the front desk of the Warm Springs Hotel in the mountains of Madison County, North Carolina—too skinny for my height and frame, too much wrist showing out of my coat sleeves, dark hair slicked back to cover my frayed shirt collar. I must have looked like the rawboned country boy I was. But even at age fifteen and never once out of the mountains, I was book learned and clever, and I could boast a few champions in my bloodline—I did boast of it! Better than that: I was born with a knack for sizing people up, for knowing what they wanted, and then being that for as long as it served me well. I have a genius for seeming.

I could tell that the stern man behind the desk was not impressed with the gangly youth who stood before him, hat in hand, seeking employment. He frowned up at me as if my very height were a personal affront to him, and I'm sure that my rustic country clothes, clean though they were, left no favorable impression either.

"I am Mr. John E. Patton, boy," he said after a long silence in which I felt that I had been measured and found wanting. "I own this hotel. It's what they call a resort, a summer gathering place for persons of wealth and breeding. Do you follow me, boy?"

"Yes, sir, I do." My eyes lit up with a spark of hope. I needed this job.

The man's eyes narrowed. "Where did you say you were from?"

"Madison, sir. My father died a few years back, leaving Mother with next to no money and six of us at home to be fed and clothed, so we had sold the farm and moved to Lapland."

Mr. Patton gave me an appraising stare. "Lapland. I see. And you came from there . . . to work here?"

Lapland is a village on the drovers road that leads over the mountains to Tennessee to bring cattle for sale to the seaboard cities to the east. At our little place in Lapland we took in lodgers to earn our keep, and I had left off schooling at Washington College in order to go to work. I understood Mr. Patton's look of surmise. There are things closer to home that a boy of sixteen might have done to earn money for his mother and the younger ones at home. With the drovers road running cattle right through Madison County, there were jobs aplenty to be had for a hardy young man. The stockman's life held many charms for a country youth with its promise of horses to ride, the freedom of the wilderness, and the adventures of a life on the trail. The spell of the drovers road was almost as bewitching as the thought of running away to sea, but I could not trade my birthright for the joys of youth. The wild streak in my nature made me long for such an untrammeled life, but the Scots practicality from my mother's side of the family kept me in the traces.

"Warm Springs caters only to the finest members of society," Mr. Patton was saying. "They come here to the mountains to improve their health by taking the waters from our mineral springs, but they don't want to experience the privations of frontier life while they are about it. We aim to make this a place that could hold its own with the establishments of Charleston or Boston or Philadelphia."

"Yes, sir," I said. I had no notion of what charms were held by the inns in those great cities, but I was happy to learn. Indeed I could not imagine any establishment more majestic than the Warm Springs Hotel. It looked like a palace to me. It was a white, wood-frame structure, two stories high, with columns and long, covered porches, and it stood in a wide meadow where the waters of a wide creek flowed into the mighty French Broad River. The front of the hotel faced the river and the mountains beyond, affording its patrons as fine a view as anyone could wish for. They never lacked for guests.

"Now, boy, I want a clerk who is honest, and who works cheap, but that's not all I want. I could have had a dozen fellows in need of employment if my requirements ended with those two attributes."

I stole a glance around me, taking in the velvet upholstery in the lobby and the white statue of three Greek goddesses sitting on the table near the fireplace, and I realized that what Mr. Patton really craved for his back-country hotel was tone. He had the cleanest water and the purest air in the world. He had a view that painters came to capture, and he had the finest game and produce to grace his dining room. All that he could wish for to make this paradise complete was an air of gentility to substantiate the claim that his hotel was the equal of any in the great eastern cities—and to justify the prices charged on account of it. Well, that suited me right down to the ground. Tone was a thing I aspired to study, for it is the passport to society and the catechism of prosperity.

That's why I was here. I knew where I was going, and a job like this would better prepare me to get there than some other occupations I could have turned my hand to. It wouldn't be the carefree existence of a stockman, but I believed I would go farther behind the desk at that hotel than they would go in a lifetime of six-hundred-mile cattle drives.

"Have you any ambition, boy?" Mr. Patton was saying.

"Yes, sir," I said, standing up straighter. Of course I did. What a tomfool thing to ask me. Why else was I here, chafing in a starched collar and new boots, instead of spitting tobacco juice at copperheads on the cattle drive. "I'm not just a—a rustic, sir."

He raised his eyebrows and looked me up and down with a hint of a smirk, but if he had planned to say something about my looks being deceiving on that score, he thought better of it. Instead he said, "Who did you say your people are?"

I smiled to show that I was not afraid of the question. Had expected it, in fact. In the end it always came down to that with the lace and linen folk: *Who are your people?* I had a ready answer. "I come from good family, sir." *As good as yours, I'll warrant,* I was thinking, but I had the wit not to say so out loud. "My grandfather was a patriot who fought in the Revolution, name of David Vance, my father's father. He wintered at Valley Forge with George Washington and fought with him at Brandywine, Germantown, and Monmouth. When he was ordered back to North Carolina late in the war, he fought at Kings Mountain with Colonel Sevier. After the war my grandfather Vance served in the state's General Assembly, and when he was done with that, he retired to farm nigh onto a thousand acres in the mountains near Asheville. Reems Creek. I was born there."

Mr. Patton grunted. "A likely lineage, if you can live up to it, I suppose. What about your father?"

"He had his war as well—the one in 1812, but he fought no battles, and thereafter he lived a quiet life as a farmer. He has been dead these past five years, leaving me with no prospects except my wits and the will to get on in the world."

"But you, I take it, have the inclination to be more than a farmer?"

"I do, sir." I wasn't prepared to say what exactly I had plans to be, though lawyering appealed to me, even then. It seemed to be the road to every means of power, and I meant to take it.

I hoped he wouldn't ask me for any more family history. There was a deal more to be said about my kinfolks, but as it was a bit colorful for as sedate a place as the Warm Springs Hotel, I thought best to leave it out. Nothing to be ashamed of, though. We are a feisty lot, my family: My great-aunt Rebecca had been scalped by Indians in her youth, but she managed to survive the attack, and she lived on to a ripe old age with no worse effects than a little bald spot on the crown of her head. We are brave, but we have tempers, as well. My father's older brother, for whom my own brother Robert was named, was so enraged at having been defeated in an election to Congress, that he challenged the winner,

Sam Carson, to a pistol duel. Uncle Robert was killed in that fight, but since Sam Carson had Davy Crockett to coach him in marksmanship, there's no shame in that, and no wonder, either. That family story did little to govern my temper, but it did counsel prudence, and made me look to resolve my disputes with measures other than dueling.

Mr. Patton looked thoughtful. "I wonder if ambition is a seed that can be planted in a child," he murmured, "or is it a trait linked to pedigree that must be bred in the bone, like the lineage of a fine blood horse?"

"I don't know, sir," I said softly, for I knew that he wasn't really putting the question to me. I have thought about that question from time to time since then, and it seems to me that much of the substance in our character is determined by the folk we spring from, for I cannot think that my success in life is due entirely to my own credit.

Much was expected of a Vance, I learned at an early age. Although my parents had little money and a mountain farm that wasn't worth much, they both set a store by learning, and they meant to see that all their children got as much of it as they could hold. From my grandfather Vance our family had inherited a fine library of five hundred volumes and my mother put it to good use, for though she had no great pretensions to learning herself, my mother valued education above all else. When we were small she would gather us around the hearth each evening and read to us from the classics. Sitting in a circle of lamplight, her head bowed over a volume of Roman history or a book of sermons, or the plays of Shakespeare, she would read us the long sonorous sentences, filled with words that we had never heard from neighbors or folk in the town. We would sound out these words and puzzle them out from their roots in Latin so that we would know them again if we met them on a page. I heard a wealth of such fine words at my mother's knee. From listening to the tides of oratory that swept over me there, I learned the art of public speaking at an age when humbler boys are learning to shoot or track deer through the forest.

"And you can read and cipher, you say?"

"As well as any," I said. "Better than some. I have some Latin as well. From Washington College."

At this Mr. Patton looked more impressed than he ought to have been, for my early education was haphazard at best. In the rural backwoods where we lived, good schooling was not easy to come by. When I was six my brother Robert and I were sent off to school some seven miles from home at Flat Creek. There we boarded with Uncle Miah—Nehemiah Blackstock, that was—and I reckon we learned more discipline than book lore in his tutelage, but still I managed to scrape together a few crumbs of knowledge to build upon later on. It was in 1843 that I was sent to over the mountain to Tennessee to Washington College near Jonesborough as one of eighty students. Calling it a college did not make it one. I don't suppose anybody ever emerged from there with more than a secondary school education, but it was miles ahead of the places I'd been before. It was there that I found that I had a love for debate and a gift for making speeches, but my training there was cut short when Daddy died and the money ran out.

I had no money for further study, much as I wanted to continue. There was much of life that I could not learn in a frontier cabin, and I reckoned that some of it could be found at that fine hotel on the banks of the French Broad River.

James Patton frowned at me while he thought. At last he said, "Well, you're young, but you look like you can do a man's work. See that your hands are clean and your boots shined, boy, and go home and fetch your belongings. You start tomorrow."

That was the opening of the first door, and perhaps

the first time that I had used my wits and charm to impress one of the patricians. I would see to it that it wouldn't be the last, because I knew there were a good many more doors between our cabin at Lapland and the mansion I was bound for.

I settled in to work at the hotel then, and I put my whole heart and mind into my duties, for I wanted to give satisfaction and to earn my wages, but really I thought myself simply continuing my education with a different kind of studying. Getting paid for it was just gravy on the meat, as far as I was concerned. Right away I learned not to say "horse overs" for *hors d'oeuvre*, and to use the word "limb" instead of "arm" or "leg," for the guests were delicate in their sensibilities. Just about any kind of plain speaking was out of bounds there. I knew that swearing was not to be thought of, but I did think words like "got sick" and "died" ought to pass muster, but no: you had to say *indisposed* for the one, and *passed away* for t'other. It beat Latin for sheer perplexing obscurity, but you can learn a foreign language tolerably well by sheer perseverance, and it was a foreign language, and by God I learned it.

Pretty soon I could tell the governesses and the French maids from the highborn ladies by the gowns they wore and their manner of speaking, and a week or so after that, I could tell Charleston from Raleigh, planter's daughter from judge's wife, with a glance at their apparel.

I was right to seek employment there. Warm Springs was a wondrous place for a mountain boy to get a look at the world beyond these hills, for in the summer the hotel catered to the gentry from the flatlands to the east. Rich men from Wilmington and Richmond and Charleston sent their families to the mountains for the summer, often coming themselves for as much time as their businesses would permit. In lace and linen the summer people came to the high country to escape the breathless heat of a Southern summer and all the miasmas that went with it. They brought their fine city ways with them, and their magazines and their talk of the world outside, and I took it all in, stored it up like treasures in heaven, for future use.

It was a marvel to me that women who had daughters about my own age could still look like girls themselves, with pretty, unlined faces and soft, white hands. I was accustomed to seeing the farm wives of the settlements hereabout—old at thirty, with gap-toothed smiles and sun-browned faces as wrinkled and sere as dried apples. There wasn't such a difference in the men, I thought, for our mountain people run from lean to gaunt, so the men carry their years with grace and vigor, while many a city merchant I see here looks like a tusk hog in a tailcoat, and he pants for breath after one flight of steps. They are a sorry sight, but I will take my chances on ending up in a similar fashion if attaining prosperity means acquiring such a wife as theirs.

I had not been in the employ of the hotel for very many weeks before I began to be in search of a likely candidate, in fact. One could work for a hundred years at honest labor and never make a fraction of the money one could acquire by uttering the simple phrase "I do." I said as much one evening to Sam Robertson, a local farm boy who worked in the stables at the hotel. One evening when our duties were over, the two of us walked down to the banks of the French Broad River for a smoke and a little time off from being so damned civilized. Sometimes when it got too hot for comfort, we'd go for a swim in the river. The guests bathed in a special pool filled with water piped in from the mineral spring, but we were "the help," and we weren't allowed in the pool. That was for the quality folks who paid to stay here, and truth to tell, we weren't too keen on the thought of soaking with the guests anyhow. You had to wear too many clothes to use their pool. When we went for a swim in the river, we were careful to do it out of sight of the hotel grounds, though, because I am sure that if they had spotted us, there would have been complaints about our lack of decorum. I think those people sit up nights trying to think up new rules to keep folks from acting naturally.

I stretched out on the bank and gazed up at the stars. "It's peaceful out here," I said, taking a deep breath of cold mountain air into my lungs. "Still, I ought to be back at the hotel studying the guest register. Half a dozen newcomers arrived today. I like to know all the guests by name. The middling folk set a store by that, and the really rich ones expect it as their right."

"So you will oblige them." Sam laughed. "I swear, Vance, you run yourself harder than anybody I ever saw. You're like a stray dog with tin cans tied to its tail."

"Ambition," I said. "I must have been born with it. It's a curse, isn't it? Why I could'a been a stockman or a card sharp if it weren't for that. That'd be the life, wouldn't it, Sam?"

"Not for you. You haven't got the hang of being poor."

"I ought to have," I said, trying not to sound bitter about it. "I've had a lifetime of practice."

"That may be, but I don't reckon it suits you." Sam was one of eight children who grew up on a steep and rocky mountain farm. Getting a couple of square meals a day of hotel cooking and a bed to himself was his idea of luxury, and he had no higher goal in life. He knew that I was different on that score, and he viewed my eternal discontent as a pitiable affliction in an otherwise boon companion. Sam was generous enough to overlook my failure to be content with my lot, and I in turn did not try to convert him to diligence, for I judged him to be happier in penury and obscurity than I was in my attempts to escape it.

"You don't like having the quality folks outrank you, do you?" said Sam, sounding amused about it. "It galls you. You never say anything, but it shows. You're always watching 'em and studying 'em, trying to find a way in. You watch them like a fox, Vance. I reckon this hotel is your henhouse."

That stung. He was so right that I had to be careful to give a soft answer so that he would not know his barb had hit home. "Well, now, ambition is a virtue, I've always thought," I said. "Don't they preach from the pulpit against idleness and wasting one's God-given talents?"

"I don't know," said Sam. "I always thought that if God had wanted me to be a gentleman, He would'a made me one."

"Heaven helps those who help themselves," I shot back. "Anyhow, we don't have royalty here in America, so I don't reckon the hotel guests we see here are aristocrats. Just because their ancestors saved them the trouble of having to rustle up their own money, that doesn't make this bunch of folks into lords and ladies."

"Well, they sure act like it does."

"I know they do. They behave like they all belong to the same club, don't they? They have their secret rituals and their code words to keep outsiders at bay. That's how they can tell who belongs and who doesn't."

Sam said, "What kind of code words?"

"Well, I only know some of them, but I'm working on it. They say a thing in French when putting it in English would sound too harsh, or else they'll throw in a phrase in Latin—like saying *tempus fugit,* when they mean 'it's getting late.' Or they set a store by whether you put the milk in your teacup before you put in the tea."

"Huh!" said Sam. "What difference does it make? It's all going to get mixed together anyhow."

"I told you, Sam. It's a code, so they can tell who belongs and who doesn't."

"Well, it sounds like foolishness to me. I can't see any way to make sense of it, or any reason to try."

"Somebody who is young, and smart, and willing to learn ought to be able to get inside that charmed circle. I hope so, anyhow. I'm studying about it."

"I think you need to be rich, though," said Sam. "It can't be as easy as just learning fine words."

I laughed at that. Rich went without saying. It was the first necessity. "That's true enough, Sam," I said. " It's a safe bet that my wages as a hotel clerk aren't going to get me very far in their estimation. No, I see only one way in that will work for me. I have to marry a young lady who has money and who does belong to their society. I have the bloodlines for it." I sat up and looked at him. "Doesn't it really bother you any, Sam? Being looked down on by the likes of them? Being left out?"

He shrugged. "Makes me no never mind," he said. "What they think don't hurt me none. I'm not saying money isn't a fine thing, but I sure could do without all the rules that come with it. Starched collars, peculiar food, and all that bowing and scraping to people just because they might be useful to you someday. I'd just as soon stay poor as come to that."

Bowing and scraping didn't appeal to me, either. "I suppose you get used to it," I said.

Sam laughed. "You might, Zebulon, but I wouldn't. Still, I can see you're bound and determined to try it anyhow. Have you picked out a likely young lady yet?"

I hesitated. Talking philosophy with Sam was one thing, but telling real secrets involving a certain young lady was quite another. "Well," I said. "Perhaps I have had the honor and good fortune of enjoying the favorable notice of a young lady of good family . . ."

Sam roared. "Lord God, Zebulon!" he gasped between peals of laughter, "when you start talking like a gilt-edged hand-tooled, calf leather volume of Presbyterian sermons, I know you're up to something. You do have a likely lady in your sights, haven't you? Now, who is she?"

I smiled and shook my head. "I was only speculating," I said, which was not quite a lie. I had made no declaration, I told myself.

Sam Robertson was no fool—not about horses and not about people. He wasn't deceived for an instant by my carefully worded denials. "You do have someone picked out," he said, peering at me as if to read the truth on my face. It was dark on the riverbank, though, and if I blushed, you could not tell it by moonlight. "Now I wonder who could it be?"

I didn't say a word, but he wasn't listening anyhow. The Warm Springs resort is a small world, and he thought he had a good chance of working out my secret. "I don't see how it could have been one of the lady guests. All the likely-looking young ones come with mamas in tow, watching over them like she-bears in a cave. And the guests don't stay more than a couple of weeks, anyhow, which oughtn't to give you time to make much headway into their affections. But if it isn't one of them . . . there aren't many rich young ladies in Warm Springs. Not single ones, anyhow. Well, except for Mr. Patton's daughter." He laughed, but I didn't.

I still held my peace.

"No, it must be somebody who lives hereabouts." He fell silent for a bit while he mulled this over. "I don't suppose it is Mr. Patton's niece Louisa?"

I laughed. "I believe she is playing with dolls yet, Sam. She is at least six years my junior."

"No. She won't do. And if it's a guest, she'd have to know your family connections. She . . . It's Miss Garrett!" By the tone of his voice, Sam must have been green to the gills. "Miss Sara Garrett."

"I did not say so," I said.

"No, and I don't hear you denying it, either." Sam was laughing now. "Her grandfather was the first owner of the hotel, and her people still own a passel of land in these parts. She'd be a catch for you."

"She is by way of being a relation," I said carefully. "My brother-in-law, Dr. Neilson, is her first cousin."

"All to the good then. If her cousin married a Vance then I reckon she can, too. And with all that land and money, she's bound to be what you're looking for."

"Well, looking is about all I can do, Sam. I have no money and no prospects at present, so it will be a while before you hear my name coupled with that of any young lady. But I promise to keep you informed. I'm going back to the hotel now."

I resolved to be less forthcoming in the future, even with a trusted old friend like Sam. He travels fastest who travels alone, and I did not want my plans or my future derailed by idle gossip. Sam was right about one thing, though: The right wife was the cornerstone of my ambitions. Young as I was then, I knew that although I could be bodily reckless—and indeed I was a gambler, a brawler, and a daredevil on horseback—I must treat my affections as if they were made of glass.

Nora Bonesteel

It was the only grave that Nora Bonesteel ever visited.

She never attended funerals, and in the little mountain community where she had lived the whole of her life, no one had seen her set foot in a cemetery—except that one time, when she was a child. Death was no stranger to Dark Hollow, Tennessee, though, and as a neighbor and a church member Miss Nora felt she had no right to ignore the ceremonies of life regardless of her reasons. Long ago she had reached a compromise that seemed to suit everyone. Although Nora Bonesteel did not go to funerals or buryings, whenever there was a death in the community she tried make her absence unobtrusive and express her sympathy in other, more tangible ways.

In a time of bereavement the family of the deceased always needs people around to cook and clean and generally carry on the business of living so that the loved ones have time to mourn. Nora Bonesteel was always the neighbor who came to the house to tidy the parlor, water the flower arrangements, and set out the cold ham and biscuits with the neighbors' covered dishes for the buffet, while the family went to the funeral and then on to the cemetery. When the family came home, they would find everything ready so that they could receive visitors in the evening in a tidy house with a cold buffet laid out to feed the multitude. If there were children too young to attend the services, Nora Bonesteel looked after them as well. As the years went by, people in the community took it for granted that Miss Nora could be counted on to tend to the funeral supper while everyone else was doing the mourning at the graveside. They saw it as a self-imposed duty, a sacrifice made for the good of her neighbors, and they were grateful for it. Custom obscured the real reason for her absence, and they did not wonder.

By the time Nora Bonesteel was sixty, she had outlived everyone who would have remembered the last time she set foot in a graveyard. She had been five years old at the time. The old man who owned the neighboring farm had died of pneumonia in late March. He had been cantankerous in age and bitter in ill health, widowed and estranged from his grown-up children, so that no one really mourned his passing, but he had been a boy soldier in the Civil War, and the men respected him for that. Besides, he had been a church member and a landowner, and for that the neighbors' respects would be paid as much to honor the rite of passage itself as to memorialize the dead man.

On the day of the funeral the Bonesteel clan joined the rest of the community in the little country church to pay their respects. Dressed in their Sunday-best they had filed into the sanctuary, solemn and silent, men taking up the pews on the right, women and children on the left, in accordance with an ancient custom that no one ever thought to question.

Young Nora had sat through the funeral in a shaft of sunlight, still and alert in her starched white pinafore, for she was accustomed to having to behave in church.

Big-eyed and quiet, she held the hand of her grandma Flossie and stared straight ahead at the flower-decked oak coffin that had been set on a trestle at the base of the altar. Nora seemed a bit pale, but nobody thought anything of that. A funeral was an emotional time, and even if the child didn't understand what was taking place, she might be frightened by the sight of the grown-ups weeping.

She held her peace, though. Before they left the house, Nora's parents had explained to her what was happening, and she had understood well enough. Death is no stranger to a farm child. She had seen the grown-ups wring the necks of the chickens for Sunday dinner, and a few months earlier she had watched the pigs dispatched by throat-slitting in the autumn ritual of hog-killing, so she knew all about dying. Since Nora had not been close to the elderly neighbor, her family assumed that for her the experience of his funeral would be an exercise in politeness rather than an expression of grief.

When the church service was over, six solemn pall-bearers in dark suits and string ties walked to the front of the church, hoisted the casket between them, and carried it down the aisle and out to the waiting wagon at the front steps. The wagon was there because the old man's burial would take place in the family cemetery on his farm rather than in the graveyard beside the church. World War II would come and go before sleek funeral parlor hearses replaced the horse-drawn wagons at country funerals.

Most of the mourners lived within a mile of the church and they had not brought their own wagons to the funeral. For the burial service, they walked together down the dirt lane to the farm. The early spring day had warmed up by midmorning, and the congregation was glad of a chance to bask in the sunshine after a long winter indoors. The mood was lighter now, enlivened by blue skies and the sight of the first meadow grass dotted with yellow coltsfoot, while on the hillsides the redbud bloomed among the yellow-green of new leaves heralding spring. Now that the funeral was over, their duty to the old man was done, and it was time to return to the business of living. People began to talk among themselves, in solemn undertones at first, and then there were smiles as they admired a new baby sleeping through its first public outing. Young Nora let go of her grandmother's hand and skipped along ahead of the slowpoke grown-ups. She was hoping to catch up with the wagon so that she could pat the horse. Her grandmother called out to her, but she was restless after a long morning of sitting still, and the warm day was too perfect to resist.

The old man's family cemetery lay on a hilltop above the farm in accordance with local custom. People said that high places were closer to heaven or lookout posts for Judgment Day, prettier notions than the original truth: that hillsides were not needed for the growing of crops, and that corpses placed so far above the water table did not contaminate the nearby wells and springs.

As the procession began to wind its way up the steep slope toward the burying ground, Nora hurried past the wagon, her curls bouncing and her white pinafore flapping in the spring breeze. She sprinted up the path toward the two stone pillars that marked the enclosure to the graves. It couldn't have been more than three minutes later when the hearse wagon, followed by the gaggle of mourners, crested the hill to enter the gate. Young Jim Wade who was driving the rig gave a shout and sprang to his feet, pulling hard on the reins to stop the horse. Before the crowd could see what had happened, he jumped down from the cart and ran into the graveyard. Flossie Bonesteel pushed her way past her neighbors and edged past the wagon and the stone pillar.

Beside the newly dug grave little Nora was lying, still as if she herself were the dead one, with her eyes closed and her arms flung out. Jim Wade reached her first, and lifted her up to a sitting position, but the child's head fell forward and she did not awaken. "What happened?" he asked as the crowd encircled him. "Did she trip and hit her head?"

"No," said Flossie Bonesteel, kneeling beside him. She examined the child with the deft fingers of one who is both midwife and healer. "There's no mark on her. She didn't trip. She fainted."

The boy stared at her open-mouthed. "Fainted? But what—" Then he remembered. This child was a Bonesteel, and the Bonesteels were known for having the Sight. Everybody knew that they saw things that other folks didn't, and most of the time, you wouldn't want to know what it was they had seen that you couldn't. Jim Wade swallowed hard and looked around at the green sward of grass studded with gray headstones—a bright, peaceful, sunlit hill. But a graveyard, nonetheless, where a little girl had seen—what? He didn't want to know.

The cold stare of Flossie Bonesteel made him shiver in the sunshine. "I reckon she got a touch of the sun and passed out," he said at last.

"I reckon so," said the old woman. She stood up and stared at the encircling crowd. "Sunstroke," she said, pulling her shawl close about her to shut out the wind. "Help me get her to the wagon."

It was the last time Nora Bonesteel ever went to a funeral or a burying ground.

Nora was nine when Grandma Flossie first took her to visit the solitary grave on the ridge behind the Bonesteel farmhouse. It was a sunny morning in late May. First they had gathered flowers from the garden beside the smokehouse, and then Nora's grandmother took her hand and said, "Bring those flowers along with you, child. We must go up now and tend the grave."

Nora caught her breath and turned, as if to run back to the house, but her grandmother laid her hand on the child's shoulder and said, "It's all right, Nora. There's nobody up there."

It was the same reassuring phrase that grown-ups always used to calm a fearful child, but Nora knew that Grandma Flossie was not one for making soothing noises. When she said a thing, she was stating a fact. Sometimes things were there and sometimes they weren't. She knew that. She could see them, too. Sometimes they talked about the visions that looked as real as ordinary objects: the black ribbon on a beehive or the traces of blood on a hunting knife. Nora had seen such things all her life. It took her a long time to understand that other people didn't see them, too—not at first, that is. After a few days, when whatever was going to happen had come to pass, then everyone would see the signs— the empty chair, the black cloth over the mirror—but Nora and her grandmother saw these things beforehand. It drew them close, a secret to be shared and a burden to be endured. So Nora knew that when her grandmother said a place was all right, it would be safe for her to go.

The grave stood by itself beneath a canopy of oaks on a ridge overlooking the back pasture. It was marked by a low slab of granite, its edges rounded and its carving softened by decades of exposure to the elements. A circle of fist-sized stones encircled the little plot of land around the headstone. Six feet of hilltop were clear of bramble bushes and locust shoots. Spring grass grew within the circle, mixed with a new crop of weeds and dandelions.

Nora stared at the tombstone for a while and then looked away. It didn't do to stare too long at some things. She set the flowers on the stone and then sprang back as if she were afraid of what would happen next. "Who's buried here?" she whispered. "Is he kin to us?"

"He's a stranger," said Grandma Flossie. "We never knew him. My daddy was the one buried him, but the boy was dying before he ever saw him." She knelt down beside the stone, and began to pull up the tendrils of weeds that had invaded the burial plot.

Nora peered at the stone, trying to make out the faint lettering of the name. She leaned close, careful not to touch it, but the letters were too worn for even her young eyes to discern.

"He was a young soldier," said Grandma Flossie. "He died in the war."

The old woman didn't have to say which war. To her generation *The War* always meant the one that happened here on home ground decades back when their own parents were young: the Rebellion, 1861–65. For those who lived through it or grew up on tales of the suffering and hardship brought on by that war, no succeeding conflict could ever supplant its terrible memory.

"There was some fighting close to here," Flossie Bonesteel was saying. "Nothing big enough to call a battle, even, but there was an ambush, shots got fired, and this young fellow was hit. I was a babe in arms back then, so I don't know the rights of it, but the way I heard tell it he was brought here to the farm to be tended, and it was here that he died a couple of hours after that. My daddy dug the grave and buried him up here on the ridge. It was summertime so there couldn't be any delay to the burial. You'd know about that?"

Little Nora nodded. She knew about meat spoiling in hot weather, but it didn't seem fitting to talk about such matters in front of the headstone here.

"Before he died that soldier told my mother his name and where his people lived, and it was his dying wish for her to write them a letter, sending his love and bidding the family good-bye. Mother wrote the boy's people, telling them that their son had died in the fighting in the

Tennessee mountains, but that he had not suffered or died alone. She told them that the soldier had met a peaceful end in a proper bed in our house, and that though his body could not be sent home on account of the distance and the weather, he had been given a Christian burial on a high wooded hill facing east so as to be ready for Judgment Day. He was from the mountains up in New England, so he would have liked this place and felt at home, with a view looking out over the valley."

"From New England?" said Nora. "The soldier was a Yankee?"

"He was," said her grandmother.

"But I thought our people were on the Confederate side."

"We had people on both sides in that war. Most folks did in these parts," said her grandmother. "My brother fought for the Confederacy. Maybe my mother was thinking how she'd want him treated if he were dying far from home."

"Roy ... something," said Nora, working out the faded inscription.

"Thompson. His name was Thompson. When I was your age, those letters were easy to read." The old woman sighed. "Well, time passes on."

"Did your daddy carve that lettering?"

"No. A stonecarver over in Jonesborough did that. Charged five dollars to do it. The soldier's family sent money, you see. They wrote back and thanked us for seeing to their son's burial, and they asked if we'd put a headstone over him and keep the grave tended, since they could not do it themselves, being so far away and all." She pulled up the wooded stem of a sapling sumac and tossed it away into the underbrush. "And so we have ever since. My mother tended that grave until she died, and then the task fell to me."

Nora looked again at the weathered stone. She stood

up and turned slowly around in a circle with her eyes
shut, arms straight out, palms up. After a few moments
she opened her eyes again, and, taking a deep breath, she
dropped to one knee and placed her hand against the
lettering on the cold headstone. She looked up at her
grandmother and shook her head wonderingly. "But . . .
he's not here," she said.

Grandma Flossie nodded. "No, child. He's not here.
And as long as I've been coming up here, he never has
been."

"And his folks . . ." Nora thought for a moment . . .
how long had it been since the War? People talked
about it like it was last week, but it must be sixty years
at least, she thought, for the Spanish-American and the
Great War had come and gone since then. "This boy's
folks must be dead themselves by now."

"Surely they are," said Grandma Flossie. "It's been a
long time."

"It's just a stone on a hill now," said Nora. "He won't
know. They won't know. So why do you bother to look
after the burying place?"

The old woman continued to stretch and pull, tearing
the weed shoots from the stone circle. "I suppose we do
it for ourselves, Nora," she said. "Because a long time
ago this family made a promise to some people who
needed our kindness, and I reckon we do it to prove to
ourselves that our word is our bond. It's what little we
can do to keep kindness and honor alive in the world.
What better way to practice charity than to keep a
promise made to an enemy?"

Decades had passed now, and more wars had come
and gone. Now Nora Bonesteel herself was the old
woman who tended the soldier's grave. The edges of the
stone were no longer sharp and the lettering was no
longer readable, but the plot itself was as well-tended as
ever. Over the years Nora had made a little garden of
the burial plot, so that flowers marked the changing sea-

sons. Surrounding it grew yellow forsythia bushes to herald spring, scarlet hedge roses for summer, and bronze chrysanthemums and Michaelmas daisies to mark the autumn. Winter took care of itself, she thought, by frosting the bare branches with spun silver that glittered in the cold sunshine. It was a peaceful place and over the years Nora had grown fond of it. She wondered if the soldier had known where he was laid to rest and if the spot would have pleased him, but she didn't suppose it mattered. Her ancestors had tended it as a kindness to the soldier's family, and she kept it because it linked her to the Bonesteels of the past—and because it pleased her to turn a place of death into a garden.

Zebulon Vance

War is a great equalizer. It shakes up the stagnant pond of society and offers opportunities to those not formerly on top. If one is bold enough, one can rise in military endeavors, and to be an officer is to be a gentleman. But when I was twenty, war was a decade off and not even hoped for by the most ambitious young scoundrel. I could not wait for that tide to carry me forward. It took a good deal of paddling my own boat to further my ambitions in those early days.

For all the ambition I professed to own, I had little enough to show for it by my twentieth year. Becalmed in the backwaters of Madison County, twenty-six miles from Asheville, I passed my adolescence in happy obscurity. I had a great many friends among the rough lads on the mountain farms, and if I could not outdrink or outfight most of them, it was not for want of trying. Mostly, though, I was drunk on my own youth and good health, savoring the pleasures of the freedom of manhood, with little thought to what I would do when those days came to an end. I was having too much fun to grow up. Perhaps I was no burden to my

doting mother in those days, but I was not much credit
to her, either.

That pattern began to change when my mother sold
our house on the drovers road in Lapland, and moved
the family the twenty-six miles back to Asheville. She
despaired of getting a good education for my younger
brothers and sisters in our mountain village, and so she
sold up and moved to the city. My father had left her
with six children and an estate consisting mostly of
debts, but through Mother's own shrewd business sense
and her diligence, she had managed to increase her
property holdings and to maintain and educate the family without owing anything to anybody. She was a re-
markable woman. How could I be content to drift
along, wasting my youth and my talents, when the example of her steadfastness reproached me at every
turn?

And what if she were to die young, as my father did,
and leave me with the task of caring for my brothers
and sisters?

All right, then, I thought. *I will make something of myself.* Asheville was the place to do it. It was a bustling
town with a population of more than four hundred, and
a goodly number of summer visitors who came there, as
they had come to Warm Springs, for the cool, healthy air
of a mountain summer. Since Asheville was the county
seat of Buncombe County, the circuit court met there,
and the political power of westernmost North Carolina
was concentrated within its borders. The representatives
of the people who were elected and sent out to serve in
the governments in Raleigh or in Washington were cho-
sen here and by and large they resided here. The place
was an orchard of opportunity, and if I did not avail myself of that bounty, I would be a fool as well as a sluggard.

When I was younger it was easy enough to glory in
the idleness of sleepy Madison County, for I felt neither
envy nor inferiority to the farmers and drovers that con-

stituted society in those parts—I quite liked them—but Asheville was a different story. The people at the Warm Springs Hotel had been easy to charm for a day or a week, and they were kind enough, but perhaps it was because I was not part of their real society. They always went away, back to Charleston or Richmond or Wilmington, leaving me little but a few more lessons in how to comport myself among the gentry. Asheville society stayed put, and that was another matter altogether.

The city contained a veritable ladder of society, and it was soon clear to me that I was not many rungs from the bottom. At eighteen I had no money and I had trained for no profession—thus I had no prospects. As I walked along the streets of Asheville, I saw the fine carriages of the local gentry and visitors from the eastern seaboard. I gazed at the stately, pillared homes lining the tree-lined boulevards, and I thought of our family's humble little frame house on a less fashionable street. I knew myself to be a plebeian cast adrift among the patricians. Every week the city's two hotels, the Buck and the Eagle, would hold elegant dances for the local young people of good family. It did not matter that I could dance as well as any fellow in the county or that I counted myself a tall and handsome fellow. The hotel soirees were events from which I—a nobody—would be barred.

It didn't take me long to learn that I could not abide the feeling of being outranked and excluded. The very idea of being disdained by people no smarter or better bred than I was unendurable, but I thought that I had sufficient wit and determination to alter my situation, and in Asheville my pedigree should be sufficient. When the town was first founded, the land on which it stood was purchased in part from the Bairds, my mother's people, and from my grandfather David Vance, so for all my shortcomings, I counted myself a prince in Buncombe County.

Soon after our arrival we heard reports of gold being discovered in far-off California, and quite a few young blades went west to seek their fortunes there, but, though I cheered them on, I was never tempted by the tales of great riches lying on the ground out there just waiting to be picked up. I felt that my future lay in North Carolina, and anyhow, probably owing to my strict Calvinist mother, I distrusted all that talk of easy money. In the North Carolina hills people still told tales about the flurry of prospecting fever that had occurred here and in north Georgia back in 1832 when gold was discovered. I was two years old then, so I remember none of it, but I have heard the stories of neighbors who gave up all they had for a chance at a prosperity that did not materialize. Back then there had been a great stir of excitement about the prospect of easy pickings, causing the gamblers and the dreamers among us to abandon their farms and their shops and head out into the hills for the lure of the gold fields. A few months later the boom went bust, for the vein of gold had proved small and hard to extract. I thought it likely that the recent strike in California might prove equally ephemeral, and I determined not to risk my life on the chance of it. Besides, when I clerked at the hotel in Warm Springs, I had seen my share of rich men who rejoiced in material goods but lacked the respect of their fellows. Their wealth had brought them neither power nor social position, so I resolved to advance myself by more reliable means.

I decided that my own "gold field" would be the study of law, for it was universally acknowledged that the law was the practice of gentlemen. It was also the gateway to politics, and thereby the path to power and influence. Oh, even back in the backwater of Lapland, I had begun to take an interest in politics. Everyone did in those days, but my youthful involvement had been no more than a country ruffian's excuse for drink and discord.

On one memorable election day I headed a procession on mule back, traveling some sixteen miles through the mountains of Madison County to the election precinct. I was filled with patriotism, zeal for the Whig cause, and hard cider. There and then I participated in fifteen separate and distinct fights, for all of which I might be set down as the proximate cause. I doubt that I did much to advance the cause of my party, and certainly I was doing nothing to improve my own prospects.

So, at the age of twenty, I resolved to abandon my boisterous ways and to devote myself to the study of law, so that I could contribute more to politics than a drunken advocacy at a country polling site. Most people seemed to like me. I thought I had a fair shot at getting them to cast their votes for me, if ever I should be in a position to run for office.

Thus one December afternoon in 1850 I found myself hat in hand in the parlor of Mr. John W. Woodfin, one of Buncombe's County's most able attorneys. Mr. Woodfin, a wealthy and socially prominent gentleman of thirty-two, was a tall and elegant figure of a man, characterized by the local ladies as regal in his bearing. I thought that I could learn as much by observing him as I could from his tutelage in the law. He shared his practice with his older brother Nicholas, and the two were as close as any brothers I have ever seen. It would never have occurred to me to link my fortunes with my own brother Robert. He travels fastest who travels alone, perhaps, though occasionally I found the road was lonely.

John Woodfin stood before the fireplace now, looking me over as dispassionately as if I had been a saddle horse up for auction. I stood up straight and was careful to look him in the eye, so that he should know me to be forthright and unafraid. I was rubbing my boot against the back of my trouser leg, hoping to get a bit of the mud off the heel before it fell on Mr. Woodfin's Turkey carpet.

The gentleman gave me a tight smile that was more perfunctory than reassuring. "So you want to study law, Mr. Vance?" he said. "May one ask why?"

I grinned, thinking to captivate him with my charm. "Well, sir, I do believe I'd have a gift for it. I'm good with words and I'd just as soon argue as eat."

He raised an eyebrow. "I have heard some reports of you on that score," he said, "but lawyers do not generally argue with their fists, you know."

"No, sir," I said. "I have resolved to mend my ways."

"Lest it mar your fortunes." He nodded. "And what do you read?"

"Walter Scott for pleasure, and Scripture, of course. Shakespeare."

He went on quizzing me for a quarter of an hour about my schooling and what work I had done, and who my people were. I told him that my father had died when I was twelve, and I was frank about my wild country upbringing, hoping that he would take my fatherless state into account, and he must have done. Indeed I think it was the subject of family that took me over the hurdle in John Woodfin's estimation. He had heard of my grandfather Vance, the war hero, and he seemed to set a store by the fact that my maternal grandmother was Hannah Erwin of the Burke County Erwins. Apparently he thought that "Erwin" was a name to conjure with, and I would be the last person to dispute him.

"My wife and her sister are kin to the Erwins of Morganton," he told me. I remembered then that John Woodfin and his brother Nicholas had married sisters. "A fine family, with more than one lawyer among their number. If you inherited any of the intelligence and character of the Erwins, you should be an asset to the profession."

"Indeed, sir, I hope to be," I said.

"Well, perhaps we will give you a try on the strength

of that, Mr. Vance," he said with a thawing smile. "Come and meet your fellow law student Augustus Merrimon."

John Woodfin led me down the passage and into a book-lined study where a gangly, bespectacled youth sat hunched at a desk, with his nose almost touching the page of a leather-bound book. He looked for all the world like a black-suited praying mantis in soulful contemplation, and as soon as he saw us enter, he sprang up looking more dismayed than pleased to behold a stranger. He regarded me for a moment with his gooseberry eyes and after Mr. Woodfin had made the introductions, he thrust out a damp hand and muttered— quite unconvincingly—that he was pleased to make my acquaintance.

Well, he's a long streak of widdle, I thought, reckoning that he would not last five minutes with those hardy fellows I had known back in Madison, but nonetheless I never make an enemy without good cause, so I gave him a blazing smile and professed absolute delight at being allowed to join him in the study of law.

"I'll leave the two of you to get acquainted," said Mr. Woodfin. "Merrimon will acquaint you with the order of the law books, Mr. Vance, and he will bring you up to speed on the work at hand. I shall see you both later this afternoon." And with a brief preoccupied smile, he was gone.

Merrimon looked at me doubtfully and sniffed, as if I were a joint of meat that had gone "off." I hunched forward a little so that the gap between my pants leg and my shoe should not be quite so evident.

"I don't believe I've heard of you," he drawled. "Who are your people?"

Well, I was getting tired of having my bona fides questioned every whipstitch, so I grinned at him, and said, "I don't reckon Mr. Woodfin is thinking of putting me out to stud, but I seem to be distantly related to his wife, if that's any help to you. As for my own qualifications, I think you'll find that my wit and perseverance will speak for themselves."

He blinked. Augustus Merrimon was a slow and careful sort, always thinking before he spoke, and weighing his words carefully, while I charged ahead full tilt and thought better of it later. "You are a connection of Mrs. Woodfin?" he said. "One of the McDowells of Morganton?"

"My grandmother was a daughter of Mr. Alexander Erwin of that city," I said. "And how about yourself? Or did you spring full grown from the head of George Washington himself?"

Well, humor was wasted on the plodding Mr. Merrimon. He took my question at face value, and proceeded to recite his pedigree, as if I cared, but I was civil to him anyhow, because old Augustus looked like the sort of fellow who did not make friends easily, and I'm sure he cherished his enemies all the more for their steadfastness. "It seems we are connected," he said. "My own maternal grandmother was a sister of Captain Charles McDowell of Morganton."

"Well, I'll buy you a drink on the strength of that anyhow," I said. "Where do the lawyers drink around here?"

Merrimon looked alarmed. "I cannot think how men can waste their time in drinking and carousing," he declared.

"Well, I could show you . . . ," I drawled at him.

At that he drew himself up like a freshly staked beanpole, and said, "My father is a Methodist minister. We do not indulge in the pursuits of the lower classes. They are a frivolous waste of time."

"I expect they are at that," I said in all humility. *Except maybe they aren't,* I was thinking. It seemed to me that if a man had aspirations in politics, he would have to get himself elected in order to govern, and there were certainly more members of the lower classes than Methodist ministers making up anybody's constituency.

I thought that learning to be at ease with the common man might go a long way toward winning you some future election, but I did not say so to that boiled owl Merrimon. Let him do it his way, and eventually we should see who was right.

So I settled down to read law in the company of that walking sermon, August S. Merrimon, and I found him to be quite a scholar in his pettifogging way. He worried every case we covered like a hound with a marrow bone, and he could wrest facts out of his memory better than I could read them from the page. He studied and I polished my wits and my oratory to get by.

Once John Woodfin was quizzing us on a point of law, and he said to me, "Vance, if you please, give us the definition of a contingent remainder."

I was happy to be asked that, for I had just read that very page in Blackstone, and so I was able to reel off the passage, more or less word for word from my memory of that page in the book.

When I had finished, Woodfin nodded and I thought he would give me a rest and go after Merrimon, but just as I let out my breath, he said, "Yes, Vance, you have summed up the gist of it from Blackstone, but what does Fearne have to say on the matter?"

Merrimon would probably know that, but I most certainly did not, so before he could jump in and flaunt the facts, I said, "Well, Mr. Woodfin, Your Honor, I was so fully satisfied with the definition of the great master, Blackstone, that I did not care to examine any other authority." It was pretty thin ice, but we skated on to the next topic.

I made myself agreeable to the Woodfins and even to Merrimon, as much as I could manage, and by degrees they began to include me in the far-flung society of frontier gentry that stretched between here and Morganton to the east of us.

Like water, money and power seem to flow downhill,

so that the closer one got to the flatlands, the more of it there was. Thus, in Morganton there were plantations and an island of polite society, set at the very edge of the pale, as it were. Merrimon was forever being invited to parties in Burke County, and, once he discovered that I was presentable and could handle a knife and fork in a satisfactory manner, he began to ask me to go along, for eligible young men with prospects were at a premium on the frontier. His thawing of manner toward me might also have been occasioned in part by my decision to leave the tutelage of the Woodfins and to study law at the University of North Carolina—if I could find the money to make it possible.

It was on one of these occasions, at a party in Morganton at the McDowell house, Quaker Meadows, that I met the woman who would change my life.

"Have you met Miss Harriett Espy?" Merrimon asked me, tilting his laden plate until I began to be afraid for my frock coat. "I fancy she is fond of me. She, too, is the child of a minister, but orphaned in infancy. She has no fortune, but her connections are excellent. She is a cousin of the Woodfins. After the death of her parents, Captain Charles McDowell raised her here at Quaker Meadows as one of his own."

"He has a brood of six," I murmured. "Perhaps he had lost count."

Merrimon was not amused, of course. "Zebulon, I will not introduce you to Miss Espy if you are going to be flippant," he said at his most severe. "She is a lady."

"I shall be as solemn as a dyspeptic deacon," I assured him, and we threaded our way through the throng of silk dresses and tailcoats to the table where a silver punch bowl rested on an expanse of starched white linen. Beside the table, ladle in hand, stood a tiny young woman with auburn hair, a kind face, and earnest gray eyes. I did not notice them light up at the sight of Augustus Merrimon, but she gave both of us a gentle smile and when

Merrimon presented me as his fellow law student, she said that she was glad to make my acquaintance.

I was even gladder to make hers. It was a relief to know that someone else at this party besides myself was of "no great fortune," and I felt at once at ease in her presence, though as tiny as she was, I felt like a Hereford bull exchanging pleasantries with a field mouse. Merrimon was hailed by other friends just then, and he excused himself, promising to return as soon as he could, though I for one was not sorry to see him go.

"And you are reading for the law with my cousin Mr. Woodfin?" she said. "Such a noble calling, the law."

"I don't know about noble," I said. "It can be almighty tedious." Then I remembered my manners and added, "But nobody could be more inspiring in his instruction than Mr. John Woodfin."

She smiled. "Mr. Merrimon says the same. He is so dedicated to his studies. I am sure you must be as well, Mr. Vance."

"It doesn't come naturally to me," I said. I had made myself a lot of fine promises about hard work and self-discipline, but it was hard to buckle down to a pile of dry-as-dust legal tomes when there was a raucous county town outside, beckoning to me with fiddle tunes and bright lights spilling out of the dance halls, and jugs of hard cider. "I'm thinking of going to the university to continue my work there."

"Well, that is a fine thing," Miss Espy said primly. "My own dear father attended the Princeton Theological Seminary, and I am a great admirer of learning. I will pray for your success, Mr. Vance."

"Well, I'd be grateful for that, Miss Espy," I said, "but I think I'll need more moral support than that if I am to succeed. Diligence does not come easily to me, and I feel that I could profit from your fine example. Would you write to me inspiring letters?"

She hesitated for a moment, but I must have looked

quite forlorn, and, as it was not within her nature to refuse such a heartfelt request, at last she said, "If you think that my encouragement will benefit you, Mr. Vance, then of course I will correspond with you. I shall consider it my Christian duty."

I chafed a bit at being someone's cross to bear, but her sweet face was such a picture of earnestness, that I did not essay a jest, but merely replied, "Miss Espy, you are an angel unawares." Over her shoulder, I saw that long-faced Merrimon scowling in our direction. "I will take you at your word."

I know that it was said forever after that Hattie Espy was the apple of my eye, and the impetus for my determination to better myself, and I have never disputed it, for just as the apple in Eden imparted knowledge to Adam and Eve, so did my Hattie enlighten me to the possibilities open to an able fellow with money and powerful friends. As I said, I have never disputed her influence on my destiny—but to return to the metaphor of Eden: I am mindful that *any* apple from the marvelous tree would have imparted to Adam the selfsame gifts.

I had learned much during my sojourn with the Woodfins, not only about the law, but also how the world works, and some of it went against the grain of my mountain heritage. Now, the folk I was raised with have a horror of charity, and if they ever find themselves in anyone's debt, they will lie awake nights thinking up ways to square the obligation. Higher up the social ladder, though, the rules are reversed. The gentry always want to be under the protection of someone higher than themselves, and they take care to do favors for the rest, in case they ever need a service from those folk in turn, or in case one of the lesser mortals should confound expectations and someday become important after all. Much as it went against the grain to put myself in anyone's debt, I soon saw that if I wanted to play society's game, I must abide by its rules.

I wanted to go to the state university, but we had no money to send me. I cast about for someone in power who might be willing to help me get on in life, and presently I mentioned this difficulty to my mother, in hopes that she might suggest some Morganton cousin who might be willing to do me a good turn. I learned that the ideal person was very well placed indeed, but our connection was a most unexpected one—at least to me.

"Of course, I have heard of David Lowry Swain," I said, when my mother had put his name before me. "He was governor in the year I was born, was he not?"

My mother smiled, keeping her eyes on her needlework, but I knew of old that her attention was entirely upon the matter at hand. "He was quite an ambitious fellow in his youth. He is from Asheville, too, you know."

"Of course, I know," I said, pacing before the fireplace. I think better when I pace. "In his early twenties Swain became a circuit judge, then a state legislator, and by the time he was thirty, he was the governor of North Carolina. A path I wouldn't mind taking myself. From the way they invoke his name, you'd think him the patron saint of lawyers in these parts. I did not know we were related to him, though, or I'd have bragged on it."

My mother smiled. "You are not kin to him, Zebulon," she said, "but it was a near thing. He was once my sweetheart."

That sat me down. How strange to think of the pious and heavyset widow and parent of six, my mother, ever being a frontier belle. I could not resist teasing her, for she had chided me often enough about my waywardness. "Why, Mother," I said, "this is a revelation. You never told us that you'd had an ardent young *swain*."

"Nonsense!" she said, stabbing her needle at the linen. "David Swain and I were at Reverend Newton's school together. When he was a young lawyer from

Asheville, and before I chose to wed your father, Mr. Swain had some hopes of winning me himself. It was not a serious romance, though, Zebulon. Just a fondness between young schoolmates, and we parted friends. It has been a good many years since I saw him, but I fancy that he will remember me as fondly as I do him. He is a good man. Write to him of your situation. Your trust in his kindness will not be misplaced."

"I will," I said. "I could not ask for anyone better placed to help me." When Swain's term as governor was over, some fifteen years ago, he did a most unusual thing, I thought. Instead of aspiring still higher—to Congress or even the presidency, as I might have done, David Swain went to Chapel Hill and became chancellor of the University of North Carolina. There he had remained ever after.

I wrote to Chancellor Swain, reminding him of my family connections, and explaining quite frankly that my ambition had outstripped my purse. Perhaps the thought crossed his mind that but for a twist of fate he might have been my father, or perhaps he really was the patron saint of western lawyers. Anyhow, he told me to come ahead, and that he would see to it that a loan of $300 was made available to see me through. I was to take a partial course of study at the university, and at the same time pursue my legal studies with Judges Battle and Phillips.

So, in July of 1851, in my homemade shoes and trousers so short that they showed three inches of my hairy ankles, I arrived in Chapel Hill. It was never far from my mind that since my true calling was politics the distinguished people I met there might be considerably more important to me than the late Messrs. Blackstone and Fearne of the law books.

The university was in its fifty-seventh year of existence when I arrived, a beautiful place indeed. The main college buildings are three in number, each three stories high, colored yellow and surrounded with neat terraces of earth thrown up and platted with grass. In addition to these are three other buildings: the ballroom, chapel, and recitation hall, all situated in a beautiful oak and poplar grove, checkered off with splendid white gravel walks, set out in shrubbery, and the whole, I suppose about twenty or more acres, surrounded with a stone wall.

I began to get myself noticed the moment I arrived in Chapel Hill. The western stage pulled up in front of Miss Nancy Hilliard's Hotel, and as my fellow passengers alighted, they were overwhelmed by greetings and backslapping from old acquaintances, for they were all returning students from the previous term. I stood there in the dust of the road, alone and ignored for about half a minute while I sized up the situation, and then I noticed an elderly colored gentleman idling nearby, so I went over to him and shook his hand, and hailed him as if we were the oldest and dearest of friends. I was not mocking the fellow, you understand, just seeking a welcome from the only soul there not otherwise occupied at the time, and he was kind enough to bid me how-do. In less than five minutes every man on the street had sought my acquaintance, and the story of Zeb Vance's droll entry into the village preceded me, and made people take note of me, which is what I had intended.

There were an unusually large number of students in attendance that term—251 young men, vying for rooms and places in classes. After some difficulty, I managed to get myself assigned to Number 5, West Building, where I roomed with Robert Johnston of Haywood County. He, too, was reading law, but I doubted whether he would have much call to practice it, because of his family's great wealth.

After a few hectic days during which I set about putting away my few possessions, making the acquaintance of my fellow sufferers, and beginning my studies, I settled down with pen in hand to write to Miss Harriett

Espy, assuring her of my safe arrival, but as it was early
in our correspondence I spent the majority of the letter
expressing my undying devotion and urging her to give
me hope that this sentiment might one day be returned—but in case it wasn't, I asked to be remembered
to other likely ladies back home in the letters I wrote to
others.

I settled into a routine at the university, rising at five
and going to bed at ten, and working the whole of that
time except for two hours of recreation, which I considered necessary for my health. I was taking a "partial
senior course," which in the first term required me to
take course work in chemistry and mineralology, political economy, and moral philosophy. Besides that regi-
men I was reading law in a comprehensive course
covering *Blackstone's Commentaries, Stephen on Pleading, Greenleaf on Evidence, Chitty on Contracts, Cruise's
Digest of Real Property,* and *Williams on Executors.*

Letter writing took up a good bit of my time as well.
I kept in contact with my cousins Martha Weaver and
John Davidson back home, and from them I heard the
political news of the western district and the news about
mutual friends—particularly the eligible and pretty
ones. They kept me abreast of the engagements, the
duels, the elections, the parties, and the camp meetings.
I in turn talked about my visits with the family of Judge
Battle, and the various young ladies I encountered in
the social round of the piedmont—always avowing that
my heart was given to one in the mountains. I did not
speak of these social activities to Miss Espy, being no
fool. I kept assuring her of my undying devotion with
great single-mindedness.

By late summer my correspondence with Miss Espy
had progressed to an exchange between "My dear Harriett" and "My dearest Mr. Vance," and I had begun to
feel quite secure in the young lady's estimable affections. Then in mid-October, the thunderbolt hit.

With a thrill of anticipation, I opened the letter from Morganton addressed to me in that familiar schoolgirl hand, but instead of the usual salutation of endearments, the letter began coldly: *Mr. Vance.*

I skimmed it in a bate of anxiety, wondering how I had put a foot wrong this time. Harriett Espy was a prickly young lady, fierce in her religious principles and quick to take exception to any laxity on my part. I once called myself her idolator, and she responded with such a ferocious rebuke that I was groveling on paper for the next month, trying to sweet talk my way back into her good graces. I was more careful in my choice of flattering phrases after that, but the bare salutation of her letter of October 13 told me that I was in trouble again.

I read on.

". . . I have been informed by disinterested persons that you were, when you addressed me, engaged to a young lady near the Warm Springs—& that you have since you addressed me, treated her very ungentlemanly . . ." I scanned the chilling phrases, with half my mind casting about for the identity of those "disinterested persons," whose necks I would gladly have wrung. Word had got to Harriett that I had written a letter intended for her, speaking slightingly of the other young lady, and that by mistake the letter had been sent to the wrong young lady, causing her great distress. Harriett took a dim view of such cruelty, and said so, ending with, *". . . I have placed the greatest degree of confidence in you—& will be grieved to know that you have acted in such a manner as this. I call upon you Mr. Vance, for an explanation . . ."* I skimmed the rest of the page.

The letter concluded: *"May the choicest blessings of a Heavenly Father abide with you is my sincere prayer—"* That sounded like a hopeful sign, but it was several shades cooler than her previous valedictions, and, sure enough, the letter was signed with a frosty "H. Espy," instead of the intimate "Your sincere and devoted Harriett," with which she had ended her previous missive.

I would have to talk fast to get out of this one, and I would have given a week's worth of dinners to be closer to Morganton so that I could explain in person, but I realized that Harriett might refuse to see me anyhow, and so I was better off scotching this snake by return mail, and using every scrap of lawyerly logic and eloquence in my possession to extricate myself from this snare.

There was just enough truth in this accusation to tell me that someone had deliberately set out to make mischief between myself and Miss Espy, and I knew that even if I managed to salvage our understanding, I would have to be constantly vigilant in case another attempt should be made to part us.

I began my brief for the defense with a confession. Yes, I told her, I had been paying my addresses to a young lady from Warm Springs before Harriett ever made my acquaintance. I had indeed corresponded with that lady, out of careless conviviality, but I absolutely denied that I was ever engaged to her, and it was at that lady's request that the correspondence between us was closed. The cause of the breach between us was indeed a misdirected letter, but it was not a letter addressed to Harriett Espy, but to a male friend, Mr. R. P. Deaver of South Carolina, in which I made comments not unusual between intimate male friends, but these remarks offended the young lady who received them by mistake, and so we parted. But all that had occurred before I began to exchange letters with Harriett, and I told her so, adding that I could prove my innocence, because I still had in my possession the letters from that original correspondence, and others of our mutual acquaintance could testify that the lady and I had parted as friends with no ill will on either side.

So I had been falsely accused, and although I could establish my innocence, I was not willing to let the matter go at that, and I wanted a message to that effect to reach my mysterious accuser. In no uncertain terms, I fired back: *"Now, Miss Espy, I know not as to the motive which led to the fabrication of these infamous lies against me, but I do know your author . . . and may the God of Heaven have mercy upon him, if without proof of his innocence, he falls into the hands of a deeply injured man . . ."*

I named no names in my letter, nor did she in hers, but there was no doubt in my mind as to the identity of my enemy in the matter.

Augustus Merrimon.

Only weeks before I had begun to pay my addresses to Harriett Espy, that oily weasel Merrimon had written to her, asking her permission to pay court to her himself, which she very sensibly declined. I suspected that Merrimon had not accepted his defeat as a sportsman and a gentleman should have, but by then I was convinced that he was neither of those things.

There is a line in the Bard's *Romeo and Juliet* that has always struck a chord with me: *My only love sprung from my only hate.* The reverse was true for me, for I flatter myself that I had no ill-wishers upon this earth until I set my cap for Miss Harriett Espy of Morganton. No doubt she was too great a prize to be won uncontested.

In her reply to my letter, Harriett assured me that she had not believed the accusations, and she thawed sufficiently to sign herself "Your sincere Harriett" again. She had guessed the object of my suspicions and went to great lengths to assure me that Augustus Merrimon was not the mischief maker I sought. I did not believe her, though, and I resolved to settle the score between myself and Merrimon if it was the last thing I ever did.

I have a constant heart. If you doubt that, pick a quarrel with me, and you will learn that I never forgive an injury or an act of treachery. But my affection and my friendship, once won, is never forfeit. I am as loyal in love as I am in enmity, and neither friend nor foe has ever disappointed me in returning the sentiment.

Perhaps I am hard on others, but I hope I am hardest on myself. I had a long way to come in this life, and in my journey I could afford neither weakness nor idleness nor the burden of treacherous associates. I found my truest friends and my greatest foes early in life, and they served me so well that I never saw the need to change them. They are my compass points in this sea of troubles.

Tom Gentry

Tom Gentry began his diary in the shelter of a laurel thicket in the Cherokee National Forest. On a windy day in late spring he had walked into the park from the two-lane blacktop in Sams Gap, and although he knew that he was either in North Carolina or in Tennessee, he could not have said which state he was in, because he had wandered so far from the boundary lines of the forest that he no longer knew where he was or where the state borders lay. It did not matter, though.

He had no plans ever to come out again.

He had reached the decision to come to the Smoky Mountains to die so gradually that he could not pinpoint the exact day that an idle daydream became a working plan. At first he had evolved the scheme as an alternative to the frustrated boredom of his life and his undemanding job. He would thumb through the road atlas, page through travel articles in *National Geographic,* looking for the end of the road.

He was weary of life, but he could not have given any reason for this condition—no reason that would have satisfied a psychologist anyhow. He supposed that a doctor would have heard him out on the emptiness of modern existence, and then prescribed the anodyne of the month to take the edge off reality. Prozac. Xanax. Valium. But Tom didn't want life-once-removed. He wanted life removed, period.

He made his way across the country from California as far as Nashville, and from there he came to the high country by bus, alone and unremarked by his fellow travelers. He spoke to no one, and they returned the favor. From the convenience store that serves as the local bus station, he carried his few camping supplies and walked deep into the national forest. Hikers are common enough in east Tennessee, and in worn hiking clothes and work boots he was neither good-looking enough nor distinctive enough to leave a memory in his wake.

From the small town where the bus set him down, he walked several miles into the Cherokee National Forest, first on the marked trails, and then simply wandering whichever way took his fancy. He remembered a line from a television program on finding people lost in the woods. Lost people take the path of least resistance, the narrator said. They go downhill. He thought he had been lost for a long time, then.

He did not pitch his tent until he came to a place from which he could see no sign of human habitation: no distant houses, no power lines, no man-made lights bleeding into the night sky. He believed he was as far from civilization as it was possible to get in the twenty-first century—beyond the pale physically as well as spiritually.

This place was not his home. He was not born or raised here. He would not go home to die. He came here instead. It was more fitting.

In his first campfire, he burned all his identity papers: military ID, driver's license, all the little markers on the paper trail of humanity. If in the years to come, some lost hiker stumbled across this campsite, he would find no clues to tell him the owner of the bleached bones herein. Tom Gentry did not wish to be disturbed, not even postmortem. He did not intend to be shipped back to the faceless midwestern suburb that would be called his home just because he had happened to be raised there. He did not belong anywhere. Perhaps that was the problem.

If he had to plead for his life, he could think of no mitigating circumstances to offer as proof that he should be spared. He was not clever, or handsome, or beloved. He had painted no works of art, written no poems, contributed no music to the spheres. He had not made the world a better place, not even for the select few individuals denoted as friends or family. He had acquaintances, nothing more.

He was a pleasant person, insofar as anyone bothered to pass the time with him. He let them come and go without complaint. He was polite to salespeople and uncomplaining to his coworkers, because conflict is a form of intimacy, and he did not want to be close to anyone. He had no snail trails of emotion clinging to his life, and he had left no one behind. Perhaps that was a sin of omission. Nature does not approve of creatures who resign from their species. He had committed no crime to warrant death, but he had done nothing to make him worthy of life either. He was dying by default, and he accepted that.

But he didn't think that he deserved to suffer. Anyhow he didn't intend to. In the end all we can ask of death is a measure of control in our own demise. He decided that it was the indignity which frightened him rather than the act of dying, and so he would take control.

He had brought a few necessities, a very few. And a journal in which to record the last days of his life. They had already begun.

Zebulon Vance

The plan was for me to spend nine months or so studying law and general courses at the university and then
go to the December meeting of superior court in
Raleigh during the winter-term vacation to apply for my
license to practice in the county courts. My preceptor
Judge Battle very kindly allowed that I should have
them like a deer in a walk, and I was looking forward to
getting that qualification out of the way, and returning
to Asheville, for from the sound of the letters I was getting, everybody back home would be married, killed,
elected, or brought to Jesus in a tent revival before I
could get back.

I studied hard, and duly traveled to Raleigh to join
the contingent of petitioners asking to be admitted to
the bar, and whom should I meet there in attendance
for the same purpose but Mr. Augustus S. Merrimon
himself, all starch and smugness. I was civil—well,
mostly I was, for I had promised my Harriett that I
should be if ever we met, but I could not resist one jibe
at the examination.

I was let off with only a question or two, but Merrimon, who had been reading on his own rather than in university, came in for quite a grilling by the learned judges. Their barrage of questions revealed his shaky grasp of Blackstone, and Merrimon became more distressed by the minute as the interrogation rolled on.

I could not resist remarking about Merrimon to the fellow beside me, "He came in a merry mon. He goes out a sorry mon."

The pun pleased me so much that I was only slightly sorry that Merrimon managed to squeak through the examination, so that all of us passed that day. I congratulated him upon his good fortune, but I told Harriett in a letter thereafter that he will never succeed in making friends in this life unless he alters his carriage and deportment. He is possessed of an infinite amount of self-importance, and I had the leisure to observe it. Merrimon was in the company of Sam McDowell, the son of Harriett's guardian, and also a candidate for a law license—he for the second time. A few years back Sam had gone to California to seek his fortune in the gold fields, and when that failed, he came home and read law, with no more success at first than his prospecting had been, but this time he prevailed, as did Merrimon and I. Then, on account of wanting to be in Sam's good graces, I took him and the aggravating Mr. Merrimon back to my boarding house for dinner and to stay the night, as they had no other planned accommodations.

At breakfast on Sunday, my landlady, who has made quite a pet of me, began to sing my praises to my guests. "Laws, Mr. Merrimon," she said, "your Mr. Vance is a great one for visiting the ladies. Why every lady in Raleigh is greatly taken with his charm, and I have high hopes of finding him a wife before he leaves our fair city. Why, if he has been paying his addresses to any young lady in the mountains, you go right back and tell her that I intend to have him married before he leaves my premises."

Merrimon egged her on in this immoderate chatter, and while she ran on, he caught my eye and gave me a poisonous smile that made me want to throw him against the nearest wall, but I remained civil, knowing that every move I made would be a tale for Sam McDowell to carry back to his foster sister, Miss Espy. But I chalked up another black mark on Mr. Merrimon's account, and knew the time would come to pay him back.

That chance was not long in coming. In the spring I began to receive letters from my friends back home saying that there would soon be a vacancy for the job of Buncombe County Solicitor for court of pleas and quarter sessions, and a considerable number of well-wishers suggested that I should run for that office. Not least among them was my older brother Robert, who had served as clerk of that court for several years now. The duties of that office, as I understood them, were not only to prosecute criminal offenders, but also to act as adviser in the finances of Buncombe County, which I reckoned I could do, as long as they didn't expect me to contribute any of their spending money personally.

Any hesitation I might have had about putting myself forward was immediately quelled when I learned who the other candidate was: none other than Augustus Merrimon. That happy news added spice to the meat of my ambition, and I agreed at once to stand for the post. That decision put an end to my idyll at the university, and in mid-March I was once again outside Miss Nancy's, boarding the western stage while my friends wished me godspeed. I teetered there upon the wheel of the coach, and essayed some feeble pun on the word wheel, for I hated the solemnity of long farewells, but I knew that I would miss the place and the people, and I should never again have so carefree an existence.

I went back to Asheville by way of Morganton, where

I stopped awhile to visit with Harriett, and to persuade her to agree to an engagement. In that campaign I was successful, and I felt that it boded well for the skirmish awaiting me in Asheville. I had to travel all night to make the last leg of my journey that Thursday night, but I was sustained by the memory of my last glimpse of my betrothed, standing on the piazza at Quaker Meadows, waving farewell to me with her handkerchief. I spent the journey building castles in the air and ruminating on my destiny, full of the ambition and boundless optimism of youth.

Bright and early Monday morning I went downtown to announce formally my candidacy for the position. The election to the post of solicitor was not a matter with which the local judiciary cared to trouble the general populace. They cast the votes among themselves to determine the appointee, and there would be nineteen local officials there on March 29 to decide the matter between Mr. Merrimon and myself.

"I wish we had known you were coming back, Zeb," said John Woodfin, my first legal mentor. "You're a bit late entering the race."

"Well, I hope to make up in ardor what I lack in foresight," I said.

"I have no doubt of your ability," said Woodfin, "it's just that Merrimon has been campaigning for the last three months to get himself appointed to the post, and he has extracted pledges of support from several members of the court."

His tone of voice suggested that he had been one of those persuaded to back Merrimon, but I did not remark on that. I merely said, "We must see how it goes then, Mr. Woodfin, but even if the outcome of this vote is bad news for me, it will be overshadowed by far happier news from Morganton." I favored him with a shy smile. "Miss Espy has done me the honor of consenting to be my wife. Indeed I would hardly strive at all for this appointment except for my wish to succeed on her account. I must provide for her as she deserves, of course."

Woodfin wished me good luck in an abstracted voice, and then he wandered away, looking much preoccupied, as well he might, for my fiancée was a kinswoman of his, and now he must consider how his vote would affect her future as well as mine. I knew that this news would make its way around the court before the morning was out, but just to make sure, I planned to impart the happy news to a few more well-wishers for good measure.

Merrimon appeared presently, and he looked as nervous as a pigeon in a shooting gallery. He approached the lawyers with a worried frown, speaking in an urgent undertone, while he darted nervous glances left and right. I did no politicking or speechifying upon this occasion, and one of my great gifts is a complete lack of nervousness upon any occasion, which may either be confidence or a blissful ignorance of the hopelessness of the situation.

Since every man there was either a friend, a relation, a neighbor, or at the very least an old acquaintance, I contented myself with shaking each one by the hand and declaring myself heartily glad to be back among home folks. It wasn't long before I found myself the object of much back-slapping and hand-wringing as the news of my engagement spread among the crowd. My brother Robert already knew, of course, and he must have told the half of the crowd that I hadn't yet got to, for all and sundry seemed to know about it.

Merrimon continued to look so stiff and nervous that you would have thought him on trial for his life, and perhaps from that the learned gentlemen received some idea about the misery involved in having to work with him. At any rate, deliberations were short, and the vote, which was taken after dinner, came out eleven to eight in my favor.

I thanked my roaring well-wishers for the honor. "Well," I told them, "I suppose since I have been made a solicitor for the county, I had better see about getting somebody to swear me in as an attorney so that I can take the job."

They all laughed heartily at that, but Merrimon took his defeat with his characteristic bad grace. He bowed stiffly before me, ignoring my outstretched hand. "I suppose I should congratulate you on the post of solicitor," he said. "For that at least has been verified."

His meaning was clear: He was accusing me of lying about my engagement to Harriett. Duels have been fought for less provocation, but before I could make a reply to that, he said, "I don't accuse you of any impropriety in this contest, Vance, but I do say that your friends have acted badly in this affair, and they have elected you with questionable means."

His attitude was as foolish as it was ungracious, and I would not have behaved so, not only because I would not have wanted to display my disappointment at losing, but also because it is unwise to alienate a powerful opponent. He would have done better to wish me well and hope for my support in some future endeavor.

My temper is as hot as his spirit is cold, and I had all but forgotten my resolve to be a magnanimous winner. At that point, I might well have wiped the resentment off his face with my fist, but before I could utter, John Woodfin appeared at my elbow, and murmured, "Mr. Merrimon is also deserving of congratulations, Zeb. He may have lost the appointment, but he has recently gained a fiancée as well. Miss Margaret Baird has agreed to marry him."

I swallowed my rage and held out my hand to my erstwhile opponent. "We must not fight, Merrimon," I said. "It seems we will be doubly kinsmen, for I am marrying your cousin and you are marrying one of mine." We shook hands then, and privately I resolved to try to like him better, for it would be a stain on my character to behave as an ungracious winner. Besides, if I am to stay in Asheville for my career, I will forever be stumbling over Augustus Merrimon, and I'd rather have his goodwill than his enmity.

As we were leaving the meeting to go out and celebrate, Woodfin again appeared at my elbow. "You must learn to govern your temper, Zeb," he said, "else some day it will do you irrevocable harm."

"Well, I will make the effort," I said, "but some fools would try the patience of a saint."

"Saints can afford enemies. Young politicians cannot," Woodfin replied.

Shortly thereafter I wrote formally to Mr. McDowell in Morganton, asking for the hand of his ward in marriage, and after more than a week's deliberation, he gave it, saying that since I had no patrimony, as he put it, he might have held his consent, but the fact that I spent my inheritance on an education showed ambition and a determination to rely on my own resources for a living. Because of that, he would entrust Harriett to me. He did not mention my recent appointment to the solicitorship three weeks previously, but I have never doubted that it was the deciding factor in the matter.

On August 2, 1853, Miss Harriett Espy and I were married at Morganton's Presbyterian Church in the presence of God and more frontier gentry than I could count. We were also within sight of the home of my great-grandfather Brank and near the place where David Vance, my father's father, had lived. I knew that both these redoubtable gentlemen would look with favor upon our union, for Harriett was a lady by birth and breeding. That she was a slight and pretty woman with a pious nature and a lionlike faith would have pleased them as well, but for me those virtues were ever secondary to her worldly connections.

The next half dozen years flew by for both of us with

scarcely a moment to draw breath and contemplate our situation. Harriett and I settled in Asheville, and I began to work toward obtaining my license to practice law in superior court, which was granted to me in the same month we were married. I was spurred on by ambition, for which the practice of law was only a means to an end. Lawyering in the thirteen counties of the Seventh Judicial District was hard work for little money, and I had not set my sight's on a judge's bench as my eventual reward. There was not enough population or wealth in any one of the mountain counties to support an attorney, and so in company with the rest of the members of the bar, young and old, I became a circuit rider, attending court in each of the county seats in turn, county court and superior court, despite bad weather, indifferent roads, and the meager financial recompense for our trouble. The only mitigating factors in this endless pilgrimage of poverty was the opportunity to enjoy the society of my brother attorneys and the festive atmosphere of a town on court day, a carnival of politics, gossip, and horse trading, spiked with corn liquor and the occasional brawl for seasoning. I was not the greatest lawyer God ever made, but I tried to do right by those that depended upon me, and I made up my mind to enjoy my sojourn in the courts, though I felt like a bondservant awaiting the day of his emancipation, and to profit from the example of older and wiser attorneys—William Waightstill Avery, John and Nicholas Woodfin, Burgess Gaither, and the rest. Of course, I had to endure Merrimon as well, and a few other young bucks of my own generation, who were shaping up to become rivals of mine in future endeavors.

One of the ablest of the pack was David Coleman, another bright fellow who viewed the law as a stepping stone to politics, and I knew that sooner or later our paths to power would intersect, and he would be a more formidable opponent than old sobersides Merrimon.

The entire decade was for me a long series of political adventures, and I could go on about that in exquisite detail, but since the succeeding decade brought the war, it would seem petty to dwell on those bloodless campaigns that ended at the ballot box instead of the later ones that ended on the battlefield.

Once, though, there nearly was blood shed.

In all likelihood it would have been mine.

I was a Whig in those days. People called me a damn fool for it, since voters were deserting that party as if it were a sinking ship, but the Democrats favored Southern secessions and the Whigs held for the Union, so I stuck with them, too stubborn to change to suit the prevailing wind. In 1854 I ran for a seat in the North Carolina House of Commons as a regular-built, old-fashioned Whig against Colonel Daniel Reynolds, who is married to one of my Baird cousins—in fact, a sister of the one who married Merrimon. I do not seem to be able to scratch my nose without bumping into some form of relative. I wish they would all find something better to do than run for office. Reynolds is a Methodist preacher; that ought to keep him busy enough with all the souls that need saving out here on the frontier.

Anyhow, I beat him by 110 votes, and to crown my success more completely Harriett promptly gave birth to a blue-eyed boy who weighed ten pounds at birth. I could have sat by his little crib from morning to night and been content to do nothing else, but my duties were ever more pressing. I was rising in the world: a lawyer, a member-elect of the legislature, and the father of a ten-pound boy. I thought myself quite content—for now.

We lost the child a year later. Harriett declared that he was such a lovely little creature that he was better fitted to live with the angels than here on earth with us, and if that brings her comfort, I will not dispute it. I kept myself occupied with my work and trusted that in time there would be other sons in that little crib, and so there were.

I entered the North Carolina House of Commons, hoping that I might do a little good for my state and my constituency, but I found that serving in a government run by majority rule is like trying to swim upstream in molasses. Independence will get you nowhere. I said as much to one of my fellow delegates, William Graham, when I was particularly exasperated about the way things were going.

"Well, they are all pig-headed on this railroad vote," I said. "The great majority is dead set against approving the bill for the Greenville and French Broad Railroad. We need railroads in the west. They're not even asking for any state money, so what business is it of these eastern representatives to oppose them?"

"Well," said Graham, "I believe they claim that a railroad that runs from Charlotte to Sparta, South Carolina would make the South Carolina port of Charleston more accessible to the mountain people than our native North Carolina ports."

"That argument is based on gross ignorance of the provisions of the bill *and* of the geography of the country. The railroad would run from Paint Rock on the Tennessee line through the valley of the French Broad River, toward the Greenville and Spartanburg line. The gauge of the road is to match the Central Road—which the North Carolina Railroad does *not*. So the Greenville and French Broad Railroad could link to railroads in Tennessee and Virginia, and from there we would have connections to Chicago and Cincinnati. Think of the trade opportunities!"

Graham smiled. "It is like the game of chess, Mr. Vance. You must learn to look two moves ahead. The others think that if the Greenville and French Broad is approved, then it will become troublesome competition for the existing railroad. The state itself is a large stockholder in that venture, you know. The best way to avoid such an issue is to prevent the formation of any other one."

"I shall support the railroad," I said.

"Just don't plan to ride it home," said Graham with a smile, "because you haven't a hope of getting it approved."

He was right, of course. I got to where I could see what the majority were up to, but I couldn't stop them. Later on they voted to approve an education bill that apportioned school funds by the general population of the county, and not by the white population. Now, that would be fine if a cent of that money ever went to the nonwhite population, but it doesn't. It can't. It's illegal in North Carolina to educate slaves and colored persons. So the eastern counties use their slave populations to get the lion's share of the education money, and then spend it on only a fraction of their citizens—while the mountain people do without!

I complained bitterly about that injustice, and wrote letters to the newspaper outlining the facts, but it came to naught, of course. There are more of them than there are of us. I keep voting for unpopular measures, and I end up on the losing side. About all I can do for the folks that elected me is to complain loud and long when the rich men's representatives cheat them out of their rights, but I am learning, and no doubt I shall do better in the future, for despite all my setbacks, I am perfectly happy in the melee of party politics. I have found my calling.

In 1858, when Thomas Clingman vacated his seat in the U.S. House of Representatives to fill the unexpired term of a senator, I decided to stand for the office, and sure enough I found myself running against another one of my innumerable kinsmen. This time it was William Waightstill Avery, whose mother was one of the Morganton Erwins, as was my grandmother Baird. Even my friends called me a fool for running against Avery. The fellow had already served three terms in the North Carolina House of Commons, and he had many richer and more powerful relatives than myself, all of whom were no doubt rooting for him to win. But I was beginning to get the hang of campaigning by now, and I saw that there was no point in being dull when you were debating with your opponent in front of a passel of ordinary farmers in the district. They like a show with their electioneering, and they like to laugh every now and again. I've no doubt that Avery was an able and learned gentleman, but on the stump he was a good deal duller than I was. He'd have called it "dignified," I'll warrant, but it doesn't win you back-country elections. He was a secessionist as well, and so much to the Democrats' consternation the unbeatable Waightstill Avery lost to this little old Whig by more than two thousand votes.

That sent me to Washington in December of 1858, and as a newly fledged congressman, I did what I could to learn the ropes and to speak in favor of holding the Union together, not that anybody paid much attention to a brash upstart from the backwoods of Carolina.

I did not have much time to enjoy my newfound prominence or to rest on my hard-won laurels, for no sooner did Congress adjourn in March than I was challenged for the selfsame seat I had just taken such pains to get myself elected to.

This time David Coleman threw his hat in the ring. I had run up against him before in 1856, because he had been trying to get his party's nomination when Waightstill Avery stepped in, but now that Waightstill was no longer in the picture, Coleman stepped up to challenge me again. I don't mind a good political battle, but I'd sure druther have had more time to enjoy the office, and less time spent fighting to keep it. The months leading up to the fall general election were one long wrangle, as Coleman and I debated from one end of the district to the other, questioning one another's policies, veracity, and competence.

I enjoyed myself hugely. The voters liked a good set-to on the election platform. I thought everything was proceeding normally for a back-country election, when in late summer, Coleman ups and announces that I have sullied his honor, and that he wants to fight a duel with me over the insult.

If he had come to me privately, bearing a brace of pistols, I suppose it would all have been over with by now. I'd have gone and shot it out with him then and there, but that is not the way gentlemen operate, even on the frontier. Social life is not unlike Congress: They must temporize, and confer with their associates, and pass carefully worded letters back and forth, and so on, until you are likely to die of suspense before the thing ever comes to a head. So, of course, my associates must jump into the matter as well as his, which is how I came to be back in John Woodfin's study in Asheville, being lectured at again, as if I were still a gangly adolescent reading law, instead of a U.S. Congressman, trying his damnedest to pass a few.

I paced the hearth rug while Woodfin sat in one armchair and Colonel Hardy in the other, though the colonel was content to leave most of the talking to Woodfin.

"Do you know what it is that you did to give offense to Coleman?" Woodfin asked me.

He probably already knew, but only wanted to be told my side of it. "He's unhappy about the way the debate went in Waynesville," I said. "He didn't like the way I questioned him, and he complains that one time I pressed him to answer a question so that I could prove his answer false."

Woodfin raised his eyebrows. "Hardly the way for gentlemen to treat one another in public," he said, watching me carefully, as if I were upon the witness stand.

"Well, I can't help it if his feelings are delicate," I said. "Politicking is a man's game."

"It does, however, have rules," Woodfin replied. "Be they unwritten, they are no less binding. Did you publicly berate David Coleman in Waynesville?"

"He thinks so. He began it, though. He claimed that I supported that Connecticut scoundrel Galusha Grow in his Post Office Appropriation Bill, which—"

"Thank you, Zeb. I am acquainted with the bill."

"I only wanted Coleman to commit himself over whether he thought that I supported Grow."

"But instead of asking the question and waiting for his answer, I expect you harangued, and shouted, and waved your fist, and did your best imitation of a tom turkey strutting in front of a rival. I've no doubt that the crowd cheered you on, which would be like kerosene on a brush fire where you are concerned."

"I may have got taken up in the heat of the moment," I said. "And now instead of shouting back, Coleman wants to slink off and fight a duel over it. And now I am bound to do it."

"Have you considered apologizing to Coleman instead?" John Woodfin asked me, still in that quiet voice as if we were discussing fence posts.

"I wrote him explaining my position, and expressing regret that I had given him offense. Colonel Hardy knows that. He has been carrying the letters."

Hardy nodded. "Yes. It's true that I have delivered the letters between the aggrieved parties."

Woodfin smiled. "I don't suppose you sounded very sorry for what had transpired?"

"No, perhaps not, but I took great pains to explain to him—"

"He's angry, Zeb. You have insulted him in front of his neighbors and constituents, and now you want to *explain* to him why he shouldn't resent it?"

"He said he didn't like my tone, damn his impudence!"

Colonel Hardy sighed. "The letters have not had the effect that I had hoped."

"I sent John Hyman to confer with Coleman's friends. Here's Hyman's letter." I handed it over to Woodfin, who read it aloud for Hardy's benefit—certainly I had no wish to hear it again.

> *The parties will meet at Waddell's cabin, Cocke County, Tennessee, near the North Carolina line on Tuesday, 30th August, instant, at 8 o'clock A.M.*
>
> *Each party may be accompanied by not more than two friends and a Surgeon. The ordinary smooth-bored duelling pistol shall be used— each to be loaded on the ground in the presence of the parties. Distance twelve paces. The choice of position and the giving of the word—*

Woodfin looked up, alarm showing on his face for the first time. "What do you intend to do about this?"

I shrugged. "Sam Brown has been out practicing with me on pistol shooting in the woods in Arden."

The two of them looked at each other for a minute, and then Colonel Hardy cleared his throat and said quietly, "Perhaps you should apologize, Zeb."

I set my jaw and narrowed my eyes. "I can't see my way clear to do that, Colonel," I said. "I spoke as I found."

"I know," sighed Woodfin. "It runs in your family— same as politics. Have you considered the family precedent, though, Zeb? Have you considered it carefully?"

I couldn't help scowling, because the shot had hit home. "I suppose you mean my uncle—Robert Brank Vance."

"Of course, I do. Why, a horse could see the parallels between that episode and this one. Your father's brother ran for Congress against Sam Carson, and during the debates, Robert Brank Vance criticized Carson for voting government money for the relief of a burned-out town in Virginia. When Carson protested that the vote was an act of charity, your uncle said—what? Do you recall this story?"

I supplied the answer grudgingly, because he would have told me anyhow. "I believe he said something about not admiring a charitable urge that caused a man to put his hand in another man's pocket."

"Fighting words."

"Platform rhetoric. He wasn't accusing Carson of stealing. Just of being too quick to offer charity with the public's money as if it were his own to give. It was a fair comment, surely."

"No. It was an insult. And don't forget that your uncle followed that slur by then accusing Carson's father of impropriety during the Revolution—of having asked Lord Cornwallis for protection of his property during the British occupation of the area. That charge amounts to an accusation of treason, I should think. Anyhow the Carsons thought so, and they called him out."

"The incident cost Uncle Robert the election, too, as I recall," I said.

"Yes, you would be concerned with that, wouldn't you? But you'd better give prayerful thought to the other consequences. The duel they fought at Saluda Gap."

I knew all about it. The two of them had met on the Greenville Pike at the state line between North Carolina and Tennessee, each man accompanied by a second and a surgeon, and at a remove of ten paces they faced one another—my Uncle Robert with a rising pistol, and Carson with a falling one—and on the count of three they fired. To distract myself from this ominous prospect, soon to be repeated with myself in my uncle's stead, I said to Woodfin, "It's said that Davy Crockett himself was present at that duel. Had you heard that tale?"

"Yes, and so was the Angel of Death, and while the late Mr. Crockett will not be present to witness your folly, I believe you can count on the Angel's faithful attendance again."

"I'm not afraid," I said.

"No, you haven't the sense to be," sighed Woodfin. "We surmised that when you shot off your mouth on the stump and accused Coleman of being dishonorable. What did you expect him to do when you insulted him, Zeb? Concede the election and kiss your hand?"

I continued my pacing up and down across Woodfin's hearth rug until I fancied I had worn a path through it. Robert Brank Vance was shot through the body by Sam Carson—who left the field unharmed—and later went on to become the secretary of state for the Republic of Texas. They said that it took my uncle Robert two days to die from his wound, and that he went bravely and without rancor. Very commendable, no doubt, but the prospect of a similar demise for such an inconsequential matter did not appeal to me. I had more to achieve in life before I could contemplate the leaving of it.

"It was a remark made in the heat of the moment," I said at last. "I didn't mean for Coleman to get so worked up about it. Emotions run high when you're politicking. I am given to hyperbole at the best of times, and in front of a crowd of voters perhaps I am prone to overstating my case. If that is a fault, I admit to it."

"It could be a capital offense if you mean to carry this duel through to its fatal conclusion."

"I can't back down, Woodfin. That would finish me as sure as a bullet."

"Think of your wife and your boys, Zeb," said Colonel Hardy. "Surely you remember what it was like to grow up without a father. Do you want them to live through that as well? Of course you don't!"

"As to backing down, as you put it, there's no question of that," said Woodfin. "You are new to the game of politics—well, relatively new, anyhow. And we are all lawyers, are we not? This is a time for clarification, for expounding upon the meaning of your words. You need only say you are sorry that Coleman misunderstood what you intended to say—not that you are sorry you said it. I propose that you let letters fly between you instead of bullets."

"Will that satisfy Coleman?"

Woodfin gave me a grim smile. "I'll warrant that Coleman even now is attended by his own friends who are advising a similar course of action. But you should write the first letter."

"What should I say?"

Woodfin smiled. "Take a seat at my desk, and I will dictate the letter for you—word for word. We have all had enough of your improvising."

I won the election to fill Clingman's seat in the Thirty-sixth Congress, and with the intercession of Woodfin and the colonel, David Coleman was kind enough to accept my explanation of high spirits and ignorance of campaign etiquette, and my expression of regret for having given offense. The matter was mended without our having to repair to Cocke County with loaded weapons and stern-faced surgeons. I was a brawler in my youth, and I've often wondered if I would have let my pride lead me into the duel if it had not been for the example of my uncle's untimely death. Or perhaps the circumstances were simply different: Uncle Robert was a stunted man, left crippled by a wasting disease in childhood, and anyhow he had lost the election to Carson. Perhaps he had even wished to provoke Carson into hastening a death that he welcomed as a surcease from suffering. Perhaps he did it all on purpose in order to die, while I had blundered into harm's way in my exuberance because I was so full of life. I was glad that I did not have to leave it yet—for all Harriett's rhapsodies about the joys of heaven, I was not yet persuaded to want to visit there.

Anyhow I got sent back to Congress, hoping that this time I could serve a little longer before somebody picked another fight with me, and I did have about a year's peace as a North Carolina representative, but a continued period of calm was not to be. It seemed that the nation was spoiling for a fight even more than I was.

Rattler

When our Wake County sheriff, Spencer Arrowood, showed up at the reenactors' next encampment, people pretty much figured that his visit was more business than pleasure. He had never heretofore showed any interest in the war, so the sight of him pulling up in that marked patrol car made some folks nervous. Not me, though.

The reenactors are a generally law-abiding bunch, so I doubted there'd be much out here for a sheriff to worry about—an expired car inspection sticker, maybe. It seemed more likely that he was politicking, but since I never have any idea when the next election is, it was only a guess. Anyhow I was glad to see him again.

I have known Spencer Arrowood all his life. He used to come out to my place in the woods when he was a skinny twelve-year-old with a crewcut and a wobbly voice. He was always tagging along after his older brother Cal, the one who got killed in Vietnam not too many years afterward. Young Spencer had a hankering to learn wood lore—plants, tracking animals, tanning hides. His father didn't take much of an interest in that kind of thing, on account of his having been a town kid himself. Old Hank Arrowood thought nature was something you took a lawnmower to. He never did take much interest in either one of his boys, except to yell at them when they didn't live up to his expectations, which usually meant making the honor roll at school and staying awake in church, to hear Spencer tell it. Hank was the kind of man who thought his obligations to the world began and ended at the office. When he went home it was to be waited on, fed a hot dinner by a wife he outranked, and then to be left in peace to watch the television until he decided to turn in for the night.

So the two Arrowood boys took to hanging out in my neck of the woods, and I can't say that I blamed them. Truth is, I didn't mind the company. Children and animals are always easier to get on with than regular folks. They're not so quick to pass judgment on where you live or what you look like, and they don't set such a store by money. They're no trouble to talk to, and they don't tell lies and call it manners. Besides, you can feed 'em just about anything. We had some fine times in those days. I taught them how to track deer through the underbrush, how to fish for trout without all the fancy equipment the tourists use, and I made sure they could recognize the leaves of every plant in these woods that was likely to do them good or ill. I taught them the name of every mountain you could see from my cabin door—in English and in Cherokee. If you're going to hang on to the old ways, you might as well make a job of it.

I told them stories, too, about how I was raised in a cabin up the holler, which they thought sounded like a fine thing, because boys always have a hankering for living rough and dirty, especially when they have a nice brick house to go home to. I don't reckon their father ever knew beans about either one of those boys, but he did see to it that they got an education, and they turned out just fine anyhow.

Spencer was a smart boy, quick to learn and grateful to be taught, and I was sorry to see him go, but the time did come when he needed learning that I couldn't teach him—like which fork to use and who wrote which book. Stuff I never learned. He drifted in with the town boys in high school, and then he went off to college and the army, and oftentimes I wouldn't see him from one year to the next. He never forgot me, though. Every now and again I'd find a six-pack of beer on my porch or an almost-new wool blanket draped over the railing, and I'd know he'd stopped by and left it while I was out, so as not to embarrass me with his charity. And now he is the high sheriff of Wake County. We could do worse.

So, still hankering to learn something he didn't know, Sheriff Arrowood came out to the Civil War encampment. This time the camp was on a two-lane road that led into the national forest, not on the site of any real skirmish, but just a picturesque and convenient place for a grown-up camporee. Another couple of miles would have put the encampment across the state line into North Carolina, where it would have been some other peace officer's problem, but as the toy soldiers were still in Wake County territory, the sheriff was within his rights to stop by, and he could even pass it off as working. Besides, the drive is a pretty one in early summer, and there wasn't much else to occupy his time, because things were relatively peaceful elsewhere in Wake County. They generally are—or else the tragedies come to light when it's too late to do anything about it except clean up the blood and see to the survivors.

The camp was a tranquil place that afternoon. Bill Nance had his bluegrass fiddle out, playing "Bonaparte Crossing the Nolichucky," which is his own honky-tonk version of "Bonaparte Crossing the Rhine," and he had a semicircle of listeners, polishing boots or cleaning weapons in time to the music. I had dropped in for want of anything better to do myself—and maybe to keep an eye on things in case the Ravenmocker was about. I had volunteered for KP duty, and I was chopping up some wild onions for the stew pot when the sheriff and his deputy LeDonne showed up. They nodded to me, and went over to say hello to one or two of the men they knew.

"I just came out here to check up on you fellas," Spencer Arrowood told Jeff McCullough, who was playing a Confederate again this time. "Make sure there's no drugs or illegal firearms around."

"I don't think we're allowed to carry Uzis," said McCullough with a straight face. "It's an out-of-period weapon. But as for drugs, I do think Bill Nance brought his glycerin tablets, in case his heart goes to acting up."

The sheriff shrugged. "I didn't really expect any problems," he said. "But this seemed like an interesting place to enjoy a beautiful summer day."

McCullough smiled. "You might find it educational, too, Sheriff. We give demonstrations on everything from cooking to nineteenth-century medicine. There's a Scout troop coming out at four for a living history lesson. That's the whole point of this exercise, isn't it? I mean, we all want to know what it felt like to live through those times."

Sheriff Arrowood didn't answer straightaway. "I've never had any particular curiosity about the Civil War," he said at last. "I'm certainly not a war buff."

"Me either," said his deputy, Joe LeDonne. "I lived through one war. That cured me of wanting to hunt one up uninvited."

"It is strange, isn't it?" said McCullough. "How people stay fascinated with this war? The surrender at Appomattox happened a century and a half ago, and yet interest in the subject flourishes. And people still *care*. Not just as an intellectual exercise, like, say the Fall of

Troy, but really in an emotional sense, as if they could somehow change the outcome. It's odd. I'm thinking about writing an article on the subject."

"Better not," said Spencer. "Nothing you could say would make any difference to either side, and you might start a whole new battle—with yourself in the cross-hairs."

Sheriffs are politicians, whether they want to be or not, so we knew what he was getting at, though you wouldn't catch him saying it out loud to a journalist. When Spencer was a kid, the Confederacy was a romantic lost cause, celebrated by people who naturally rooted for the underdog and glorified in the movies. Like the Alamo before it, the Southern "Cause" was made romantic by virtue of its own doom. Since then, though, the concept of political correctness has been brought to bear on public opinion, and it is no longer fashionable even in Tennessee to show respect for a Confederate heritage. Regardless of what people might think privately, most of them no longer talk about the war or display the Confederate battle flag (which any reenactor will tell you is not the "Stars and Bars") openly the way folks did when this bunch were youngsters. Nowadays people who do not distance themselves from their Confederate heritage are suspect. They make other people nervous. They leave themselves open to the assumption of racial prejudice, and nobody wants to be tainted by that. Especially not a local politician. The best opinion for Spencer to have was no opinion at all. He saved his enthusiasm for University of Tennessee football—which isn't politics, but might qualify as religion.

"Are you running for office again?" I asked him, because it seemed to me that he was being even more hard-to-pin-down than usual.

He looked surprised at the question. "This November," he said. "You planning on voting for me, Rattler?"

I grinned at him. "Well, if I ever do vote, it'll be for you."

So Sheriff Arrowood was running for re-election in the fall. That explained why he was gadding about the county. Politicking is an awkward, humbling process, and Spencer would hate it more than most, because every time he ran he had to overcome his own solitary nature and spend a few awkward months trying to act like a glad-handing politician. All through the summer and early fall before the November election, he'd have to spend his off-duty hours meeting and greeting the voting members of the county, which did not include me, because I don't much like anybody. If you could vote for bears, I might go to the polls; otherwise, not.

I didn't envy Spencer the rest of the year. He would be visiting the county fair and the Ruritan meetings. He'd make himself visible at the Fourth of July fireworks, and in between there'd be brief, cordial stops at weekend family reunions and church picnics in order to remind the citizens of Wake County that they could count him as a friend.

So that's why he turned up. The reenactors' encampment was a good place to meet a group of male voters without having to go door-to-door to meet each one individually—a practice that Spencer would dread. I pictured him standing hat in hand on a doorstep facing folks who would either be suspicious and hostile, thinking that he was making an excuse to invade their privacy, or else they'd be patronizing or just plain rude.

At least this bunch could be counted on to be civil. He knew a good many of the reenactors in their ordinary lives as lawyers or teachers or whatever, and he was aware that they did not fit the redneck stereotype that outsiders often assumed they were. Still, I was willing to bet he'd be careful not to appear in any photos with this bunch. That was just the sort of thing that a political opponent might make an issue of, and there would be no explaining it away in this world of sound bites and snap judgments. Once somebody has called you a redneck or a racist, no matter how untrue it is, the tears of the angels themselves will not restore your character. Still, he has to meet the voters, and by now there aren't too many male gatherings that wouldn't arouse the ire of some special interest group. Hunters? The animal rights people would pillory him for that. Boy Scout camporees? Then the gay crowd would be up in arms. Was there a gay segment in his constituency? Spencer wasn't sure, but he didn't want to discover their existence by provoking them.

"Sometimes I think that the country is even more divided now than it had been by the War Between the States," said McCullough.

The sheriff smiled. "That's another sound bite I'll take care *not* to use."

Some of the other reenactors had ambled over to the patrol car, apparently forgetting that they weren't even supposed to see an automobile if they were staying in character. I had to smile. They were like a bunch of little kids come to take a peek at a police car. I bet they'd even sound the siren if he'd let them.

"Mr. Arrowood, you ought to be out here reenacting!" said Fred Yarby. "Seeing as you had kinfolk in the War."

"Well, I suppose I did," said Spencer. "Don't know of any, but my people settled these mountains in the 1790s so I expect some of them must have served in one army or the other."

"Don't you know?"

"No. My dad never talked about family history. It didn't interest him at all. Besides, my dad fought in World War II, and he considered that the be-all and the end-all of all wars. He never bothered to bone up on any conflicts before or since."

Fred Yarby looked over at McCullough and me and smirked, which was a waste of time as far as I was concerned because I didn't know what the joke was either. "I bet he doesn't know," he said.

"Know what?"

"About a soldier named Arrowood."

Spencer shook his head. "I never heard him mentioned. I don't suppose he was a famous general that I somehow missed hearing about?"

"No, he certainly wasn't a general," said McCullough. "We're not sure what rank he held. Not much of one, I gather. But I can tell you why the name rings a bell with us. He was from the North Carolina mountains, by the way, but we don't know anything about him aside from that."

"All the Arrowoods are kin," said Spencer. "My grandfather came through the Iron Mountain Gap into Tennessee in 1915 to work in the railroad shops in Erwin. Nobody ever said anything about a Civil War hero in the family, though."

"Hmm," said McCullough, who looked like he wanted to take issue with something in that statement, but thought better of it. "Sheriff, have you ever heard of the Battle of Waynesville?"

"Well, no. You mean the town of Waynesville over in North Carolina? South of Asheville."

"That's the one."

"It's a small town."

McCullough sighed. "So were Sharpsburg, Gettysburg, and Chancellorsville. They loom large because of what happened there, that's all."

"Well, Waynesville doesn't loom, Jeff. At least, not to me."

"Not worth fighting over," said LeDonne. The deputy was born and bred in Ohio, and he wasn't inclined to obsess about the War the way Southerners do.

"You can say that again," said McCullough. "Oh, it's a fine little town, but worth fighting over? No. Not when you consider the fact that the battle took place in *May* of 1865."

"That can't be right. The war ended at Appomattox in April."

"Well, it did. Mostly. Took a while for the news to get around. I guess Waynesville was the last to hear, because that turned out to be the very last battle of the War."

"Unless you count some fools out in Texas or New Mexico who had no business being in it at all," growled Yarby.

"They do seem rather irrelevant somehow," McCullough agreed, "but, yes, New Mexico did have a battle, and for the strict nit-picking accuracy essential to a Civil War fanatic, we do have to specify that Waynesville was the last battle in the Civil War fought *east* of the Mississippi."

"More of a skirmish, really," said Yarby. "But it has its points. Thomas's Legion fought in it."

"That was the Cherokee regiment," I said to the sheriff, in case he wasn't up on the fine points of tribal history. "They're always interesting."

McCullough nodded. "I *love* them! Remember when they got sent out to attack those troops from Indiana?"

"Baptist Gap," said Yarby, and then they both nodded as if everybody ought to know the whole story from just that reference, but of course the rest of us had no idea what they were talking about. My knowledge of Cherokee lore is wide, but it ain't deep.

I wouldn't have minded hearing the story, but when the conversation seemed like it was going to drift away from the matter at hand, the sheriff seemed to recall that he had more hands to shake that afternoon, so he said quickly, "About the Battle of Waynesville. This Arrowood fellow distinguished himself in it?"

"No. He wasn't even on the winning side that day. It wasn't much of a skirmish, but I'd say he was definitely the loser. His claim to fame, in fact, is that he was the only soldier killed in the entire battle."

Fred Yarby laughed. "Unluckiest man in the world," he said. "Only man killed in a battle that took place some three weeks after the war ended."

"Sheriff, you might not want to mention him on the campaign trail," LeDonne said, deadpan.

"I don't think having a Confederate soldier as an ancestor would help no matter what he did," said Spencer.

"Oh, but he wasn't a Confederate," said McCullough. "Didn't we mention that? The Confederates may have lost the war, but they sure as heck won that particular battle. Thanks to the Cherokees. But Arrowood was a soldier in Kirk's Legion. He was Union."

You could tell from the expression on Spencer's face that he hadn't seen that coming. People in these parts just naturally assume that their people fought for the South, and for a long time after the war, nobody talked much about who was on what side—it was safer not to—so gradually most folks just forgot the whys and the wherefores of their family's role in the war. What they remembered was half Hollywood and half gossip.

Spencer managed a smile, and said something like, "Union, huh? That's a story they never told around the table at Thanksgiving."

"Well, it could come in handy," said LeDonne. "The next time one of the Florida people goes on about Southern rednecks, you can invoke your sainted Union ancestor to shut him up."

Spencer said he'd be sure to do that, and we all knew he wouldn't, and the two of them left then, but I could tell that the news had stuck in his craw, and we hadn't heard the last of it. He'd be back.

Malinda

Sometimes when you climb the mountain that folk around here call the Grandfather, and you crawl out to the precipice of a rock ledge to look out, you can see before you a patchwork of woods and fields stretching way into the distance with dark skeins of clouds hanging over them. Then you know that there is a storm happening somewhere off in the valley. Down below folks are getting rained on—maybe even struck by lightning—but you are safe, far above the storm, sitting in the golden sunshine, just watching it happen.

That's how the war felt to us, at first.

Nobody could have cared less about that war than I did. The rights of it was just something the menfolk argued about, that's all, and if it hadn't of been that, they'd have found something else to bicker over. Did Carolina have a right to leave the Union? Did the Northern states that sold the slaves in the first place have the right to declare them free without giving back the money they made a-selling them? Which side was in the right? Oh, the men argued loud and long about it, and a few

resorted to fistfights to settle their differences, same as
the states themselves would come to do, but it made me
no never mind. I had me a young husband and a home-
stead to tend.

For all the men's quarreling about it, nothing changed
up in the hills—not then. Nobody I knew went off to
fight, and life here around Grandfather went right along
just like it always did. Keith's stepdaddy Coffey said the
war was just a squabble over whether rich men could
keep their slaves or not, and since up here in these hills
we had neither rich men nor slaves, we paid it no mind,
except as a wedge for an argument. It was all happening
a long way off.

It was somebody else's storm in the valley.

Then it wasn't.

I was the first one Keith told when he decided to go
off to the war. Lots of men in these mountains ain't like
that. They'll talk to their daddies or their uncles or the
rest of the menfolk in the family, and the wife gets no
more say in her man's business than a yard dog, but me
and Keith talked everything over just like I was a
brother to him, even if I was just a girl and two years
younger'n him to boot.

"Malinda, I'm heading off to the war," he said.

It was a gray afternoon in early March, and the two of
us were hunting up on Grandfather. Keith was born in
the shadow of that mountain, and I reckon he loves it
more than he does me, which is saying a lot. He says he
can see the face of the Grandfather in the ridges of rock
at the summit of the peak, and sometimes it smiles
down on him in the morning sunshine as if to bid him
good day. Keith's daddy run off when he was little, and
he likes the man his momma married well enough, but I
guess he feels like the mountain is kin to him more than
they are, something that belongs just to him, though I
think it's the other way around, myself.

We were hoping to shoot a deer or at least a couple

of squirrels for the stew pot. Most men up here don't take their wives along when they go hunting, but Keith does. I can shoot as good as him anyhow. I can put a ball clean through a squirrel's head. You just about have to, if you're going to eat it. Otherwise you spend so much time picking shot out of the carcass that it's not worth the trouble to cook it.

We hadn't found any game yet, but the wind was blowing so cold up there on the ridge that our faces got numb and our fingers felt like sticks against the stocks of our muskets. We crawled back into the shelter of a laurel thicket, and snuggled up to one another to take the chill off our bones. I put my nose up against the hollow of Keith's neck, and he put his hands up under my shirt to get 'em warm, and then one thing led to another and we were in there for quite a spell.

Afterward, I was hitching up my britches—I don't wear no skirt when we go out hunting and I'd as lief not wear one the rest of the time neither, but needs must. I picked the leaves and twigs out of my hair, and said, "Come on out, Keith. I'm ready to go looking for game again, but I bet just now we made enough noise to scare every beast out here clear over into Tennessee."

"Rabbits won't run far," he said. "They have so little spirit that there's not too awful much sport in shooting at 'em. I'm out for bigger game."

"Too early for bear," I said, squinting up at the pale winter sun. The leaves were still yellow-green in the valley, and up here on the mountain the buds were tight knots on the tree limbs, waiting for longer days and warmer winds before they'd open. "Still too early for bear."

"Wasn't talking about bear," said Keith. He was standing underneath a cloud shadow just then, and all of a sudden he looked as gray as that great stone face on the top of the mountain behind him, and his voice got all quiet and solemn. I stopped walking then and turned to look up at him, trying to hear whatever it was he wasn't saying. Keith is head and shoulders taller than me, and I stepped back a pace so I could look square into those blue eyes of his, looking for truth. He wouldn't look me in the eye, and I felt the cold curl right up in the pit of my stomach, a tapeworm of fear.

"Malinda, I'm heading off to the war," he told me.

I sank right down on the slope of the hill then, not feeling the cold any more. I looked up past Keith at the mountaintop, but Grandfather had hid his face in the clouds. I should have known this would come sooner or later. We had heard that the state had passed a new law forcing the men to join the army. Before that I hadn't thought much about the war. There didn't seem to be any reason to. I was content to leave the subject to the men. Let 'em talk, I thought, for the subject didn't seem important enough to waste women's time on it. The men would bring it up time and again, chewing it over like a cow with a cud.

Things had already started to happen over the line in Tennessee. Four months ago, in November of '61, the U.S. government was gearing up for the spread of the war, and they ordered all the bridges in east Tennessee to be burned and all the railroad lines taken up from Chattanooga on up. They didn't send regular soldiers in to do the job—maybe they couldn't spare an army. Anyhow, they knew that a lot of the east Tennesseans were still loyal to the Union, so they sent word in secret for the local loyalists to do the job in the night, and to try not to get caught. The plan was to make it hard for the Confederate army to get into the area from the South, and then the Federals could slip in through the Cumberland Gap and occupy the area.

What happened over in Sullivan County was so terrible that everybody in these parts got to hear about it, and it made some people even stronger for the Union than they had been before. It also told them that they had better be both careful and pitiless, because this was indeed a cruel war.

The east Tennessee partisans went over to a town called Union in the night to destroy the bridge over the Holston River. There were a handful of local Confederate soldiers posted there to guard the bridge, but the raiders captured them first, and then they proceeded to burn the bridge right enough. But then they had to figure out what to do with those Rebel guards. They knew each other, you see. They were neighbors. Common sense said to kill them, of course, but the war was only eight months old and still happening far away, and it isn't easy to kill people you know in cold blood when their only offense is being on the other side.

The Rebel soldiers begged for their lives. Swore they wouldn't tell who did it, if they were only let loose and allowed to live. So the partisans took their oath of silence and let them go. The Bible says, *"Blessed are the merciful, for they shall receive mercy."* Well, from the Lord maybe, but not in this war. As soon as those treacherous Confederates got back to their own lines, they told the officers the name of every man they knew who'd had a hand in burning the bridge, and those they didn't know they were able to guess at.

The Rebels sent troops into east Tennessee, captured the bridge burners, and hanged them next to a railroad track over in Greeneville. Folks said that their bodies were left dangling so close to the railroad tracks that folks in passing trains used to lean out the window and swat at the dead men with their canes. When the news of this reached us over the border in North Carolina, we were reminded how perilous a thing it was to talk about politics. Being loyal to the Union in a Rebel state would put you and all your kinfolk in mortal danger. But it didn't make us loyal Confederate citizens. It only made us careful.

The menfolk knew the war was coming here. There

was as yet no fighting within fifty miles of our settlement and no slaves in the whole of the county, but yet
they must thrash it all out as if that war had something
to do with us. Men have time to talk when sunset ends
the farm chores or the hunting party, but women work
right along. In the daylight hours, there is the washing
and the churning to do, livestock to tend, a garden that
needs looking after, and three meals to cook for the
menfolk. After supper is over, there is sewing to be
done by firelight until your eyes are too heavy to stay
open anymore. If I'd a had any say in the matter, I
would have asked to have been born a boy, for it seems
to me that menfolk have the best of it. Leastways I
thought they did, until the government started telling
them they had to go off and die for some bureaucratic
notion whether they believed in it or not.

And now here was my own husband saying he was
going to join up, telling me—not asking or caring what
I thought about it—even though we had been man and
wife five years now.

"I thought you didn't hold with secession," I said. I
kept my fists balled up and my eyes narrow and I stared
him down like a dog. I wasn't going to stand there and
cry like some skirt-bound old biddy. I'd like to have
punched him in the jaw, except that there wouldn't be
no sport in it, 'cause Keith'd never hit me back. He was
funny that way. He'd as lief hit a man as look at him, but
he never raised a hand to me.

"They'll give us some money, Malinda," said Keith,
trying to smile me back into a good mood. "Ten dollars
the very day I join up and more to come."

"Ten dollars—and your daddy Coffey would half kill
you, Keith. You know how much he hates secesh."

"No, I'll square it with him. See, Malinda, I got a
plan."

I rolled my eyes heavenward. "Oh Lord deliver us from
L. McKesson Blalock's plans," I said, and he knew I was

boiling then, 'cause I hardly ever call him by his given name. He's been known as Keith to all and sundry since he started fistfighting at sixteen, when folks said he was almost as good as Alfred Keith from over in Burnsville who made a living at it. "Well?" I said. "What kind of plan starts with going to war on the enemy's side?"

"It's not like they give you a choice. You know about the conscription, Malinda? That's a new law that says men have to serve in the army. No choice. Now, I reckon I could try to run off to Kentucky where the Federals are, but h'it's a good ways away, and I might get caught on the journey. And then they'd hang me."

I looked around at the curtain of trees stretching away down the mountain and covering all the other mountains as far as the eye could see. "I don't reckon anybody could find you if you was to hide out here," I said. "And I could bring you up some food. I know all the deer trails same as you."

"But they might take our land if I was to go missing. They'd make it hard on you."

"Let 'em try," I said. If this war was going to tear holes through my life, I would look forward to putting buckshot in somebody to even the score a little. Just let some government toady set foot on my land.

"Besides, Malinda, I couldn't stand to sit up here like a penned-up hog while everybody else was off doing the fighting. I ain't no coward." He shook his head. "My way is better."

"And your way is—what exactly?"

He beamed. "I join up with the Confederates, and we get the money. I go to their training camp, and they give me a new musket and teach me soldiering. Then they send me up to Virginny where the war is, and then—then—we'll be camped just a short walk from the Union lines, so I'll slip away in the night and join t'other side."

Keith grinned at me then like a shit-eating possum, and I reckoned he was waiting for me to shout hallelujah and amen, but I didn't. I just sat there staring up at him, as stone-faced as the mountain I was sitting on, a-waiting for him to finish being so pleased with himself. When his smile dimmed a little, I said, "What if they catch you slipping off, Keith? Or what if there's a battle before you ever have a chance to get away? What if you was to catch the fever down in the flatlands and die?"

He sighed. "Well, maybe it's not a perfect plan, Malinda, but I swan it's all I know to do. If I could stay home and be let alone, I would, but they'd just come and get me. At least this way I get a chance to fight for what I hold with, instead of what I'm told to fight for."

I nodded. When Keith is set on something, it's a waste of breath to argue with him. I could see his mind was made up, and he was probably right about not having a lot of choices in the matter. I shivered in the cold mountain sunshine. Part of me wished the war would go away and leave us alone, and the other part of me was fit to be tied because Keith was going to go off and have an adventure and see the world and leave me home—like men are always doing. I could tell that he expected me to be a good girl and keep the house swept, and the garden weeded, and the hogs tended while he was gone.

Back when I had gone to school the teacher had told us stories from *The Iliad* about a Trojan War, and they were fine tales and a treat to listen to, all except the part about the hero's wife. Ulysses went off to war and stayed gone for twenty years, having a fine time soldiering and sailing around after the war ended, but his wife had to stay home and wait for him for all those long years. The teacher said she did needlework the whole time while she waited, and I thought she sounded too pitiful for words. If Keith thought I was going to do needlework while he went off to fight, he had another think coming.

"The only thing that's worrying me, Malinda, is you," Keith was saying. "I hate to think of going off to war and leaving you all alone here. Nobody to help you with the livestock. Nobody to protect you."

"Oh, don't you fret about me, Keith," I told him all cold and solemn. "I reckon I'll be all right—one way or another."

Rattler

After the sheriff drove away, I got Yarby back on the subject of Thomas's Legion, on account of my Cherokee bloodlines. People never say much about the Indian presence in the War, but I knew that at least one Confederate general—Stand Watie—was a Cherokee. If you look at pictures of the signing of the surrender at Appomattox, you won't have any trouble picking him out of the crowd. Thomas's Legion is mentioned in passing every now and again by one of the reenactors. Anyhow, I wanted to hear what had happened to the Indiana troops.

It wasn't hard to get Yarby started on the subject. Primed with one of Bill Nance's home-brewed beers, he settled back on a camp stool and told the tale off so pat that right away I spotted it as a party piece of old Fred's. This is one he tells the sightseers, I thought. Or anyhow he used to. In these times, a lot of people wouldn't find it funny anymore, but I did, and I figured I was entitled, because I might even be related to those old boys in the story. I thought I might tell it to Maggie Raincrow anyhow. She'd claim to be horrified, too, but I bet it would make her smile. McCullough hung around because listening to people talk is what he does, and he said he wished he could write about Baptist Gap in the newspaper sometime, but he knew he'd catch hell if he tried.

"It's an atrocity story," Fred Yarby warned me. "Some folks might not care for it."

McCullough smiled. "To the thinking man, it is a comedy. To the feeling man, it is a tragedy."

"Well, I know some about William Thomas," I told them. "Little banty-rooster of a feller—*Wil-Usdi,* they called him in Cherokee. White man who grew up in the Carolina mountains near the Cherokee nation, and befriended the tribe. Ran a trading post early on."

McCullough nodded. "Later on he went to Washington and became a spokesman for the Cherokee."

"What was left of them," I said.

"What was left of them," Yarby agreed, taking a pull on his beer.

In the 1830s when gold got discovered in these hills, the U.S. government aimed to move all the Cherokee out to Oklahoma so the whatchamacallit—"ethnic majority"—could claim the land and pouch the gold. Sometimes I think the summer people from Florida would like the rest of us up here to join them. Anyhow, when most of the tribe was marched off to Oklahoma on the Trail of Tears, about five hundred Cherokee hid out here in the hills and managed to get left behind— long, sad story—and William Thomas took up for them every chance he got.

"He tried to get the government to pay the Eastern Band for the land they took. Finally he had to buy it himself, because the Indians weren't allowed to have title to the land."

"Don't get me started, Fred."

He smiled.

McCullough said, "After that Thomas got himself elected to the state senate, which is a pretty shrewd move for an activist. Back in the 1850s he tried to get them to run the railroad through the mountains, but either the money was lacking, or the technology, or both."

"Then the war came along, and all the money and the technology went to that instead." What with one thing and another the railroad didn't cut through these mountains into Tennessee until the 1880s.

"Well, so did William Thomas," said McCullough. "He sided with the Confederacy—"

"Which, considering how the U.S. government had treated the Cherokee, makes a world of sense—"

"Don't you get started, Rattler," said Yarby.

"Sure, it made sense, though," said McCullough. "Since all of Thomas's influence was in North Carolina, he really didn't have any other option if he wanted to stay important. He ran for office in the new Confederate legislature and lost, so he decided to establish his little empire in the army instead. They needed all the troops they could get."

"And he knew where he could get a whole bunch of recruits who'd follow him anywhere," I said. And people wonder why I live alone in the woods.

Yarby looked disgusted, too, but it turned out to be for a different reason. "With Thomas's prestige, he becomes a colonel on Day One. Nice work if you can get it." He looked a little shamefaced. "I speak as an ex-corporal, you understand," he said.

"Why, Fred, I thought you were a captain," I said, eyeing his uniform.

"No, I mean in the army I was a corporal. The real army." Then he looked around, like he was afraid somebody would overhear and give him grief about saying this wasn't the real army, but McCullough just grinned, and personally I was relieved that he remembered.

"Thomas's Legion," I prompted them.

"Right. A battalion of Cherokees and mountaineers commanded by Thomas. Remember nobody has any military experience there, not even Thomas. What a sight they must have been! Early on, his troops were armed with everything from squirrel guns to steel-tipped spears and bows and arrows. The Confederacy as a whole was never well-equipped, but Thomas's men must have been exceptional even by their standards."

"Originally," said McCullough, "the battalion was attached to Major General Kirby Smith, over in Tennessee."

"The trouble with reenactors and newspapermen," I said, "is that they are prone to getting bogged down in details and politics. If there's a good part to this tale, get to it."

Yarby took over. "September 15, 1862. Union forces under the command of General George W. Morgan had ventured south of the Cumberland Gap, heading for upper east Tennessee, where the local populace strongly favored the Union. If the Federals could establish a military presence in upper east Tennessee, they could obstruct communication between the Confederate forces in Kentucky and those in the rest of the South."

"Obstruct?" said McCullough.

"Well, you know, keep 'em from conferring with one another. Divide and conquer."

"I'm with you," I said. "Go on, Fred."

"Well, the Confederate scouts found out about this little invasion, and the army ordered a force of Partisan Rangers into the area to observe the Federal troop movements."

"Thomas's Legion," I said.

"Well, two companies of 'em, anyhow." Yarby stopped and looked at me. "One group went into Baptist Gap, which is about ten miles north of Rogersville, near the Kentucky line. Do you want to know who led them?"

"No," I said.

"First Lieutenant William S. Terrell," said McCullough.

"Don't sound Cherokee to me."

"No, he wasn't, but the guy who led the charge was. His name was As-too-something-or-other. I've only seen the name written down."

"He was Chief Junaluska's grandson," McCullough added.

"And you can only pronounce *his* name because there's a big lake named after him," I said.

"Okay," said Yarby, "but the point is—here's this dark-skinned soldier in a turban, probably doing some kind of wild yell—"

"Not the Rebel yell, I bet," I said. "Cherokee warriors did something like—" I cut loose with a long, loud rolling howl that would raise the hackles on a wildcat, until they shushed me on the grounds that we weren't more than ten miles from town.

"The Indiana troops were transfixed, I expect," said Yarby, when his ears stopped ringing. "The problem was that Second Lieutenant As-too-ga-something . . . well, Junaluska's grandson . . . goes charging at the Indiana troops. Nobody seems to know why he did that. The logical way to fight in a narrow mountain gap is to lay up in the rocks and ambush the enemy as he walks past."

"Well, I'm sure he was sorry about it later, because the Indiana boys blew him away," said McCullough.

"Graveyard dead," said Yarby solemnly. "After that, the Cherokee soldiers just lost it. They all attacked, running full tilt at those astonished Union soldiers, splitting the air with that eerie battle cry, and just hacking left and right. The Federal troops weren't up to that, and those that could get away took off running for their lives."

"Okay, stop there," said McCullough. "It makes a better story this way. So, the Cherokee Confederates made their way back to their camp, and went to camp headquarters to report to William Thomas. *Sir, we engaged the enemy in battle and we won,* they said.

"That's good, boys, said Thomas.

"And we brought back proof of our victory, they told him, just as pleased as punch. *Here it is, Colonel Wil-Usdi.* They held up a big, wet-looking burlap sack and plopped it right in the middle of Thomas's desk. He opened it up, and there was—"

"A pile of scalps," I said.

"Yep. They scalped the Indiana regiment, and brought the results home as war trophies. Well, Colonel Thomas was *hor-ri-fied.* He often said that he aimed to make not savage warriors, but Christian soldiers out of his troops, and this little escapade was definitely a sign that he was not making progress in that direction."

"Chewed 'em out, did he?"

"Worse than that," said Yarby. "After he finished giving them down the country, he ordered a deputation to go back north to the Cumberland Gap under a flag of truce, and return those scalps to the Indiana regiment's commanding officer."

"That's the scene I'd like to have witnessed," said McCullough. "A couple of Cherokee soldiers under a white flag walking up to the Union colonel, handing him that dripping sack, scuffing the dirt with their boot toes, and mumbling, *'We're sorry.'* Just the looks on everybody's faces." With his hands he framed an imaginary headline in the air, 'The Nightmare of Ethnic Diversity.' "

"I don't imagine they'd find that story overly amusing in Indiana," I said.

Yarby nodded. "Might even make 'em regret naming the state that."

"The Legion didn't keep doing that, did they?"

"Well . . ." McCullough looked uncomfortable. "Don't forget that it was the white settlers who invented scalping in the first place. They used to pay bounties for wolves or Indians killed, and that was the proof."

"It figures," I said. "But you didn't answer the question. Did Thomas's Legion quit doing it?"

"They didn't stop altogether."

"But not at the Battle of Waynesville, right?"

"Well, I don't think so, Rattler. It was so late in the war. *After* the war, to be exact. And only one guy died, after all."

"Yeah," I said. "Private Arrowood. I hope to God they didn't scalp Arrowood. I'll never hear the end of it."

Zebulon Vance

I was, at the age of twenty-eight, the youngest member of the Thirty-sixth Congress of the United States, and a member of the minority American Party, to boot, so that in the House of Representatives I had all the influence of a barking dog upon a freight train. I could see the train wreck coming, though—by God, I could.

The talk of war grew louder with each passing day.

The Secessionists were hell-bent on derailing the Union, and though I spoke against it, and wrote against it, and did what little I could politically, I still saw the collision coming at all deliberate speed. In February, at the behest of the Virginia Legislature, twenty-one states held a peace convention in Washington, and after much wrangling the delegates submitted their recommendation of measures to avert war, but nobody paid them any mind, and the talk went on as before.

I still argued for reconciliation. I suppose it seems odd that the man who would have walked into a duel only months earlier would now exert all his energy toward preventing a duel between the states, but, while I did not doubt a state's right to leave the Union, I questioned the necessity of it. I couldn't see any percentage in it for the mountain people, and that's who had sent me to Congress.

In the spring of 1861, still fighting the inevitable, I had agreed to go on the stump in the mountain counties to urge the voters to oppose secession. It was close on my thirty-second birthday, and I was holding forth to a goodly crowd back home in Marshall, trying to prevail upon my constituents to see the sense of remaining in the Union, and trying to keep the secessionist wildfire from spreading into the mountain territory. After all, we had few enough slaves in our territory, and import tariffs do scant harm to folks who buy little except salt and nails. The South may have had legitimate complaints against the rest of the country, but what business was it of ours?

The crowd was restive, and I knew that it would be a job convincing them. They were only listening to me because no other entertainment presented itself that afternoon. One good dogfight would have cost me half my audience. A goodly number of the listeners had pistols on their hips and the sullen expressions of men who don't like what they are hearing. They muttered among themselves at how the government was supposed to do what the people wanted instead of the other way around. But they heard me out, civilly enough, with occasional expressions of anger and excitement, where they ought to have been showing somber concern, for they knew the gravity of the situation as well as I did. Blood had been shed over slavery in Charles Town, Virginia, and John Brown hanged for it. We were all mindful of the consequences, should war come, and the ones with joyful anticipation were graven fools.

"At the very least," I said, "North Carolina could do as some have suggested in the event of war: Withdraw from the North and constitute ourselves an armed neutrality. I think the border states would join in such an attitude of neutrality, and then the fight would whittle down to a boil between New England and South Carolina and such states as are mad enough to join them. I think the war might even be prevented entirely if the government would withdraw its troops from the Southern forts—"

A tow-headed boy in overalls came running out of the telegraph office across the street, shouting and waving a bit of paper as he ran. He hardly seemed to take any notice of me up on the speaker's platform, but he came barreling on toward that cluster of townspeople, braying as he went. When I saw the look on the boy's face, I ceased to speak and the crowd subsided into a frozen silence.

I stood there immobile—literally with my hand in the air, for I had been gesturing to heaven about the point in my speech—and the boy's words carried over the heads of the crowd: "Fort Sumpter has been fired upon. Mr. Lincoln calls for volunteers to suppress the insurrection. Seventy-five thousand volunteers!"

Slowly I let my hand fall.

Slavery was no longer the issue. Now we were being asked to invade our sister state to the south, and that we could not do. The telegram was passed from hand to hand, and finally offered up to me. I read it while the buzzing over this thunderbolt of news subsided, and at last the crowd fell silent, and they turned back to me still standing there alone on the platform, like an oak tree waiting for the lightning.

I found my voice again. "If war must come I prefer to be with my own people," I said. "If we have to shed blood, I prefer to shed Northern rather than Southern blood. If we have to slay, I prefer to slay strangers rather than my own kin and neighbors. And so it is better— right or wrong—that communities and states should go together and face the horrors of war in a body—sharing a common fate . . ."

A great cheer went up then, I think, but I scarcely heard it.

"A war is mighty like a hog killing, Mr. Vance," the fellow said to me, pumping my hand and grinning up at me. "I reckon it just pulls all the neighbors right in close, and all of 'em working alive for a common cause."

"Mighty like a hog killing," I said, managing to repress a shudder. Mighty like before long, that's what I was dreading.

But for now in Asheville—on the fourth day of May 1861—the newly-declared war had all the air of a carnival, with cheering crowds and blaring trumpets. The streets flashed with gold braid and bright leather, polished swords, and shiny gun barrels, and the gleam of freshly curried saddle horses. The town bubbled with the thrill of knowing that something was about to happen, and even if that something should prove terrible, it was nonetheless new and exciting, and therefore welcome.

I began the war on the speakers platform, and spent many of its early days there, for as a man of substance in the district, I was expected to raise a company of soldiers and then to lead it. There was no going back to Congress, since I could hardly represent a state which no longer belonged to the country of that governing body. I supposed that another such Congress might soon materialize in the new Confederacy, and I thought I might try for it, but for now all the able-bodied young men seemed bent on taking up arms.

Even August S. Merrimon had gone for a soldier.

When I went back to Asheville, and announced my intention of raising a company of men from the mountain counties, Merrimon was among the first to answer the call to arms, and he was made an instant officer under my command. My brother Robert had joined a different regiment, perhaps thinking that we could both rise farther and faster if we were not in one another's shadow.

In all the excitement no one seemed perturbed that precious few of the Confederacy's newly fledged commanders had a lick of military experience. I did not even have a uniform yet—Harriett was seeing to that—but by God I had troops to command. They signed up in droves, intoxicated at the thought of martial glory, and apparently unperturbed by the fact that their commanding officer had no more experience at soldiering than the least of them. I marveled at their trust, for in their place, I would have been mightily perturbed.

"It's quite feudal, isn't it?" said Merrimon, as we stood watching the company clerk swear in some grinning farm boys. "One of the duties of a nobleman is to furnish troops at the king's behest. In this country we claim to be a democracy, but the rules for the aristocracy remain the same."

"I don't feel all that much like an aristocrat," I said. "I always thought they ate better than this."

Merrimon raised his eyebrows. "But who else could join the army one minute and be made the company commander the next?" He pointed at the gap-toothed ploughboy swaggering toward the recruiter's table. "That fellow there . . . He may be a better shot than you. Even a better, braver warrior. But he will wait a long time for a promotion—if he ever does get one."

Merrimon had nettled me—as usual. "I suppose training and leadership count for something," I said. "I have been to university and served in both the state legislature and the U.S. Congress, so perhaps I know a thing or two about authority that cannot be learned plowing furrows in Buncombe County."

"Well, I hope that may be true," Merrimon said, nodding toward the newly formed Rough and Ready Guards milling about on the cobblestones. "For their sakes."

By the eighteenth of May the Rough and Ready Guards had got as far as camp in Statesville, where the men drilled, and donned their newly made uniforms, and got accustomed to life as soldiers. I sat in my tent in the cool of the evening, listening to a whippoorwill off in the woods, and penning a few lines by lamplight to my wife and family. The people of Statesville had been wonderfully kind to us. The ladies brought me cakes and pastries and bouquets enough to fill a trunk. I shall send them back to Harriett in Asheville as a token of my love and remembrance. In the morning we would start for Weldon, where the train would take us east to camp.

I was tired and chilled with the night dew, hearing occasional bursts of laughter and fragments of tunes from my newly made soldiers as I wrote, and I was mindful of the dangers that lay ahead. Not the enemy armies. I had scarcely had a thought to spare for battle. Foremost among my concerns were the powers that be in the state capital, where the Democrats in power seemed bound and determined to appoint their own henchmen to all the state offices, while those who had opposed their secessionist policies would be made to do the hard work and to make bricks without straw. It would take all my luck and skill to prosper in such a climate, but a more immediate worry lay in the prospect of seeing the summer months through in an encampment, where fevers could run rife, and disease made cowards of us all.

We arrived in Raleigh, and I was so peppered with letters from citizens back home until I did believe I'd rather face bullets. Soon after we got here Private Joseph Randle was in a state, claiming that his wife had nothing to eat since his absence, and I sent his letter on to my brother Robert, for I'll not have the families of my soldiers on my conscience if I can prevent it. Robert says it is all nonsense. He has looked into the matter himself, and in his latest letter to me he reports that Mrs. Randle has shoes, two or three dresses, and plenty to eat. Robert has made himself responsible for the well-being of the Rough and Ready Guards' families. He says he gave Newton Patton's wife some bacon and flour as well. I must urge the men not to believe these rumors, for such morale-killing tales would fell an army as fast as a fever.

I was assigned to the Fourteenth Regiment of North Carolina Troops with my merry men—but not with my Merrimon, for he had got himself transferred to the commissary general's department with the rank of captain, and I have no doubt that he will fight the war from a leather-bound chair in the state capital, dodging requisition forms and firing paper salvos at all and sundry. My Harriett could wish nothing more for me, but I am satisfied to be a soldier for the foreseeable future, though I doubt I shall escape the paperwork, for not a day goes by without my receiving some urgent letter from a constituent, asking for a soldier's discharge, or a favor of some sort. I do what I can, but sometimes I think kindly of the enemy for wanting nothing more of me than the sight of my chest for target practice.

By mid-June we found ourselves in Virginia, where the war was.

The Fourteenth settled in at Camp Bragg, at a railway crossing some two and a half miles from the town of Suffolk, though I for one would be gladly further from it still. It is a straggling, ragged, old-fashioned town about the size of Asheville. Our camp is sixteen miles from Yorktown, eighteen from Norfolk, and about twenty-six from Newport News, where the enemy have landed a large force. Camp Bragg commands the junction of the Petersburg & Norfolk & Roanoke & Seaboard railroads—quite an important post, for should the enemy strike across the country and seize our position no more troops north or south could be thrown into the relief of Norfolk. We do not anticipate any attack here though for the present, as everything seems tending toward Manassas Junction and Alexandria, and we look for a tremendous fight there in the course of ten days. Our time may come sooner than we expect.

We sleep with our weapons at hand, and have picket guards thrown out one mile and a half every night. And in late July, while we are waiting for the Union army, who should turn up first? Augustus Merrimon.

He had been visiting Yorktown as part of his duties for the commissary office, and being in my neck of the woods, of course he came to the camp, and we were able to scare up a decent meal in his honor, but nothing compared to what he is used to back in Raleigh, I'll warrant. Still, he seemed a little shamefaced at being offered even that.

"The troops at Yorktown are in a bad way," he told me, when we had repaired to the out-of-doors with a jug of Virginia whiskey to talk of home and better times, but inevitably our conversation turned to matters at hand. Merrimon drained his glass and looked up at the stars. "It seems strange to think that there should be war on such a night as this."

The moon was full and the night was pleasant, with the scent of distant roses borne on the breeze. "I've no doubt that you think it a fine evening," I said, "but I take a more jaundiced view of it, as I am slated officer of the day, so I will be spending the remainder of this balmy night tramping around our lines and pickets."

"I suppose you must," said Merrimon, "but from what we hear, the battle took place last week—not at this railroad junction but at one much closer to Washington. Manassas Junction. They say that Thomas Jackson leading Virginia infantry made a great success of it. I had thought the war would be over by now."

"Well, nobody told me about it," I said.

Merrimon gave me that maddening superior smile of his. "You are somewhat off the beaten track here," he said. "And generals do not share their thoughts with lesser officers—even if they happen to be former congressmen. Now, where I am situated—in Raleigh—I hear things."

He saw me winding up to protest that while he was hearing things, I was actually in the war, and he cut me off with, "Oh, you are soldiering, right enough, but you only see the little patch of war where you are posted. Back in the capital we get a larger picture. And indeed we thought the war would be over last week. Manassas Junction is only thirty miles from Washington. The dispatches say that people from the city drove out in their carriages with picnic baskets to watch the fighting—and, when the tide of battle turned, they were nearly trampled by their own retreating army! If our forces had simply pressed their advantage and invaded the capital, we could have forced Lincoln to capitulate."

"Well, that's too grand for me," I said. "I am but a lowly officer of the day, fit for pacing out the lines of an evening."

Merrimon smiled again. "That may change. There are new regiments being mustered in next month, some from the mountain counties. Your supporters have not forgotten you, Zebulon."

I had supposed this bit of confidence to be simply more bravado on Merrimon's part, boasting of his inside knowledge of the workings of war and politics, but I am bound to say that he was correct. Well, even a broken clock is right twice a day. But sure enough before another month was out, I had a special dispatch from James G. Martin, the adjutant general of North Carolina troops:

> *August 27, 1861*
> *Official information received at this office that you are elected Colonel of the 26 Regiment*

*N.C. Troops. Will you accept? If so report here
in person without delay.*

Would I accept? Why, I believe that if I had set out on
foot, I could have beat the train to Raleigh. I arranged
for Philetus Roberts, another lawyer from Asheville, to
succeed me as captain of the Rough and Ready Guards,
while I proceeded on to Raleigh to assume my new
posting. I had hopes of transferring the Rough and
Ready from the Fourteenth to the Twenty-sixth, so that
they might be under my command again, but it is difficult to reason with the military bureaucracy about anything, and the change has not yet been effected. I
accepted my new command, managed to wrangle a fur-
lough in the deal, and went home to Asheville for a few
weeks' respite and a visit with Harriett and my boys.

    In early September I left my home in the mountains
and went east to join the Twenty-sixth at Camp Burg-
wyn on the Atlantic coast near Morehead City. Our
forces were about two thousand strong in the area, and
we could see the Yankee vessels sailing past every day,
but they did not attack, which was odd, because they
could easily have moored out of range of our guns and
thrown shells into our camp if they felt like it. We decided that they must be intending to attack at Wilmington, or in one of the inlets closer to the Virginia line. So
we sat there eating figs and scuppernong grapes, while
the war snubbed us again, but Merrimon's words about
my not having been forgotten resounded in my memory
more than once. In mid-September I had a letter from
an innkeeper in Macon County, asking if I would be a
candidate for the Confederate Congress, but I told him
no. He is a good fellow and means to honor me with his
request, but I think it best that I stay out of politics yet
awhile. I softened my answer to him by reminding him
how strong for the Union I had stood, and that when my
efforts to keep us from secession failed, I had pledged

myself to defending my homeland. Now having acquired sufficient knowledge of military affairs to begin to be useful to my country, I cannot escape its obligations by seeking, or even accepting, a civil appointment, I told him. But I am glad to be warmly remembered back in the mountains. Now if only my sister Hannah would stop agitating within the family for a promotion for her worthless husband, I would be almost content. He went into the Rough and Ready as a private, and so he should stay, but they are deviling Harriett about it, and I won't be bullied through the womenfolk.

The war whirled on—elsewhere—and 1861 gave way to a new year while I grew exceedingly tired of watching and waiting behind ditches for battles that never happened. I even wrote to Congressman Davidson, offering to go back to the mountains and raise up some new companies of soldiers from our citizenry there, for I truly thought I might be more useful employing my influence for recruiting rather than whiling away the war in drizzling, leaden idleness on the Carolina coast.

The answer to that prayer came not from the Confederate Congress, but from the Almighty, who seemed to say, "If you want to see battle so awful bad, boy, we'll send you one." Roanoke Island fell to Federal forces on February 10, and the coastal sounds and inlets were then open to invasion. Ten days after I wrote to Allen Davidson asking to go recruiting, my regiment was ordered inland to the town of New Bern, thought to be the target for General Burnside's advance. We were put under the command of Lawrence Branch, who had been my colleague in Congress before the secession, and who was elected colonel of the NC Thirty-third last September, about the same time I took on the Twenty-sixth. Last month he was promoted to brigadier general, commander of the Pamlico district of operations, but I wonder if he takes any pleasure in it, for when the war did let us in for the show, it left us reeling.

At seven o'clock in the morning on Friday, the fourteenth of March, Burnside's forces attacked New Bern. I was stationed on the right wing, with a swamp in front of my position, and the enemy hit us hard. By eleven o'clock, every regiment but mine was in retreat and gone, and the enemy crossed over our trenches and swept through my camp. From the shelter of the woods Burnside's troops were advancing on my position. They would have taken me prisoner, but Captain Young, my quartermaster, told me of the danger and urged me to retreat. The newly minted "General" Branch had not sent me any orders. (Well, afterward he claimed he did, but I never got them.)

Anyhow, we fell back, and when I got in sight of the River Trent, I saw that the railroad bridge was in flames. My fellow officers had all run off and got their troops safely away, and then they had fired the bridge to keep the enemy from following them!

Left us to our fate.

Fortunately for all of us, I knew something of the terrain, and, seeing that the river was impassable, I struck out for another route of passage. I found Briers Creek—at seventy-five-yards wide and too deep to ford, it was almost as big as the river itself—and I knew that it was navigable for steamboats. I wish there had been some steamboats available, for we were sorely in need of swift passage. All we found was one little wooden craft that would hold three men at a time. And I had hundreds to ferry to safety.

The enemy had advanced to within a mile of us. The smoke of their cannons mingled with the fog, and the ground trembled. There was no time to mull over the situation. I spurred my horse into the stream, but partway across he refused to swim any further with me astride, and I had to jump off and swim to the other side—with my sword, pistols, and cartridges boxes all fighting my efforts to stay afloat. One of the enlisted men grabbed the horse's reins, and now that he was unburdened of his rider, he consented to make the crossing. On the other side, I mounted him again and rode half a mile to a house, where we secured three boats for the evacuation of my forces.

We had to carry those three boats back to the creek on our shoulders, and then set out across the river amidst smoke and shell fire to rescue the men a few at a time. After four hours of hard labor, we managed to get all the soldiers across, except for three poor fellows who were drowned. The danger was great, and we knew it. It was a dark and foggy morning, and to hold off the enemy while the boats made the crossings, the men were situated in small half-moon redans, firing by company, beginning on the left, and the blaze from the muzzle of their guns lit up the darkness as we worked.

Balls whizzed around us in the fog, and at times men fell mortally wounded right at my feet, and I expected to be terrified, but oddly enough I felt only pleasure and excitement, for my soldiers fought gloriously in that continuous roar of small-arms fire, and they did not abandon their comrades to the enemy. The earth shook from the great guns of our own batteries and the answering salvos from the attacking ships, and the roar of the cannons made my ears ring. Deserted by the other regiments, and outnumbered by the enemy, we stood our ground as long as we had to.

"That's the last of them, Colonel!" said Roberts, my second-in-command, when the last of the boats was pulled ashore with its final load.

I was helping to pull a wounded soldier up the bank. He was bleeding badly, and when we let go of him, he started to pitch forward into the mud. "Put him on my horse," I told the men. "He can ride behind me."

When that had been done, I turned back to Roberts. "How do we stand?"

"Thirty-two killed, included the ones we lost in the

river, Colonel. Maybe thirty wounded. Many more than that missing. Perhaps a hundred and fifty all together. I fear that many of them will prove to be dead as well."

I nodded. "We took a beating, but it was the first real test of the men's resolve. I think we acquitted ourselves with honor."

"Well," said Roberts, "we did what we could, sir—without much help from either side."

Malinda

Keith joined up with the Confederates near the middle of March 1862, just like he said he would, but if he thought I was going to stand by the road, a-twisting my apron and crying as he marched away, he had another think coming.

He stood there in the yard next to the cabin with his boots all polished and his greatcoat pulled around him and a scarf I knit him around his neck. He's so tall I had to stand on the stone step to kiss him good-bye again. I like a tall man. I remember my grandaddy Gragg, who had been a soldier in the Revolution. He was a great tree of a man, full seven feet tall, topped off with a shock of red hair. He died when I was little, but I remember him telling stories about how his pappy came over from Ireland, and I used to think to myself that when I was a grown girl I wanted a man just as tall and strong as Grandaddy Gragg. And now that I had one, the war was fixing to take him away.

"Well, Malinda, are you sure you don't want to come?"

To see him off in the town, he meant. I had kissed him good-bye like an older sister, and he knew I was none too pleased that he was joining up with the Rebels after all his fine talk about the Union.

"I got chores to do up here at home," I said, worming my way out of his arms. "There's a sow about to pig, and since it is her first litter, I want to stay and see her through it. We can't afford to lose any stock with the war on."

Keith grinned and touched my cheek. "You don't want nobody to see you bawling on the street, do you, girl?"

"Well, it's a long way down the mountain to Lenoir," I said. "I'll stay right here and tend the farm. I got me some sewing to do, besides." Well, that was true enough.

"You should be all right here," he said, all solemn again. "Most folks are secesh, and when they hear I've joined up, they'll not bother you. Might even help if you was to need it."

"I'll take care not to," I said.

He didn't press me any more about going to see him off. He knew I didn't hold with secession, and if I'd had to traipse all the way down the mountain to Caldwell County, and stand in the streets of Lenoir next to all them people a-hollering for the Rebels, I'd get myself in trouble for certain. I'd be likely to tell them what fools these backwoods farmers were being for fighting a rich man's war. Ten dollars for joining up. Why, I reckon them planters pay more than that for their boots, and I would have said so. Why, I could turn that seeing-off party into a free-for-all in no time flat. Keith knew how I felt and that I wasn't shy about saying so. I don't suppose he wasn't in any hurry to see fighting—leastways not by his wife on the street in Lenoir—so he didn't try overmuch to make me go with him that morning. We said good-bye in the yard, and I told him again to be careful.

"Don't be a damn fool," I said. "You know you're only going 'cause they made you. Don't go getting carried away and get yourself shot on their account."

He smiled, even though he looked a mite shaken at the thought of going. "Why, 'Linda, I had it in mind to come home a beribboned hero," he said, and I knew he was poking fun at me, and so I reckoned he'd be all right on his own for a little while anyhow.

I watched him go down the hill until the laurel bushes blotted out the last little glimpse of his hat, and then I set out to chopping firewood, not because we needed any—Keith had seen to that—but because it felt good to bring that blade down on something hard, and I reckoned the wood-splitting would do me as much good as crying—maybe more, because at least I'd have some kindling to show for it afterward.

I had made up my mind what I must do not long after Keith told me he was going to enlist, but I kept going over things in my head just to make sure I had worked it all out and that I could manage it.

Keith left in early morning, and I spent the rest of the day setting the place to rights. I turned the hogs out of their pens and drove 'em off into the woods to forage for themselves. They lumbered past me, noses to the ground, already on the scent of chestnuts. The young sow that was fixing to farrow didn't want to go, but I made her. No point in her hanging around here, a-waiting for me to tend to her. The chickens were already loose, wandering all over the yard, so I gave them some scratch feed and they hovered around my feet, cocking their heads at me and hoping for more.

"You're on your own from now on, boys," I told them. Maybe the hawks or the bobcats would get them, but I couldn't worry about that. At least they wouldn't be penned up and starving. It was March: Out in the fields there would be worms and seeds aplenty to keep the hens in feed without any help from me.

The horse was different, though. He was a good bay saddle horse, just five years old, and Keith set quite a store by him. That horse would come like a puppy

when Keith called him, and he was as good-gaited as
any horse in these parts. He was fast, too. Keith had
once turned down an offer of thirty dollars cash money
for that horse, though he said later he wasn't any too
sure that the fellow doing the offering was good for
the money. I knew he'd never forgive me if I was to
turn a blood horse out on the mountain. Whether he
broke his leg, or foundered, or got caught and taken
away by somebody else, we'd never see him again, that
was certain.

You might think that neighbors wouldn't steal from
one another, and there was a time when I thought that,
too, but this war has cut deep into people's feelings, and
now they see your politics as an excuse to act against
you. They probably told themselves that stealing your
horse was an act of war, and the fact that they wanted it
anyhow was by-the-by. There weren't too many people
I could trust these days. They were mostly secesh, and
even if they thought we were on their side on account of
Keith joining the Confederacy, they might remember
the days when he argued loud and long for the other
side. Or else our Union neighbors might think he had
turned traitor on them, and so they'd set out to do us
harm. It seemed to me that there was no right side in
this war—only a choice of enemies.

After the hogs and chickens were sorted out, I went
out to the corral and saddled that horse. I'd miss him,
but at least he wasn't going to war. I didn't see why he
should suffer for people's foolishness. We didn't have
far to go—just a couple of ridges over and through the
fields to Austin Coffey's place. Daddy Austin wasn't
Keith's real father, but he was all the daddy that Keith
could remember, and I reckon he was about the only
person that Keith would listen to about anything. Part
of the reason that Keith was so strong for the Union was
that Daddy Austin was staunch against secession and
said so for as long as anybody would listen to him. If I

had to farm out Keith's horse, there wasn't any other
place I'd feel right about taking him.

As I rode into the gap toward the Coffey place, I
could see plumes of smoke coming out of the rock
chimney, so I knew Daddy Austin was there in the
cabin. I had figured he would be. I couldn't see a hard-
shell supporter of the Union going off to town to watch
a bunch of poor fools join the Confederate army, not
even if Keith was among them.

The bay horse's breath made little clouds in the cold
air that day, and at the outset I kept him going at a
goodly pace to keep us both warm. I steered him along
the low ground below the ridges where the wind wasn't
so fierce, and after a few minutes I drew rein and let the
bay amble along at his own pace in the afternoon sunshine, me enjoying my last ride for a long time, I reckoned. At least Keith's horse would be kept safe and
guarded at the Coffey's farm, where secesh people
couldn't steal him for an army mount. The maple
trunks were still white against the bare hills, their
branches tipped red with the buds of leaves to come.
Only the evergreens broke the bands of brown and
white. Nobody was out planting yet, and I didn't see a
soul along the way, only a couple of rabbits and a
glimpse of a deer high-tailing it into the woods when
she heard us coming.

As I rode up to the cabin, Daddy Austin hobbled out
to the porch, and waved to me. He must have seen me
through the window and known who I was, 'cause he
wasn't holding his gun. These are perilous times. "He's
gone then, is he?"

"Left first thing this morning," I said.

He curled his lip, and I couldn't tell if he was sad or
disgusted at the thought of Keith's joining up—maybe it
was some of both. Daddy Austin was past forty—too old
for the armies to want him, so he didn't feel the pressure
like we did. He acted like Keith had a choice in whether

or not to go, but Keith said it didn't feel like much of a choice to him.

"Well, the whole damned family's turned secesh, seems like," said Daddy Austin. "All three of my brothers have turned Confederate, and McCaleb's son Jones has enlisted, too. I never did think I'd see Keith go, though."

I dismounted and tied the reins to one of the narrow posts of the front porch. "Well, he felt like he had to," I said. "He wanted you to keep the horse for him."

Daddy Austin raised his eyebrows. "Keep the bay? He never said nothing to me about it. Why? Don't he trust you with him?"

I had the answer thought out already, so I shrugged and said careless-like, "Well, Keith said he thought a lone woman couldn't protect a horse if raiders came to steal it. We worried about the secesh neighbors before, but now that he has joined up with the Rebels, we thought that some of them that's strong for the Union might make a run on our place."

"Make war on women?" Daddy Austin's voice trembled. "I hope we have not come to that."

"Well, I figure we will," I said. "So I turned the hogs and chickens loose in the woods, and I've brought you the bay. I got people in Tennessee. Maybe I'll go and stay a spell with them, so if they raid us I won't be in harm's way."

"You think they'll make a run on your place." The old man looked like thunder. "I suppose they would, too," he said. "There's pickings to be had, and an excuse to take it, isn't there? The meanness that people will do on their own is nothing compared to what they'll do when a cause fires them up. This damned war will stir up enough bad blood to keep us at one another's throats for generations to come—even if we never see head nor tail of an army up here."

"Do you think the war might pass us by?" I said.

"I hope so, but you can come and stay with Mary and me if you'll feel any the safer for it."

I shook my head. "I got people over the mountain, thank you all the same."

He sighed and stood up. "Let's put this fellow down in the pasture with my mules."

He stumped down the steps and I followed along behind him, hoping that he wouldn't think to ask me why I didn't simply ride the horse over into Tennessee where I'd said I was going. I hadn't thought up an answer to that one, except maybe that a lone woman without a horse would be safer than with one. "Maybe the war will be over soon," I said.

He scowled. "Not soon enough, girl. The poison is already in us. Well, at least, you're out of it. I hope nobody around here is low enough to make war on women."

"Let 'em," I said. "I can shoot good as a man."

He stopped and looked hard at me then, and I was afraid that he knew some of what was in my mind, but I started talking about the horse again, and how Keith thought the world of him, and how he liked apples come fall. After we had pastured the bay, we walked back up the hill together and Daddy Austin asked me to come in and sit a spell, but the sun was slantwise in the sky and I had a long walk home before dark. He never did ask me why I would ride the horse to his place and then walk back home. If he thought about it later, it would be too late. Come sunup I'd be long gone.

That night I pulled on my hunting boots and britches and Keith's old coat, and I made my way up on the ridge to look at the stars and think. The night was clear—still winter up on the mountain—so that the cold air burned my insides as I walked, and I had to keep blowing on my hands to keep my fingers from going numb. Spring was coming, though. I would miss the mountain. Up there I almost felt like I could talk to Keith and make him hear me. I wasn't too sure about God.

The black sky was spangled with stars, looking like frog spawn scattered across a deep, still pond, making me wonder what laid 'em and when, but this wasn't a time to be thinking about stars. They had been a long time up there, and they'd still be there after I had gone to dust. I thought about praying, but I didn't have too much to say to God, either, so I set my mind to figuring out what to do about Keith Blalock, who was a fool for fighting, and might go charging off into battle and get himself killed, even if it was for the wrong army. Or else he might get het up in a political dispute in the Rebel camp and tell the soldiers what he really thought about this tomfool war, and then I reckon they'd hang him.

I couldn't lose Keith, too. Once already I lost somebody to death. I'd not live through that again without a fight. Four years ago we had us a baby, Keith and me. We got married that June, and the young'un was born that next spring. I remember him as a red-faced bundle with eyes shut tight and fists balled up like he wanted to be a fighter like his daddy. The minute I held him, I clean forgot how mad I had been on account of it hurting so much to bring him into the world, and I just wanted to sit there and look at him from one hour to the next. But he didn't thrive. He was awful little, and the midwife said he might have come before he ought to have. It was still cold up the mountain in late spring, so I reckon the cabin wasn't warm enough for a tiny, frail thing like him, but we weren't much more than young'uns ourselves, and we didn't know what to do for him when he took sick. I just sat there by his basket, watching him thrash in his feverish sleep, and not knowing what to do. He held on to my finger with his little fist, as if I could drag him back into life, but I didn't know how, and just before sunup one morning, that little hand went slack and the fever went away, and my baby was gone.

Well, it was God's will, folks said, and they told me it would have been wrong to question His ways by grieving overmuch for my boy, so I shut it away inside my heart, and ever after I tried not to think on it too much. Keith wasn't nearly as tore up about it as I was, and I reckoned that men didn't hurt as much as women did. Didn't hurt Keith none to bring that baby into the world; didn't hurt him overmuch when it left it. So I just shut up my sorrow, and I thought, "There ain't no percentage in being a woman." Then I resolved not to be like one any more if I could help it. I went hunting with Keith, and I wore britches and learned to shoot straight. I stalked deer and skinned rabbits, and I worked as hard as a man. Sometimes what I did made the hurting stop, and sometimes it didn't, but the free life of menfolk suited me, and was a deal more interesting than the cooking and sweeping that was a woman's lot. I could tell Keith was happy that I was his friend as well as his wife, so we . . . soldiered on.

Soldiered on.

And now the war has come and the government wants Keith to go off and fight on their say-so, and I am supposed to be the little wife, a-tied to hearth and home while he's off fighting. But I can't go back to that, to washing floors, and sewing shirts, and waiting, and watching babies die. What is there to war as terrible as that?

The way the Confederacy rounded up men for the war was that they would put out a call for soldiers, and offer a cash bounty, and men would go down to the nearest fair-sized town to get their money and be sworn in. Then the army would send some officers down to pick them up, and they'd all march off to the next town to pick up some more recruits, and so on, 'til they got to a town where the railroad stopped, where all the new soldiers could be put on the train and sent to camp to be trained in soldiering.

Keith joined up in Lenoir, which is down the mountain east of here, in the general direction of the army training camp, way east, clear on the other side of Raleigh. Once they had gathered up all the new recruits from the mountain towns, I reckoned the place they were headed for would be Morganton, because that's as far as the railroad goes, but there were one or two towns in between, and I meant to find out which one the recruiters were headed for next. The towns aren't more than a day's ride from here, but as I wasn't fixing to come back, there was no way I could have taken the bay. I made up my mind to start out walking, and hope that somebody with a wagon was headed down the mountain and would give me a ride. Either way, I knew I could get there faster than a whole herd of new-made soldiers, trying to keep together on the road.

I hated to leave the farm, but I thought the land could take care of itself for a while better than Keith could. At sunup, I headed off down the mountain, traveling east. The next town where the Rebels might be signing up men was more than twenty miles away, far enough away for me to be a stranger to all and sundry, which is what I wanted. I knew that in a day or so we'd meet up with the bunch from Lenoir that Keith had joined up with, but until then I was on my own.

I walked alone most of the morning, because I wanted to get some distance between me and home, so as not to meet anybody I knew. I was wearing Keith's black hat and my own boots which looked like a man's anyhow, because I hunted too much to traipse around in lady's slippers. The night before I had sat in front of the fire, sharpening my hunting knife and cutting down a couple of Keith's old shirts to fit me. Next I cut an old sheet into strips and wound it around my chest so my shape wouldn't give me away. Last of all I took the knife to my long hair, sawing off hanks of it with a bowl set down over my head to get the ends as even as I could. When I was done I had a pile of brown hair that had taken me years to grow out. I gathered the tresses up in both hands, and then I went and threw them out into the yard for the birds to take and use for their nest weaving. That way at least a part of me would stay here.

Now I had on one of those cut-down shirts over my leather hunting britches, and around my neck I had knotted a red kerchief to hide what I didn't have: an Adam's apple. The hat still fit me, but it felt loose around my ears with all that hair gone, and I thought I might have to practice shooting some to get my balance righted again.

I carried an old haversack with some supplies I'd need for soldiering. I had a bit of lye soap and a sewing needle, the last of the food from the larder, a tin cup, a wooden plate that Keith had whittled, and a real silver spoon kept from my wedding day. My folks had given us four of them, and I buried the others out behind the cabin to keep them safe while I was gone. I kept the rest of that cut-up sheet in case my time of the month should come while I was soldiering. Keith had taken some paper and swore he was going to write me a letter while he was gone, but I didn't need any paper, because I had nothing to say to anybody but Keith, and I planned on doing that in person.

Along about mid-morning when I had passed through the woods and down the mountain to where the land was flatter, the air was warmer, and the trees were more in leaf. The people in the flatlands get the first and most of everything—even spring—but that's a fair trade for they have nothing to touch our land for beauty, and I'd not swap with them. A few miles into the greenwood, I saw an old man out plowing his field with a sorry excuse for a mule. He waved me howdy, but since I didn't know him by sight, I figured it would be safe to speak to him. I climbed over the fence and threaded my way along the furrow to where he was standing, taking a rest from his labors, or maybe letting that mule rest. He looked like he needed it. That was one mount the armies wouldn't bother to steal, I thought. Not unless they were awful hungry.

"Mornin'," the old farmer said, mopping his brow with a grimy kerchief. He didn't seem to be paying me any particular attention, so I figured I looked all right.

My cap was pulled down low on my brow, and I remembered to pitch my voice low and not talk too loud. "How-do, sir," I said. "Fine day for plowing."

"Well, if you are of that opinion, I'd be happy to let you take a turn in my stead," he said.

He didn't crack a smile, but I knew he was joshing, so I laughed to be civil. "Well, sir, I would," I said politely, "but the fact is I'm a-hunting the army, so I'd best be heading on if you can point me the way."

He gave me a sharp look then, and I hoped he wasn't seeing too much. "The army, is it?" he said. "Why, you ain't old enough to shave. You taking provisions to your daddy?"

"Older brother," I said, not wanting an argument, just information. I held up my rucksack to bolster my tale. "He joined up in Lenoir a couple days ago, and I'm hoping to catch him before the train takes them off to camp. Would you know which way they was headed?"

"You just keep going down that selfsame road," he told me. "They passed this way this morning, and I hope they won't ever be coming back. Armies is worse than locusts for farmers. Two of my hens is missing, and I know which way they went, too."

I said I was sorry about the chickens, but I reckon any army would have done the same and thought the farmer was getting off cheap if all he lost to this war was a couple of hens. I had lost a husband, though I was aiming to get him back. This fellow is lucky not to be hauled off to join the fighting himself, I thought, but I bid him good day and headed back for the road, thinking that tracking armies wasn't much work at all. You couldn't hardly hide one.

I walked into town about midday, with an aching shoulder from carrying that sack, and a throat full of road dust, but I didn't mind that. I reckoned a little dirt would make me look boylike, since I never saw one that set much of a store on being tidy.

The soldiers weren't hard to find. You could hardly see the town for them. A roaring, back-slapping crowd of farm boys was milling around in the mud of the main street, acting as if they were being given a ride to the county fair instead of having been taken away to war like calves to market. I didn't see what they had to be so happy about, but then men seem to get pleasure from a raft of things that women find foolish . . . Spitting contests come to mind . . . and hitting each other with their bare fists . . . and tying two dogs' tails together to make 'em fight . . . The best I can figure is that they like noise and disorder where a woman craves peace and quiet.

I hung back awhile in the shadows between a bank and a storefront while I studied the faces of those new-made soldiers. They were a scruffy lot, and some of them looked like their clothes had been pitched on them with a hay fork, but many of them had chins as smooth as mine. I reckoned these boys were really as young as I must have looked, a bunch of fellows drunk on war, and a-thinking that a uniform and a drumbeat would make them men. A couple of them were so skinny and raggedy that they'd probably be glad of government-issue clothes and army rations, and like as not they'd see both as an improvement over what they were used to. None of them looked like they were thinking about dying. I don't suppose they figured there was much chance of it, young as they were. Even Keith thought the war was more of an aggravation than a hazard, and he was nigh on twenty-four years old, which is old enough to know better. I knew better. Women are born knowing better.

The important thing about the faces, though, was that I wasn't familiar with any of them. None of these recruits came from my settlement, so that was all right. I didn't see Keith or any of the fellows from our county, so I figured they were either camped elsewhere or in some other part of the town, which was all to the good. Once I was sure that no one there would know me, I pulled my hat down lower to shade my face, and sauntered out onto the road to mingle with the crowd.

"I hope the war don't end before we get there," one scrawny boy was saying as I drew near.

"If we would of took Washington after Bull Run, it would be over by now," another one said in a high-pitched boy voice. "I reckon we better hurry and get in it."

A red-headed fellow a little ways off took a harmonica out of his coat pocket and puffed out a jaunty tune, and his playing joined with the shouts of children and the barking of dogs to make such a din that I could scarcely hear myself think, much less talk to anybody else, but that was just as well, because talking leads to questions, and I didn't dare let on too much about where I came from or who my people were. Nobody was taking any notice of me.

After a while the music maker traipsed off toward a gaggle of girls up the road, and a tall, grinning soldier stepped up to me and said, "Ain't it grand? Not only do we get to be in the war, but our commander is a mountain man hisself."

"Who would that be?"

He cocked his head and looked at me as if I was crazy. "Don't you know what outfit you're joining?"

I shook my head. "This here's the one my brother Keith took up with, that's all I know. He left out of Lenoir a day or so back, and I made up my mind to meet him here, and go along as well. Didn't matter to me who the commander was, long as I can serve with my brother."

He nodded, and I knew my answer would serve, because we set a store by family in these parts.

"Well, who is the commander?" I asked.

"Why, Colonel Zebulon Vance," he said. "He was made commander of this here regiment you're joining up with—the Twenty-sixth North Carolina."

That figured, I thought. Zeb Vance was our man in Congress until the war broke out, and now he has quit and come home to raise troops. Being one of the quality folks, he'd join the army by starting out at the top and working his way up even higher.

"Well, I hope he knows about soldiering," I said, because it seemed to me that having money and serving in Congress might make you a colonel, but it didn't guarantee that you'd be any good at it. I knew better than to say so, though, so I nodded and wandered off to find a real soldier who would put my name down in his book and pay me the ten dollars enlistment money.

Across the street there was a wagon and a flag with a circle of stars in the corner. Beside it a man in a new-made gray uniform with ginger side-whiskers stood over a barrel that he was using as a writing desk. Another soldier stood by him, trying to keep order in the crowd. Men and boys were grouped around them, calling out their names and asking questions nineteen to the dozen, so I sidled in amongst them and waited my turn to join up.

People were pushing and shoving me, and I shoved back some, but finally I got to the head of the line, and stood facing the whiskered soldier, who barely looked up from his papers when I stepped forward. "Name?"

"Sam Blalock," I said.

He looked up then, and peered at me with squinty eyes. "How old are you, boy?"

I cleared my throat and set out to answer him in a deeper voice. "Seventeen this month, sir," I said.

"You don't look it. Where's your father?"

"Dead, sir. But my brother has done enlisted in this here regiment, and I am fixing to join him. We'll look out for one another."

He was about to say something else, but the line got to pushing again, so he just wrote down my name and pointed to the group that was already signed up. There was another soldier there, looking over the recruits, but he wasn't making much of a job of it. You'd do more poking and prodding on a hog you were fixing to buy than he did on those new-made Rebels. I figured I'd get past him if I didn't have to take my clothes off, and I was satisfied that I smelled better than most of the rest of that crew, anyhow. Mainly the soldier looked into our mouths.

"Why is he so all-fired worried about teeth?" I whispered to the tall fellow beside me. "Is the food bad?"

"Bound to be," muttered the recruit, "but he don't care about that. You have to have an upper tooth and a lower tooth that meet so's you can bite the top off the powder cartridge. Our powder and shot comes already put together in little paper pokes called cartridges, and you tear it open with your teeth. So you don't need no powder horn like we use when we hunt up home. That's all they care about—in battle can you open that poke fast enough with your teeth."

So when the inspector came to look me over, I bared my teeth at him like a mule, and he barely broke stride before heading on to the next soldier. I have strong teeth—reckon I could bite his head off if I had to. I knew I could pass any test they cared to give me—except a pissing contest, maybe. But I could shoot and ride and tear cartridges with my teeth, and they didn't think to ask for more, so I was duly sworn in as a soldier of the Confederacy.

That recruiting day was like a horse fair, except that it was us folks that got bought up instead of horses. They paid us a portion of our enlistment money, swore us in, and then the local parson prayed over us, asking God to keep us safe in the battles to come—which didn't seem likely. When the signing and the speeches were over, the uniformed soldiers marched us down the street with the townspeople singing and waving us all good-bye, and then we were out on the open road with nothing but woods and mud between us and Morganton.

Raiders

Stanley Ritter always walked in his garden at twilight. He liked the peace and solitude of his North Carolina place, and the fact that he could see no other houses from the property. He had bought the place simply as a refuge from the summer heat, but now he found himself wondering if he could give up the other place entirely and live up here year-round.

There was so much space up here, and so much quiet. At his other place near Tampa, he could stand in his yard and tell what the neighbors were having for supper, even what channel they watched for the evening news, but up here in the cool serenity of his 1840s farmhouse he felt that he wanted no news more current than a geology textbook. Up here the only news that mattered to him was the local weather report, and it was usually comforting: never too hot, never any tornados, hurricanes, mud slides, earthquakes, or any other natural catastrophes that plagued other forms of paradise. The mountains just drifted on immutable in a sea of time, and if they changed, one lifetime was scarcely enough to notice it.

The green sward of valley visible from his cliff terrace, and the curtain of mist against the distant mountains had become the most precious things in the world to him, at least while he was in residence here, before winter's harsh winds and ice storms drove him south again. After all, hadn't he moved to Florida to get away from the Connecticut winters? Strange now that he would find himself edging his way back north, and loath to leave. Or perhaps it was not so strange after all: He missed the seasons in Florida. He could not get used to Christmas in Bermuda shorts and autumns without the riot of color of the oaks and maple. Fall in the North Carolina mountains was so spectacular that people drove for hundreds of miles just to creep along the Blue Ridge Parkway and peer out at the season's reds and golds: *Leaf peepers* the natives called them, cursing the traffic jams. Stanley, who did his leaf peeping on his own five-acre property, felt superior to these day trippers, conveniently overlooking the locals' other derisory designation: *Snowbirds*—the ones who fly south for the winter.

The snowbirds had other names for the locals. One of the more perceptive bridge-widows in the nearby gated community had once remarked that they were the new pioneers, kicking out the Indians all over again. Stanley could not tell from the tone of the woman's voice whether she was pleased about this fact or apologetic, but after an uncertain pause, the conversation had flowed over her strange remark, and soon it had been forgotten. Only Stanley had been left musing about what happened to some of the settlers when they encroached on Shawnee land.

The prospect of Stanley's winter exile was only a distant cloud on the present horizon. It was early June, and he had six more months to be lord of all he surveyed.

He looked around the garden to see if there were any projects he wanted to complete over the summer. When he had bought the white clapboard farmhouse three years back, the realtor had stressed the historic significance of the property. The house had belonged to a prominent local family, whose members had included a state legislator, two lawyers, and the inevitable Confederate colonel, whose name escaped him. Stanley wasn't much interested in the Civil War. Nobody who *was* anybody came from these mountains, he thought. Not like Connecticut, which had a host of colonial notables. He couldn't actually remember any, but it was common knowledge. They had never talked about the Civil War back in Connecticut. Most of Stanley's own ancestors had been in Russia until the early twentieth century, so perhaps he should more properly take an interest in the Crimean War, but he couldn't even remember when that one took place or who won it.

Anyhow there hadn't been any real battles in this part of the country, so the farmhouse's distant warrior owner was hardly a selling point for the property. Stanley reserved his reverence for whichever woman of the family had planted the fragrant lilac bushes and laid out the rose beds along the brick walk that led to the edge of the cliff. The only real alteration he had made to the garden had been the addition of a stone terrace that clung to the edge of the precipice. There he had set out his wrought iron patio furniture and there he worked on his watercolor landscapes, a hobby he had acquired since retirement. Mountain scenes in deep greens and silvery blues dotted the walls of the farmhouse, while he waited for a local arts and crafts show to give him the opportunity to display his new skills.

The gathering twilight deepened the colors of the distant hills against the pewter sky. Soon the color would be drained from the landscape altogether, leaving only shades of gray as substance turned to shadow in the darkness. He saw a movement at the edge of the woods.

Horses?

But he had not heard anyone approach. He peered into the shadows of trees at the edge of his manicured lawn. There were riders making their way through the woods—at least four of them. One of them, a tall man, was riding a dainty white horse, or perhaps it was a Welsh pony, which seemed most incongruous. How many were there? He couldn't be sure. It was too dark to see faces, but that didn't matter. They were locals and they were trespassing.

The tranquil vista forgotten, Stanley marched across the lawn shaking his fists at the interlopers. "This is private property!" he shouted. "You rednecks get your horses away from my house!" Since Stanley would never have dreamed of using the word "nigger," he did not consider himself to be a bigot. Had he not been angry with the trespassers, he might have been more diplomatic verbally, but he would still have thought the word.

The riders appeared to have heard him. The procession slowed, and then turned and headed directly toward him.

Stanley spluttered with rage, afraid to speak because he had a stammer that surfaced when he was very angry and made him sound weak and foolish. He contented himself with shaking his fist again, but the riders kept coming. They were still indistinct in the twilight, but he could see now that they were wearing costumes—part uniform, part cowboy garb, he thought. Perhaps they were musicians taking a shortcut to some other home for an evening gig. Or actors, scheduled to perform at the community clubhouse? He had heard of no such programs scheduled for that evening.

"Are you lost?" he said.

They did not answer. The lead rider, the one on the white pony, emerged from the trees, and stopped, perhaps a dozen feet away, staring at him in silence. The other riders, still shadowed, clustered behind him.

Stanley realized suddenly how quiet it was. He heard no sound from the horses, no birdsong in the trees, no music from the radio in the kitchen, tuned as always to the local classical station.

He tried again. "Who are you? Can I help you?"

The rider shook his head.

Stanley felt his anger ebbing away to be replaced by a stab of fear. Suppose this rag-tag band were vandals or burglars? Had they come to rob his house? He began to back away, mentally gauging the distance between his present position and the back door of his house. He must keep them talking, he thought. Never show fear.

"I'm sorry if I was abrupt," he said, willing himself not to stammer. "You startled me, that's all. What an interesting outfit. Are you a performer?"

The man continued to stare at him as if he were the odd spectacle. Then he slid off the white horse and took another step toward Stanley, who began to back away. The man's face was just visible now in the twilight, and Stanley could see that the side of his face was shattered and caked with blood. One eye was missing. But he did not seem to be in pain. He was grinning as he came forward, and he had pulled a knife out of his belt.

Stanley felt himself falling, and he thought, *I am fainting, but perhaps that will frighten them away.* He lay motionless on the manicured grass of his lawn, and the twilight deepened.

Malinda

Well, I finally met up with Keith on the new-made soldiers' march to Morganton.

After the Rebel officers swore us in and marched us out of town, I kept close to the boys I'd joined up with, keeping myself deep in the pack, and trying not to let myself get noticed by anybody. I knew that it was a long march to Morganton and a long train ride after that to the army camp, so I was in no hurry to find my husband, especially not with a crowd of people around. I was afraid that if he did spy me, he'd yell out my name and then ask me what the devil I thought I was playing at. As long as we were so close to the mountains, he might even tell on me himself if he spotted me, just to get me sent home, where he reckoned I'd be safe.

I made up my mind to concentrate on being a soldier and to postpone Keith Blalock's discovery that I had become one until we were well away from Watauga County in general and Grandfather Mountain in particular. A time or two on my way out of the hills, I had looked back over my shoulder, expecting to see that rock-hewn face scowling down at me, but by now we were out of sight of it, and into flat country.

As we went along, some of the boys sang "Wait for the Wagon" and some other fine tunes I hadn't heard before, and I was fixing to join in with them, when I remembered that my singing voice might sound an alien note amongst all these deep voices, so I contented myself with humming low and watching the sights as we went along. There weren't any Federals within a hundred miles of us, so I reckoned they could sing loud enough to wake up Moses and it wouldn't make any difference. Sometimes I'd catch a glimpse of a deer, fading back into the woods at the sound of our coming, and more than once a young rabbit would spring out from the tall grass by the roadside and run zigzag along in front of us for a few yards before diving back into the weeds on the other side. Rabbits lose their minds in the spring when they are courting—not that they are too awful bright the rest of the time, neither. I wondered if I had any more sense than the rabbits, to be doing what I was—running willynilly alongside an army with no more business to be there than the rabbit had. Only thing was, I wasn't terrified. As long as I didn't get caught, I figured I could do anything the rest of these boys could do, just as good as most, maybe better'n some.

They let us rest every hour or so, for some of the men weren't used to long walks or else they were too full of hard cider to go much longer without taking a piss. I hadn't drunk any cider back in town, but I knew that sooner or later, I was going to get the call of nature, too, and I was going to have to be careful how I went about it, for if anyone saw me taking down my britches I would be caught out for sure. I wondered if they shot people for joining the army under false colors. I know they shot folks who ran away, but I judged that the officers would deem deserting a worse sin than false enlisting, but I wasn't sure enough to stop worrying about it.

It was all I could do to march after a while, with my bladder feeling tight as a drumhead so that I couldn't think about anything but that. Just about the time I decided that I couldn't hold it in anymore, the officers called for a rest period, and I sat down with some of the farm boys on the grass, thinking about what to do next, for if I went off by myself into the woods, they might think I was trying to run away and come after me.

The redheaded fellow that had played the harmonica back in town solved the problem for me. He leaned back against a tree stump and pulled a chaw of tobacco out of his coat pocket, holding it out to the rest of us.

"Anybody want a pull of this?" he asked.

I stuck my hand out straightaway, knowing there wasn't much time to a soldier's rest. "I'll give it a try, boys," I declared. "Seeing as how I'm a soldier now."

One of the older men shook his head. "He looks awful young for tobaccy, don't he?" he said to the red-haired fellow.

"Old enough to get shot, old enough to chew," another man said.

The others nodded. "Best to grow up now, right, boy?"

"Never did this afore," I said, stuffing the brown wad into my cheek, like I'd seen folks do up home. I bit down on that plug of tobacco, feeling the bitter juice mix with my spit, and then I clapped my hands over my mouth and pretended that it had made me sick—well, it tasted god-awful, but I wasn't as sick as I let on. I jumped up, still holding my hands over my mouth, and I dashed off toward the trees as if I was a heartbeat away from throwing up all over them. I could hear the rest of them laughing and calling out after me as I crashed through the underbrush, and quick as I could, I spit out that tobacco, unhitched my britches and relieved myself into the pine straw. I guess just about everybody had noticed me by then, but after a few minutes I walked on back to the others, wiping my mouth with my sleeve, and looking shamefaced while they all laughed fit to kill and slapped me on the back, and said what a plucky little lad I was.

Then the captain sang out for us to fall in, and we took to the high road again. I was ambling along, light-hearted over having cleared that first hurdle so easy when a tall man edged his way up past one of my comrades and fell into step beside me.

"How-do little fella," he said quiet-like.

I didn't look up. Knowed the voice.

"How are you liking the army so far, young man?"

I tilted my head back then, the way I always have to do when I want to look Keith Blalock in the eye. "It's tolerable," I said.

"You want to tell me what you think you're doing?"

"Looking out for you," I said. "Now, hush!"

"Well, what about the farm? And where's my horse at?"

"Farm can look after itself awhile, and Daddy Austin's got your horse," I said, walking a little faster.

One or two of the others looked around to see me talking to this stranger, so I said out loud to the nearest one, "This here's my brother Keith. I come looking for him so we could serve together."

"You never mentioned no brother, Blalock," one of them said.

"Well, this one here is just a young'un," said Keith. "I never figured on seeing him here. He's so little I thought the army would throw him back."

They all laughed then, and somebody slapped me on the back and said, "He's a brave boy!"

"I've already been sworn in," I said, giving Keith a look that said don't waste your breath. "I've got just as much right to join up as you do."

"You took the oath?"

"Took another one a while back. 'Til death do us part. Remember?"

"Yeah, and I hope it doesn't come to that. You that worried about me?"

I shrugged. There were plenty of other men in the mountains; bound to be fewer though when this war got going. "I already have you broke in," I said.

Keith leaned down and whispered close in my ear, "Thanks—what did you say your name was?"

I hissed back, "Sam!"

"Well . . . Sam . . . this'll take some getting used to, but it's a long march to Morganton," said Keith. "I'll think on it awhile."

"Think away," I said.

It seemed like a lark to me. I was with Keith again, and I knew we wouldn't be staying long in this army anyhow; meanwhile I was getting to see different country—going farther from home than I had ever been in my life. In a way it was two journeys at once: coming down from the mountains to see new places, and coming out of my apron strings to see a man's world. I knew that once Keith got used to the idea, he wouldn't mind having me along. If I was the kind of wife he could send home, I wouldn't be here in the first place.

It would have been nice to have a pair of shiny knee boots and a fine saddle horse to ride, like the officers did, but they didn't make officers of the likes of us, and there was no point in wishing for it. Since the Confederacy was a new country, they had to get up an army from scratch, so some of the officers were new at soldiering. Others had been regular army, but they had quit and come home when North Carolina left the Union. I reckon those fellers got first pick at being officers, and maybe they would know enough about fighting wars to keep from getting their soldiers killed. The rest of the officers were rich men from the towns, people with powerful friends and enough money to buy a dress sword and a blood horse.

Some of the officers looked too young to be ordering

other folks around, but they seemed to have got the hang of it well enough. I hoped Keith had made up his mind to behave himself around these boy lieutenants, but he would have to work at it, because he wasn't very good at letting other people tell him what to do, and he was the best bare-knuckle fighter in six counties, so people didn't usually try to boss him around. Since I was a woman, I was more used to having people tell me what to do, and I had learned to get my own way without making them mad, so I figured I'd have less trouble taking orders than Keith would. I reckon officers are like horses: They're bigger than you and stronger than you, so you have to think around them to get your way.

We were passing through a patch of woods and I saw a white-shirted hawk sitting high up in the bare branches of a poplar tree. He was watching a flock of little brown birds skittering around in the bushes, and after we passed him I turned my head, hoping to see him swoop down and snatch one up, but he just kept sitting there, watching us go. You mostly see hawks alone, and they live up on the mountain—same as us. I wondered what that hawk would do if somebody forced him to join the flock of sparrows and made him take orders from the head bird.

The march was easy enough for most of us. We were used to walking, but having to keep pace with a hundred other folks hobbled us some. I felt like a guinea hen, waddling along in a slow-moving flock, seeing heads or tails of strangers every which way I looked. Pretty soon one new recruit started complaining that his feet hurt, and the sergeant, who had been regular army before secesh, said that he'd better enjoy this stroll while it lasted, because he'd never have it so easy again. After the army got us trained, they would load us down with a weapon and a field pack, and then we'd find out what marching really felt like.

We might have been more mindful of that warning of

those darker times to come if we hadn't had the prospect of a train ride coming up in the next few miles. Most of us had never ridden on a train before, and some of the boys had never even seen one. There had been talk for years about laying track through the mountains, but it hadn't happened. You could take a train almost clear to Morganton from the east, or to Knoxville, Tennessee, from the west, but in the mountains between them the only choices were a horse or shank's mare.

Some of us would have run to Morganton if we could've, just to get a ride on that train. We weren't thinking about the war. Some of the old folks who remembered the Mexican War or the old days before the Indians went away, they knew that war was no lark, and maybe they had an idea of what lay ahead for all those mooncalves who skipped away to army camps, and who would come straggling home, if they came at all. We would learn by and by, but we didn't know it then. Wouldn't have believed it if anybody had told us.

We were all young enough to live forever.

I never heard anybody talk about the politics of the war, or the problems of fighting against an army that not only outnumbered the Confederates but out-supplied them by a country mile. Or that the doctoring was worse than hog butchering, and the fevers would fell you faster'n an enemy bullet. There was a lot the young soldiers didn't know, and most of it would kill them.

But the train ride was glorious.

Spencer Arrowood

Spencer Arrowood was having supper with his mother. He had grown up in the white frame house with the well-tended garden, and his mother, widowed for nearly twenty years now, still lived there. She was a spry and slender octogenarian, firm in her determination to remain in her home, despite her son's concern for her in case of accident or sudden illness. She refused to consider giving up her home for a retirement community, and although both of them recognized that this Indian summer of her health and vigor could not go on forever, Spencer was reluctant to force his mother to give up her independence before she had to.

Dinner was not yet ready, so after setting the table—the one task entrusted to him for the evening—Spencer walked around the living room, comfortable in the fact that it had changed little since his youth, unaware that its museum-like permanence was achieved for his benefit. When the old carpet or the upholstery fabric wore out, Jane Arrowood installed the most similar replacement she could find. The colors, the pictures, and the arrangement of the furniture stayed the same, year-in and year-out. It gave both of them a sense of serenity, as if the years were not rushing past, leading inevitably to less happy times.

He had always loved the pictures that hung in the parlor: R. Atkinson Fox prints of idyllic landscapes of sapphire lakes and marble pavilions, peopled by nymphs and shepherds. The pictures were like illustrations in a story, but since the story was not provided, he had spent many idle hours as a child trying to imagine his own legends to explain the scenes. Tonight, though, Spencer was looking at the wall of family photos above the bookcase. The pictures of his parents as young people were so familiar to him that he barely had to look at them anymore: his father in an army uniform with his new bride in her corsage and big-shouldered "forties suit." His mother in a summer dress posing in the seat of a tractor, as if for a calendar picture. His mother, her red lipstick and pageboy hairstyle proclaiming the era, holding a red-faced baby in a swaddling blanket. And then the pictures of his own childhood, himself and Cal in a progression of snapshots from toddler to early twenties, which, thanks to the Vietnam War, was as far as Cal ever got.

Tonight, though, Spencer was drawn to the older family pictures, those stretching back more than a hundred years to people his parents had known only when they themselves were children. His Arrowood great-grandparents, photographed in middle age, stared grimly out from an oval wood frame lined with convex glass. They stood tight-lipped and stern: he gaunt and wiry, with a handlebar mustache, wearing a thin tie and a dark suit, reminiscent of the outfits associated with the Old West; she, severely handsome with a pleasant unlined face, wore her still-dark hair in a bun at the nape of her neck, and her high-collared dress evoked an era of kerosene lamps and horse-drawn buggies.

There were smaller studio photographs of the broth-

ers and sisters of that generation, including his favorite
scene—two handsome youths in cowboy hats and boots,
seated at a round table, and looking like the popular
conception of Old West desperados. They had been
brothers, a pair of North Carolina farm boys, preacher's
sons, whose lives had been as blameless and unexciting
as a mother could wish for, but, frozen in that sepia
image, they crackled with youth and bravado. That was
as far as the photographic record would take him, and it
was not far enough. The oldest of these ancestors was
born in 1870, too late to be involved in the Civil War.

As a child he had glimpsed some of these people at
family gatherings, ancient wraiths of their former selves,
dull-eyed and nearly deaf, unreachable strangers to the
lively boy he had been then. He remembered a picnic in
a shady grove by a cold mountain stream. He had
played tag with some of the younger cousins, and as
they darted in and out among the trees, squealing in the
excitement of the chase, someone had grabbed his arm
and pointed to a wizened old woman, swathed in blankets and sitting in a lawn chair near the picnic table.
"Don't make so much noise!" the grown-up had hissed
at him. "She can't abide noisy young'uns!" The old
woman had been Spencer's great-grandmother, and he
remembered avoiding her for the rest of the afternoon,
so that no one else would scold him for disturbing her.
He never saw her again, for she had died the following
winter, but Spencer told himself that he would have
been too young at the time to have asked her any intel-
ligent questions anyhow.

By the time he had grown up enough to take an interest in the histories of his oldest relatives, they were
all dead. He wondered if his father had ever been told
any of the old stories, but it was several decades too late
to ask him. Probably not, he decided. His father had
shown no interest in family history, and precious little
interest in any living representatives of it. A prosperous

and self-made businessman in the small town of Hamelin, he always seemed to be afraid that some of the farm-dwelling cousins would try to cadge money from him. Besides, he would never have been interested in anyone else's war stories: he had his own.

Hank Arrowood had been a veteran of World War II, the war that finally banished the specter of that earlier, more terrible war that had been fought here in the mountains. In Spencer's youth it had been better to talk about World War II, when everybody in the country had been on the same side, than to hark back to that earlier time, to the war that had so divided the region that some wounds had still not healed.

Now people had mostly forgotten the little scars that had been still visible a generation earlier. Nowadays there were people who had attended the Union Baptist Church all their lives yet had no inkling of the fact that the name of their church was a political statement, harking back to an old schism, when the area's one Baptist church had split into two, because in 1861 a congregation composed of both Union and Confederate sympathizers could scarcely find a unanimous prayer.

Now the memories had faded so much that people could not even remember which side their ancestors had fought for. Spencer supposed that was a good thing, because people certainly found enough to disagree about without worrying about a war that ended in the century-before-last, but the news about the Union soldier named Arrowood had still unsettled him. Somehow this unexpected link to the invading army had effected a subtle change in his identity. *I am not who I thought I was,* he told himself, but whether this might be a good thing he had not yet worked out.

"Dinner is ready, dear," said his mother from the doorway. "Is anything the matter? You're wandering around as if you've forgotten something."

"No, I'm fine," said Spencer, following her into the dining room. "Just a bit tired."

"How are things in the county?" This was a perfunctory question, since Spencer seldom discussed his work, and in truth his mother was not particularly interested in the small instances of law-breaking that constituted the major part of county law enforcement.

Spencer focused his attention on carving the ham before he replied. "Things are pretty quiet, I guess. Stanley Ritter had a heart attack and died last night. I'm not sure if you were acquainted with him or not. He was a retired fellow—been here about three years. Well, half that, I guess, since he wintered in Florida."

"Yes, I'd met him. He came to our book discussion group once or twice. He seemed surprised that any of us could read, as I recall. Still, what a shame! You never can tell about heart attacks, can you?"

"I guess not," said Spencer, who thought that a lot of times you could. After another few moments of companionable silence he said, "The Civil War reenactors have set up camp again. I rode out there to see them this afternoon."

"I expect the children will enjoy that," said his mother. "Anything with weapons. Do they have horses?"

"I didn't see any."

"Well, I'm sure the children will be interested anyhow. I hope they notified the schools."

"I suppose someone did. Being out there got me thinking. Do you know anything about our relatives back then? Did any of them fight in the war?"

Jane Arrowood smiled. "My great-grandfather lived in eastern North Carolina—near New Bern. He was only sixteen when he enlisted in the Confederacy, so I don't suppose he was much use. I told you about him when you were little."

"I remember. What about Dad's relatives?"

She thought for a moment. "Hank always made a joke about his relatives back then. It's hard to know what he really felt about anything. The one story he always told was about one of his great uncles who had been a draft dodger. The way your father told the story, his great-uncle had been out in the hills, on the run from one of the armies—"

"Which one?"

"I asked him that once. Hank said that he didn't know, and he wasn't sure if his uncle John knew, either. Anyhow, according to the family story, while John was out in the hills, he discovered a vein of silver out there in the wilderness. He didn't have much time to investigate it, because the army scouts, or posse, or whatever they were called, were only a few miles behind him. He knew he had to keep running, so he marked the silver vein so that he could find it again, and kept going. He managed to outrun his pursuers, but a few weeks later when he went back to find the silver mine, he never could locate that clearing again."

"He never found the way back?"

"Never did. To hear your father tell it, the rest of the family has spent years trying to find that site, but no one has ever succeeded. And that's the Arrowood Civil War story, as told by your father, dear."

Spencer frowned. "There had to be more to the story of the family's war experiences than one abstaining great-uncle. Everybody had at least six children in those days. Surely somebody actually fought in the war."

"I suppose, dear." His mother looked thoughtful. "Why are you so concerned about it all of a sudden? You've never seemed interested before. You're not trying to join some society for veterans' descendants, are you?"

Spencer laughed. "I wouldn't know which side to apply to. But there is a reason for my asking. I heard something interesting while I was out there, by the way.

It turns out that the last soldier killed in the Civil War east of the Mississippi was named Arwood or Arrowood. The battle was over in Waynesville, so I think he must be kin to us somehow, don't you?"

"Well, it's not my side of the family, but I would think that if you go back far enough all the Arrowoods in this region are related somewhere along the line. As you said, they all had hordes of children. I'm not sure if you'd be able to trace the exact kinship though. Could you check the Confederate enlistment records to see if his parents are listed?"

Spencer smiled. "Not Confederate," he said.

Malinda

Back when we were first in camp, I'd hear one or two of the soldiers playing a particular tune on the fiddle or maybe on the French harp, and as it was a lively tune and caught my fancy, I asked them what it was. "Soldier's Joy," somebody told me, and at that I wondered even more. It struck me as a strange thing to name a tune, because it didn't seem to me that soldiers had too awful much to be joyful about. The military life was hard and lonely, with young men carted away from home and fed on sorry rations, with the prospect of dying thrown in for seasoning. A man may think this is fine sport, but a woman knows better. She will never mistake resignation for bravery, nor discomfort for adventure. I do not complain, though, because all the fellers seem set on seeing battle, and they would flush me out sure if I was to say any different. I had to talk like a man in sentiment as well as in the pitch of my voice.

Now that I have been in camp a couple of weeks, I believe I can hazard a guess as to what a soldier's joy might be. Clean socks. Fresh springwater. Dry ground to sleep on. A hot meal with no worms in the meat. At least those are the things that give me pleasure, or would if I ever got any of 'em, but, to hear them tell it, the boys in camp all long for purer things, and usually by that they mean some sweetheart back home or the sound of their mother's voice. Or else they long for baser things, which they talk about as if they were rutting hogs, and more than one of them carries a picture of a naked woman next to his heart, where he ought to be carrying a letter from them that loves him.

What they mostly mean when they talk about "soldier's joy" is women the like of the laundresses that are to this post what buzzards are to a dead deer . . . A sorrier-looking bunch of women you never did see, all scraggly hair and weasel faces, but they have special permission from the army to make camp near the entry gates so as to be able to do the washing for the soldiers. Laundresses, my hind foot! Some of them have come to be with their husbands, but the rest of them wouldn't know a washboard from a buckboard, that's what I think. They are here to service the troops all right, but cleaning is no part of the bargain. Camp-followers. They are whores, swarming after this stockade full of men like flies to a dung heap, sashaying and hollering out at every man who passes within fifty feet of them. The laundresses are here for their cut of the army pay, and I'll wager that they give more than carnal joy in return. They pass the pox around the encampment from sick soldiers to well ones, and the very sight of them makes me ashamed to be a female. I'm glad the mothers and sisters and wives back home don't see the spectacle of their menfolk, lonely, swaggering boys, trying to drown out the fear of dying in the arms of these strumpets.

I hold my peace about the laundresses, though, and I stay well away from them, because women are more noticing than men, and I reckon it wouldn't take two shakes of a sheep's tail for that brazen bunch to figure

out that young Private Sam Blalock wasn't the beardless boy he claimed to be.

In the evenings around the fire, I stayed out of my
comrades' woolgathering about hearth and home, too,
because the less I talk around here the better. I'm always afraid that I will forget to deepen my voice, and
the sound of it will give me away. There's also the danger that one of these mooncalves will say something so
foolish that I will commence to giggle and be unable to
stop myself, and then I will be caught for certain. Then
they would send me home, and Keith would have to go
to war without me, so I am mindful to keep to myself
and to stay quiet.

When they're not talking about home and family or
talking dirty, then they're wrangling over politics, which
is another thing I must keep quiet about, because I
think we are fighting somebody else's war for him, and
I must not say such a thing to these poor fools who
haven't worked that out for themselves. After all, some
of them are bound to die, and they might as well be
proud of the cause they're giving their lives for. I respect that anyhow. But they talk a lot about how the
government can't tell them what to do, but now in place
of the American government, they have the Confederates who are writing down their own rules as fast as they
can think them up.

I reckon some of the men think I am a simpleton because I say so little, but because I am smooth-faced and
little, they think me very young, so it seems only natural
that I would hang back when older and more experi-
enced men are holding forth. I stick as close to Keith as
I can, and he does the talking for both of us.

We share a tent together, too, and that's something
else to be careful of, because sometimes Keith gets to
feeling so homesick for his mountain and his farm and
all that he wants is the same kind of comforting the
laundresses give out. I'm glad to oblige him on that

score, because like as not I need solace as bad as he does, but I'm always afraid we'll make too much noise with our loving, and bring the rest of them poking their heads into the tent to see what's the matter.

Keith is in a worse way than I am. He is homesick nearly all the time, and so poor in spirit that even having me here is no recompense for what he has lost. He felt like he had no choice but to come, and he hated leaving his land up home, but I came to look after him, so I am content to be here as long as I am with him. The marching and the soldiering is hot and wearying work, but no more so than what I do on the farm. Keith hates flat country, though. Between the heat and the biting bugs, he curses this end of the state with his first breath every morning. He says that if he owned Kinston and hell, he'd live in hell and rent out Kinston.

I see him looking up at the sky, squinting at thunderclouds, trying to pretend they're mountain peaks hazy in the distance. He minds not being able to see more than a few hundred yards in any direction, too. Here the trees block your view every which way you look, and there's nowhere to climb to let you see where you are or what's a-coming at you. Keith says breathing the wet, stifling air in this marshland is like trying to swallow cotton through your nose.

"Malinda, I can't take much more of this," he told me one night as we lay side by side in our tent on the edge of sleep. "It ain't what I bargained for."

"What? The army?" I said, yawning.

"We're just as far from the war as we were back home. Maybe farther. And we just keep drilling and marching with the heat and the bugs until I can't hardly stand it. I want to go home."

"I think we're stuck here," I said. "Once you take your oath, you belong to the army, and they don't care if you like it or not."

"Well, I don't like it," he said. "It ain't the real war.

Besides, every day we stay here is a danger to you. Every time you go out in the bushes to take a piss, I'm scared to death somebody will see you squatting. They'll find you out for sure if we stay here too long."

"What do you reckon they'd do?" I asked in a small voice. "They wouldn't hang me, would they? Do you think they'd put me in the stockade?"

"No telling what this bunch would do. We ain't officers, so we got no rights and no friends. They can do whatever they want. That's what scares me."

"We could run away," I said. "Wait for the new moon, and slip out through the woods."

"Then they *would* shoot you," said Keith. "If they let one soldier escape, pretty soon they'd lose the whole pack."

"Maybe they wouldn't catch us. We know our way around in woods."

"In our woods back home," said Keith. "We're more'n a hundred miles from Globe, though, and we don't know every mile of flat country well enough to stay hid until we got there. They'd catch us sure. I wish I could make 'em want to get shut of us."

"I reckon you'd have to get shot to get sent home," I said. "Or sick, maybe."

"They got doctors here. If you get sick, they'd patch you up and keep you 'til you get well enough to fight again. Unless you get some kind of pox that could spread to the rest of the encampment. I reckon they'd send you home, then, to keep you from wiping out their whole army. I wish I could get pox."

"Well, I don't," I said. "You might die before they made up their minds to send you home. Or you might get something that would mark up your face for life and leave you feeble. What you want is to look sicker than you are, so they'll figure you're no use as a soldier, but you'd still have the strength to get home."

Keith got all quiet then. I think he must have been

mulling over what I said, seeing the sense in pretending
to be sick, and trying to figure out a way to make it
work. I drifted off to sleep then, because the bugle
would rouse us at sunup, and then they'd run us off our
feet for most of the morning. I didn't think any more
about what Keith had said, because every enlisted man
in the whole camp was always complaining about
something—the food, the red bugs, sore feet, a belly-
ache. I thought he was just talking to let off steam, so I
never thought much about it, but the next day he was
gone for an hour or two while I was down at the creek
washing our clothes—I made sure that we steered clear
of the laundresses, so I did our own washing. If anybody
asked me, I always said that Keith and I didn't have the
money to pay anybody to do our chores for us.

The next afternoon he slipped away for a couple of
hours, and came back at dusk, looking dirtier and more
scratched up than usual. Wouldn't say where he had
been—not the truth anyhow. He said he had been out in
the swamp hunting berries, but he didn't take anything
to put them in, and he didn't come back with any—
probably because there aren't any berries to be had this
time of year. Then when I went down to the creek to
wash up before bed, Keith wouldn't go with me. Said he
was too tired.

That evening at supper Keith looked happier than
that sorry plate of beans could account for. "I went and
done it, Malinda," he whispered to me, when somebody
started playing a mouth harp and nobody was paying us
any mind.

"Done what?"

"Made myself sick," he said, and his eyes glittered
like they always did when he was spoiling for a fight.
"You'll see in a day or so."

"What did you do?"

"Never you mind," he said with a sly smile. "I don't
want you trying it, too."

"I hope I won't have to take care of you," I said. "They'll make me keep on soldiering, you know. And if you get carted off to the hospital, they might put somebody else in this here tent with me."

"No hospital," said Keith. "I'm going home."

"But, Keith—"

"Malinda, it's too late to argue about it now. It's done."

I spent that night wondering what tomfool thing Keith could have done to make himself sick, and most of the things I came up with could have killed him— tainted meat, bad water, swallowing lamp oil, or eating poison berries. I hoped he hadn't done any of that, because the regimental surgeon had too many men to look after to pay much attention to one sick private. I was willing to bet that more than one poor soul had died because medicine was scarce and the doctors were too busy to figure out what was ailing their patient.

Keith came down with his pox a day or so after that.

We shared a two-man tent together. The army was good about letting kinfolks stay together, and we were the most devoted brothers you ever saw, but that night between the smell of him and the tossing, there wasn't much brotherly love in my heart.

All through the night Keith thrashed and scratched and swore until I thought I'd have a better chance of getting to sleep on an anthill. It was a warm night, but the mosquitos didn't seem no worse than usual to me, and I was too tired to care if they bit me or not, so I hunkered down in my bedroll, and tried to ignore the twitching lump of humanity laying next to me.

The next morning when I shucked on my uniform and crawled out of the tent, I saw what all the turmoil had been about in the night. Keith was standing there in front of the tent, yawning and stretching—and scratching—with a smile on his face like a wave on a slop bucket. He was a sight to behold. His face looked like a snow-laden holly bush—the white cheeks were streaked with little red bumps, going down toward his chin and some bigger red bumps, stretching sideways toward his ears, and his eyes were almost swollen shut. It hurt to look at him.

"What happened to you?" I said, standing up on tip-toe to get a closer look at him, but keeping my hands behind my back, because the thought of touching him gave me gooseflesh.

Keith tried to grin at me, but he was snaking his left arm up under the back of his shirt trying to scratch his shoulder blade, and kind of hopping from one foot to the other while he scratched one leg with his other foot, all of which kind of distracted him from the conversation.

"I got it, Mal—Sam," he said. He mostly remembered that I was supposed to be his kid brother and that he had to call me Sam. "I got it good."

"Well, whatever it is, you got it all over, from the look of you," I told him, backing up a step. "I hope you don't feel as bad as you look, 'cause if you do, you won't last out the morning. What is it—measles?"

"Naw." Keith shook his head. "I did this a-purpose. You won't get it," he said, "but don't tell nobody else that or you'll spoil everything."

"Do you feel sick?"

"I feel like eating breakfast, Malinda." He looked around, but nobody was within earshot. "—Sam, I aimed to say—and then I'm going on sick call and let these army doctors tell me how sick I am. Maybe you better walk me over there. I can't see too good with my eyes swole shut."

Keith did his best to look pitiful at roll call, but even though he was itching fit to kill, I think he was enjoying all the consternation he caused with his pox face and his piggy eyes. He groaned and swayed so much while we were standing at attention that the sergeant took one look at him and told him to report to the camp doctor.

"Can I go with him, sergeant?" I said. "He's mighty weak."

The sergeant hesitated, and Keith started moaning again. "All right, Sam," the sergeant said to me, "but after you get your brother to the infirmary, see that you come straight back. You will carry on as usual."

I gave him a smart salute, and when we broke rank, I put my arm around Keith, and he stooped down so he could lean on my shoulder. We hobbled away like that across the drill field toward the camp hospital, a touching sight of a soldier tending to his sick brother. Keith felt somewhat worse after I elbowed him sharp in the ribs to stop him chuckling. "You'd better pull yourself together before we get to the doctor," I told him, "else they'll put you in the stockade for trickery and you can sit there scratching yourself until the war ends."

Keith grunted. "I couldn't stand it that long. This itch is about to kill me. Malinda, could you just reach down my britches, and—"

"No!"

I left Keith outside the medical quarters, and told him to hunt me up when he knew something. I wasn't as worried about him as I might have been, because he seemed so all-fired pleased with himself that I figured he had gone to some trouble to come down with this affliction, whatever it was. I went back to the company then, and tried to keep out of everybody's way. I had got used to Keith talking for both of us, and taking the lead when we were with the rest of the soldiers. Maybe they thought Private Sam Blalock was a little slow-witted, or else that he was too young to be on his own, a beardless boy tagging after his big brother. But they had got used to me, and now they hardly paid me any mind, except to make a pet of me. It was always, "Sam, fetch this," or "Sam, get the water bucket." I never argued. They weren't harsh with me—reckon Keith wouldn't have stood for that—but, without thinking too much about it, they were offhand kind to me, the way a good man treats a stray dog. Even the sergeant didn't yell at me too awful much.

We were drilling with the Springfields that day, so I was all right on my own. I could shoot as good as any of 'em, and target practice is about the loudest and yet most solitary thing you can do in the army. Nobody could talk to me with all those weapons firing, and nobody could find fault with my aim, so I was satisfied to stand there and load and fire for an hour if they had the shot for it, which they didn't. The officers didn't exactly admit to being short on supplies, but most of them were as careful as housewives with the provisions. But it was just as well that shooting practice was kept short, because the barrel of the musket got so hot after the first couple of shots that I had to wrap a rag around my left hand so I could hold the barrel steady. I could see where that might be mighty distracting in a pitched battle. Pistols make more sense. They might not be as good for distance as these long barrels, but you can't aim with a burnt hand and a weapon as full of soot as a blocked-up chimney, which is what happens after you fire enough shots. Good aim is a fine thing, but there's plenty of other things to worry about in a battle.

I was peppering a painted target one shot at a time with my muzzle-loader when the sergeant called me out. "Come say good-bye to your brother, boy," he said. "The doctor is sending him home."

I ran to the tent, and there was Keith, stuffing his blanket into a knapsack. "I'm going home!" he roared, grabbing me by the shoulders and just barely stopping himself from making it a hug.

"What happened?" I said, wiggling out of his grasp. It looked like Keith was peeking out at me through a berry bush, and I looked away.

"Well, I went in and the doctor examined me, and at first he thought it was poison oak, then he thought poison ivy, and then he said he had no idea what it was. 'It's the Unaka fever, Doc,' I told him. 'We have it up home. It spreads like wildfire.' 'Contagious, is it?' he says. 'Oh, it will lay this army low, sir,' I says, pulling a face. And then he says, 'I'd best send you home then, son, before you kill more of our men than the Yankees . . .'—and then he wrote me a chit, and said to show it to the officer, and I could be on my way."

"Well, how sick are you? Do *you* know what's ailing you?"

"I ought to. Took me long enough to find the right plants. It's all of 'em. Poison oak, poison ivy, poison sumac. I rolled in everything I could find. The reason the doc couldn't put a name to it is because he'd never seem them all mixed up on one body before."

"So you've just got an old rash, then?"

"That's it. Nothing a couple of weeks of mud baths won't cure once I get back home."

"Well, I'm glad you ain't dying," I said. "Have a safe journey."

Keith's grin faded. "What do you mean *a safe journey?* You're going with me!"

I shrugged. "I ain't sick."

"Well, no, but you're—" He made a fiddle shape in the air with his hands.

"And they don't know that, do they?"

"Well, you're going with me. I'm not leaving you here and that's flat."

"All right. I'll get them to let me go, and I'll go back with you," I said. "If they don't hang me."

I left him there in the tent, trying to pack and scratch at the same time, and I went to hunt up the sergeant. He wasn't much older than Keith, I don't reckon, and he hadn't been too many months in the army either. Some of the Confederate officers had been in the Federal army before the war started, but they generally got higher ranks than sergeant, on account of they knew what they were doing. A year ago this big fellow with a face like cheese had been plowing a field somewhere, and not thinking about killing nothing 'cept tobacco worms. When he was hard on us, I think it was because he was scared—of doing his job wrong, of getting us all killed.

I went up to him and held myself to attention, ramrod straight, staring over his shoulder with my eyes narrowed and my mouth tightened up like a drawstring purse. "Sergeant, I have to go home."

He looked down, smiling at the little boy he thought he saw. "Why, Private Blalock," he said, "are you requesting permission to leave the army?"

I didn't know how to use fancy military talk, so I just said, "The doctors are sending Keith home, so I have to go, too."

"Why, Sam," he said, sounding amused, "the doctor gave your brother a medical discharge, and that's why he's allowed to leave. But, Sam, you're not sick."

I nodded. "No, sir, I'm not sick. But I'm not Sam, neither. My name's Malinda." I pulled off my cap then, and shook out my hair, which was still too short to make much of a difference, but he could see by my expression that I was serious, and I could tell that nothing in the hasty military training he'd been given covered situations like this.

He stared at me open-mouthed for a long minute, and finally he whispered, "You're saying that you're a woman, Sam?"

I nodded. "Keith ain't my brother, sergeant. He's my husband. So you see, I have to go home now."

The sergeant shook his head. "I can't sign off on this, Private," he said, and suddenly I could see that I was talking to a rule book, and there'd be no point in trying to argue with him. He stood there looking at me for a minute, opening and closing his mouth like a fish, and then he said, "I'll take you to see the lieutenant."

So we went over to the officers' part of the camp and hunted up a lieutenant. The one we found looked to be younger than we were, so I figured his family must have some money, which is mostly how you got to be an officer, since capes and swords and saddle horses don't come cheap. He was a soft-faced fellow with blond curls, and I'll bet there were broken hearts back home when he went off to war. He was almost pretty enough to be a girl his own self, but he wasn't about to take my word for being one. Or maybe he didn't know what the army's rules were for a situation like this.

Anyhow, he hardly looked at me. The sergeant went to explaining the situation, and after hearing him out, the lieutenant narrowed up his eyes and said, "Sergeant, do you mean to tell me that you've had this soldier in your ranks for several weeks and you did not notice . . . you did not discover that he—that *she*—"

"No, sir," said the sergeant. "She looks more like a boy than one or two of the drummer boys I've seen. These here Blalocks said they were brothers. You never saw one without the other."

"Well, I think the captain ought to hear this tale," said the lieutenant. "I wouldn't want him to have to take my word for it. Dismissed."

The captain wasn't any happier to see us than the lieutenant had been, and he seemed personally affronted that the fates had tried to dump this problem into his lap. "Discharge is a matter for the camp commander," he said, turning his back on both of us before the sergeant could get out another word.

When he had walked away, the sergeant shrugged and muttered, "Well, you heard him, Private—er, ma'am. Whatever. We're going to see the colonel."

I trailed along after him to the house that was the colonel's headquarters. He had commandeered it from the people who had lived here before the camp was set up, and it was a fine-looking house. I'd never been close to it before, and even though I was scared the colonel might be mad enough to have me hanged, I was interested to see what the inside of the place was going to look like. I was hoping for red carpets and wallpaper and marble statues, because it stood to reason that colonels were even richer than lieutenants, and they might live in palaces for all I knew, but I was disappointed in my expectations, because the house wasn't anything special. It had scuffed wooden floors that could have used a scrubbing, and plain old whitewashed walls. We walked down a narrow passage to a desk where a soldier looked us up and down and asked the sergeant what his business was. I understood that as a plain old private I was as much beneath his notice as a cockroach, so I kept quiet while the sergeant launched into his tale yet again. It went faster this time, on account of all the practice he'd had. He had almost got it off by heart now.

When he had finished explaining the situation, the colonel's aide did look at me, and he let out a low whistle and kind of rolled his eyes. "Wait here," he said, and he tapped on the closed door behind him and then darted inside without waiting for an answer.

The sergeant looked down at me. "Why did you do it, Sam?" he asked.

I didn't correct him. He was used to calling me Sam, and I didn't look no different now. "To look out for Keith," I said. "Him and me, we're a team. Not just wedded folks. Partners."

He turned away, and I heard him mutter something that sounded like, ". . . my wife . . ."

The colonel's door opened just then, and the aide came out and shut it behind him. "Go in," he said in that cold, formal tone of his. When the sergeant stepped forward, he said, "Not you, Sergeant. The colonel wants to see the alleged female. Sergeant, you are dismissed."

The aide and I stood there for a minute, listening to the sergeant's boots clattering down the wood hall toward the front door, and then he opened the colonel's door again and motioned me in. "Just you, Private," he said. "The colonel will see you now."

I went in then, and stood to attention in front of a big oak desk. The colonel wasn't behind it, though. He was standing over by the fireplace, poking at the logs, and scattering ash on the carpet. I thought it was too warm a day for a fire, but the encampment sat in the middle of a piney woods and there were plenty of folks to fetch the firewood for the colonel, so maybe he just had it for show.

I kept staring straight ahead, but from what I noticed as I came in, the office wasn't no throne room, either. It had a Turkey carpet spread out in the middle of it, and a couple of leather chairs over next to the fire, but the desk wasn't nothing fancy, and he just had an ordinary oil lamp instead of a crystal chandelier.

Out of the tail of my eye, I saw him come up beside me and look me up and down, like I was a horse he was thinking about buying. He wanted to see if he could tell by looking at me. Finally he came around and stood in front of me, and said, "At ease, soldier. I understand you are a most unusual recruit."

I looked up at him then. So this was the famous Colonel Zeb Vance, who had been our Congressman before the state left the Union and put him out of a job. After that he left Washington and went back home to Asheville to get up the Rough and Ready Guards. I had seen him from a distance at the camp, but up close he didn't look all that much older than Keith. It seemed funny to think of him being in charge of older men like the sergeant, but I guess he had got practice in ordering people around, being in Congress and all.

He was a big man, at least six feet tall and big-boned, looking like he might run to fat one day if he wasn't careful. His uniform, a fine gray broadcloth with stars on the collar and the embroidered chicken guts that officers wore along their sleeves, fit him so well that I figured somebody had made it special for him. I saw that his right hand was bandaged up, and I wondered if it was a war wound. That set me to thinking about Keith trying to get home with just a rash when the colonel himself was injured worse and staying put, but then I didn't reckon colonels would ever want to go home on account of being hurt. Old Zeb had thick black hair, dark eyes under low, straight eyebrows, and a bushy mustache that made a pyramid with his lower lip and came to a point under his nose. It was twitching at the moment, like he was holding back a smile.

"What's your name, soldier?"

"It says on the rolls I'm Sam Blalock, sir."

"And you're not Sam Blalock?"

"My name is Malinda. The Blalock part is right, though."

"Malinda," said Colonel Vance. "I see. You look about fourteen—for a boy, that is. How old are you?"

"Twenty-two, sir."

"You don't look it—not for either sex. Well, then, soldier, what have you to say for yourself?"

"My husband is sick and the doctors are sending him home, so I must go with him."

"That explains why you want out of this man's army, but, tell me, why did you want in to begin with?" His face looked stern but there was a kind of a lilt to his voice that made me think he was going to bust out laughing any minute.

"I joined to be with my husband, sir. He went off and

enlisted, so I cut my hair and went off to the next town and signed up."

"Yes, I see your haircut. Most convincing. But what about the rest of you?"

"Bandaged up, sir."

"And you've been here how long?"

"Couple of weeks."

He sighed and shook his head. "You went through training? Marching? Shooting? All of it?"

"Yes, sir. Weren't hard."

"Where are you from, soldier?"

"Watauga County, sir."

"I see. My brother Robert married a Yancey County girl," he said. "It's not far from your neck of the woods, is it?"

"No, Colonel." Not far in miles. But between that other Mrs. Vance and me—probably a mighty far piece in other ways. "I hope your brother is well, sir?"

"I hope so, too," said Colonel Vance. "My brother is also a colonel, you know. He's off in Tennessee with the Twenty-ninth these days, and he reports himself in good health and spirits." He commenced to studying me again. "A mountain colt. I know Watauga County. Indeed, I do. That would go far toward explaining this situation, I'll warrant. Well, Private Blalock," Colonel Vance sighed and commenced to pacing back and forth on his Turkey carpet. "What's to be done?"

"I hope you won't hang me," I said.

"No, don't worry about that. It's not a crime to break into the army—just to break out." He sighed. "I'd sooner hang the fools who let you slip past their vigilance. Who'd believe it?"

I stood still and waited while he thought it out.

"Well, soldier," he said at last. "If you are indeed of the female gender, of course we must let you go, but I am mindful that it is an old trick, you know. As old as Troy."

He glanced down at me then, and it must have showed on my face that I had no idea what he meant.

"*The Iliad,*" he said. "No? Well, it is a fine tale about an ancient war. There was a warrior named Achilles who did not want to fight, and so he dressed himself as a woman to hide from the soldiers."

"But I didn't do that—sir."

"No, but you might now be claiming to be female just so the army will let you go home. How are we to know? Men will do many peculiar and terrible things to avoid conscription. Some are cowards, I fear, and some are simply loath to leave their families to the uncertainties of life on a farm with no one to tend it. I've heard tell of men who have chopped off a foot with an ax or shot themselves in the leg so as to make themselves unfit for soldiering. Compared to those acts of desperation, how easy it would be for a smooth-faced boy simply to claim to be a girl so that he can go home with his ailing brother."

I nodded. "You have to be sure," I said. "I can see the sense of that. Reckon I'll have to prove it then." Before he could say another word, I hitched up my shirt, and started tugging at the bandage-wrappings I had wound around my chest.

"Would you not prefer to have a doctor examine you?" asked the colonel. I noticed he didn't look away, though.

"Colonel Vance," I said, pulling at the white strips of cloth that held me in, "I reckon if you're smart enough to be the commander of this whole encampment, then you can tell for yourself whether a body is a man or a woman. There." I finished unwinding the wrappings and let them fall on the floor. Then I stood there before him at parade rest with my shirt up and I let him look.

It did him credit that he didn't look any longer than he had to in order to verify the truth of my gender, and he didn't blush, either. Nor did I. I was doing my duty and he was doing his, and that's all there was to it.

He was quiet for a long minute, and then he said—real quiet—"Mrs. Blalock, if you would care to turn your back while you rearrange your clothing, I will have my adjutant fill out the necessary papers to effect your release from military service."

"I can go home?"

Then he did smile. "Madam, we dare not keep you."

Zebulon Vance

Three days after the Battle of New Bern found us encamped some five miles out of Kinston on the Goldsborough Road, assigned to General Ransom's Brigade. Although reinforcements arrived daily, we were weakened by our losses in battle and by sickness. I had cut my hand by falling on a log of the breastworks, and it pained me, but my own troubles paled beside my concerns for the men under my command. They were in a bad way. On their behalf I was obliged to write an urgent appeal to Mr. Holden, the editor of the Raleigh newspaper *The Standard: "Will you please announce to the good people of the State that my regiment is here in a most destitute condition. Any persons that will send a coarse cotton shirt, drawers, or socks, will be doing us a great kindness, as it will be weeks before the State can supply us."*

Other newspapers picked it up, especially those in the western part of the state, and many citizens did what they could to aid us. I was most touched by the donation given by Mr. Kemp Battle, my old friend from my days at the university and the son of Judge Battle, my tutor when I read law. Kemp sent $114 to be used for the purchase of clothing for my regiment, bless him.

In April, with the example of General Branch's rapid advancement uppermost in my mind, I set about trying to raise a legion—that is, to add twenty companies to the ten I already had, plus a complement of cavalry and artillery. The commander of a legion carries the rank of Brigadier General. It was the fastest way I could think of to advance my career—and to ensure that I wouldn't be swimming any more creeks in a hailstorm of Yankee bullets. I even ran another notice in the newspaper, offering a one-hundred-dollar bounty to anyone enlisting as a new recruit. Cavalry enlistees had to furnish their own horses, but the government paid each man forty cents a day for his keep, and the full value of the animal should he die in battle. (I wrote to Harriett, urging her not to lend my horse to anyone, and to see that our servant takes good care of the brute. Horses may soon be at a premium in the Confederacy. In fact, they may be outnumbered by brigadier generals.)

My recruiting venture did not prosper, for within a few weeks the Adjutant General informed me that since the Conscription Act had just been enacted, the army felt that North Carolina had already raised her full quota of troops, and thus they were not inclined to authorize the formation of any more companies, but I am not a lawyer for nothing. I looked for a loophole and I found it. The Conscription Act provided a grace period of thirty days for new companies to be formed before the practice would be prohibited, so I continued to advertise, and to make my lists of recruits, hoping to reach a sufficient number to float me up to the rank of general before the time expired. I was spurred on by thoughts of General Branch. It deviled me that he had been made a colonel in the same month as myself, and then promoted to general four months later—and a sorry one at that. I felt I had been left in the dust—not a sensation I am accustomed to.

As badly in need of soldiers as I was, there was one new recruit that I had to turn away. A few weeks after we had set up camp near Kinston, a young soldier was brought to me requesting a discharge on account of *her husband* was sick and being sent home. Turns out she had fooled the sergeant and the rank and file of her unit for several weeks about the truth of her gender. It was all I could do to keep from laughing and slapping her on the back for the audacity of it. She was a mountain colt, a sturdy little thing who looked you straight in the eye and carried herself like a proper soldier. Probably she wouldn't have been any more scared at the Battle of New Bern than I was, though I am glad she was spared such an experience.

I am afraid that the worst ordeal she faced in the whole misadventure was the interview with me, for I required her to prove the truth of her assertion by partially disrobing, which she did without a blush or whimper. At that presentation of proof, I wished Mrs. Blalock well and sent her home with her husband to Watauga County. I shall not mention anything of this episode in my letters home to Harriett. My dear wife would be shocked to hear of such goings-on, and she already thinks this army a godless enough place without being told about women in breeches ensconced in this man's army.

I wish I could talk about it back home, though. Even with the Conscription Act we are having the devil's own time raising troops from the mountain counties, for the folks up there don't see it as their war. That may be counted as one of my transgressions, for wasn't I stumping all over those hills a year ago speaking out against secession? Well, I am paid for it now, but I do think that news of a woman enlisting might have shamed those proud and brave fellows into joining up.

Not that it would have helped the outcome much, I fear.

In March I had the Yankees vexing me with cannon fire at New Bern, but by mid-May I believe I preferred their company to that of our Confederate bureaucracy. First the government tried to deny me permission to raise my legion, and then when I got around that and had sufficient numbers of men ready to join up, my commanding general refused to give me permission to leave the camp at Kinston to go and muster them. I spent the weeks from mid-May until mid-June trying to get the enlistment rolls up to date and ready to submit to the bureaucrats, trying to meet the deadline for the formation of new companies, but it was like trying to swim in molasses. Some of my newly enlisted troops were immediately assigned to other commands, and then that rascal of an upstart general—Holmes—the very one who refused me permission to go and muster my new recruits—wrote to the War Department advising them to disband my troops, on the pretext that North Carolina had filled her quota in the field. So I gave it up and wrote to the bureaucrats advising them that I had quit trying. Theophilus Holmes must have had five minutes' satisfaction in thinking that he had prevented the creation of yet another general to crowd his limelight. If so, his pleasure must have been short-lived, for like the French Broad River back home, I could be diverted but not stopped.

It's a poor hen that has only one chick, and I left off being poor some time back.

Another avenue of advancement soon opened to me, and the messenger of my deliverance was none other than Augustus Summerfield Merrimon himself—as unlikely an angel as ever rode into an army camp.

"You have had some perilous times these last few weeks," he said to me, after we had exchanged pleasantries and asked after kinfolks. "The ladies of the fam-

ily never cease to worry about you, and they say so
many prayers for your safety that the Good Lord must
be tired of hearing your name."

I smiled. "Tell Him I'd be less of a nuisance to Him if
there wasn't a war on."

"Well, I have come with news," said Merrimon, "and
perhaps I can do the Almighty the favor of getting you
out of harm's way, so that He can concentrate on other
folks' needs for a while."

Merrimon had my full attention, and my muscles felt
like guy wires in anticipation, but I didn't let on. "It's always a pleasure to see you, Merrimon," I said. "News
from home would be more than enough kindness for
you to bring a poor, weary soldier."

I was surprised at how truly glad I was to see him. I
suppose that having married cousins made us kinsmen,
and so we had many friends and loved ones in common.
Besides, I had known him nearly half my life. Perhaps
we had matured past our old rivalry and into an alliance
based on mutual ambition, for we both realized the advantage of having well-placed friends. Since we both
were becoming well placed, it was best that we be
friends.

"I have weightier matters than home news to speak
to you about," Merrimon said. "You know that the election for governor will take place in a few weeks' time."

"I know it," I said. "The vote will come in August." I
would rather talk politics than eat, so I settled down
happily to thrash the matter out with him. I suppose
that a soldier ought to be respectful of the civilian government he's supposed to serve, but I thought the men
in power were a sorry lot, and I had a hard time not
showing it.

"The Confederates are backing William Johnston of
Mecklenberg, aren't they? I'll bet I know the wherefores of it, too. Johnston was a solid Conservative until
secession, and now he is a staunch Confederate, so they

are hoping to get both sides to support him. It might work to get him elected, but it will be politics as usual if he gets in."

"He may not get in," said Merrimon. "The government's opponents saw through the ploy of putting Johnston up as a candidate, and they countered with a candidate of their own: William A. Graham. But he has declined the invitation to run."

"Did he, by God? Begging your pardon, Merrimon." The man never could forget he was a preacher's son. "But you astonish me. Senator Graham turned down a nomination to be governor? Damned if I would."

"Well, Mr. Holden will be glad to hear that. He's the editor of the *Raleigh Standard*, you know."

"I do know. I am always firing off salvos in his direction, asking for supplies for my men or correcting one of their tomfool editorials."

"Well, you must have impressed him, Zeb, for he's all set to back you for governor. And so is Mr. Hale, who edits the Fayetteville paper. They sent me to sound you out on the matter before they endorsed you in their newspapers. I wasn't sure you'd be interested. I know you're trying to raise a legion, and since that would make you a general . . ."

"I don't think I'm cut out to be a general," I said hastily. No need to go into all the exasperating bureaucratic details with Merrimon. "I am too impatient, and not over-fond of taking orders from idiots who happen to outrank me. At least in politics you have to convince somebody to follow you. You can't *order* him to."

"Well, I know that cousin Harriett would be glad to have you out of the army, so I said I would sound you out on the matter. But what about all those recruits who are signing up to serve in your legion?"

"Well, I don't think the army means to let me have them," I said. "Perhaps I can do more good as governor than I could as a beleaguered colonel."

I was beginning to think it might be easier to win an election than it would be to win this war.

On the fifteenth of June I wrote to the army relinquishing my request for the command of a legion. The very next day, I fired off a letter to the Fayetteville newspaper, acknowledging that many interested persons and a number of newspapers throughout the state had recently put forward my name for the office of governor, and I felt that it behooved me to respond to this summons. I pointed out that I had refused a request to run for a Confederate congressional office only a few months earlier, but, I said: *"A true man should be willing to serve wherever the public voice may assign him. If therefore my fellow citizens believe that I could serve the great cause better as governor than I am now doing, and should see proper to confer this great responsibility upon me without solicitation on my part, I should not feel at liberty to decline it . . ."*

The vox populi had called, and I had thought myself on the way out of hot and swampy Kinston with my brass-bound trunk, but my superior officers had one more task to devil me with before I could leave their ranks: They ordered my company to the front.

On June 20, the Twenty-sixth North Carolina was carted off to Richmond, where we became part of Ransom's Brigade—just in time for the Seven Days' Battle.

The odd thing about war is that when you are actually in it, you cannot see it as clearly as you can from behind the lines. Merrimon was right about that. Up close war is all noise and smoke, shouting men, thundering cannons, and the stench of blood and powder. It is only after everything is over that you might get a copy of a *Harpers Weekly* and find out what you had been doing—if you were still healthy enough to care.

My regiment started out on picket duty on the Williamsburg Road, and the fighting began, but the woods were full of generals, so I, a mere colonel, had very little to do with what transpired during those seven days—just as well, for we lost every battle save one, and the deaths were many and terrible. This much every foot soldier knew: The Union commander, George B. McClellan, had landed a mighty army on the Virginia peninsula, and he was intending to march that army into Richmond, or else kill a bunch of them trying. We had no doubt that our General Lee had a brilliant overreaching plan to coordinate the attack, but we couldn't see it. The fighting seemed to break out in patches with no particular pattern to it. Orders didn't get through. Reinforcements failed to show up.

The only good thing was that McClellan didn't seem to know any more details about the fighting than we did. He didn't know that his forces outnumbered us two to one. He didn't realize when his army stood between the enemy and the very capital city they were defending, and he didn't seem to know that he was winning. So he gave up trying to take Richmond, and he started to pull his army back to the James River, so that they could sail away to safety and put the peninsula behind them. We were chasing the Yankees to the river, and the last piece of high ground before the James where they could turn and fight was Malvern Hill. And, outnumbered or not, we were supposed to take that hill.

The Yankees had a line of cannons strung out across the top of Malvern Hill, with siege guns positioned behind them, and plenty of infantry to punctuate the intervals between bursts of artillery fire. Our orders were to try to charge up that hill with our infantry and take out those guns.

Wasn't a battle. More of a hog killing.

Men would run across that open field, try to make a run up the hill, and a shell would come whistling down and blow them to pieces. Or a swarm of bullets from the hilltop would pick them off as they ran. The blood and the roar and the screams sickened us where we stood.

I was as dismayed as anyone, but I tried to keep up the spirits of my men. Once when the bullets were peppering our assault, a rabbit ran out of the brush beside us and scurried across the field seeking shelter. I spied him, and yelled out, "Run, you sorry rabbit! If I wasn't the governor of North Carolina, I'd run, too!"

The story made the rounds of the encampments, and its wit and sentiments pleased the soldiers. A few weeks later when the ballots were handed out to the North Carolina troops, they must have remembered that Vance had seen combat with them, while Johnston was safe at home in Carolina, and perhaps they recalled, too, that a year or so ago, Vance had urged them not to get into this war at all. The Wilmington and Charlotte newspapers made much of that last point, questioning my patriotism and even claiming that I had not taken part in the Battle of New Bern, but I hoped the general populace would know enough about me to discount those lies.

All the campaigning was done in the newspapers, except for the little electioneering I was able to do in Virginia among the North Carolina regiments. Perhaps I was helped by one story that I would never tell which made the rounds of the encampments: As we were marching back from the Battle of Malvern Hill, I noticed a young soldier, staggering along the road, looking ready to collapse from the heat and the weight of his pack. I dismounted, and helped the poor fellow up on my horse, while I walked along beside him for a couple of miles, much to the relief of my saddle sores. My men set a great store by that small gesture, and told it far and wide, though I had no thought of profiting from a simple act of charity toward a fellow soldier. The men fought gallantly and suffered much. I wish I could do more for them.

Anyhow, when the votes were counted in mid-August, I learned that, thanks to the soldiers' votes, I had won the election almost two-to-one.

I would take the oath before a judge of the superior court on the second Monday in September, after a few weeks spent in Asheville, trying to restore myself to health after the privations of military life. It was a bittersweet victory though, for while I was being carried to new heights in my political career, the Confederacy was being cast down by a shattering defeat at Antietam Creek in Maryland. I was hardly cognizant of it at the time, of course, for having just taken office as governor, I had hornet's nests of my own to contend with, but later I came to realize that the Confederacy's death knell was sounded at Antietam Creek: In that September battle in western Maryland, Lee lost one fourth of his army, and was forced to abandon his presence in Maryland and fall back across the Potomac to the Virginia side. Thus ended any hope of European alliances with our new government, and without such help we could not prevail against the populous and well-equipped Union.

In the autumn of 1862 I had neither the time nor the information to ponder such military consequences, though, for I was being inundated with requests, and demands, regulations, and prohibitions, until I thought I should be buried in the sea of correspondence. The governor needs a secretary to dig him out from under all those letters, and I awarded the job to Captain Richard Battle, the son of Judge Battle of the university at Chapel Hill and the younger brother of my friend Kemp. Another of the Battle boys, Junius, had been killed at Antietam just weeks earlier, and mindful of that, when I heard through mutual friends that Richard was with the army in Virginia, and that he was ill and unlikely to survive the rigors of military life, I asked him to make the sacrifice of exchanging his commission for a government post, and he readily agreed. Perhaps he thought me facetious for calling it a sacrifice to leave the dangers and deprivations of the front, but I meant

what I said. I knew from experience that once he had recovered from the knotted belly and lice-ridden squalor
of combat duty, he would miss that life, and the tedium
of handling a barrage of letters and appointments
would be a poor substitute for the exhilaration of soldiering.

Richard Battle is too fine and promising a youth to be
consigned to cannon fodder. As was I—though I would
never utter that thought aloud to a living soul: *as was I*.

Tom Gentry

Here at the world's end . . .

Tom Gentry wrote the line in his journal with a flourish. For a moment he considered adding the word "Agricola" beneath it, but since he would never meet the person who discovered his journal—assuming that anyone ever did—he preferred to imagine his reader as some kindred spirit who would be familiar with the works of Tacitus.

Here at the world's end . . . A good phrase with which to begin his musings. He wondered if the phrase conjured up an image of a solitary cliff overlooking the sea, but such a place would not have been private enough for his purposes. The forest was better. Hundreds of miles inland, hundreds of thousands of acres of trees, underbrush, and briars, all sentinels to keep out the curious, the officious, the would-be rescuers. This forest was itself once a sea—a green expanse of trees stretching all the way from Alabama to Canada in an unbroken wave, but the pioneers began to reduce that vastness in Washington's time and by the late-nineteenth century the lumber business finished the last remnant of virgin timber in the eastern mountains. There was little enough of the wilderness left now, but perhaps it was enough for his purposes.

This was the world's end for him, anyhow. He had been camping in the solitude of the national forest for two days now, and he found that he loved it here. He loved the deep green of the oaks and poplars, and the taste of the springwater in the shallow stream. Sometimes he saw rabbits and squirrels, even a deer sometimes at twilight, but they respected his solitude and he theirs. It could be cold here at night, even in summer, but he was deep in the forest, far from the boundaries of the park, and if he wished he could make a campfire without fear of being detected.

He had not eaten for two days.

At first he had felt the churning of his stomach, and even a stab of pain as his body protested this treatment, but he fought the emptiness with water from a nearby stream that looked clean enough. It had been hard at first to distract his thoughts from food. When he tried to concentrate on his journal, he would find his mind conjuring images of his grandmother's chocolate cake, with pecans studded in the chocolate frosting. He would work back from there to the turkey and cornbread stuffing that had been the centerpiece of the Thanksgiving meal.

A cup of water would banish such reverie for an hour at most.

Then he would write again . . . memories of his life . . . a record of what he was seeing, what he felt at that moment . . . lists of things he had loved . . . the music of Sibelius; his grandfather's old leather armchair, smelling of pipe tobacco; a little town west of Innsbruck called Zirl . . . Thai food . . .

He scratched out the last entry. Food again. He must not dwell on food. What about a list of people he had loved?—He scribbled down four names and then paused, realizing the problem with that list. Will Rogers ... Winston Churchill ... Ingrid Bergman ... He had never seen any of them in the flesh. Of course he hadn't. They had all been dead for years. They were strangers, and yet he felt closer to them than to anyone he had ever actually met. He admired their work, he had spent many happy hours reading their words or watching their images on film, and most important of all: None of them had ever hurt him. Tom Gentry could have added another twenty names to that list before he would even consider putting down the name of an actual acquaintance. All the people he knew were so fallible, so prone to selfishness, to anger, so indifferent to the feelings of others. Or else they were boring. How could ordinary people bear to spend whole evenings sitting in small, overfurnished rooms and listening to other people tell stale jokes or hold forth with opinions in matters they knew little about?

He could never see the point of the human community.

What on earth had possessed him to join the navy? He supposed that he had been attracted by all the recruiting commercials, picturing earnest young men working sophisticated electronic equipment. He could have done that. If military service had consisted of himself and a room full of steel boxes studded with flickering lights, he would have been the best man they had. What he could not do was find a comfortable niche in the hierarchy. Authority either made him bristle with irritation or cringe in fear. They sensed this, he was sure, even if he gave no outward sign of his disturbance. He had read somewhere that people could smell fear, as dogs could. Anytime he heard his name, he had to make a conscious effort to keep from wincing.

Finally he had gone to see a shrink, but that hadn't helped. The doctor seemed to be listening with the impatient air of someone waiting to see which pigeonhole this patient could be shoved into. Judging from his leading questions, the doctor's diagnosis seemed to be inclined toward latent homosexuality or repressed memories of an abused childhood, or—hey! Why not both? And the problem with shrinks is that if you tell them they're wrong, it becomes just another symptom.

So Tom gave up, because the doctor didn't like him much, either, and by the third session Tom was even more depressed than when he had first arrived.

That's when he had started to idly plot an escape. In his off hours he pored over maps and bus fares. He looked up information on subjects like camping, the Great Smoky Mountains National Park, and suicide. That last inquiry had posed a bit of a problem. The poet Dorothy Parker had been right about that ... *Razors pain you, rivers are damp* ...

But then at supper one evening he had overheard Ramirez talking about San Juan de la Cruz. Saint John of the Cross had proved to be a very interesting Net search indeed.

So now ... and it amused him to put it like this ... Tom Gentry had embarked upon the Way of the Cross.

Malinda

So there we were, turned a-loose from the army a good hundred miles from home, and just as far from the war as we were to begin with.

"Well, that didn't work, did it?" I said to Keith, as we strolled away from the army garrison, carrying our pokes over our shoulders. Nobody came out to see us go, and I was grateful to the sergeant for not bandying the news about to the men that their comrade Little Sam Blalock was really a woman. I know what soldiers are like, all grouped together in camp with no ladies or parsons to tone them down, and I was glad to escape the whistles and catcalls that might have followed us down the road.

I wondered if Colonel Vance would ever tell the tale of how he made me prove I wasn't a boy. I thought he might, because sometimes a gentleman is less of a gentleman than an ordinary fellow, especially when he's dealing with people he thinks he outranks, but I figured that it didn't matter as long as Keith never got to hear about it. The colonel let me go, anyhow, and he didn't put neither one of us in the stockade, so I figured I owed him a tale to tell at least.

I was still dressed as a boy, because I didn't have any dresses with me, and I was just as glad of it. I'd be freer and safer on the road if folks thought I was a young boy called Sam. Folks in these parts had strange notions about what was fitting for ladies. They had to wear long skirts too cumbersome to move in and wire cages under their dresses that made them look like tom turkeys in full strut. They rode their horses side-saddle, which could get your neck broke at anything above a trot; and they had to talk like butter wouldn't melt in their mouths. All the silk dresses in the Confederacy couldn't get me to behave like that, so I'd best keep on being Sam yet awhile, at least until Keith and me got back to the mountain. We figured on walking to the Kinston train depot and buying tickets for Morganton, which was six miles past the end of the line. After that it wasn't more than two days' walk home.

"What do you mean 'that didn't work'?" said Keith, rubbing his cheek with the back of his hand. He had as many ways to scratch as he had places to scratch. Sometimes when the itch took him in the leg, you'd have thought he was dancing down that road. "I got us out of the army, didn't I?"

"Yeah, but it was you that got us into the army in the first place. And you said it was so the Rebels could give us weapons and then transport us up to the front lines so we could join up with the Union."

"Not we," said Keith. "I never said one word about *we*."

"Well, you, then. But the outcome is the same. You are out of one army and not a whit closer to the other one. And all you have to show for it is a face like a berry patch."

He clouded over at that, and I could tell that arguing on top of itching was too much for him to tolerate. "We got our pay, didn't we?" he said.

"Thanks to Colonel Vance being partial to mountain boys, we did, but it's going to take most of that money to get us back where we started from, Keith. And then what?"

"Well, I've been studying about that," said Keith.

"I hope you have, because those discharge papers you got are only good for six months. After that, the Confederates can make you go back to the army, and they will, too, because of that conscription law. Once we are back home a week or so, it will be pretty obvious that you aren't sick. Those Watauga County Rebels will be counting the days until they can ship you out again. So unless you plan on having a permanent case of pox . . ."

"Well," said Keith, "I ain't never going back to the regular army. They about wore me out with their rules and their ranks, and having to be amongst strangers all the time. I'll just have to find another way to be in this war. It seems to me that if we can't get to the war, then we'll just have to bring the war to the mountains."

I opened my mouth to argue with him from force of habit, but then it occurred to me that if we stayed on our own in the mountains, then there wouldn't be any army officers or regulations to trouble us, and nothing could stop me from fighting right alongside Keith. I thought I might keep quiet about that part, though, until he got the idea set in his mind.

"All right," I said, "we'll go home." It seemed a fine idea to me then, and I didn't stop to think who it was we might be fighting if we carried the war back to Grandfather Mountain. All I knew was that I couldn't get shut of the flatlands fast enough, even if it was spring here and still winter up home. I knew that Keith was going to be too sick to fight anything for a couple of weeks, and I knew that I'd have to be tending to him, but that was all right, too. It needed doing, and he'd do the same for me if I was to take sick.

It wasn't no great shakes getting home. Keith had his discharge papers, but he only had to show them a time or two, and I stayed dressed as his kid brother Sam, so we had an easier time getting back than we did going. It was the middle of April when we finally walked up the lane to our farm in the shadow of the mountain. It gladdened my heart to see our land, rich with a patch of spring grass, with the trees leafing out a pale green and the redbud showing pink at the edge of the woods.

I let out a sigh of relief when I saw the cabin still sitting peaceful up there on the rise. "I was afraid somebody would'a burned it," I said.

"No, they wouldn't," said Keith. "They think I'm a good Confederate, remember? That's not to say there won't be trouble—just that it hasn't caught up with us yet."

I reckon Keith took about a year's worth of baths in the next couple of weeks, some in mud and some in brine, trying to dry the poison out of his skin. He sit there in the big old washtub, soaking in brine for an hour or more at a time, hunched over, and trying not to scratch the red patches all over him. Sometimes I'd sit there with him and talk to keep him company, and then I'd set to on some small chore, peeling potatoes for supper or cleaning the guns, because I never could sit still without having something to do with my hands, but he liked me keeping him company, because Keith hates to sit still doing nothing as much as I do.

I got the horse back from Daddy Coffey, and set his mind at rest about Keith's ailment. It didn't take long before word went around the county that we were back, and that no doctor had been sent for to tend the supposedly stricken soldier. Directly one of the county bigwigs rode out to see for himself whether Private Keith Blalock was fit for duty. Keith hobbled out on the porch, hoisting his suspenders over his shoulders as he went, trying to look as feeble as he could, but the man made him take his shirt off so he could see the rash. It struck him funny, seeing Keith standing there trying not to scratch, leaning up against the porch timber, and rubbing his back against it like a tomcat.

The stout old man grinned at us through his ginger beard, and said, "Do you know who I am, boy?"

Keith nodded. "Sure do, Mr. Green."

Robert Green had a house in Globe and a finer one in Blowing Rock, so it stood to reason that being a rich man he'd take to this war like a maggot to a dead cat. He took his time, sizing Keith up before he said, "Well, Blalock, I see that soldiering didn't agree with you."

Keith scowled at him, but he knew you don't sass people that can send you to your death—at least, not if you can help it. He said, "I reckon the spirit was willing but the flesh was weak."

"You don't look particularly ill to me," the county man said, but I noticed that he took a step back when he was looking at Keith's rash, which was oozing now. "You know, we'll keep an eye on you, Blalock. You know the Conscription Act's in force now. Do you understand what that is?"

Keith looked mulish. "It means you have to join the army, and I did," he said. "They sent me home because I was sick."

"Oh, indeed. And you are a good Confederate, then?"

"I'm a veteran," said Keith, and his tone of voice was saying that he had done more for the war than the fat county official ever had or would.

"Well, you're not off the hook yet, though. We'll keep checking on you, and when you have returned to health, you will be sent straight back to the war." Then the old stoat turned and leered at me. "That, of course, does not apply to you, Miz Blalock. You have gone well beyond the call of duty for one of the fair sex, and you shall stay home hereafter."

I thought to myself that we'd see about that, but I knew better than to talk back to the likes of him, so I just stared him right back same as I would a snarling dog, and he dropped his eyes first.

As he started back across the yard to his horse, he called back, "Times are going to be hard around here for traitors. You mark my words!"

"They will be if I have any say in the matter," muttered Keith.

We knew we were living on borrowed time, though. In the earliest days of secession Keith had spoken up for the Union too loud and too often to be let off with just a month of army service, and we knew that they weren't going to forget about him. Every county had to furnish men to the Confederate army, and there was nobody they'd rather get shut of than Keith Blalock.

Sure enough, somebody in the community must have been watching us. Keith's rash cleared up after some more brine baths, and he was out plowing, looking like his old self. I wished the war would either end or pass us by, because farmers always have enough to worry about between bugs and drought without having the government come meddling, too, but sure enough, soon after Keith got better we had more company.

I was out weeding the garden when I heard hoofbeats coming up the road, half a dozen shod horses from the sound of it. I dropped my hoe, and crept alongside of the cabin to get a look at them before they could see me. They were Confederates. One or two of them looked familiar, and I knew that they were headed to see us, but not to pay a social call. Keith was off in the field, but he must have seen them about the same time I did, because I saw him hurrying down the hill toward the riders, with his pistol in his belt. I wondered if I could sneak into the house and get the long gun, but before I could make up my mind to do it, the leader swung off his horse, and pulled a piece of paper out of his belt, so I figured they weren't here to start a fight, but just to deliver more printed warnings from the government.

The one with the paper headed up the path to the cabin, and the rest hung back, still mounted, with their guns at the ready, in case we tried to ambush the messenger, but they need not have bothered, because there's no point in killing somebody with half a dozen witnesses sitting there watching you do it. I don't know if Keith would have shot the officer if he'd come alone—I doubt it—but anyhow, he didn't make a move toward his weapon. He just came across the yard, mopping his brow with a rag, and walked up to the Rebel messenger like he was meeting him after church. I was close enough to hear, and I stayed hid, but I wished I'd had a weapon on me just in case. I thought to myself that from here on out I would start toting a pistol everywhere I went.

"You McKesson Blalock?" the officer said, all squinty-eyed and rude, the way they are.

"You're standing on my land," said Keith. He said it quiet and civil, but there was a stillness all around, the sort of frozen minute you get just before two dogs jump one another.

The officer didn't look fazed by the cold stare Keith was giving him. I've seen Keith give rattlesnakes that same look, only maybe a shade more friendly.

One of the other riders spoke up. I recognized him, all right. I knew that voice. It was William Coffey, one of Daddy Austin's brothers. The other one—Reuben—was right alongside of him, and I recognized one or two other neighbors in the party as well. This war was already setting us at each other's throats, and we had yet to see a stranger.

The officer said, "I am major of the Caldwell company militia. You know about the law that says ablebodied men must serve in the army?"

"I did join the army," said Keith. "Got sick, so they

sent me home. I got my discharge papers, you want to see them."

"It doesn't matter," said the officer, taking a step back and looking Keith up and down. "Looks to me like you're well again."

"I went, and they sent me home," said Keith, quiet as ever.

"Blalock, the county folks know about you. They say you're a Union sympathizer and a shirker. Some say you got sick on purpose to come home. That's by the by. We came here to give you a message."

He thrust the paper at Keith, who took it without even glancing at it.

"I'll tell you what it says," said the officer, and I wanted to slap the grin off his face. You could tell he thought Keith couldn't read. I wanted to tell him that Keith could read just fine, but that the Confederate county bureaucrats didn't have anything to say to us worth looking at. Keith wouldn't say that though. He just kept staring at the man sweating in his gray wool uniform, waiting for him to cough up all he had come to say.

"Blalock, this document says that you have two choices. You can either go back into the army and serve the remainder of your enlistment, or else you can suffer the full penalty of the Conscription Act."

When Keith still didn't move a muscle, the officer blinked at him, and barked out, "Did you understand what I said to you, boy?"

Keith nodded slowly. "Go back or get lawed," he said.

"That's right." The officer looked around at the cabin and then back at his men, and he jerked his head, as if to say to them, "Watch this." They were close enough to hear, loud as he talked.

"And them's my choices?"

"Why, not entirely," said the officer, in that tone of voice folks use when they think they're about to be funny in front of their friends. "If you don't want to go back to the army your own self, you can hire a substitute to go and fight for you. Fifty dollars in gold ought to about do it." He started laughing. "Or if you teach school or own yourself twenty slaves or more, then we'll just say no more about it." He nodded toward the house. "This here y'all's slave quarters, boy?"

Keith shook his head, and his face was as blank as the back of that paper, so you couldn't tell if he understood the insult or not.

I wondered if the officer was saying all that on purpose to get Keith riled enough to jump him so that the rest would have cause to shoot him, but I reckon Keith figured that out on his own, because he just kept stock still and stared at the officer, who was laughing fit to kill. Fit to kill, indeed, I thought. I wondered if the militia man knew that Keith was kin to some of his soldiers. I didn't think the Coffeys would shoot Daddy Austin's boy, even if he was just a stepchild. That joke about our house wasn't wise, either, because most of that officer's men lived in places just like ours. It was no plantation, but it was clean and sturdy, and I'd liked to have gone out there in the yard and told him so, but it wouldn't have helped matters any.

"Well, I'll have to study on it," said Keith, sounding like he wasn't too awful sure what was going on, and the officer must have thought that Keith was slow-witted. He probably thought everybody was stupid who didn't live in town and talk like he did, but playing dumb is like playing possum—sometimes it fools your enemy into leaving you alone. You can always fight later if you have to.

"You mean you want to think over our ultimatum?" Some of the rest of them laughed when he said this.

Keith just nodded.

The major was probably beginning to wonder if Keith was making fun of him behind that stone face.

Then Reuben Coffey spoke up. "Let the man have a while to set his house in order afore he leaves," he said. "It's fair. He did enlist once't, mind."

The commander was none too pleased about that, but he must have realized then that he was more of an outlander than Keith was, and that it wouldn't do to be too harsh on one of their own. "Three days, then," he said, turning on his heel and walking back to his horse. "We will be back for you in three days, and you'll be going with us—one way or the other."

They would, too. That was two government visits since we got back, and I knew there was no use to lay low on the farm and hope they'd forget about us. I stayed hid where I was until the Rebels rode away out of sight, and then I went running up to Keith to see what he wanted to do. He was just standing there next to the porch, staring after the riders like he wasn't quite awake.

"They're coming back," I said.

He nodded. "I know. It's peculiar, ain't it?"

"What is?"

"Well, they claim to be fighting this war so as to make the United States government leave them alone. But they aren't too good at leaving other folks alone, are they?"

"I reckon one government is pretty much like another," I said. "Soon as folks get in charge, they start ordering people around. I wish we had the money to buy you out, though."

"Well, we don't, and I wouldn't give it to them if we did."

He looked down the road, where the last bit of dust was settling in the wake of the horses. "I won't forget the Coffeys being there. Letting that happen. By God, I won't forget."

"But they're coming back in three days, Keith."

He set his jaw and scowled. "Let 'em come. I won't be here."

He was looking up, past me, to the dark cloud-hung shape in the distance. Grandfather.

We didn't know it then, but Keith wasn't the only one who was unhappy with the Confederacy's meddlesome ways. There's nobody braver than a mountain boy, and you'd never see one run away from a fight on account of being scared (more's the pity about that, sometimes), but he don't like being bossed around neither, so when the new government started telling the mountain men what they could and couldn't do, a lot of 'em laid their ears back, dug their heels in, and refused to budge. They understood about fighting for freedom, but they could not figure out how you could force somebody to fight for freedom, and they began to suspect that freedom in the Confederacy was going to be a one-sided affair.

Keith took his gun, a haversack of provisions, and another shirt, and got ready to set out for the mountain-top, where he could see any army coming clear into the next state. "You can't go with me this time, Malinda," he said.

I was rolling up his clean socks to put in the bag. "I know that," I said, and I was beginning to think there were reasons that Keith didn't even know about. "Somebody has to stay here to give the soldiers something to watch, and to take supplies up to you. Take another quilt. The winds up there'll be fierce. Do you know where you're going?"

He smiled. "I'm spoiled for choice," he said.

Maybe it was better if I didn't know for sure where he was, and maybe he didn't know himself exactly where he was going. There were enough caves and thickets and stock pens dotted across that mountain to hide a hundred men, and nobody knew the terrain better than Keith did. On the very top of the Grandfather, there is a bare outcropping of rock the size of a church, and from there you could watch soldiers coming from as far away as Tennessee. Then farther down the slope were the laurel thickets and caves, and lower still was a flat meadow bounded by a stream. Even from there the valley was so far below that the houses looked like squares on a quilt. It would take searchers a week to cover that terrain, and if their quarry kept moving, they'd never trap him.

It was hard to let Keith go, but I knew that I'd be busy enough tending to the farm by myself, and trying to keep the Rebels from deviling us too much.

A month or so later I slipped away from the cabin early one morning and climbed the mountain to make my regular visit to Keith and to take him a flour sack full of provisions. The militia had taken to patrolling the roads, and laying out up in the rocks to ambush fugitives. The word was out that the major had put out a bounty on Keith, dead or alive, and I took care to see I wasn't followed when I went up the mountain.

I had my hunting clothes on, and a pistol stuck in my belt, and I walked up and down on the open space of the meadow, whistling bird sounds, and hoping Keith would spot me so that I wouldn't have to spend half the day getting up to the rocks at the summit.

Finally I heard an answering whistle from the big rocks in the woods west of the meadow. I stood still for a couple of heartbeats longer, listening for the sounds of soldiers, or to see if the whistle I'd heard had come from a bird, but then it came again, and I recognized it as one of Keith's signals, so I headed for the rocks, and sure enough there he was, looking as dirty and scraggly as I'd ever seen him, but none the worse for wear.

After we'd done hugging and saying how-do, Keith sat down on the wet leaves and opened the sack. "I made you some biscuits," I said, but he had already stuffed one in his mouth. "The militia came back."

"Figured they would."

"They were fit to be tied when they found out you were gone. I think they went over to Daddy Austin's place, too, a-hunting you. Said I'd be seeing them again, so I don't reckon it's safe for you to come home."

"It wasn't in my mind to come home. I'm not the only one up here, you know."

I nodded. People didn't talk openly about the conscript dodgers, but word gets around, and it figured that they would all head for that mountain, with its high ground for lookouts and its old trails that led through the gap into Tennessee. I hoped they weren't thinking about shooting it out with the militia, but I knew it was galling Keith to be coon-hunted by his own uncles.

"I hope you ain't planning to do anything foolish," I said.

Keith finished swallowing the last of the biscuits before he said, "I'm not running from a fight. If the militia wants trouble, they'll get it."

"There's other things to consider besides your itch to get even. What if they were to kill you?"

He gave me a puzzled look, and I know he was thinking it wasn't like me to be afraid.

"Why, if anything was to happen to me, you'd be all right," he said. "You're as tough as a half-starved wildcat. You know you are."

"It's not me I'm worried about. It's the baby I'm carrying."

Rattler

Not too long after that first encampment with the sunshine soldiers, I took an early morning walk in the woods, not looking for anything in particular, but carrying a poke-sack anyhow, in case I spotted some wild mushrooms or ginseng or suchlike along the way. A walk in the woods is my version of grocery shopping. It's also my way of checking on the neighbors—to see how the fawns are doing, or whether the rabbits are still courting in the pine woods.

I have other neighbors, too. Retired stockbrokers build glass-and-timber nests halfway up a mountain, and dot-commers who hate people even more than I do hole up in newly constructed log cabins, complete with solar panels and wine cellars.

After an hour or so of meandering without much to show for it, I came to the bank of the Little Pigeon River, which looks like a footpath of flattened boulders edged with narrow channels of white water. Anybody who saw that rock-strewn rivulet would be likely to call it a creek unless they knew better. In these mountains, what constitutes a river is its length not its size. Anything that flows a hundred miles or more is a river, even if you can step across it—and you surely could cross the Little Pigeon and keep your feet dry, for it was more rocks than water and not much more than five yards wide. It gets wilder with the spring runoffs, but there hadn't been much rain lately, so crossing the river wasn't much of a problem.

I was just picking myself a path across the steadiest, driest stones, when downstream of me on the far bank I spied an old acquaintance. It had been a long time since I'd seen him, but right off I knew who he was. If I hadn't, I might have been looking around in the shrubbery for some movie people, for there he was, perched in a patch of sunlight on one of the flat rocks, his skin as brown as broom sedge, and that long black hair that put me in mind of crow feathers tied back with a length of deer sinew. He was naked to the waist, and from there on down he had on deerskin breeches and moccasins. More Hollywood than Cherokee, I thought: Tonto by Cochise, out of Pocahontas. I shook my head at the sight of him.

He was leaning back on that rock, holding the end of string that went deep into the water to the crannies under the rocks where rainbow trout linger in the heat of midday. I didn't think he was fishing, though. Not with that string, anyhow, and not for trout. I wondered what had brought him out in broad daylight with nothing better to do than dangle a string in the water.

Oh, he was a picture all right, looking more self-consciously Indian than heads on a buffalo nickel. The way he was kitted out he could have gone straight over to the Cherokee outdoor drama *Unto These Hills* to try out for a part. That play tells the story of the relocation of the Cherokee nation to Oklahoma—the Trail of Tears—so I've never cared to see it, but I reckon if they really wanted to get the story straight, they ought to let this fellow here direct it.

Since I was crossing the creek anyhow, I forded on a

line of rocks a few yards upstream from him, and once I got to the other side, I angled my way down to where he sat. He was pretending not to see me. Or maybe he figured I couldn't see him. Some hope.

"How do," I said.

He looked up at me with a toothpaste smile, and said in broadcast English, "Why good day, brother Rattler. Now I thought I heard that you didn't hold with talking to dead people."

"I don't," I said. "But you ain't dead. In fact, you ain't even an Indian."

He shrugged. "A mere detail, don't you think? They've always been proud to claim me, you know. Creek and Catawba, Cherokee and Shawnee, and even the ones before that, the ones whose names are now forgotten."

"I've not forgotten the name of your tribe," I told him. "It's *Ravenmocker*, ain't it?"

He winced when I said that, and I could tell that was more plain speaking than he cared for, being used to dealing with the Cherokee like he was. They're a courteous people, which is not a trait that came down to me in my pint and a half of Indian blood. I never got the hang of all that diplomacy and wheel-greasing lies. Maybe that's why I live alone in the woods. Not that I get much peace and quiet, mind you. But at least my neighbors don't stay around much. Some of them hibernate, some fly south for the winter, and the once-in-a-blue-moon ones like this fellow here seem to come and go without rhyme or reason. None that I can see, anyhow.

"We go by many names," he said at last.

"And many faces," I added, just to keep the record straight. "I do believe you were a bear last time I saw you in these parts."

"The last time you recognized me, perhaps," the Ravenmocker said with a tight little grimace that might have been a smile. He had set down his fishing line, and anchored it under a flat stone, which wouldn't have held it if a fish had hit the line, but I didn't think either one of us was worried about that. Now he held a finger-sized flat stone in his hand, and he was sliding it around, through his fingers and back into his palm as if he were working a puzzle.

"And what brings you back here today?" I asked him. I set down my sack of fresh-picked herbs and eased down on the flat rock a little way away from him. I wasn't scared of him, mind you. If it had been my time to die, he wouldn't be the one dropping by to fetch me.

He had more on his mind than the fate of one no-account human being, that was for certain. Still I decided that my meeting him today was no accident. He had a bone to pick about something, and I waited out a long silence until he got ready to tell me.

"There is a storm in the mountains," he said.

"No argument there," I said, knowing we weren't talking about the weather. "Any amount of them, I expect. Which one did you have in mind? Clear cutting in the forest? Strip mining? Acid rain? That monstrosity they built on top of your favorite mountain? Or is it the wine and cheese crowd over in Asheville that's annoying you?"

His frown deepened when I mentioned the desecration of his mountain, but after a couple of heartbeats (mine, anyhow), he spat out the words, "The soldiers are back."

"Oh, *them*." I almost laughed and said "Is that all?" but then I saw him giving me a look that could sour milk, so I went solemn again. "Shoot, I wouldn't worry about *them*. Those old boys are reenactors. You must have seen them out in the woods staging one of their mock battles. But they're only play-acting, you know. It's not a real war. That's long gone. I guess it might seem like yesterday to you, 'cause I've heard that your time doesn't run the same as ours, but you can rest assured that in this world that particular war has been over for a long time."

"It is not over at all," he said.

He tilted the flat stone between his fingers, and I could see now that it was an arrowhead. A second later he flicked his thumb against the edge of it and sent it spinning out to land between the boulders in the deepest trout pool. As it spiraled down toward the bottom it left circular ripples on the bright surface of the water.

I got the point.

"They're shooting blanks," I said.

He looked up and scowled in my direction. "They are shooting .69-caliber Springfield muzzle-loaders and Spencer carbines. They are carrying the weapons of the *time* and they are fighting in the *place*. Whether or not they are killing anyone this time is not the point. They are . . . striking a chord."

"Striking a chord." I smiled. "It sounds funny to hear you being so precise about the reenactors' weapons. You know, being dressed like you are. I thought you'd say something like *fire-sticks*, to stay au-then-tic."

"I am talking to you on your level of understanding," said the Ravenmocker, trying not to look stung by my comment. He scowled at me. "If I were speaking to someone with more education—to your neighbor with a wine cellar in his log cabin, perhaps—I might quote the American president of that era . . . *The brave men living and dead who suffered here have consecrated it far above our poor power to add or detract from it* . . . Ah, how right he was." He smiled, savoring the fine words. "Or to a physicist I might explain what is happening with a reference to *string theory*."

"Well, Chief," I said, "I expect you could find some folks around in these woods who'd understand all that if you want to try it out on them. You might even turn up a professor or two on the hiking trails. I'm just having trouble understanding what you're upset about."

He looked thoughtful for a moment. Probably trying to get the idea small enough to fit into my head, I thought. At last he said, "Have you ever seen the wooden ducks that the hunters put out on lakes in the autumn?"

"Seen one or two on coffee tables," I said. "Not in action, so to speak." I don't hunt with guns, and I'd never heard tell of people going duck shooting on Watauga Lake, but I knew what he was talking about anyhow.

He nodded. "Those wooden ducks—what are they for, then?"

"Well, hunters use them to attract the real ducks," I said. "I reckon the real ducks are flying high over the lake, and when they see the decoys they swoop down to visit with them, and . . ." My voice trailed off there, because I didn't like the way he was smiling at me. I thought back over what I had said.

"Now do you see?"

I nodded. "What you're saying is: *Things that look like things are likely to attract the real things.*"

"Just so."

I started to say, "Can they do that?" and then I remembered the fellow who came looking for the Fifteenth Mississippi in the reenactors' camp. "Well, I don't see what I can do about it," I said. "I don't go playing soldier, and I doubt if they'd listen to any warnings from me on the subject."

"They would be wise to do so."

"Or else what?"

The fishing line jerked just then, hitting the trout line so hard that the flat rock slid right over into the water. I made a grab for the string and missed it. When I looked up again, he was gone.

Malinda

"It's this baby I'm carrying . . . ," I said to Keith.

Did you think he'd tell me to go home, put my feet up, and commence to embroidering baby clothes? I didn't. Wouldn't have done it anyhow. There was a war on, but even if there hadn't been, I wasn't one of those delicate females like the ones down in the flatlands. He just stood there looking at me while the news sunk in, and then he threaded his fingers through his hair, and let his breath out in a long ruffled sigh—like a horse—and then he wrapped his arms around me.

"Lord God, Malinda," he said, "you've got no more nesting sense than a cowbird."

"I'll manage," I said.

"I can't come home."

"I know that."

"Look. I'll try to slip home ever chance I get. You need anything, you go tell Daddy Austin, all right?"

I nodded.

"It'll be fine," Keith said, but he wasn't talking to me.

* * *

Keith and the rest managed to keep clear of the conscription guard for mos' the rest of the summer. They lived like the deer up on the mountain—venturing out at night and laying low in the daytime when they were likely to be seen—and shot at. Now and again one or another of them would slip away to see his kinfolks, or somebody would take provisions up to them. A quilt on a clothesline or one rock placed on top of another one beside the path would signal safety or danger. We worked out the signs as time passed, and by and by we got so good at it that we thought we were safe for sure.

We were wrong about that.

The county militia wasn't about to let a bunch of farmers and cove-dwellers make a fool of them, and they never was going to let up on them. The raids went on all summer, and there were some close calls, times when the boys had to scatter for the rhododendron hills or the hog pens, but they generally kept a sentry posted high on the bare rock outcrop atop Grandfather, and he could give a hog call to warn all and sundry that danger was on its way up. The dodgers got better at hiding out, but the searchers got better, too. Stands to reason. Not a man in these parts but hunts, and hunting men ain't harder than tracking beasts.

One night when I was alone—which was mostly these days—there was a banging on the cabin door. I crawled out of bed, grabbing the pistol as I went. "Go away!" I yelled through the closed door. "I got a gun—and besides, he ain't here."

The pounding stopped and a quiet voice said, "Yes, he is."

I flung open the door, and near 'bout dropped the pistol, 'cause there was Keith standing there in the moonlight, swaying like an stripling poplar. "What are you doing here?" I said, dropping my voice to a whisper, which was foolish, because the nearest neighbors were miles away, but I was used to hiding and sneaking by now, and the sound of my own voice would have made me jump. "The quilt ain't out on the line."

Keith tried to smile, but couldn't. "Figured I'd risk it," he said. "Not much to lose." He staggered over the threshold, and sank down in the chair next to the hearth.

In the firelight I could see the dirty strip of white cloth wrapped around his left arm above the elbow. It was oozing blood. "They damn near got me, Malinda," he said.

Keith nodded, and swayed a little in his seat.

I set the pistol down on the table, and lit the candle. "I need to unwrap it," I said. "Shall I fetch the whiskey?"

"I can stand it," said Keith. "Let's save the liquor for hard times."

"If you change your mind, say so," I said. I got a dipper of water out of the kettle on the hearth—it was still warm—and I poured it into a wooden bowl. I got a clean cloth out of the scrap box and sat down beside Keith, feeling as wide-awake as if it was midday. I started to untie the knots on the bandage. "You want to tell me about it?" I said, figuring that talking might take his mind off what I was doing.

"Not much to tell. The sentry missed them, and by the time we spotted them, they were almost up on us. I managed to lose them in the woods, but not before they put a ball through my arm. I'm going back directly. They might show up here."

"Well, you'll have to come back tomorrow as well, so I can change this dressing."

"Ow!" he roared and pulled away from me. "Lord, God, Malinda, you should'a been a blacksmith."

"Seems like I'm working on a mule as it is," I said right back. "Now hold still while I see about this wound." It had bled right smart, but when I palpated the arm, the limb seemed sound enough. "You were lucky. The ball missed the bone. It should heal up all right if you don't get flesh rot. It's a big gash, though. Better if I was to get my needle and sew it shut."

"Malinda?"

"Yes, Keith?"

"I believe I'll take some of that whiskey now."

I spent all the next day worrying about Keith. He had slipped out well before dawn, but I was afraid that they might be using dogs this time, and the blood scent from his wound would give him away for sure. I did the washing first thing in the morning to get rid of the blood-stains on the sheets and the old bandages so that nobody could tell Keith had been home. As I did the rest of the chores around the place, I wondered how he was doing, and if I ought to go up looking for him, but that would be dangerous, too, so I made up my mind to wait for nightfall and see how he was then.

He didn't come, though.

Well before sunset I hung the quilt out back of the house so he'd make sure to see it if he was hiding nearby. It was a red and yellow one in a bear-claw pattern, and I had made it myself the winter we got married. I had used one of my old dresses that had been dyed in madder for the red pieces, and an old skirt dyed in snuff weed for the yellow. The quilt was still bright, for we had sot the dyes in salt to make them hold fast to the thread. Keith knew that old quilt. We had slept under it many a night. He couldn't miss it.

But he didn't come.

I sat up by the fire until the moon had risen and set, mending shirts until my fingers bled, and running to the door at every sound, but there was no sign of him. Come morning I woke up by the cold ashes of the dead fire, still alone, and fearful now that something had befallen Keith on his way back up the mountain.

I was right about that, but it was ten days before I

knew what happened. I didn't sleep much for the first couple of days, and I must have eaten, but I don't remember what. I paced, and cleaned the pistol, and did what chores had to be done, having no heart for the rest. Finally I got tired of pacing from one end of the cabin to the other, and I made up my mind to head up to the mountain myself to see if the rest of the outliers could tell me what had befallen my husband.

I kitted myself out again in boots and breeches though I'd had to let the waist out because my belly stuck out so far nowadays. I put on Keith's old coat to cover my shape, and I set off up Grandfather with the same sack of provisions I had taken when I went off to war. I knew there wouldn't be no trick to finding the rest of them as was hiding up on the mountain, for they would find me soon enough if I made no move to cover my tracks or move in secret. I didn't think they would shoot strangers without asking questions first, and there wasn't no use worrying about it anyhow for I was bound to risk it. In fact I decided to make as much noise as I possibly could just to show them that I wasn't trying to ambush anybody.

There weren't any new-fallen leaves to crunch underfoot yet, it being early September, but up on the high slopes the locust trees were already turning brown, and I knew that the world was holding its breath just waiting for the days to get a little shorter, and then summer would be over. Nights were already cold, and I had brought the red-and-yellow quilt with me as well as a dyed-wool blanket, for it wouldn't do to fall sick while I was carrying a child.

There was a farmhouse in a meadow partway up the mountain, and I had just given it a wide berth, and headed on up past a clump of boulders when I heard a rustle in the bushes behind me. I stopped walking and held my hands out away from my sides. "I'm looking for McKesson Blalock," I said loud enough to be heard twenty feet away.

The moving stopped, and it got all quiet. Off in the distance a crow screamed. You'd think they'd be used to strangers on their land by this time. Finally I heard steps again. Somebody was coming up behind me. "Who wants McKesson Blalock?" said a cold, quiet voice.

I squared my shoulders and stood up straighter. "*Mrs.* McKesson Blalock."

I heard the outlier sucking breath, and then he walked around in front of me and peered up under my hat. "Is it Malinda?"

I recognized the fellow now. It was one of the Pritchards, kin to me, so I reckoned I could trust him as much as anybody.

I nodded. "Is my husband here? He come home after he got shot, and I patched him up, but I ain't seen him since."

"We heard tell they got him again. Gonna take him east to a prison camp."

"Did anybody go after him?"

The boy shook his head. "Not as I've heard. They's too many of 'em for us to take on in flat country. It ain't safe up here neither." He stepped back, looking me over, and I knew my belly was sticking out enough for him to know how it was with me. "Why don't you go on home and we'll send word if we hear anything."

"I'll stay up here," I said. "I don't want Keith to get caught a-trying to get home to me. You show me where he hid out, and I'll wait there."

He hesitated, so I said, "I'm three months away from needing a midwife, and I don't plan on staying with you boys. Nobody has to look after me or give me a share of the vittles. I can shift for myself. Now show me where he beds down."

That shut him up. He jerked his head for me to follow him, and set off through the woods toward Grandfather's chin, and a good while later we ended up at a laurel thicket back in amongst some chestnut trees.

Pritchard stooped down in front of that stand of laurels, and pulled aside some fallen branches, and I could see a crude door, fashioned out of wood scraps, it looked like. Pritchard tugged it open, and I could see the inside of a low-hung hut fashioned of bark and branches, built there in the heart of the thicket. There wasn't hardly enough room to turn around inside it, but I reckoned it would be dry and sheltered from the wind. I just hoped the rattlesnakes hadn't chanced upon it yet. Then I saw Keith's bedroll inside, and I reckoned I'd be safe enough.

"I'm obliged to you, cousin," I said to Pritchard. "I'll be all right now. I brung my horse pistol." I pulled the Navy Colt out from under my coat, and showed him. I figured he'd tell it around to the other outliers, and nobody would come bothering me—not that I was in much shape to be an enticement anyhow.

I spent the rest of the day waiting, and trying not to think too hard about what I would do if Keith didn't make it back. He had left some deer jerky in the hut, so I ate on that, when I remembered to be hungry, but mostly I just tried to keep still. I sat in the opening of the shelter and watched the birds scrabbling on the ground for seeds and fighting amongst themselves, just the same as if they was people. I was hoping that bigger birds—maybe a turkey or a bobwhite—would happen by, or even a rabbit, so I could pot them with my horse pistol, and have something to make a meal on, but I reckon there were so many men a-hiding out on this mountain that easy pickings were getting scarce. I tried to sit as long I could sit without moving to see how close I could get the birds to come to me. It didn't take my mind off the knotting of my belly, but it was all the distraction I had.

After all those sleepless hours, Keith finally came when I had crawled into the bedroll and drifted off from bone weariness. Being six months along now, I knew the baby needed all the rest I could give it. I came to in pitch darkness with Keith a-shaking my shoulder and whispering, "Malinda! What do you think you're doing up here?!"

I sat up, wide awake in a heartbeat. "A-waiting on you," I said. "What happened?"

"They got me again, but I stole away," said Keith. "Did you bring any provisions with you? I hope you took everything you want to keep from the house, 'cause we ain't going back there."

I rubbed my eyes. "Can I have some light then?"

"Not a fire. I'll light a tallow for you. I don't think there's anybody out there, but I don't care to risk it. They damn near hanged me."

"Who did?" I was on my knees, hauling one of Keith's shirts out of a saddlebag, for the one he was wearing looked to be held together with blood and dirt. I had put some of our clothes in the pack, along with a couple of the baby dresses I had made for the first one we had that died. Keith was rooting through the other gear— knives, flints, and what little ammunition we'd had for the guns.

"Green!" Keith spat the name. "That Robert Green from over to Blowing Rock. He was the worst one of 'em all—treated me like I was dirt! They damn near strung me up. Would have, if Green'ud had his way about it. But then they changed their minds, and trussed me up, and took me along to their camp at Cove Creek. They got some huts thrown together down there and a stockade fixed up for prisoners, and they hove me in it while they went hunting more dodgers, I reckon, but they didn't find anybody else."

"How's your arm?" It was too dark for me to tell, and I didn't want to hurt him by feeling it.

"Tolerable. I kept it clean as I could. You can see to it when we get where we're going. No time now."

"How come they let you go?"

Keith laughed. "They never did. Not if they knew it! I reckon I'd be keeping company with them yet if they'd left me in irons at the militia camp, but after a week or so they took a notion to deliver me to safer quarters east of here. I reckon they thought some of the outliers here on Grandfather might try to rescue me, but I never saw a sign of it." His face clouded over for an instant, but I reckon he figured you could only hate just so many people at a time, so he gave up on holding that grudge. "Anyhow, I didn't need 'em, did I?"

"How'd you get loose?"

"Slipped my bonds and stole away while they were a-sleeping. Another time they'll have the sense to post a better guard, I reckon, but I judge us to be safe enough up here on the mountain—leastways for now. I can't see the militia finding their way up here."

Not without help, I thought, but Keith had already stretched out alongside of me, and was halfway asleep, so I didn't say any more.

So we settled in to life with the outliers up on the mountain. It put me in mind of being in the Rebel camp back in Kinston, except that we were in more danger here as civilians than we had been with the regular army back east. We posted sentries up on the rocks of Grandfather's brow, watching the valleys to the east for a plume of dust that would signal riders on the way, or for the smoke of campfires along the river where there didn't ought to be settlements.

We had to take care to keep our own fires small, so as not to be spotted from afar, and we were mindful not to use green wood or rotted branches, on account of the smoke they give off. I don't know that I'd care to pass a winter up there, when the wind cuts across the summit like a razor and the snow buries everything to your boot-tops, but in the gold of Indian summer, that old mountain was a fine place to hole up. Oftentimes the men would sit out together and share the evening meal over one campfire. One or two of the boys were dab hands at catching trout out of the streams, and we'd roast them over the campfire on whittled sticks, or else we'd cook a bird or rabbit that someone had snared in a string trap, for we didn't care to waste bullets on such as them. The families in the valleys would send up provisions, too, when one of us snuck down into the valley to visit and get news. We might get a loaf of bread or a mess of greens and onions out the garden, but the news was just as welcome as the food, as it was the only way we had of knowing how the war was going.

Joe Franklin came back one evening with a tale to conjure with. He made us give him the biggest piece of trout before he'd open up about it, but finally he wiped the grease off his chin with his sleeve, and rared back and said, "North Carolina has got itself a new governor, boys! Keith, you ought to be glad of it."

Keith scowled. "Why? I don't know any of those fancy vote-rustlers."

"Well, you know this one. It's old Zebulon B. Vance from Buncombe County—erstwhile colonel of the Twenty-sixth."

I could feel myself blush, but it was dark, and nobody was paying me any mind. It seemed funny to think that I had taken my shirt off in front of a governor. Not a tale I was ever going to tell, though.

"Well, I hope he'll remember where he came from," somebody said.

"So do I," said Joe. "It could make a world of difference to the mountain counties to have a friend in office."

I wasn't sure how much say-so a governor had in war time, but I thought Zeb Vance was a decent man, and I figured it was as good a news as we were likely to get for a while.

Somebody hauled out a fiddle and commenced to playing Saint Anne's Reel, and the men passed a jug around and drank to the health of old Zeb Vance. I didn't take any, though, for I was more worried about our health than his.

The weeks rolled on, with the days getting shorter and the wind turning sharper, and the leaves going from red and gold to muddy brown. Some nights were so cold we all had to go and huddle together in the cave to keep warm, and when I felt the baby kicking inside my belly, I wondered if he was trying to tell me he didn't want to be born up here in the wild wood.

He got his wish.

One day when the clouds rolled in so low over the mountains that it was like walking in a white shroud, and all the sounds were muffled inside that fog, we were up high near the laurel thickets, gathering brush for a fire, fixing to cook a mess of beans, when we heard the clip-clop of horses' hoofs—coming close.

The militia. Maybe Daddy Austin Coffey's brothers. Raiding our camp.

Somebody yelled for us to take cover—wasn't no time for bird calls or fancy signals. They'd be in sight of us in a heartbeat. I started to run to the hut for the pistols, but Keith grabbed my arm, and said, "There's no time to get your weapon. I've got mine. They're toting Enfield rifles. Now you get gone!"

I stayed where I was and faced him down, with the others running past us like rabbits in an owl's path. Nobody made a sound, though: There was just the crunch of boots on dry leaves, and then they were into the trees and gone. All except us.

"I ain't running unless you do, McKesson Blalock," I said—formal, to show him I meant it.

"There's no time to wrangle about this, Malinda."

I jerked my head toward the tangle of laurels against the rocks above us. "You first."

We heard the crack of a pistol shot, and then some shouting from below us, and then a volley of rifle shots all at once. Keith grabbed me by the shoulders and shoved me headfirst into the laurels, and I scrambled forward to give him room to follow me. The branches tore strips down my arms and snagged my clothes, but I never made a sound, just kept scrabbling forward on my hands and knees, flinching every time I heard the snap of rifle shots in the clearing. I hoped they wouldn't think to aim a bullet into the brush, else they'd get us for certain.

We crawled as far back into that thicket as we could go, and then we sat stock still, with me trying not to think about them setting fire to the brush, and wishing I'd gone after my Navy Colt, so's I could fight back if I was going down. And what if they'd brung dogs with them?

Keith put his lips against my ear and said, "It's Robert Green. I hear him. Somebody led 'em here."

I nodded. They came right to us. Left their horses a ways down the hill and walked up to the camp. Knew where to look. But we couldn't study about that now. I wanted to be a long way off and upwind of that crew before I thought about anything except getting away.

Keith had his gun out, and he was starting to scoot back out of the laurels, but when I made a move to follow him, he shoved me back in. I couldn't see nothing from the inside of that laurel thicket, but from the popping of shots and the burnt smell of the air, I knew there was a right set-to going on out there.

By and by the shooting stopped, and Keith was scooting his way back toward me. "They ain't gone," he said. "Likely they'll try to surround us, but I think they're south and east of us for the nonce. Our best chance is to make for the trail toward Tennessee."

"What about the others?"

"I hope they'll have sense enough to follow us. We can't go to rounding 'em up."

Keith took the knife out from his belt and started hacking away at the branches of the laurels. We were going to come out on the other side of the thicket, and head for the balsam woods where the path lay. We pushed and slashed until finally the branches weren't so tight against us, and we heaved ourselves out onto the mossy ground.

The shooting had started up again, closer now.

Keith pulled me to my feet and shoved me ahead of him toward the trees. I was hightailing it as hard as I could, and thinking six things at once—about keeping my footing, and how the shooting put me in mind of musket drill back in camp, and that the baby I was carrying would have to be tougher than wet rawhide to live through this. Then I heard Keith stumble behind me. I half turned, but he yelled, "Go on!" and I went.

After a few more yards, I heard his footsteps behind me, and I ran on, but when we got to some bushes, Keith grabbed hold of my shirt and pulled me down through the leaves. "Need you to bind my arm," he said through clenched teeth, and then I seen that his sleeve was wet above the elbow. Must have been a stray bullet, I thought, because nobody was on our tail.

"Just stop its bleeding for now," Keith said, quiet. He kept shaking his head, and closing his eyes and then opening them again real fast.

I knelt down and took the knife out of his belt, and cut a strip off the tail of my shirt. Then I tied it as tight as I could above the wound. "Bone's not broke," I said as I worked. "Just a flesh wound. Lotta blood; not much harm."

Keith grunted. "Ain't your arm."

Tending to the wound cost us some time, and we could tell from the shouts and the gunshots that the fighting was between us and the path. "They'll catch us if we make for the path," I whispered to Keith.

"Well, we can't stay in here. You already got shot once't."

We kept stumbling forward while we talked it out in whispers. They could fire the camp, and even the woods, but I had thought of one place that ought to be safe. "The hog pens!" I said.

There was a farmstead in a meadow alongside the creek about midway up the mountain, and they let their hogs have free range over the mountain all summer. Now they had got them penned up ready for the fall hog killing, and we weren't far from the pens. I could hear the hogs squealing at the noise and the blood smells that had 'em spooked. Noise and hog stench and a pen with a lean-to shelter. It was our best chance, and we ran for it.

Keith pitched headfirst over the rails of the hog pen, and then scrambled up to hoist me and my belly over the side, and then we dived for that jumble of hog flesh, and commenced to muddying up our faces and arms so we wouldn't stand out so much in the crowd. The hogs didn't seem to mind the company. "Good thing you're the only one here that's in farrow, Malinda," said Keith, grinning.

He was right. Sows with piglets will stomp you to death if you get near their young'uns, but it was too late in the year for that, though I didn't much care for Keith's way of putting it. These here hogs just figured the more the merrier, especially with it turning cold as evening came on, so we crept over to the lean-to and hunkered down in the pile, taking care not to get trampled on by those sharp trotters of their'n. It seemed like the longest day of the year, I was wishing so hard for the sun to set, but finally the shadows bled into darkness, and the shouting faded out below, and we figured the militia had done all it was going to.

"I wonder how many they got," I said.

Keith shook his head. "Won't help to dwell on it. I'm studying about getting even."

I leaned back against the hog pen, and shut my eyes.

"You and me and your busted arm against the militia, McKesson?"

"No. This is personal. I want Robert Green and I want William Coffey."

"William? I didn't see him in that fight. Did you?"

"No. But who else could'a led them to us? William Coffey knows this peak as well as I do, and you know he's secesh. He's done betrayed us all, and I mean to get him."

"How? They already got most of your men. You're lucky they didn't get us, too."

"I ain't waiting around for them to get any smarter," said Keith. "We're going over to Tennessee—get some help."

"Who from?" I had people over in Carter County, but I couldn't see us going hat in hand to them, 'cause for all I knew they might be Confederates their own selves.

"The U.S. Army's over there somewhere. I heard my uncles and the rest of the men talking about it before. I aim to find 'em. Are you with me?"

I nodded. "I knowed we was leaving," I said. "I done put the fire out." That made it final. There was no telling when we'd be back, or if the Rebels would leave our place standing if we did come home. All I knew for sure was that I was three months away from having a baby, and I'd likely be on the run when he decided to be born.

Leaving this time was a solemn thing, worse than when I went off to war. What made me feel it the most had been putting out the fire when I went up on Grandfather to find Keith. The fireplace was the heart of the cabin—it was light and warmth and hot food. We never let the fire go out, for it was troublesome to have to strike flint to bits of grass to get it alight again. Sometimes we'd even go and borrow coals from another household, rather than have to start over from scratch to rekindle our own. Putting it out on purpose was like stopping the heart, like leaving the cabin for dead.

"Where's the horse?" said Keith.

"Soldiers took him last time they came a-hunting you."

Keith clouded up for an instant, but then he shrugged and hoisted the saddlebag up on his shoulder. "That's all right. There's plenty of Rebel farms between here and Tennessee. We'll steal us a couple of choice ones. I figure they owe us."

Governor Vance—1863

I can't say I cared much for the way 1863 began. If there hadn't been a war on, I daresay I might have enjoyed the office of governor as much as anything I ever did. In September I moved into the Governor's Palace which stands on the south end of Fayetteville Street, facing the State Capitol building, a dueling stance probably unintended by the architects, but symbolic nonetheless.

Once I was reunited with my dear ones, my personal happiness was as complete as one can have in the face of our country's tribulations. Harriett was much pleased with our new residence. It is a fine white-columned edifice with windows as tall as I am, a fan light over the front door, and a portico on the second story—quite a change from the log house of my boyhood, but I am glad for the chance to have lived in both.

Certainly the Governor's Palace was more commodious than a colonel's tent at the front, but one quickly gets used to one's surroundings, and I was indifferent to the grandeur. What pleased me most was the idea that I was in control, instead of having to bend at the whim of every fool and rascal above me on the ladder of command.

Some may marvel at the idea of a boy from a frontier log cabin moving into such a mansion in his thirty-second year, but to me the transition did not seem abrupt. I counted two former governors—David Swain and Frank Graham—as my friends and mentors, and I had often dined in their company, so the "seats of the mighty" held no terrors for me. Here in Raleigh—only thirty miles from Chapel Hill, I knew I was never far from old friends. Besides Mr. Graham and university president Swain, there was Mr. Burgess Gaither of Morganton, a kinsman on my mother's side, who sits in the Confederate Congress, and a host of other old friends that I knew from my days in politics and the law. The only stars missing in my firmament are my brother Robert, in command of Confederate forces in east Tennessee, my fellow lawyers John Woodfin and Waightstill Avery, likewise serving in the army, and Augustus Merrimon, who had got himself appointed solicitor of the western district, so he is back in Asheville, seeing that justice is done in the mountains, while I try to hold the state together in the face of new disasters from every quarter.

In late January I had to issue a proclamation ordering all deserters to return to their units, and promising that if they did so by February 10, they should not be punished for having deserted. I know that desertion is rife within the mountain counties, and I hope that they will realize that this proclamation is an effort to throw them a lifeline. I cannot exempt them from the army, but at least I can try to protect them if they will but do their duty. They are worried about their families, and their farms. Of course they are. War is terrible for all of us, not just those on the battlefield. I did what I could to allay the deserters' fears, though, by inserting a pledge into the proclamation: *"As your Chief Magistrate, I promise you that the wife and child of the soldiers who are in the Army doing his duty, shall share the last bushel of meal and pound of meat in the State."* I meant that vow, but it chilled me to write it, for it had about it the air of prophecy.

If the crises of war were not enough to keep me humble, there is always the reminder that I am not the only governor of North Carolina. The United States government in its meddlesome efficiency appointed a military governor of the state, in their perpetual defiance of our wish to conduct our affairs without their interference. I wonder that they found anyone base enough to take the job, but even a gilt brass trophy will have rascals chasing it, I suppose. The scoundrel who called himself the military governor was Edward Stanly, a New Bern–born politician, who had served in the North Carolina House of Commons and then as state's attorney general back when I started out in politics. But nearly ten years ago he ran for Congress against Thomas Ruffin, and was beaten so badly that he tucked his tail between his legs and hared off to California. Now that the war is on, Stanly, sensing pickings to be had, no doubt, has come slinking back, proposing to lord it over the state he abandoned a decade ago.

A few weeks after I took office, Stanly actually had the effrontery to write to me, asking for a meeting between us two holders of the same office, and he seemed to be hinting that he wanted to end our citizens' sufferings in this war by having North Carolina make a separate peace with the Union, exclusive of her sister states in the Confederacy. His presumption did not endear him to me, and I replied brusquely that I did not see it as my duty to meet with him, and that as I had no authority to end the war, it seemed pointless to hear him out.

I had thought that my reply would have ended our correspondence, but less than a week after I wrote him,

Richard Battle came into my office waving a letter and saying, "Governor, you seem to have lit a firecracker under the tail of our *military governor*. Old Stanly goes on for pages about it!"

With a sigh I held out my hand for the letter. "It would seem that I have yet to learn to give soft answers to people I can't stand," I said. "Why, once a political opponent challenged me to a duel on account of my plain speaking. I don't suppose this scoundrel has that much sand in him?"

Richard laughed. "Mr. Stanly? I'd say not. Remember when you said that the people of North Carolina would not be so base as to abandon her sister states? He takes exception to that, but he doesn't proposal a duel. I think he means to hector you into an apology."

"Some hope," I said, taking the proffered letter. I was reading the spidery handwriting, taking little note of the man's expostulations until the name of General Lee leaped out at me. "Now he has done it," I said to Richard. "Now the weasel is claiming peerage with Robert E. Lee. He says that when General Lee went into Maryland . . . at Antietam . . ."

Richard winced as I said that, for his brother Junius had been killed in that campaign. Junius Battle's commander had written to say that Junius had been wounded at the Battle of South Mountain, and, although his leg had been amputated, his life could not be saved. Junius spent the last few hours of his life reading to the crowd of Union and Confederate wounded who lay around him, faltering only when his eyes were glazed with death.

After a moment, he said, "Yes, sir? When Lee's army went into Maryland . . ."

"Stanly will have it that Lee asked the Marylanders to abandon their sister states and join the Confederacy, and that the general tried to persuade the Marylanders with the sword, while Stanly says that he himself came and asked nicely for our allegiance, without an army to back up his request, so he claims the moral high ground. And he goes on to call our government *a disastrous tyranny*."

Here I said a rude word, and Richard pretending not to hear, said, "Shall I put the letter in the fire, Governor?"

"Oh, no. Official correspondence. Matter of record. Let's answer it." I got up with the letter still in my hand, ready to dictate while I paced. I always think better on my feet—a holdover from my days in court, perhaps. "And, Richard, you'd best make a copy of our reply, because I expect Stanly will burn his copy once he reads it. Have you paper with you?"

"I do, sir."

"Too bad we don't have a rattlesnake to use as an inkwell, for I think my reply will be venomous." I paced and dictated awhile. "Read that last bit back to me, Richard."

"*. . . Your mission to North Carolina was a failure, miserable and complete. Coming to the people who had often honored you, in the wake of destroying armies; assuming to be governor of the State by the Suffrages of abolition, bayonets red with the blood of your kindred and friends, how could you expect it to be otherwise . . .*"

"Good. I think we must make things very clear to poor Stanly. He does not seem to realize his position."

"People hate him, sir. He sits there giving himself airs in the eastern counties while the Federals pillage his own hometown."

"Well, let's tell him so. Write this down: *Do you not know, sir, that your name is execrated, and only pronounced with curses in North Carolina?* We'll come back to this part in a bit, and give him a sample of the atrocities committed in his jurisdiction. I have thought of a good ending, and I want to set it down before I forget it."

"He thinks that the North is going to win the war, and then he will have the whole state to despoil."

"Well, he may be right, but I can remind him that it will be a hollow victory. Take this down . . ." My voice took on the cadence of the lecture platform as I warmed to my wrath: ". . . *North Carolina . . . may be subjugated . . . You may reach her Capitol and take possession of her government. The fortunes of war are fickle. But I assure you, upon the honor of a Son, who will follow as he has followed and maintained her, whether right or wrong . . . that you can only do so over the dead bodies of the men who once respected you, through the smoking ashes of the homes which once greeted you with hospitable welcome, and through fields desolated, which once gladdened your eye, rich with the glorious harvest of . . . of . . ."*

"Peace," said Richard.

I nodded. "Peace."

The first crisis I had to cope with after New Year's was Mr. Lincoln's Emancipation Proclamation.

"Mr. Lincoln," said Harriett, pronouncing the name with careful precision. "You know, back in Morganton, people said that he was a Lincoln in name only. Everybody knows his mother was a servant girl for the Enlow family down in Swain County, and all of them are tall and gawky-looking, just as Mr. Lincoln seems in the pictures of him. They say that when the Hanks girl was married off to Tom Lincoln, she was already in the family way. Odd that the Enlows have produced a president and cannot claim him."

"I don't expect they'd want to claim him," I said. "He has just made his emancipation proclamation official."

Harriett nodded. "Half the state seems to be living in fear of a slave revolt."

"The other half is living in fear of the Conscription Act," I said with a sigh. I found that every now and

again I could sympathize with Mr. Lincoln's plight, since
the cares of leadership had been thrust upon me as well.
It was my predecessor who issued that proclamation,
but I was sworn to enforce it, and to sit here before my
well-tended fire and read the pitiful scrawls from those
whose lives had been ruined in its wake.

Every day I receive letters, many of them from the
mountain counties, because the folks up there regard
me as a favorite son, and see me as a protector more so
than they would a governor from the eastern part of the
state. They ask me to secure promotions, report foul
deeds committed by both armies—as if I could do anything about them!—or they report their neighbors for
hoarding blankets or leather. One correspondent
wanted to know whether a lady from North Carolina
may exchange embroidery thread with a lady from
South Carolina without running afoul of some Confederate supply law. (I granted my sovereign permission for
this momentous transaction.) And the letters from the
humblest of our citizens are heartrending.

> *Dear Gov. Vance,*
>   *this is to no of you whether ther should be*
> *any chance for me to get my Two sons Dis-*
> *charged or furlowed home or not that is Harri-*
> *son & Paton Gibsons that formerly belonged to*
> *your Regement they are both Sick and has been*
> *for along time not able for Service and I am fer-*
> *ful they never will again if you please instruct*
> *me how to Get them home if I had them home I*
> *could nurse them up and maybe save their lives*
> *or Recrute them up so they wold be able for*
> *service again my Boys has been in ther War over*
> *fifteen months and have don all they cold in*
> *defince of there contry of you please to assist me*
> *in tryin to get them home for Iam a poore*
> *widow woman . . .*

Of course, it is useless for these poor souls to appeal to me on behalf of some friendless recruit from the backwoods. He is exactly the sort of fellow who does get killed in this war, and everybody seems to take that as a matter of course. Except his grieving relations, I suppose. I know how proud these mountain folk are, and what it must cost them to come begging to me for assistance. Indeed I wince to be the recipient of such pleas. It does not come easy to them to ask favors, and moreover they will not understand why it is that I cannot help them. In the most humble and courteous tones they make reasonable requests of someone with whom they think they have a connection, and it is utterly useless for them to do so, but I cannot bear to tell them so.

I temporize. *Well,* I say, *thank you for your letter. Be sure that I will do all I can for your Henry . . . your Jim . . .*

All I can. Which is nothing.

My erstwhile constituents think that I am powerful because I am governor. Useless to explain to them that I cannot intervene with generals—or even captains—on behalf of one lowly foot soldier, no matter how much my sympathies may lie with the plight of his family.

I detect no hint of reproach in these carefully scrawled, earnest letters from simple folk on hardscrabble farms. No one seems to say, or even to think: *Here, Zeb Vance of Reems Creek, you got out of the war fast enough! One day you were a colonel being shot at in Virginny, and the next you were sitting in the governor's mansion in Raleigh, having your food brought on silver trays and sleeping on eiderdown.*

It's true, of course. The world—and certainly the Confederacy—seems to think one man is worth more than another. The Union does, too, though. Three hundred dollars is the price they put on a gentleman: For that sum he can pay a penniless Irish immigrant to take his place on the front lines. *Harpers Weekly* reports that there have been draft riots in the city of New York, and upward of fifty Negroes were lynched by angry mobs who felt that their menfolk should not be sent out to die for the rights of such as these.

If anyone from the mountains should ask me about my deliverance, I'd say it was merely unintended good fortune on my part to have been spared. True enough that when I got myself to the university and began to cultivate powerful friends, I did not see the war coming. But I was running from the impotence of poverty all the same; to be poor is to die, war or no war.

Richard Battle came in with the morning post, looking stricken, but since he reads the letters first, there is nearly always something in the correspondence to grieve him, so I did not inquire, but he held back the rest of the stack and handed over only the topmost letter. "From Augustus Merrimon, sir."

Harriett had risen to go, but upon hearing her cousin's name, she said, "Is there family news? Dear Augustus and Maggie! Shall I stay while you read it?"

Richard warned me off with an almost imperceptible shake of his head. "No, my dear," I said heartily. "Just dull old legal matters. If you have trouble falling asleep tonight, I shall regale you with it then."

We managed to keep up this pose of indifference until my wife had departed for her duties elsewhere, and then I slid the letter out of its envelope and began to read the message aloud. *"I learn that the Laurel expedition is about over . . ."*

"You remember, Governor," said Richard. "The Unionists broke into the storehouse in Marshall and carried off some salt and other supplies. We had a telegram on the twenty-first from General Heth in Tennessee, saying that Confederate troops had attacked the Tories of Shelton Laurel, killing thirteen and capturing twenty."

"Yes. We telegraphed back, didn't we? Agreeing that the insurrection should be dealt with, but not too harshly?"

"Yes, sir. I fear that your words were not heeded. Read on in Mr. Merrimon's letter."

"*. . . I learn that a number of prisoners were shot without any trial or hearing whatever. I hope this is not true but if so, the parties guilty of so dark a crime should be punished. Humanity revolts at so savage a crime. Our Militia had nothing to do with what was done in Laurel. I am glad of this . . .*" I looked up from the letter then. "Yes, by God, if there are monsters, let them not be our monsters!"

"No, Governor."

"Shot without a trial! In my old home county." I wavered between sitting down to take the weight of this news off my shoulders and the urge to pace out my wrath until the Turkey carpet was threadbare. "We must have more news of this. I'll show the army that they cannot slaughter our citizens with impunity."

Telegrams flew back and forth, and inquiries were made. We learned that the soldiers who carried out the execution were in the command of James Keith, a resident of Marshall. I had been acquainted with him in my youth. He is an ambitious man, aspiring to be a prosperous farmer. He married well, and he counts himself a leader in the county, so of course he sides with the well-to-do Confederates of Madison County, and he has only contempt for the poorer citizens in the back country. He would say that their loyalty to the Union is little more than a hatred of their wealthier, slave-holding neighbors. And now he has slaughtered thirteen of them. I wonder if there but for the grace of God go I.

I wrote back to Merrimon, asking him to investigate the shooting in Shelton Laurel. *I intend to look into the matter myself,* I told him. I was much less reticent about the matter in my remarks to Richard Battle.

"I want to know who did it, and I want him hanged!" I said every time he brought the matter up.

Two weeks after the first reporting of the Shelton Laurel incident, I said it again when Richard told me that there had been more communications from Madison County in relation to the massacre. Richard usually tolerated my outbursts with an expression of discreet neutrality, but this time he blanched and said, "There are extenuating circumstances that you need to hear about, Governor."

"I don't care," I said. "I don't care if the archangel Michael himself provided the sword and signed the order—" But I stopped then, for I saw that Richard was still looking at me like a stricken calf. "Well, what are they? These extenuating circumstances?"

"The men who raided the salt warehouse in Marshall numbered about fifty, and some of them were deserters from the Sixty-fourth. After they had taken the salt and whatever else they could lay their hands on, they advanced on the house of their erstwhile commanding officer, Colonel Lawrence Allen . . ."

"I know him," I said. "There has been some trouble about him, I hear from home. The raiders attacked Allen?"

"No, Governor. Colonel Allen was absent from home, but Mrs. Allen was in residence with her children. And, sir, two of those children . . . Romulus, age six, and Margaret, four, lay gravely ill . . . with diphtheria."

I was silenced, thinking of my own dear boys who were about of an age with the poor Allen children. "Tell me the rest," I said.

He sighed. "The report we received from Marshall states that the marauders pillaged the house, taking whatever food and clothing they could lay hands on. They even invaded the sick room, and took the children's clothing from the drawers as they lay there."

"I see. And the children?"

"They were badly frightened, of course, by these brutal strangers invading their home. They heard their mother crying and pleading for the intruders to leave . . . They did leave without harming Mrs. Allen or the children . . . but . . . the shock cannot have helped their condition. Colonel Allen was sent for, and told that his son had just died. Allen rode all night from the encampment and he reached home just before dawn . . . in time to hold his dying daughter in his arms before she, too, departed this life. It was after the Allens buried their children the next day that the Colonel rejoined his soldiers in pursuit of the marauders. They were camped at Shelton Laurel that night . . . in the bitter cold . . . and during the company's march out from town they had been shot at by bushwackers hiding on the hillsides."

I sat down, and put my hand over my eyes, letting the silence fill the room. At last I said, "It's never easy, is it, Richard? It never *is* Saint George versus the dragon. Like most everything else in life, it's a choice between two wrong answers."

"Yes, Governor." Richard looked pleased that he had talked me down off my high horse. "There was indeed provocation. I'm sure the soldiers were in sympathy with their colonel in his bereavement, and they were cold and tired and frightened of ambush. Feelings were running high . . ."

"It's no excuse," I said. "Those soldiers shot thirteen men—no, by God, twelve men and a *boy*—without a trial, without benefit of clergy, without even knowing for sure that those men were the marauders they wanted to punish. The act was barbaric, and we cannot allow it to go unpunished, war or no war."

"People will say that the Tories had it coming, with their thieving and their cowardly attacks from the brush."

"And so we slaughter them? I cannot allow it. Well, I

cannot *condone* it anyhow. It is a crime. Even in war, it is a crime."

"But those men were the enemy, Governor."

I had already thought out the rights of that, and I didn't bat an eye before I answered him. "Had they been shot in battle, I concede it would be a just measure," I said. "At least they'd have had a chance. But once a soldier is taken prisoner, he must be accorded the rights of a human being again, and he may not be slaughtered like a hog. There will be a trial, and the charge will be murder, war or no war. I suppose it is all in Merrimon's hands, since he is the district prosecutor. But I intend to let him know my sentiments in the matter."

"But, sir, the men responsible for the killings were Confederate soldiers. Has Mr. Merrimon any authority over them?"

"Well, I will look into that. Meanwhile, let us write a letter to the secretary of war, demanding an investigation. We shall proceed from there until we have settled the matter."

"Of course, Governor," said Richard in his usual soothing tone, but then he said, "But keep in mind, sir: *Inter arma silent leges.*"

"Not if I know it!" I shot back at him. "As long as I am governor of this state the laws *will* be heard amidst the roar of the cannon!"

"Indeed I hope they may, sir," said Richard, with polite lack of conviction, "but we ought to bear in mind that there is a war on, and that the men shot in Shelton Laurel were technically the enemy. So many thousands are dying that it might be difficult to make people care about thirteen mountain Tories."

He was probably right, I thought, but that did not stop me from making my outrage felt. In fact, if there should ever be forgeries of my signature in circulation, Mr. Seddon, the secretary of war, could be relied upon to spot them at once, for he has seen more specimens of my actual signature than his desk will hold, I'll warrant. Not a week goes by without some salvo from me being fired in ink in his direction.

As the winter turned to spring, I had many other pressing matters on my mind—most notably the problem of how to get supplies into North Carolina through the Federal blockade of the harbors—but still I continued to pepper the army and the Confederate government with demands for an investigation. As time went on, though, I began to fear that the lack of resolution was deliberate on the part of the authorities. They wanted the matter to go away, but they reckoned without me and without Merrimon, who would worry an issue to death as long as he had his teeth in it and believed it to be his business. I was counting on Merrimon to claim jurisdiction over the case, and to hold on come hell or high-ranking officers.

I believe he would have, too, but politics often plays out in private, and the thing was settled before Merrimon or I could intervene. I had a letter from him, written the eighteenth of May: *"I am informed that the Military authorities have allowed Col. James A. Keith to resign his office, and that too, without any trial for, or inquiry into, the alleged Murder of thirteen prisoners in Laurel, by his immediate Command. Am I correctly informed on this matter? I suppose you are advised?"*

I put the letter down. "I was not advised," I said, as if he could hear me halfway across the state.

"I think there is something in the dispatches, though, from Tennessee." Richard left the room, and I paced before the empty fireplace until he came back with the telegram from Confederate army headquarters in Tennessee. I read it and scowled. "They have contrived a way to let Keith get away with it, Richard," I said, "but at least I can make them show me their tracks. Take a letter!"

With a hint of a smile, he put pen to paper, intoning aloud: *"To the Honorable Jas A. Seddon, Secretary of War—Sir . . ."*

I took up the tune, *". . . I had the honor to request of you some time since an examination into the case of Lt. Col. James A. Keith 64th N.C.T. charged with the murder of some unarmed prisoners and little boys—"*

Richard gave a low whistle, and then mumbled, "Begging your pardon, Governor."

"—And little boys—during the recent troubles in the mountains of this State. I have heard by rumor only that he was brought before a Court Martial and honorably acquitted, by producing an order for his conduct from General Davis, Commanding in east Tennessee. I have also been officially notified of his resignation. Will it be consistent with your sense of duty—Richard, don't snicker. It puts me off my train of thought—*with your sense of duty to furnish me a copy of the proceedings of the Court Martial in his Case? Murder is a crime against the Common Law in this state and he is now subject to that law. Very respectfully and so on . . ."*

Richard looked up from his writing. "What do you suppose will happen to Colonel Keith, Governor?"

"Well, he can't go back to Madison County," I said. "Those men he killed had fathers and uncles and cousins, and they will not accept an acquittal as the end of it—not from the army or even from God Himself."

"Then I suppose he'll have to wait until the war is over, sir."

"Oh, Richard, that war isn't ever going to be over."

I did what I could to help the mountain Unionists. In May I had issued a proclamation calling for all deserters and conscription dodgers to surrender to the army and return to their duties. I chided them for their dereliction of duty, telling them that their neighbors would never forget how they neglected to do their share in our time of need, but at least I promised them immunity from prosecution if they would comply without delay. While I was making that effort on behalf of my former constituents, my brother Robert was being promoted to brigadier general, and given permanent command of the western district of the army, now based in western North Carolina, but it was too late for him to exercise any authority to secure justice for those poor devils in Shelton Laurel. Anyhow, Robert promptly came down with the typhoid, so his battles for the next few weeks will be personal, fought with the aid of the regimental surgeon. I hope he won't see too much action where he is posted. If I can get the outliers and the deserters back in the fold, it should make his task much easier.

With that in mind I made an appointment of my own: I put John McElroy of Yancey County in charge of the Home Guard in the mountain counties. I have made him a brigadier general, with the unenviable task of keeping his territory loyal to the Confederacy. He is also brother Robert's father-in-law, so the pair of them ought to get on well together out there in the mountains in case their troops need to work together. Lord knows I have enough to contend with down here in Raleigh.

Rattler

I spent the rest of that morning's walk studying about what to do about the Ravenmocker's warning, but it seemed to me that things weren't yet clear enough for me to know what to do, so I decided to wait and see what developed. A day or so later another neighbor of mine brought up the same subject, only she had only a vague idea about what was going on.

I was sitting in an old ladder-back chair out back of my cabin watching a red-tailed hawk scouting my garden for field mice or baby rabbits. The pickings must have been good because she had taken up residence in the stand of trees near the porch, and I saw her at least once a day. All of a sudden though she broke off her surveillance, looked toward the side of the house, and then let go of the pine branch and sailed off toward the ridgeline. About that time Maggie Raincrow came into the backyard carrying an empty mason jar.

"Somebody stole your jelly," I said, giving the eye to that empty jar.

Maggie Raincrow lives by herself in a new little A-frame on the ridge about a quarter mile down the road.

She wears her black hair long, and she looks about twenty-five—I've never cared to ask whether it's art or nature that makes her youthful. She doesn't come from around here, but she fits in better than most outlanders, probably because she's from Vermont, which isn't all that different from here. Maggie says that we're "Vermont without the winters," which is what brought her here in the first place. She's an artist, and she's a fair hand at getting a likeness of a person, though you'd never know it from looking at most of her paintings.

Maggie looked down at the mason jar and smiled. "I'm sorry, Rattler," she said. "I didn't bring you anything. Actually I came to ask for your help. See, the deer are getting into my tomato plants, and I tried tying pie pans to a clothesline, hoping the noise would scare them off, but that didn't do it, and then the lady at the farm supply told me that the best way to keep the deer away was to put human scent around the perimeter of the garden."

I nodded. I knew where this was going, and it was all I could do to keep a straight face.

"I was all set to try it, only the clerk said that it won't work unless it's male scent." She laughed. "You wouldn't think the deer would be chauvinistic, would you?"

"I believe I would," I said, "considering the size of the buck's harem. Or maybe the deer have just figured out which sex it is that does most of the shooting at them."

"I guess so. Have you heard about this trick?"

"Oh, sure," I said. "I do it myself." I nodded toward an old wooden table I had set up. "Why don't you sit down here at the table. Do you want some tea? If I'm going to fill up that mason jar for you I'll need at least half a potful first."

I went inside and set the kettle on the wood stove, and after I got the tea made, Maggie and I sat in the shade talking while we drank it. She talked a little about the landscape painting she was working on, and some about a new kind of tomato she'd ordered from a seed catalogue. I didn't ask too many personal questions, because I always figure that sooner or later folks will tell you anything they want you to know.

I've often wondered what her real name is, though. Still, I never asked, because if she wanted to call herself something else, that was her business. Maybe her last name really was "Raincrow," but I didn't think that could be it, and I reckoned she picked it because it sounded earthy and ethnic, and maybe she wanted people to think she had Cherokee blood, too. It's quite a status symbol nowadays. Anyhow, Maggie is one of those artistic types, and they get fanciful about poetry and symbolism, and "raincrow" is one of those beautiful words that makes you think of woods and waterfalls—if you didn't know any better, that is. I did, though. A raincrow is the local mountain name for a bird that is generally known as the yellow-billed cuckoo. I figured that if Maggie knew that, she would have called herself something else, but I didn't want to be the one to tell her. Maybe she thought that a mountain artist ought to have an Indian-sounding name. She could call herself whatever she liked as far as I was concerned. She was a good neighbor and I liked her. She didn't act like she was better than the locals, and she didn't make fun of poor people or pretend that everybody who was from around here *was* "poor people." People with graduate degrees and nice homes don't make for colorful yarns, but they outnumber the other folks here by a wide margin, though you won't hear many of the new people admitting to that. The new people like to regale the folks back home with stories of their life among the savages. Most of them haven't figured out yet that they are associating mostly with the people they hire—the workmen and the house cleaners—

because a lot of people up here don't associate with the new folks unless they have to.

Maggie Raincrow was pleasant company. You didn't have to be on your guard all the time for fear that she was looking for something quaint to pounce on, or storing you up for a tale to dine out on.

"Isn't this the most perfect day?" she said, smiling and stretching like a sleepy cat. "Not a cloud in the sky, not too hot, and the laurel is in bloom on the mountain. It's so peaceful here. I'd put this day on my list."

"What list?"

"I call it my eternity list." Maggie made a funny face. "It's a silly idea, I guess, but I rather like it. You know Ben Hawkins, the potter in Hamelin? He's a friend of mine. We end up at a lot of the same art events and we get to talking when business is slow. Ben studied physics at SUNY-Binghamton, and once during a lull at the spring craft fair, he started telling me about a new theory of the universe he'd just read about."

Physics again. People were talking about the strangest things these days, I thought. I was used to holding my own in talk about the weather and plant lore, but this was new territory for me. "A new theory of the universe," I said. "Well, that's different. And you understood it?"

"Sure," said Maggie. "I took physics once—well, one entry-level course ages ago, but still I can listen with the best of them. And I read a lot. Besides, Ben is a potter, not a professor. He explained it to me in simple terms— almost poetic terms, in fact. What he said was that a scientist in England—I forget his name . . ."

"Wouldn't signify a thing to me," I told her.

"No. Well, this English physicist has theorized that every moment in time lasts forever. Ben said that even though time seems to flow from one moment to the next, it is actually just a collection of separate *nows*, each existing forever in its own dimension. Or universe. Something like that."

"Every moment stretches on for eternity in its own separate compartment?"

She nodded.

I thought about it. "So somewhere I'll be drinking this mug of tea—forever?"

"That's what he said. I think." Maggie smiled. "And I thought that maybe that's what heaven is: getting to live forever in one really wonderful moment. So the more happy moments there are in your life, the better your chances are of spending eternity in a good place. It makes sense to me. If you have no anger, no enemies, no unfinished business, then you're likely to end up in a happy moment, don't you think? Ever since Ben told me about it, I've made a point of collecting happy moments, ones I might like to live in for all time."

I just smiled at that, and Maggie said, "What do you think of that theory, Rattler?"

"Well," I said, "I think you ought to put it in that mason jar and pour it along the edge of the garden. But I don't reckon it hurts any to be on the lookout for happiness. Too many people are heading in the other direction."

"You see a lot of unhappy people, don't you?"

"A fair few," I said. People are always coming to me for poultices and tonics, and sometimes all that ails them is that they are bored, or tired, or just plain lonesome. Sometimes they'd rather dwell on their little aches and pains instead of worrying about the big ones: a dead-end job or a marriage that's gone sour—the problems that nobody can fix with a potion. So they drink their tonic and try to pretend that it'll make their troubles go away. They wouldn't believe me if I told them that, though, so generally I don't. Lots of folks tell me their troubles when they come by, and maybe talking it out does them as much good as my herb brew.

"I'll have to try that tonic of yours sometime," said Maggie. "Does it chase away bad dreams?"

"Are you having bad dreams?"

"Well, strange ones anyhow." She looked as if she wanted to say more, but then she just shook her head and smiled. "There's something else I wanted to ask you about, though. Are the Civil War reenactors out in the woods these days?"

"Off and on," I said. "They prefer to fight the war in the summertime, though I believe the real soldiers did the same. Why? Have you seen any around?"

"Yes, every now and then I'll get a glimpse of a couple of them going up the dirt road or through the woods."

I was surprised because the last encampment hadn't been near Maggie's A-frame, but I thought the soldiers might have gone out foraging in the woods, or jogging, or some such thing. Or maybe she'd been out walking far afield herself.

"Well, they don't mean any harm," I told her. "They're in their own little eternal moment, if you will—the War. It does just seem to go on forever. So they won't bother you. Nice bunch of fellas. I'm acquainted with most of 'em."

"Well, that's good to hear. Maybe I'll ask if I can do a sketch of them the next time I see them. It would make quite a dramatic picture—them on their horses."

"I expect it would," I said, and I felt a chill go through me even in the bright sunshine of that June afternoon.

Our local reenactors don't have horses.

"Tell me about the dreams," I said.

Malinda

I don't reckon anybody sets out to do great wickedness in a war. Not ordinary folks, anyhow. Maybe not even generals, but I wouldn't know what it's like to be one of them. I think that regular people just try to get along as best they can, but of course they put themselves and their families ahead of everything else, so if somebody gets in their way or makes them afraid, that somebody is going to get hurt. And there's revenge, of course. Men are not creatures to let an injury pass unanswered.

The thing about revenge, though, is that there was a lot of things that happened in these mountains that needed avenging, and there's never enough justice to go around.

After that shoot-out on Grandfather Mountain with Robert Green and the militia, we made it through the gap and into Tennessee without any more trouble, though Keith was the worse for wear with the bullet hole in his arm. He got better, though, and we went to see Mr. Lewis, who was known to be strong for the Union in Carter County. It was through him that we heard about a unit of soldiers from Michigan who had set up camp in east Tennessee.

"I reckon I'll go talk to the Michigan boys," Keith told me.

"I thought you had got shut of wanting to be in the army," I said, and I scratched at my neck in case he needed reminding of his last experience in the military.

He gave me a look and said, "I ain't fixing to join as a regular, Malinda. But I reckon I can offer them something they ain't got: somebody who knows these hills like the back of his hand."

"You want to be a scout?"

"No. A pilot. There must be a lot of other men in Carolina who want to get away from the Rebels and need guiding across the mountains. And maybe some captured Union soldiers trying to find their way back to their own lines. They need people to get them safely through the passes, and I reckon I'm the one to do it."

I thought about it. It did sound safer than putting on a regular uniform and getting shot at, and Keith was dead right about knowing the country around here, but I couldn't see where it was our business to help either one of them armies. In fact, I wished they'd all go away and take their war somewhere else, because it seemed to me that people were going to suffer no matter who occupied this territory, and no matter who won, but there's no use talking like that to a man. They always think that any contest with two sides has to have a winner, and Keith wasn't about to miss a chance to settle scores with those Rebels back in Watauga County. He has a long memory, and he'll never fail to repay a favor—or an injury.

Another reason I wasn't so keen on this new plan of Keith's to get back in the war was the fact that he wouldn't let me go with him to hunt up the Federals, on account of me being six months along. He left me with my kinfolks, and went off by himself to talk to the army commander. Although I wasn't best pleased about it, I did see the sense of it. I knew the regular officers wouldn't see me as nothing but a millstone—a pregnant woman, belly out to here, looking helpless as a landed fish. They wouldn't know what a good soldier I had been, and it wouldn't do no good to tell them. Seeing is louder than talking.

Keith was better off on his own, but staying behind meant I had to wear a dress again, and sit with the womenfolk, while they ran on about babies and needlework and all the homely things that just seemed no account at all with a war going on right outside their doorsteps.

So as fall turned to winter, Keith joined up with a Michigan cavalry regiment, unofficial, as a scout, which meant that he could do as he pleased. He got himself a new Enfield rifle and a good pair of boots—almost new—out of the deal, and he set about slipping in and out of Carolina, recruiting soldiers for the army. I stayed around the cabin helping with the hog killing, making cornbread, washing clothes, and tending young'uns. My cousins had cabins within visiting distance of their folks, so I never wanted for company—though sometimes for solitude. Keith was gone for a week at a time, and every time he left I'd know I might never see him again.

I sewed and I slept 'til I was sick of both.

When he came back in the middle of January he brought somebody with him. Keith stood there, dirty and scraggly, stamping snow off his boots, and looking like thunder. I didn't run up and fling my arms around his neck, like I mostly did, but I smiled with relief to see him come back. I was sitting in the apple-wood rocking chair close to the fire with a blanket bundle in my lap. My kinfolks gathered around the hearth, too, and they muttered how-do's to Keith, and darted looks past him at the young boy he had in tow, because these days strangers mostly mean trouble. The boy didn't look like he could do much harm, though, the state he was in. He was rail thin, dirty, and thorn-scratched, and his breeches looked more mud than cloth. He stood there swaying in the doorway, and I knew that Keith must have pushed him pretty hard getting through the mountains, and they hadn't had too many chances to eat along the way.

Keith took his hat off, and finished stamping the snow off his boots. He nodded to my kinfolks, and then he came over and said quiet-like to me, "Malinda, I need to talk to you."

I pulled the blanket back a bit so that he could see the top of the little pink head underneath. "Come meet your son," I said.

That made him forget whatever was on his mind, and for the next couple of minutes he was hugging me and making foolish noises at the sleeping boy, 'til he woke him up, and then trying to get the little one to grab on to his finger. The menfolk slapped him on the back, and for a minute everybody forgot about war and winter in that little bubble of joy. One of the younger Pritchard girls had gone over to the stranger at the door and led him off to the table, telling him to sit down before he fell down. She give him buttermilk and cornbread, and held up the tin plate to ask Keith if he wanted some, but he shook his head to say, "Not just yet," and went back to admiring his baby.

"I named him Columbus," I said.

"I reckon that's a name that won't get him in trouble no matter who wins the war. At least folks agree on who discovered the place," said Keith. "It's a good long name."

"He's got blue eyes."

"Babies mostly do. Like kittens. We'll see what he looks like come spring." Keith tucked the blanket back around the baby. "I'm thankful to find you both well. It's the only good news I've heard in a while." He nodded toward the tow-headed boy at the table, shoveling cornbread into his mouth with both hands. "He's got a story to tell, and I brung him out to make sure he lived to tell it. Something bad has happened over in Madison County."

We waited and talked of other things until the stranger had done eating, and then Keith signaled for him to come over by the fire. "Crowd around," said Keith to the Pritchards. "This boy has a tale that needs to be heard and passed on far and wide."

When the family had shepherded the boy to a place of honor next to the fire, Keith put his hand on the boy's shoulder, and said, "Tell 'em what happened in Shelton Laurel, John," he said. "You're among friends here."

My relatives were like most people in this war: that is, mainly the side they were on was whichever one would leave 'em alone. All they wanted was for their crops to be left standing and their hogs not to be stole, and their menfolk not taken—the rest of it didn't seem like any of their business. But if they met up with a hungry person who wasn't trying to rob or kill them, they'd help him best they could without worrying too awful much about his politics. I knew, though, that they were scared about what Keith was doing, piloting for the Union. They feared that harboring me might bring the soldiers down on them, and that's where mercy would have to yield to common sense. I didn't blame 'em none. They had young'uns, too.

The boy looked stronger now that he'd got some food in him, but he still had an empty look, and he stared into the fire as he talked, as calm as if he was telling us a dream from which he had not quite yet awakened.

"It was the salt," he said. "Well, first it was because we didn't want any part of this war. Wasn't our fight, but it was happening a long way off anyhow. Up in Virginny. We figured we was like moles in a cornfield—buried too deep to bother with. We figured they'd leave us alone."

Somebody passed a tin mug over to the boy, and he

took a long drink, and said, "Wasn't that what the Confederates were fighting for in the first place? The right to be left alone by a meddling government?"

He was parroting Keith word for word, but Keith just smiled and said, "No, they just want their own way, same as everybody."

The boy nodded. "You know they passed that law last spring saying men had to join up with their army, but we didn't. Finally, though, the government hit upon a way to force hillfolk to fight."

"They took the salt," I said.

Made sense. There isn't much you need on a mountain farm that you can't grow or make yourself, and if you need help, there's neighbors and kin standing by to lend you a hand. But two things cannot be had by work or skill in the back country, and that is salt and iron. Those you must buy or trade for: iron for tools, and nails, and horseshoes, and salt to cure the meat so that it will last you through the winter hanging up in the smokehouse. If the meat goes bad, your family goes hungry. Maybe they die. Salt comes out of the ground in some places, but not in these Carolina mountains, though they are rich enough in gold, mica, silver, and bauxite. The politicians in Raleigh knew it. Or maybe it was the rich people in Marshall that wanted to keep the salt for themselves.

The boy sighed, still watching the fire swallow the logs. "It was the only thing they could take away from us, and a few months back they done it."

Before the war, salt came in by wagon from Saltville, Virginia, but there are Union troops now between there and the supply depots, so the shipments cannot be made. Folks say that in Raleigh you might pay fifty dollars a barrel for salt, and it might as well be a thousand, for it is more money than we'll ever see. I've heard men say that salt could win this war—or lose it.

"The governor is said to be a good man. He comes from these mountains his own self . . ."

"He's all right," I said. I'd have boasted more about knowing Zebulon Vance personally, but the memory of our one and only meeting—Colonel Vance and Private Sam Blalock, that was—made me squirm to think on, so I held my peace about that.

"They said the governor sent what salt could be spared to the western counties," the boy went on, "but the folks in the towns there hoarded it for themselves. They weren't about to share it with them as had no men serving in the army. Some of us didn't think that was fair—join up or starve. So in January some men from the outlying settlements—"

"Shelton Laurel," said Keith to the listeners. "H'it's between the Sugar Loaf and White Rock Mountains. One of the passes to Knoxville leads through there."

"Yessir. Well, some of the men from up that way went down to the town of Marshall, where the salt was kept, and they broke into the storehouse and took some salt for the relief of the folks back up the hollers. Wasn't just our folks—a lot of people are in dire straits now for want of salt. They didn't steal it to sell or despoil, you understand. They only took what they figured was the settlement's rightful share, and we had to have it to live out the winter."

"Did you'uns kill anybody a-getting it?" That was the Pritchards' old granny asking that. She likes to make up her own mind without you leaving anything out of the telling, and she can spot a liar through a stone wall.

"They never did," said the Shelton Laurel boy. "The raiders shot one man that caught them breaking into the stores, but he lived. Then they took their share of salt, and some blankets, and ever what else they thought they could use, and lit out of there before daybreak."

"They never thought they'd get away with that," said the old woman, looking up from the shirt she was mending by firelight. "They never thought the soldiers wouldn't go after 'em?"

The others nodded in agreement. They had seen enough of soldiers by now to know that they were not to be trifled with. They could see what was coming.

"I wasn't with them," said the boy, "but I reckon they must have thought they could hide in the hills if the army came after 'em. I'd a-thought that." He looked at Keith when he said it, and I knew he was thinking that Keith had hid from soldiers often enough not to judge others who thought they could do the same. "Only turned out they wasn't running from militia. The general over to Knoxville sent the Sixty-fourth North Carolina over the mountains to catch the salt robbers."

"Heth," my husband said. "He was out west fighting the Mormons before the War started up."

"Should'a split up and hid," I said. "A man alone ought to be able to disappear into these woods so no army could dig him out."

"They did, ma'am," he said. "But they left their wives and babies and old people back on the farms. Didn't figure an army would bother them. Women and babies and old people." He looked around at the listeners by the fire— mostly women and babies and old people—until one by one they looked away. And then he went on. "So the army came over the mountain. The men they were looking for were long gone, of course. Word of the Sixty-fourth's approach reached the hollers long before the soldiers did, and them they was looking for lit out. But the homesteads were still there. Their women were still there."

I shivered a little, remembering what the army feels like. The soldiers were tired of tramping through deep snow, chasing shadows, and getting shot at, and they didn't plan on turning back empty-handed. So they'd tried to make the women tell where the men had gone.

"The women," said the boy, faltering now at this part of the tale. "The soldiers—"

My cousin, a bride last summer, laughed and said, "No woman is going to tell on her man!"

But I had seen something of what soldiers were like, and I knew they must have done more than ask. "What did they do to them?" I asked the boy.

He shrugged. "Strung 'em up. Cut 'em down. Thrashed 'em with hickory rods 'til their backs ran red. All the while shouting out their questions. One woman had a newborn son. They tied her up to a tree in front of her cabin, and they put that baby down in the snow six feet in front of her. *You can tell us how to find your husband,* they said, *or you can watch your baby freeze to death. You're gonna lose one of 'em, and if you wait too long to tell, you'll lose both.* They killed the hogs, stole everything they could carry and burnt the rest."

His voice trailed away, and for a while nobody said anything.

Finally the old woman said, "Did they catch the men?"

The boy hesitated. Then he said carefully, "They took fifteen prisoners."

"Not the right fifteen," I said.

"No, ma'am. Not the ones stole the salt. They got young'uns and them that was too old to run. Davey Shelton was thirteen, and I'm not much more."

We all stared at him. "You?"

"Yeah. They got me at home while I was feeding the cow. They shot her and dragged me away. They put me with their other prisoners—tied us all together with hemp rope—and marched us along the muddy track that led out the cove to their camp. I was so scared. I knew they'd shoot me sure if I was to run. To keep from crying or thinking about what would come next, I began to look for signs as we went. Something to tell me what was going to happen to us."

Everybody got all quiet then. "Did you see any?"

"Maybe. When they took me away, I saw a crow a-setting on top of the cow shed, and then a little ways down the valley, I saw three more crows perched on a poplar limb."

The Pritchards nodded. They didn't have to be told what that meant. *Counting crows: One for sorrow, two for mirth, three for a funeral . . .*

And four for a birth, I thought, feathering the hair on my baby's head as he slept.

"When I seen them three crows, I made up my mind to get away, first chance I got. They took us to a house they used as their headquarters and kept us there two nights, tied up. Whenever the guard went off and left us to ourselves, I'd try to tell the rest that we must make a fight of it, or else find a way to steal out while it was dark, but they wouldn't listen. The older men said that we were only going to be taken to Knoxville for a trial, and that we could get a lawyer to say the soldiers had arrested the wrong men. *At least in jail they'll feed us,* one of them said. And the Sheltons thought that if we was all to run, the soldiers would go back to our farms and take it out on the women and children."

"They would have, too," I said.

"I know that now," said the boy. "But then I was just thinking about how I didn't do nothing wrong, and that running was my only hope of salvation. And I was right about that. On the second night, after it got dark, I told the guard I had the stomach pains and the flux, and I told him I couldn't help it, but I was going to go in the corner.

"Well, he didn't want me fouling their quarters, so he yelled at me to hold on, and then he untied me and started hauling me out in the snow to do my business. I looked back at Davey Shelton, hoping he'd understand what I was doing and ask to come too, but he looked embarrassed to see me carrying on like that, and he turned away.

"I never seen him again.

"The sky was clabbered with low snow clouds, so once we got ten feet from the cabin, it was so dark you couldn't see your hand in front of your face. He wouldn't have let me go, except I was looking so sick and wobbly that it didn't look like I could go ten feet under my own power. I even asked him if he'd help me walk back when I was done. The guard said no and gave me a shove toward some bushes. I unhitched my belt, and stumbled off into the thicket, groaning loud and grabbing at my belly, but as soon as I got to the cover of the woods, I buckled up again and slipped off through the trees, trying to put as much distance as I could between me and the camp before the guard got suspicious at me for taking so long.

"I didn't care what direction I was going in or where it took me, as long as it was well away from that cabin, and I figured I had all night to put some miles between me and them. By the time I heard shouting and gunshots, I was wading a creek, and by the time there was enough light to tell one tree from another, I was across the valley and most of the way up a mountain, where the laurel thickets were so deep that you could hide a wagon in one. I stayed there most of the day, listening for searchers, but they never came after me, or if they did, they didn't come close. Another one of us got away the next day—I ain't seen him, and I don't want to say who he was . . ." The boy frowned as he said this, and gave Keith a pleading look, as if we might press him to tell.

"The name would mean nothing to us," said Keith. "And you are right not to trust anybody too much these days, I reckon. Tell the rest, John."

"Well, I sat up there in the snow until I thought I'd freeze to the ground, and then I got to thinking that I ought to try to go back and see if I could help some of the rest get away. It was Davey Shelton I was thinking about. We was friends. I didn't have no weapon, though, so I knew I didn't have much chance."

"Should have got some help," I said.

"I know it, ma'am, but I thought time was short, and I

didn't know where help might be. Anyhow, I worked my way back down the mountain and through the woods, taking care not to make any noise or to get too near the open fields. I was so quiet the deer didn't even run as I slipped past, but before I got to the cabin, I scouted out the bottom land from a ridge over east of it, and I seen the soldiers moving off down the track, following the creek, with the prisoners tied together, trying to walk in that deep snow best they could without pitching one another over into the drifts. I moved along the ridge, keeping clear of the edge, and watched them go, thinking I might wait until they stopped to rest and then edge in close and try to spirit Davey off into the woods without us getting caught.

"From up there on the hill it was all quiet, as if I was looking at a picture in a book instead of a real scene. I couldn't hear the crunch of boots in the snow, nor make out any voices. The soldiers never once looked away from the prisoners, but chivvied them on sometimes with the butts of their weapons. I thought about waving to see could I signal to one of the Sheltons, but since I was unarmed, I thought better of it. I counted the prisoners and there were only thirteen, so I knowed somebody else had got away, but it wasn't Davey. He was stamping alongside his father, looking little enough to get swallowed up by those snow drifts.

"I wish he had.

"Finally they come out of the cove and into the valley where the creek joins up with the French Broad River, which will take you to Knoxville if you was to follow it long enough. Then the soldiers turned the Shelton Laurel men into a wide meadow down by the river, and I thought that this was where they would rest before heading on toward Tennessee. Before I could set about finding a way to work my way down off the ridge without being spotted, I heard a crack in the silence, and I peeked out through the bushes and saw one of the men fall in the snow.

"The soldiers were dragging them away from the others one by one, making them kneel down in the snow, and then shooting them in the head. If the body was still moving after they'd done shooting, they would club at it with their gun until they were satisfied that the man was dead.

"I was stumbling down that hill now, taking no more care to be quiet, but between the shots and the cries, no one was listening, and so I made it to the very bottom of the hill, still hidden by a stand of laurel. Five bodies were dark lumps in the snow, with puddles of red seeping out around them.

"The soldiers were hauling five more men into a line with their backs to the river.

"*You promised us a trial!* One of the men called out.

"*For God's sake, grant us the time to pray!* said a white-haired fellow.

"I saw two of the soldiers turn and look at their commander, as if they expected him to grant this last wish, but he stood there as if their words were no more than the bawling of hogs at butchering time. One young-looking Rebel turned as if to walk away, and this time the commander did take note. *Fire on the prisoners or take your place among them, soldier!* he shouted.

"After a moment's hesitation, the Rebel walked back to the line of shooters, and faced the five weeping men, tied up and helpless by the river. The order was given, and the five weapons cracked, and the Shelton Laurel men fell down in the snow. One of them was belly shot, and he was screaming so loud I couldn't hear nothing else, but directly one of the soldiers walked over to him and put the gun barrel down next to the man's head and fired. I reckon it was merciful. Gut shot is a sure way to die, but nothing is more slow and painful, so the fellow was better off as it was, with a bullet in the brain instead of being left laying there to die for hours.

"There were three prisoners left, and Davey Shelton was the last.

"He was crying.

"My face burned for shame to see him beg those devils for his life, but I reckon I would have done the same in his place. It would have been better for them to have shot him straightaway, if they meant to do it, instead of making him watch his father butchered and letting him see what was in store for him.

"*Please let me go!* he was wailing at the soldier who had him by the arm. *You shot my daddy—shot him in the face. You shot my brother. There ain't but just me now. Let me go home to my momma, please! I ain't but thirteen.*

"But they kicked the bodies out of the way, and set him up with the last two prisoners, ready to finish them all. I thought about running out of the bushes and trying to make a stand. I thought about it, but my legs wouldn't move, and my chest was tight when I tried to draw breath, and I knew that I could not save anybody. I could only add to the pile of dead bodies, so I stayed where I was.

"Davey was still crying and pleading with those men. He knew them, too, some of them. The commander was James Keith, who does some of the doctoring in the county, and with him was another man in officer's kit: Mr. Lawrence Allen, who lawyered more than he farmed. Davey called on both of them by name and asked for the help of a neighbor, but that seemed to make them angry.

"One of the soldiers threw him on the ground, and Keith gave the order for them to fire. He had to say it loud to be heard over Davey's screams. Then the guns started snapping, and the screaming stopped. One of the bullets hit Davey in the face, and he fell forward into the snow, twitching his legs a time or two, and then he lay still in the red-streaked snow, and one of the soldiers went over and kicked him in the head, but he didn't move.

"They didn't bury the dead men. Just left them where they lay, and they sent word back up the holler that the families were forbidden to take their kin for burial. They did in the end, of course, after a couple of days had passed and the soldiers were gone, but by the time they got there to take away the remains, the wild hogs had got to the bodies—tore up what was left of them. It wasn't a sight a brother or a father should have to see.

"I was scared to go home after that. I figured those soldiers might be coming back, and they knew what I looked like. So I kept on running. I made it through the gap into Tennessee, and people helped me along the way, 'til finally I caught up with Mr. McKesson Blalock here, and he brung me this far."

"I reckon you'll be safe now," said Keith. "We'll see that you get on into Union territory, and what happens after that is up to you." Then he looked over at me and said, "I'm going back, though."

I held Columbus tight to my breast and just glared back at him, not saying *You'll go alone, then,* but meaning it.

"A-lord, I wouldn't go if I was you," said the old woman. "H'it's not safe over there in Caroliny."

"Well, I'll hold off 'til spring," said Keith, talking to me, not her. "But I've got scores to settle over the mountain."

Zebulon Vance—1863–64

"Yes sir, Lawd," said my manservant William, as if he were talking to himself. "The Confederacy may be going to hell in a handbasket, but the governor of North Carolina is taking the *train!*"

He went on packing the remainder of my lunch back into the picnic basket, taking special care to cork the apple brandy, and still muttering to himself, while I looked out the train window at the unraveling autumn countryside and pretended not to hear him.

The rest of my staff had been more diplomatic in their comments about my excursion, but they were all of the same opinion as William: that I was being a reckless fool. That was probably so, but for a year I had been sitting in that Governor's Palace firing memos at bureaucrats and setting off telegraphed rockets under incompetent army officers, until by God I'd had just about all the temperate rustication that I could stand. So here I was with William and as few staff members as I could get away with, heading westward to Salisbury on the train—to where the war was.

. The year had begun tragically with last January's

Shelton Laurel shootings, but now that incident paled beside the other calamities that 1863 had brought. In the summer the Army of Northern Virginia had attempted to take the war into Union territory by invading Pennsylvania, an unqualified disaster, culminating in such a slaughter at Gettysburg that the town's very name is enough to turn your blood cold. Instead of our setting the war in the enemy's country, the enemy had instead brought the war straight back to us with a vengeance. In North Carolina the civilians were suffering not only the loss of their men, but also from shortages of every kind—food, medicine, clothing. The blockades have closed our ports, and the war has taken what supplies we had on hand, like a great fire consuming everything in its wake. I wonder if any previous governor of North Carolina has ever felt so helpless.

To complete my torment Harriett and my son David fell ill with diphtheria in September. Diphtheria! The word puts the fear of God into a parent's heart, right enough. We feared for their lives. My wife and son spent weeks in the western part of the state, recuperating from the illness, while I paced and worried. It even crossed my mind to wonder if Providence had sent me this tribulation as a reminder of Shelton Laurel, but if so He needed to be more specific, for I can think of no other action that I could have taken to help those people or to obtain justice for them after the fact, so I let it go. Mercifully my family all recovered from the illness. It must be on account of Harriett's prayers, though, for the Lord seldom hears from me.

At the same time that we were personally besieged by diphtheria, the city of Knoxville fell to Union forces under General Ambrose Burnside, and so the Confederacy had lost the most of the east Tennessee counties for good, and in doing so we had left the western part of North Carolina in peril, a circumstance that touched me both personally and as head of state, for it was my friends and my homeland that now lay in the path of the invader. Federal troops could make raids across the border with near impunity. The Cumberland Gap had also fallen into Federal hands, so that reinforcements could be brought in to strengthen their position. My older brother Robert, commander of the Confederate army's western district, now based in North Carolina, wrote to me asking if I could arrange for him to be given a command along the coast somewhere, but I think he had better stay where he is, for the war has followed him home.

The steady rocking of the passenger car that had punctuated my thoughts faltered, slowed, and finally the train shuddered to a stop. A murmur of alarm began to rise from other startled passengers.

"Uh-huh," said William with melancholy satisfaction. "You see what has come of your orneriness now, Governor. Train stopped, and I reckon them Yankees is going to come through the windows and scalp us all."

"Not this close to Greensboro, William," I muttered. "Not yet, anyhow." I stuck my head out the window of the train to determine the source of the trouble. An elderly conductor was waving passengers off the car in front of us, but he moved with genial deliberation, with no hint of urgency. When he saw me peering out the window at him, he touched his cap, and called out, "Engine on the line just up ahead, sir!"

"An engine? Is it broken down then?"

He grinned at my unintentional understatement. "Oh, it ain't going nowhere 'til they haul it off. It's mired down like a sow in quicksand. We can't go around it on this train, nossir!"

"It's all right, Governor!" said another voice behind me. "We won't be stuck here for long."

I turned away from the window to see one of my aides standing in the aisle. His muddy boots told me that he had just descended the train to ascertain the difficulty for himself. "The tracks are blocked just up ahead," he said. "An engine has ditched itself right in the cut that divided the ridge ahead, and it cannot be moved until more help arrives, but the railroad has sent another train to meet us on the other side of the obstruction. The conductors are removing everyone from this train, and sending them over the hill. I'm afraid we'll have to walk it, though."

"I don't mind," I said. "Anything is better than having to sit here in idleness waiting. Would you make sure that the luggage is transferred to the new train?"

He nodded purposefully and strode away in the direction of the baggage cars. William picked up the lunch hamper and set off after me down the aisle. Outside the rail car we joined a stream of passengers proceeding westward to the small ridge that we would have to climb to reach the new conveyance, as the pass was blocked by machinery. The recent rains had rendered the soft earth aqueous with mud, and it was hardly a pleasant country walk to our destination. Besides, I was not dressed for rough travel, being still kitted out in my "governor suit" as William called it, and a year of sedentary life in high office had rendered me stouter and less fit than I had been as an army colonel.

I advanced upon that steep and slippery bank, made more impassable by the boots of the passengers who preceded me, and I nearly fell several times as I heaved myself upward toward the summit. At last, just a few feet from the crest of the ridge, I halted on a scrap of rock unable to find secure footing to take me further. As I was debating my next course of action— and the indignity of the state's governor being hauled over the hill like a barrel of flour—a dirty and emaciated face appeared before me on the top of the rise, and lively eyes took in the particulars of my dilemma. It was a Yankee soldier, still in his ragged uniform, a prisoner that had been brought down from Salisbury

with a large lot of captives on the train that was to be
our deliverer.

He took a moment to survey the situation, and then
he lay down full length upon the top of the bank, and
stretched out his hand, saying gallantly, "Allow me, sir."
After a moment's effort he succeeded in pulling me to
the top.

Once I had regained my balance, I thanked my res-
cuer, and motioned for William to come forward. I took
the lunch basket from him and handed over its contents
and the bottle of apple brandy to the young soldier. I
judged by his voice and demeanor that he was a "Home
Yankee," and that he might have been a neighbor of
mine in happier times.

The young fellow gave a shout of joy, pocketed the
food and brandy, and said, "May I have your name, sir?"

"Why, Zebulon Vance," I said, shaking the soldier's
outstretched hand. "From Buncombe County in the
west. I wish you Godspeed, young man."

We went our separate ways then, he to the east-
bound train, and I to the one he had just come from. As
I walked down the western slope of the embankment, I
heard a lady passenger say to William, "Wasn't it kind of
Governor Vance to give that poor lad some food?"

"Well," said William, "can't nobody say the governor
ain't a kind man—not while I draw breath—but that
there transaction just now wasn't kindness a bit. It's just
that the governor won't be beholden to anybody on this
earth for five minutes, not even for a muddy handshake
at a train wreck. He pays his debts, and if he can't do it
straightaway, he'll lie awake nights 'til he can fix on a
way to make things even. The governor was born mountain, ma'am, and the flatlanders ain't never been able to
beat that out of him."

I strode on now, dignity regained, and pretended that
I had not heard the foregoing conversation. William was
right, of course. He usually was.

*   *   *

It was ironic that my only encounter with "Yankees" on
that train ride was the helping hand of a captive soldier.
That incident was a grace note in the dirge of an otherwise grim journey. The reason I was on that train in the
first place was because news had reached me that the
invasion had come at last. Dispatches from the western
counties informed us that a Union force, led by Colonel
George W. Kirk—another "Home Yankee," an east Tennessean—had crossed through the gap at Paint Rock,
and over into Madison County. There he had made his
headquarters in Warm Springs, the village of the hotel
where I had clerked not so many years ago. They were
some six hundred strong, and within striking distance of
my mother and family in Asheville and they put danger
within sixteen miles of my old friends in Marshall. The
only opposing force in the area was a cavalry unit of
240, commanded by my first mentor, John W. Woodfin
of Asheville, now a major.

Word had come that there had been a battle at Warm
Springs and that Woodfin was dead.

Well, it is one thing to worry about an army on some
distant battlefield in Virginia, led by a West Point–trained
general, but it is quite another to hear of some home-
grown thieves and murderers poised to sack your home
county. I couldn't stand it, and I couldn't bear to sit in
my leather chair in that great barn on Fayetteville
Street, waiting for the news to trickle in by contradic-
tory telegrams half a day at a time. So I came out on my
own, heedless of my advisers.

We journeyed on to Morganton without further incident, and there the railroad ends in the foothills of the
mountains, but I would not be deterred by that. When I
disembarked in Morganton, the first words on my lips
were, "What news of Madison County?"

But nobody knew. There was rumored to have been

a skirmish with several killed, but details were sketchy, and the whereabouts of Kirk's Legion unknown. "Well, I will go to Quaker Meadows for the night, then," I said. "The McDowells trusted me with a daughter, so they might give me the loan of a saddle horse for a few days. William, you can stay there and pick up some of the local gossip for Miss Harriett while I am gone."

"I can come with you, Governor," he said. "I'm not afraid—or tired."

I smiled at the old man. "Thank you, William, but you'd best stay with the McDowells. If I was to get you killed on my fool's errand, Miss Harriett's wrath would make the Yankees seem like preachers at a camp meeting. I'd sooner face them than her."

"Well, God go with you, Governor."

"Thank you, William," I said. "I'll be grateful for your prayers. Are you one of the elect?"

He smiled with the confidence of a Presbyterian with four aces. "Yes, Governor, I believe I am."

"That's good to know." I started to leave, and then another thought occurred to me. "William, do you think *I'm* one of the elect?"

William chuckled. "Why, Governor, I never even heard tell *you* was a candidate."

Early the next morning I set off with half a dozen comrades for a hard day's ride westward through Yancey County where we picked up the drovers road that ran along the French Broad River, and followed it into my old hometown of Lapland, which had grown more sophisticated and grand with time, and now was called Marshall.

As we clattered into town, a crowd of onlookers—a few old men and a gaggle of small boys—came out into the street, timidly at first, for there was a war on, and either side would bring you trouble. A moment's inspection satisfied them that the mounted strangers were not in uniform, and perhaps too prosperous-looking to be outliers, and they ventured closer. Then one wizened old fellow called out, "Why h'it's Zeb-u-lon Baird Vance thar!"

Suddenly we were engulfed by them, all talking at once, jostling each other against the horses' flanks, and reaching up to pat me on the back or shake my hand. I don't know if they thought that I constituted reinforcements or whether they were just glad that I wasn't a Union raider, but I hastily dismounted, and returned their greetings as heartily as I could, despite the gravity of my errand. When at last the hubbub subsided, I said, "I have come for news of the Yankee invasion. Where is Major Woodfin, boys?"

Now I could hear the swish of the horses' tails and the buzzing of flies in the sudden silence. The townfolk looked at one another, but no one spoke. Then another figure came hobbling toward us from out of a nearby doorway. He was a haggard young man in the tatters of a gray uniform. He had a freshly scabbed cut across his forehead, and his right arm was cradled in a sling of dirty linen.

"You're wanting to know about Warm Springs, ain't you, sir? I can tell you. I was there."

While some of the small boys led the horses away to be walked and watered, and my escorts waited nearby, the gaunt soldier and I repaired to a bench in the shade, and some of the others followed. By their uniforms I judged them to be part of Woodfin's command as well. "Where is the battle?" I said. "I have come to join in."

The weary young man must have been ten years and fifty pounds shy of me, and, while he made no answer to my declaration, his expression was eloquent. "Sir, the battle is over," he said at last. "Such as it was. The battalion is here, and Kirk's men were occupying the hotel at Warm Springs, but they are gone now. We did drive them out, but we didn't kill enough of them. Now they have gone to make mischief elsewhere."

"You won? That is comforting news, anyhow," I said. "But what of Major Woodfin. Is it true?"

"The major was killed, sir." Seeing the stricken look on my face, the soldier said, "We rode up from Marshall—there was about a hundred and forty of us, about a quarter of what Kirk had, anyhow, and that's to say nothing of the weapons and ordnance he had and we didn't. Anyhow, the Yankees had been there long enough to dig in pretty well. They had men holding the high ground, and sharpshooters covering the road, though we did manage to take out several of their pickets afore we got to the village proper. When we reached the bridge that leads to the hotel, we couldn't see our way ahead because of the screen of trees there at the entrance. So the major, he calls halt, and then he and Colonel Allen rides on ahead across the bridge with a couple of the officers. Some of Kirk's men were hiding in the spring house, and right as the major came alongside it, they opened fire at close range and just blasted him off his horse. One of the officers beside him was killed outright, and another one was hit bad, though we couldn't tell if he was dead or not, for he was slumped over his saddle and his horse kept going.

"Seeing the major shot down like that put us off stride, but we rallied quick enough, and we charged over that bridge like the devil was after us, and the Federals fell back. We got them on the run, sir, but Colonel Allen and some of his men got separated from the rest of us. They took off into the brush, and some of 'em still ain't back."

Another soldier in the crowd spoke up. "Sir, about the major—after we routed the Yankees we sent word to Asheville, and the next day some gentlemen from there went up to Warm Springs under a flag of truce to claim Major Woodfin's body."

"That's right, they did," the first soldier said. "But the truce flag wasn't needed, for the Yankees had gone by then. The delegation went up to the hotel, and Miz Carrie Rumbaugh herself let them in.

"She's a pistol, that Miz Rumbaugh," said the first soldier. "Her husband owns the hotel, you know, Governor."

I nodded. The Rumbaughs had purchased the hotel a good while after I had worked there, but they were part of local society, and I had come to know them when I canvassed the western counties for votes.

"Well, when Miz Carrie Rumbaugh heard the Yankees was coming, she tried to burn the bridge over the French Broad. A little bit of a lady like her, firing the bridge. I never heard the like."

The second soldier smiled. "And they say she put her saddle horse in the parlor to keep the Yankees from taking him. They found him anyhow. Well, they would. I mean, *a horse* . . . Even spoons ain't safe from them . . ."

"They took Miss Carrie's horse?" I hoped to hear no worse than that.

"Tried to, Governor. Tried to. They do say she flung her arms around that horse's neck and screamed and cried and carried on until they let her be."

"I'm glad to hear it," I said, but I was thinking that Mrs. Rumbaugh was a lucky young woman. She is youthful, and pretty, and a lady. If she had lacked even one of those gifts of fortune, the soldiers would have taken the horse and her as well, and burned the house over her head to boot. War teaches you all of life's lessons, only harder and faster. "But what of Major Woodfin?"

"Well, after the fighting was over, we got him into the back door of the hotel, but the poor major didn't live long. He expired right there on the floor of the hall before anybody could even tend to his wound."

A familiar voice spoke up behind me. "The delegation from Asheville has already collected Major Woodfin's remains, and they have taken him back to Asheville for burial. You aren't in time for the funeral, though, Governor."

I turned and saw the brigadier general for the western district, looking tired and grayer than I remembered. "Hello, Bob," I said to my older brother.

"Good to see you, Zeb. Wish it could be under happier circumstances."

"Why did Kirk's men occupy Warm Springs?"

"They've been recruiting men for the Union over there, and they wanted to protect that operation. I should have sent my artillery up there, I reckon, Zeb, but we didn't know how many they had, and I didn't want to risk it without more to go on. So I sent Woodfin and Lawrence Allen with the Fourteenth North Carolina up there to see what they had—"

"Wait. Did you say Lawrence Allen?"

"Yes."

"The man from the Shelton Laurel shootings?"

"The same."

"I had hoped we'd have him in a jail cell by now."

"Well, Zeb, he's a good officer, and he did have provocation at Shelton Laurel. You heard about the deaths of his children."

"His men shot thirteen people without a trial. Old men and little boys."

"Well, it's a big war. And there's a lot of guilt to parcel out. You could blame me now for John Woodfin's death."

"I'm sorry it happened," I said. "I don't feel the need to blame anybody for it, though. I'm going to ride on to Asheville and pay my condolences to Mrs. Woodfin and to Nicholas and Eliza Grace. Will you come with me?"

Bob nodded. "I think the governor should have a military escort," he said, with a trace of a smile.

*   *   *

As we rode away from Marshall, I was thinking that a chapter of my life had closed with the death of John Woodfin. He had been my first mentor, and an able and learned gentleman. It seemed a waste to consign such men as him to cannon fodder. My presence would not have saved him—I was not vainglorious enough to think I could turn the tide of a battle or that I would have been a better general than my brother—but my sortie from the Governor's Mansion had not relieved me of the sense of futility I felt. I had thought myself powerless because I sat in an office, walled away from the war, but here within striking distance of the invaders, I was reminded that everyone is powerless in war, for chance holds all the cards.

Those of the Asheville citizenry who were not otherwise occupied with the war had gathered to meet me and to pay their respects to the Woodfins. Merrimon was among them, of course, and toward evening we had a few moments to speak privately.

"It's a bad business, Governor," said Merrimon.

He never called me "Zeb" or even "Vance" anymore, despite our ten years' association. I could not decide if he really respected the office that much or if he was just bucked up about being so close to power himself.

"A bad business, indeed," I said. "I don't suppose anyone thought that Woodfin stood in much danger, serving as close to home as he was. I confess that it never occurred to me to worry about him."

"The mountains have become a treacherous place," said Merrimon. "We thought that we were in a remote and inaccessible place, and that—like Switzerland—we would be more trouble to conquer than anybody was willing to take. But the war has found us after all. The tragedy at Shelton Laurel was a warning to us, I fear."

"I wish we could have done something more about

that, Merrimon. I don't know what Keith thought he could accomplish by killing those men. He certainly didn't stop the outliers, if my many correspondents in these mountains are to be believed."

"No, Governor. The situation is as bad as ever, but what really concerns me is justice. The war is allowing killers to commit crimes with impunity, and I will not stand for it. God did not stand for it. Did He not punish David for the death of Uriah?"

"Well, I wish He would punish James Keith, then, because we're not going to get a chance to. The secretary of war is as slippery as a grass snake, but I finally got him to admit that Keith had been allowed to resign, and now he's gone—out west, I expect. That's where people go to get away from this war—hell or Texas."

"I know," said Merrimon. "And I hope he chose the former."

"So do I. At least we can console ourselves with the knowledge that Lawrence Allen did not escape completely. We caught him in a conscription scheme—he threatened to draft men, and accepted a bribe to choose a substitute instead. He had made a fortune trafficking in such scrounging. Tens of thousands of dollars, Merrimon! I wasn't going to let him get away a second time. I wrote to Seddon and demanded a trial."

"I know," said Merrimon. "I believe they docked him half a year's pay, which apparently he can well afford."

"And yet he still has his command," I said. "He was with Woodfin at Warm Springs, you know."

Merrimon nodded. "They tell me that Colonel Allen is an asset to the army. Anyhow he is still engaged in chasing the outliers and trying to stop the robbing of honest citizens by these marauders. I suppose he is doing good work, Governor."

I grunted. "Even the devil works hard, Merrimon. Has Allen taken any prisoners lately?"

Merrimon nodded. "He has. But these days he sends

them all to us in Asheville. He may not be repentant, but at least he has become careful."

A few days later I went back to Raleigh, and continued to fight my own little wars on behalf of the civilians of my state, who were heartily sick of both armies, and for the most part simply wished they would all go away, regardless of the outcome of the conflict. That weasel Seddon, the secretary of war, heard from me as often as my mother did, I think, for there was always a new outrage to apprise him of. As my frustration grew in response to his soothing replies and his complete inaction on all my complaints, I began to wax rhetorical in my correspondence to him, knowing that the catharsis of composition would be my only reward for contacting him.

On December 21, I was in my usual state of frustration, berating Seddon with all my powers of rhetoric. "Read that back to me, Richard," I said as I paced. "Will it answer, do you suppose?"

Battle looked over his scribbled notes. "Well, the first part is temperate enough," he said doubtfully. He held up the pad and began to read: *"Dear Sir: I desire to call your attention to an evil which is inflicting great distress upon the people of the State and contributing largely to the public discontent. I allude to illegal seizures and other depredations of an outrageous character by detached bands of Troops—chiefly Cavalry ... It is enough in many cases to breed a rebellion in a loyal county against the Confederacy ..."*

"Well, that's nothing but the honest truth," I said, pausing before the fire to warm my hands. "I call that restraint, in fact."

"Ye-es," said Battle. "It is mild enough. Here's the part you may wish to water down a bit. This is after you've said that you don't want to give him specific instances or demands for punishment, but that you are just making a general complaint about the practice and hoping for some strongly-enforced regulation to keep the soldiers in check."

"Worded in civil terms?"

"Yes, Governor. But *then* you say: *I give you my word that in North Carolina it has become a grievance, intolerable, damnable, not to be borne! If God Almighty had yet in store another plague—worse than all others, which he intended to have let loose on the Egyptians in case Pharaoh still hardened his heart, I am sure it must have been a regiment or so of half-armed, half-disciplined Confederate Cavalry!*" He looked up at me, and shook his head sadly, before continuing. *"Had they been turned loose among Pharaoh's subjects, with or without an impressment law, he would have become so sensible of the anger of God that he never would have followed the Children of Israel to the Red Sea, No Sir not an inch!! Cannot officers be reduced to ranks for permitting this? Cannot a few men be shot for perpetrating these outrages . . ."*

"Well, at least I don't bore Mr. Seddon with my correspondence," I said.

"I wouldn't say there was much chance of that, Governor. Should we wish him a Merry Christmas, do you think?"

"No, Richard, let us not increase the magnitude of falsehood at this stage. Close with the usual mendacity."

Battle nodded and wrote: *"Very respectfully yours . . ."*

Tom Gentry

Tom Gentry was no longer hungry. After days of stomach pangs and thoughts obsessed with food and memories of food, his nights beset with dreams of eating sumptuous meals, the cravings fell away, and he felt like a purer, more spiritual being than he had been before. He had shed the gross animal cravings for sustenance, and now he could set his sights on more ethereal matters.

He had never been very comfortable in his body anyhow. He was awkward, sometimes clumsy, never an athlete. His mind, however, was first-rate. He had been an honor student in high school, and he showed a natural aptitude for mathematics that had impressed his teachers. This odd disconnect between mental prowess and physical ineptitude had always burdened him, and now he saw this present course as the perfect solution to that problem. Discard the body altogether.

If only he could live like this.

But of course he couldn't. A month at most was all he had before the disintegration process finally ended his existence. He had read the scientific information, trying to keep his manner detached, as if he were studying a phenomenon that would happen to someone else. When long deprived of sustenance, the body begins to digest itself. Organs break down, muscle tissue deteriorates, one by one bodily functions fail . . . At some point—he wasn't sure when—perhaps it varied with each individual—the process would become irreversible. Well, that was all right. The medical sources he had consulted had said that the death was relatively painless, and he didn't want to go back anyhow.

He felt a great joy, a sense of becoming one with the forest and the sky. Sometimes he thought he could float upward past the oaks and poplars and look out over the valley as the hawks did.

He recorded all these feelings in his journal, writing pages of speculation on the meaning of life, and he recorded each symptom of his condition. As his concentration began to waver, he began to intersperse these essays with little lists. What was the last nonfood item he had purchased? He could no longer remember, but he thought it might have been the map of the National Forest. What were his favorite songs? Five places he wished he had visited?

On the fourth day he had moved his tent out of the forest clearing and into a large thicket of rhododendron. The sun had been oppressively hot around midday, and he thought the concealment might help.

He would sit out a few feet from the thicket and write in his journal, watching for animals and observing the changing face of the woodland.

It was late evening of an otherwise uneventful day when he saw them. People moving through the trees on the other side of the clearing. At first he thought they were hikers, and then one of them stopped and turned in his direction, and Tom saw that the man was wearing some kind of military outfit. Civil War reenactors!

He closed his journal and scooted back into the

safety of the thicket. He didn't think they had noticed him, and in another moment they were gone, but the encounter had still annoyed him. Really, there was no such thing as wilderness anymore. People—everywhere you went.

Malinda

I've never prayed so hard before or since for spring—
only in April of 1863 I was praying for it *not* to come, because Keith had said that once the weather got warm
again we'd be heading back across the mountain to
Watauga County. He was itching to go back, but even he
had to admit that it would be foolish to venture into
dangerous country with no leaf cover to hide us, no
crops to feed outliers, and the weather so cold that we'd
need a fire to keep us alive, even if the wood smoke led
the militia right to our hiding place. Keith was brave, but
he wasn't a damned fool about it.

I wasn't scared, either, but I was in no hurry to go
back. Every day that it stayed cold and bleak was another day that I got to spend being a mother to Columbus, but I knew there was no use wishing that I didn't
have to give him up, because I already lost one baby,
and I wasn't about to risk this one to the cold and danger of living rough. Every day we stayed made Columbus stronger and bigger, and I was letting my cousin
help me take care of him, so by the time we had to

leave, I figured he'd be all right even without his real momma.

All through a cold, wet spring Keith kept on doing his piloting through the mountains, getting escaped prisoners and Carolina Tories out of Confederate territory and over into Tennessee where they could join up with Union troops. There was another mountain loyalist name of Daniel Ellis who did his own piloting to the Federal lines, and sometimes he and Keith joined up. Dan Ellis is a good scout, but he's too prideful about it to suit us. You'd think he was fighting this war single-handed.

The Michigan cavalry paid Keith and gave him what supplies he asked for, and they furnished him with enlistment papers so he could sign up anybody that wanted to join the Federals—sometimes he even wore their uniform, so if he'd a been caught on one of his runs, the Rebels would'a shot him then and there, and we both knew it, but we never said nothing about it. Talking about it wouldn't change the facts.

Finally, getting on toward May, when the leaves had come out on the oaks and the maples, and the redbud and lilacs were blooming in the yard of the Pritchard cabin, Keith came riding up one morning. I was out in the grass on a quilt, trying to get baby Columbus to sit up on his own when I saw a bay horse coming up the lane, and there was Keith, wearing a big old cavalry hat and tall boots, and a kind of faded blue army tunic so streaked and dirty that it looked like the floor of a cow byre. He looked thin and shaggy-haired, but he was smiling, and he didn't look as weary as he had last time he came by. What I noticed most, though, was the Spencer rifle he had slung in a long leather holster on the side of the saddle, and a Navy Colt on his hip. He had a little chestnut gelding on a lead rein, and he waved to me, but he didn't smile. I grabbed up the baby and hugged him close to

my breast, because I knew that this was the day we
would be heading back to Carolina. Wasn't no use to
argue, but I tried anyhow.

"The leaves ain't hardly thick yet," I said. "And it's
still cold enough of a night for a fire."

He shook his head. "It's time. We got scores to settle.
Get the baby seen to, and fetch us something to eat. I'll
be out here."

I went back in the cabin and gave Columbus to my
cousin. He was so used to being passed from hand to
hand that only one of us was crying. I took some of the
corn pone in a poke to take with us. I didn't waste time
on long good-byes, because there wasn't any point in
dragging things out. I had to go, and I reckoned it was
like pulling a splinter—best do it in one good yank than
to draw it out and suffer longer. When we rode away, I
didn't look back, but I had a lock of the baby's hair
tucked in a cloth pouch in my pocket. He wouldn't remember me when I saw him again.

Going back into North Carolina sure felt different from
the way we left. Last year we had been run out of there,
footsore and shot up, creeping through the woods like a
couple of wild animals, but on that spring morning in
'63, we returned like avenging angels, ready to get our
own back. We were mounted on fine Union cavalry
horses, toting Spencer repeating rifles, and kitted out
with gear give us by the Tenth Michigan Cavalry. We
weren't going back alone, neither. Keith had rounded
up some of the other outliers from the western counties—Harrison Church, Jim Harley, and Jim Voncannon—all seasoned fighters who knew the land as good
as we did. We rode along in the sunshine, single file
along the trace that led east through the gap into Carolina, with me trying to catch up to Keith to talk to him,
and the rest of them waving their new weapons around,

just hoping for an ambush, but not even a rabbit crossed our path that morning.

Keith said we were under the command of Colonel George Kirk, who was an east Tennessean his own self, and his job was to recruit for the Federals and bring hell to the mountains of North Carolina, so those secesh politicians would think twice about bothering honest folk. Our orders were general enough: Pilot deserters and escaped prisoners through to the Union lines, and bring down misery on the Rebel citizens.

"We can't go home, can we?" I said to Keith.

He didn't take his eyes off the track ahead. "We are going home, missy."

"I mean back to the cabin."

"Well, no, 'Linda. I figure on getting killed, but I can't see making it all that easy for 'em." He saw me cloud up then, because I had been missing home all this time, and he said, "Well, maybe we'll slip back there every now and again, when things quieten down. And we can stop with Daddy Austin once in a while. But most of the time we'll be up the Grandfather in the caves or sleeping rough. If that don't suit you, Malinda, Tennessee is back that away." He pointed back the way we came.

"It suits me," I said in a little voice. Then I pulled up on the reins and let Church and Voncannon ride on ahead of me. I didn't feel like talking anymore.

We spent a couple of days fixing up bolt holes in case the militia got wind of us, but Keith was too restless to stay out of trouble for long. We stashed some food and ammunition in a cave up on the mountain, buried some more of it elsewhere, and took the lay of the land, asking folks we trusted who was on our side and who wasn't. For Keith the war was personal. If you weren't for the Union, then you were his enemy, even if you were neighbor or kin. That was it.

One night when we judged it was safe, Keith and I hobbled the horses in the woods, and crept up to Daddy Austin Coffey's cabin to let him know we were back. When Keith knocked, he yanked open the door, and I found myself staring down the barrel of his musket, but as soon as he seen it was us, he drew us inside, and grinned at me and pumped Keith's hand, while the dogs jumped up on us, trying to lick our faces and barking in the excitement. Then he sat us down and dished up stew and greens, asking questions nineteen to the dozen, about the baby, the war, and everything else that crossed his mind.

Keith showed him the Navy Colt and told him about all the supplies Kirk give us.

"But how are things faring here?" asked Keith, sopping up the stew gravy with a piece of corn pone.

"Oh, gone to blazes, just as I feared," said Daddy Austin. "My brothers are hell-bent for the Confederacy, so bad we can't hardly be in the same room anymore for arguing. And prices are going through the roof—if you can get the supplies in the first place. You know about the salt? Yes, I figured you would. Everybody knows about that. Still, I believe I could endure the privation, if it weren't for neighbors being at one another's throats over this. Puts you in mind of old tales about Indian raids."

"Well, the war can't last forever," said Keith. "I can tell you for a fact that the Federals have got better gear and more men. I seen it. It's just a matter of time."

"Well, I hope we live long enough to see it," said Daddy Austin.

I thought, *Well, he'll outlive the war anyhow, tucked up here safe in his cabin. He's not even fifty yet. It's Keith and me that's got to worry about getting our heads blown off by the Rebel soldiers and their murdering militia.*

*   *   *

The war went on, mostly elsewhere, and one morning in high summer Keith arrived back at the camp, swaggering like he had just won Kentucky in a poker game. I was sitting out at the mouth of the cave stripping leaves off field greens, so I could make our dinner meat stretch further. You'd think the men had hollow legs the way they could put food away.

Harrison Church, who was skinning a rabbit, glanced up and noticed Keith looking pleased with himself same as I did. "Who died and made you a general?" he said.

"Even better," said Keith. "I have it on information received—" He winked at that. "Information received—that Mr. High and Mighty Robert Green is going to be heading for his house in Blowing Rock this evening. I was thinking we might meet up with him along the way and ... pay our respects ... all of us." He looked around, catching the eye of every one of the men, and then he pulled out his Navy Colt and sighted down the barrel, in case anybody had missed the meaning of his words.

Church stood up, wiped the skinning knife across his pants leg, and stuck it back in his belt. "How many guards you reckon he'll have with him?"

Keith shrugged. "Don't matter," he said. "Get the horses."

The horses had been hobbled in an open grass patch in the piney woods, and the men fetched them, and saddled up, while I wrapped the greens and the rabbit carcass in wet cloths, in case we made it back for supper. While none of them was looking I tied up a lock of my hair with red thread, for luck, putting it where it wouldn't show, so's they wouldn't tease me over it. Then we set off.

The road that led into Watauga County wasn't near as busy as it used to be. There weren't any more cattle herds to be moved down to Morganton. They had either been eat or stolen. Some people would still ride out to visit kinfolks or go to town for supplies, but it took a brave soul to do it nowadays, for horses were scarce and precious, and there were people who'd kill you soon as look at you, just to get a fresh mount. I was a little jumpy myself about riding out, not because I thought there'd be anybody with enough sand to try and rob us, but because we were going looking for trouble, and I was mighty afraid that we were going to find it.

We found a bend on the steep part of the road with some bushes and an outcrop of rock on the slope above the track. We tied the horses farther into the woods uphill, knowing that we could hear anybody coming up the road in time to fetch the mounts out for an ambush. It was cool up there under the trees on the mountain, but the flies were troublesome now and again, and we had to be quiet to make sure we could hear the sounds from the road. I had sat down with my back against a tree and was sliding headlong into sleep when Keith touched my shoulder, and I opened my eyes to see the others looking suddenly alert, straining to listen for the faint sounds of hoofbeats coming up the road. Harrison Church slipped back into the trees to get the horses, while the others checked their weapons and moved behind trees closer to the road.

"Let's see how many he has with him," said Keith. "If it's more than five, we all rush them. If it's just one or two, I'll go out alone and you all cover me."

We knew better than to argue with him, and anyhow there was no time, for the hoofbeats were louder now, and in a minute or so the horse would come around the bend. I touched the red string in my hair for luck.

Keith swung up into the saddle with his weapon at the ready, and as soon as that horse's head came in sight he headed down the slope and out onto the pike, blocking the way.

We could see now that the horse was pulling a buckboard, and it was Robert Green a-driving it all right, but there wasn't a soul with him. His hat was pulled down low on his forehead, and he was staring down at the horse's head, looking as if his thoughts were ten miles away, and then an instant later he glanced up and there was Keith Blalock staring him down with a grin on his face and a rifle barrel pointed straight at his chest.

The man had come out all by himself on a lonely mountain road in the middle of a damn war. Was he cocky or just a complete fool, I wondered. Maybe he thought he was so rich and important that everybody would leave him alone. Well, he was wrong about that. Seeing as he was alone, we stayed where we were, and didn't even mount up. Keith could handle this, and all we had to do was watch.

Robert Green's thoughts passed across his face like clouds on a mountain. The first one was should he go for his gun, but he knew straight off that drawing would get him shot. Then he glanced around, trying to figure if the road was wide enough for him to turn the wagon, but the ridge side is too steep and the other side is a drop off a couple hundred feet to the valley floor, and nobody would want to chance that. So that left him with his third option, which was to try to bluster his way past us.

"I know you, McKesson Blalock!" he roared out. "You're an outlier and a traitor, and if you raise your hand against me, they'll hang you higher than Haman."

"Well, they've not caught me yet," said Keith, chipper as ever. He nodded toward the woods, and we took a step or two forward so that Green could see Keith wasn't alone. That set him back some. His eyes got big, and he kept taking big breaths like a fish does when you lay him on the bank.

"Get down out the wagon," said Keith, pointing with the rifle barrel.

"You got no quarrel with me," said Green. "I'm not the militia. You want a fight with the Major, why—"

"You shot me. In the raid on the Grandfather. You're the one shot me."

"Blalock, I swear . . ."

"Down. Out the wagon," said Keith. "Ain't gonna tell you again."

Green just sat there for a minute, trying to think what to do, I reckon, so Keith turned to look over at us and kind of jerked his head. We stepped forward out of the brush with our weapons pointed, and that decided him. The next instant he was clambering down out of the wagon, and trying to scramble down the slope, maybe looking to hide in the rocks and bushes down below, but he never made it.

Just as he was about to go over the bank Keith swung his gun around and fired, and Robert Green pitched over, squealing like a stuck pig. There was a hole in his thigh and blood was dripping out, but it wasn't spurting like a spring, so we figured he wasn't hurt all that bad. Robert Green kept hollering, scrabbling in the dirt, and trying to grab at his leg and scoot down the bank at the same time, but before he could go any farther, Keith dismounted, went over and planted his boot right on the man's shot-up leg.

He leaned down and inspected the wound, and then he nodded as if it satisfied him. "That'll do," he said. "I reckon we're quits."

Robert Green was still bawling and rolling in the weeds, and Keith walked back to us, and said, "I'm done here. Let's ride."

"You gonna leave him like that?" I said.

Keith shrugged. "He ain't worth killing, 'Linda."

"Then you better make sure he don't die," I said. "Else he's right and they will hang you for it if they catches you."

"They have to catch me first." He stuck out his lip, the

way he did when I argued with him, but I wasn't backing down on this one.

"He ain't worth killing. You said it yourself."

"All right, Colonel," said Keith giving me a sloppy salute and a lopsided grin. "We'll do it your way."

He handed me the rifle, and walked back across the road. We all stood there and watched while he bent over and hauled Robert Green to his feet. "On your way, old man," he said. "We're done here."

He half dragged and half carried Green back to his buckboard and set him back up on the seat. Keith was wonderful strong. When he was sure Green wasn't going to faint and fall out in the road, Keith slapped the horse on the rump and set it trotting off down the road in the direction of Blowing Rock. "Looks like the beast knows the way," Keith said to us as the wagon clattered on down the road. "I guess we ought to make ourselves scarce now."

We turned the horses back toward the Grandfather and cantered away before Green's buckboard was even out of sight. We had to get out of there before anybody came looking for us, because we knew that once Robert Green got to town, after he had done hollering and carrying on, and once he got his leg fixed up, he'd set the law on us for sure.

They never caught up with us, though.

The cabin was a sorry little place on that winter twilight. Only a little light flickered in the small window. Around the yard, the dry grass went unmown, the rail fence needed mending, the stock shed stood open and empty, and there were no geese or chickens to be seen. No man has been around the place for months, I was thinking. The winter of '64 was hard on everybody, but poor people felt it most. Salt was scarce, and without it there'd be no meat or butter to see them through the cold months. Nothing moved as we rode up to the porch that night.

"Let's move on, Keith," I said. "These folks ain't got nothing to give us."

"Well, whatever they've got, we're taking," said Keith. "They're Rebels." He dismounted and tossed the lead rein to me. "You stay with the horses. Come on, Jim."

Keith pounded on the door and then we waited. After a few moments a scrawny little woman came to the door with a yellow-haired girl cradled in the crook of her arm. The child was about three, I judged. Older than my Columbus, who had just turned one, but it made me think of him, and I wished we could move on and let her be, but we were having a hard winter, too.

She was giving the men a stone-faced stare. "We can't spare nothing," she said. "My man's away in the army."

"Which army?" said Keith.

"I don't reckon it matters," she said.

She tried to close the door, but Keith put his boot in it, and yanked her out on the porch. The young'un was crying now, and the woman pressed its face against her bosom, but she stood her ground. "There ain't nothing to take," she said.

"We'll see about that. Hold her, Jim." Keith shoved the woman over to Jim, who grabbed her by the arms, and held her while Keith barged into the cabin. An instant later we could hear thumping sounds as he turned over the table and went to smashing what he didn't want. Suddenly the woman looked over at me, and I wanted to kick my horse and ride out of there and not look back, but I couldn't. I was a soldier now, and my orders were to tend the horses. But I wished she'd quit staring at me, as if to say, *You're a woman, too. Can't you stop them?*

No, I couldn't. We were cold and hungry, living on game and winter apples, bone weary of sleeping rough up in the woods, and fed to the teeth with hearing about our loyalist neighbors being burned out and stole from and shot down. Anyhow this woman had her babies with her, didn't she? And my boy was over in Tennessee and wouldn't even know my face when I saw him next. So I met her stare for an instant to let her know I understood and then I turned away.

"Take the blankets, too!" Keith was saying. "It stays cold out on the mountain."

We robbed a lot of lone, lorn women on barren farms that winter, and I got used to it after a while. They all said the same thing—that there wasn't nothing left to take—and mostly it was true. Some of them cried, but mostly they just stared at us too weak or weary to put up a fight, even for their last handful of cornmeal.

One time though one of them cursed us and tried to spit on Keith. Then she caught sight of me, and said, "You ought to be ashamed helping these men steal from other women!"

I didn't answer her back, but I thought I'd have been more ashamed to be poor and helpless in a cabin somewhere than out riding with the outliers. My baby was fed and tended and my man never left me, which is more than those weak sisters could say, and if I had to sleep rough and take to stealing to pay for that, then so be it. War ain't cheap, even if you're winning.

I reckon the tables turned for good in '64. By then the war had become too much for everyone to bear. Around the campfire the menfolk talked about far-off battles and who won and who lost, and what that would mean in the next set-to, but I was never much interested in the big war. They made it sound like a horse race or a wrestling match. Who was stronger, who was ahead, who was going to win. But I didn't think anybody was going to win—not really.

Being a woman, I thought of the war as a big old quilt, patterned with a stitch for every man killed, for every one wounded, for every farm burned, every child orphaned. And I thought that if you stood back far enough and looked at the pattern, it might be crows and crosses against a background of red. A quilt so big it would cover all American territory, Rebel or Union. A quilt made of shrouds, stitched with a bone needle and dyed in blood . . . I just wished they'd hurry up and finish it, that's all.

In the early days of the war, the Unionists in the mountains had been kicked around by the Rebels and the rich folks, but by '64 after Kirk and Stoneman got to raiding the mountains with more men and more supplies than the Confederates, it was the Rebels who began to suffer. Then our jobs got easier. Nowadays men were getting tired of the war and changing to the Federal side or else deserting altogether. Those that did stick it out with the Rebels left wives and farmsteads unattended, which was a windfall for us, because being on the run, we had to keep robbing folks to get enough provisions to stay alive. We deviled them as much as we could, and I stopped being sorry about it, for I knew they did the same thing to their Tory neighbors. Them that always treated us like dirt, they had it coming.

We started wearing the blue coats of the Federals so people would know which army we sided with, because the Confederacy had been making more than its share of enemies in the mountains. The conscription laws and the salt hoarding had been bad enough early on in the war, but when the army started swooping down on farms and requisitioning food and horses and paying for them with a pittance of Confederate money—whether folks wanted to sell or not—then people got mad enough to spit.

I think most people just wished both sides would just get shut of the mountains and leave them be. They had stopped caring who won, because anybody winning was better than having the war go on any longer.

Keith wasn't ready for the war to end, though. He still had his scores to settle. I think he was afraid that he was going to run out of war before he ran out of enemies. As the year wore on, our raids became bolder, and we even rode out in daylight now and again, for though there was less to take, it was easier than ever to get it. Word had got around about us, and people were afraid, but there wasn't nothing they could do. We had permission—hell, we had *orders*—from a proper Union general to take food and horses from Rebel citizens in the mountain counties, and they needn't bother to complain to the sheriff about it, because generals outrank sheriffs. Of course, the Confederate troops were snatching horses and provisions just as fast as we were, and paying for them in Confederate money—if you could call that paying—so we never felt too bad about taking folks' property. They were going to lose it anyhow; might as well give it to us.

"Saddle up, 'Linda," Keith said to me one cold blue morning. "It's time to visit kinfolks."

"Mine or yourn?" I said, wondering if we were going to go to the Tennessee side of the mountain and see Columbus, who was walking by now.

"Coffeys," said Keith, and that told me which of the Coffey brothers he meant, because he didn't say they were his kin, and if he didn't want to claim them, they'd be the Confederate Coffeys.

I wondered what this was about. The other night Keith had gone over to Daddy Austin's place to see his mother, and he took the two new Tennesseans with him—Blackwell and Perkins. I wondered what had been said down there that set him off.

Without another word, I strapped on my gun belt and put a knife in my boot. "I'm ready," I said. "Are we going alone?"

"No." He motioned to the men who were sitting around the campfire, looking alert as hounds waiting for the signal. "Reckon we'll all go."

We must have made a fearsome procession, heading down the trail through deep snow toward Coffeys Gap, in our blue uniforms. I had me a pale-blue overcoat and a yellow flannel cape, like the ones General Stoneman's soldiers wore, and it kept me almost warm against the winds coming off the ridge. I was riding between my cousin Adolphus, who just turned eighteen, and one of the new men from Tennessee, George Perkins. Neither one of them talked much, and I was known as Sam among the outliers, so I kept to myself. Adolphus knew me, but he never let on, and I reckon most of the rest had ridden with us long enough to know better, but they never said. Still, I didn't make too free with the men, but kept in Keith's sight as much as I could. One time when we were shucking some corn we'd stole for dinner, one of the men held his up and said, *"Look, I got me a red ear, 'stead of a white or yaller one . . . That means I get to kiss a girl,"* and Keith said to him, real quiet, *"I don't see no girls around here, do you?"* Nobody said a word.

I was thinking a lot about the way men and women look at war. To the regular army Federals, like the Michigan cavalry folks, it seemed like the war was like a shooting match or a horse race. They did what was called for, but they weren't mad about it, and they didn't hate the people they had to rob or shoot. It was just business among strangers. Now a woman won't ever see

an enemy like that. To her it's always personal and hard
to forgive. It's funny that Keith saw the war more that-
a-way than he did like the regular army soldiers. Maybe
it's because we never left home to do our fighting, so we
weren't making war on strangers. It was personal, all
right. They knew it and we knew it.

All the Coffeys live around Coffeys Gap, east of the
Grandfather, over on Anthony Creek, so we had gone a
good ways before I was able to figure out which one of
'em it was we was calling on. Turned out to be Reuben.
At a bend in the road, Keith turned his horse and
started at a gallop up the trace to Reuben Coffey's
cabin, coattails flying in the wind, while the rest of us
kicked our mounts and tried to keep up.

By the time I pulled up in the yard of the cabin, Keith
was already pounding on the door. He had the Sharp's
rifle in the crook of his arm. Reuben's wife Polly opened
the door and stood there, staring Keith down as if she
had a regiment behind her. She must have known what
we'd come for, because Reuben is secesh, like his
brother William, and there had been bad blood between
nephew and uncles for years now, but she stood her
ground. She didn't look scared like those rabbitty
women we usually saw huddled on their porches too
scared of us to speak.

Miss Polly has known Keith all his life, and even
though she knew he was a soldier and an enemy, I
reckon it's hard to be fearful of somebody you knew
when he was a little boy chasing chickens across your
yard. She looked at him and then past him to the crowd
of riders waiting in her yard.

"Your uncle ain't here, McKesson," she said, loud
enough for all of us to hear.

"He and our Millie have gone off somewhere. I didn't
ask the particulars." Their breath was making clouds
there on the porch, and Miss Polly shivered and took a
step back toward the door.

"Now, Aunt Polly," said Keith, sounding as friendly as a drummer, "I don't doubt your word, but I reckon we'll have to prove the truth of it to these boys who came with me." He nodded to a couple of the men, and they ran up to the porch and shouldered past Miss Polly to search the house.

I was holding the horses, and Miss Polly took a step toward the edge of the porch and looked down at me with frost in her eye. "Morning, Malinda," she said to me. "How is that baby of yourn?"

"I reckon he's well," I said. She knew I hadn't seen much of him, but she didn't say anything else. She didn't have to. I knew what she thought.

The men came back outside. "He ain't here," Keith announced. "And we didn't tear the place up, Aunt Polly. On account of you being kin."

If he was waiting for her to thank him, he had a long wait coming, for she gave him a look that would have curdled milk and went back inside without another word. I thought there wouldn't be no use coming back here, for Reuben Coffey was warned now, and he would make himself scarce from here on out.

"Well, that was a dandy ride," I said, easing my horse up alongside Keith's. "I'm hungry. What say we—"

"We ain't done yet," said Keith. "Ride on!"

He was headed for the next brother's house—that was William Coffey, who had rode with the militia and deviled us when he could. I was thinking that someday Keith would push his luck too far. Miss Annie, William Coffey's wife, was old and scrawny, but she was kin to Daniel Boone, and I thought she just might have a gun behind the door, waiting for trouble to come up the pike.

We never got to find out, though. Before we got to their place, one of the men spied a skinny old man in a black coat running across the snow-covered cornfield, heading for the woods. Somebody let out a war whoop and they all galloped after him like dogs after a coon. I was sorry for him, he looked so little and helpless, carrying a bundle of clothes and a hunk of cornbread instead of a gun.

They surrounded him. I hung back, but I was close enough to hear Keith say, "You're coming with us, William Coffey."

He looked up at the circle of faces and tears wet his cheeks, but he saw it wasn't no use to argue with so many of them, so he just nodded and suffered himself to be led away by Joe, who had dismounted and was prodding William along with a pistol to his back.

We went about half a mile in a slow procession following the creek to Gragg's Mill, which we thought would be empty that morning. We didn't meet a soul on the way, but Keith kept looking around as if he expected a regiment to bust out of the woods and open fire. It stayed quiet, though. I didn't even hear a birdsong, only the crunch of the horses' hoofs on hard-packed snow.

When we got to the mill, there was James Gragg coming out the door. He froze in his tracks and looked from us to William Coffey and back again. "I was just going off home," he said quietly.

"I need you to get back inside for a while, Mr. Gragg," said Keith. "We don't aim to hurt you or bother your mill."

Gragg nodded and held the door open so that Joe could herd William Coffey inside. Keith got down and tied his horse to a tree. Then he turned to the rest of the men. "George Perkins and William Blackwell," he said, "you stay with me. The rest of you, go on back to camp."

He didn't have to tell them twice. Perkins and Blackwell went inside. Joe Franklin came out and mounted up, looking glad to be out of there. Then they all wheeled and cantered off back toward the Grandfather, but I didn't go with them. I just sat there, staring him down.

"What are you aiming to do?" I said.

"What has to be done," Keith said, looking away. He had pulled the Navy Colt out of his holster, and was running his thumb along the wood.

"He's your uncle."

"He's the brother of my mama's husband," said Keith. "And he's a damned Rebel. This is war."

"No," I said. I got down off the horse and went over to him so I could speak softer. "No, it ain't. War is officers telling people to take a hill or a town. It's shooting at uniforms. At a faceless line of enemy soldiers. This is a killing. Keith, you know the Michigan cavalry, what gave you that gun? Well, when the war is over . . . when some general somewhere signs a treaty that says we can all quit fighting . . . those Michigan boys will go home. They'll go far away, back to their wives and their farms, to a place where nobody was agin 'em in this war, where nobody's mad at 'em for what they did. They will go home and leave the war behind. But you will still be here—right where you fought, and the enemy will be your neighbor. And now you are wanting to kill your own daddy's brother. Keith, this ain't war. *War is better than this.*"

He didn't say anything for a long time, and I could hear the old man whimpering inside the mill. "I'm coming in with you, then," I said.

I pushed open the door and went into the mill. In the dim light I could see William Coffey straddling a wooden bench, tears streaming down his face, while George Perkins stood over him, holding a pistol to the side of his head. Gragg the miller was standing a little ways off with his fist in his mouth, as if he was afraid he might cry out if he let go.

Keith came in behind me and touched my shoulder. "I reckon you're partly right anyhow," he said. "I can't have kinfolk's blood on my hands. It ain't right. I'll take you back to camp. Go on outside."

I stepped back out into the sunshine, thinking that it was a good thing I had come along to talk some sense into Keith, and watching three crows circle down over the stubble of corn in the fields by the river, when I heard the crack of the pistol. A minute later Keith came out again, smiling. "I got George to do it," he said. "The Coffeys ain't kin to George."

Governor Zebulon Vance—1864

I wish the war wouldn't turn personal. It is just about all I can do to worry about the welfare of North Carolina's citizens in general and her soldiers in particular, but when Fate deals me a blow to the heart on top of everything else, it is almost more than I can bear.

January 1864 . . . A gray rain-streaked day in Raleigh, and I thought that things had got as bad as they were going to, excepting further invasion and ultimate defeat. Spring comes sooner in Raleigh than it did back in the high country around Asheville, but it was still a long way off, and I was feeling the discontent of winter in my bones. I managed to get through a tedious afternoon of correspondence and paperwork before the early darkness brought on evening, and I prepared to leave my office and walk back to the residence for dinner with the family.

Richard Battle came into the office then, just as I was struggling into my overcoat, and I said, "Won't you come and eat with us tonight, Richard? It's just the family." Then I saw the stricken look on his face, and to forestall whatever-it-was, I said, "It won't be that bad,

Richard. I believe there may at least be a few potatoes and a scrawny rooster to grace the table."

He did not smile at my feeble jest, and I saw that his look was more of sympathy than shock. "There's an officer to see you, sir," he said quietly. "Headquarters here has had a dispatch from—from Tennessee."

"I see," I said. "You'd better send him in." I sank back down in my chair, quite forgetting to remove my coat, and waited for the bearer of bad tidings.

He was through the door an instant later, a short, corpulent fellow whose grave expression seemed out of keeping with his appearance. I saw that he was a captain, and I thought, *This is bad. Routinely grim news is brought over by a sergeant or even a corporal.* "Well, soldier," I said, as he stood there searching for words. "You'd better get on with it."

"It's General Vance, Governor. Your brother."

I forced myself to stay seated and to keep the emotion out of my voice. "Yes, Captain? General Robert B. Vance—is he—is he killed?"

"Sir, no, sir! Captured, Governor."

I could tell that despite the fellow's horror at the bad tidings, this ruddy fellow was enjoying his part in this drama, and I had not the heart to scold him for this touch of nature. He stumbled on into his tale. "We had a telegram just now from Colonel John B. Palmer." He handed it to me, which he could have done in the first place, and he stood there while I read it, perhaps waiting for some Homeric reaction with which to cap his tale of bringing bad news to the governor. I was sorry to disappoint him, but nonetheless I murmured a few words of thanks for his trouble, and Battle ushered him out of the office while I read the message.

"What happened, sir?" said Battle, when he returned alone moments later.

"According to this, he was attacking a Yankee wagon train. He had a force of two hundred men . . . two hundred! Why, he should have three times that many soldiers . . . Oh, I see. They have been trying to cut a road through Indian Gap. They managed to get themselves and the artillery through the gap into Tennessee . . ."

"In January, Governor?" said Richard. "The weather must have been terrible."

"I reckon they thought it was urgent," I said, and went back to reading the message. "Once they got over into Tennessee, Robert sent Colonel Thomas and the Cherokees and Lieutenant Colonel Henry and the cavalry on toward Gatlinburg, while the General himself took the remaining troops, bound for Sevierville." I looked up. "Well, I don't know enough about the details of that campaign to make any sense of the strategy. I suppose he'll tell me himself one day, God willing. Anyhow, on the thirteenth of this month, the scouts nosed up a wagon train . . . doesn't say how many . . . and they attacked it. Of course they would."

"Supplies," said Richard. "They couldn't resist it. I suppose they were going to herd the wagons toward a rendezvous point with Thomas and Henry?"

"Apparently so. But they ran into some bad luck, according to Colonel Palmer. Wait . . . I thought Palmer . . . Ah, it seems there are two Palmers mixed up in this tale, and the second one is a Union officer, a *William* Palmer, who commands the Fifteenth Pennsylvania Cavalry, and is currently making a nuisance of himself in east Tennessee. It seems he and his men got wind of the incident from some of the local Union sympathizers, and they were trying to slow down the procession—felling trees across the road—"

"Where were they headed, sir? Gatlinburg?"

"Road to Asheville, it says here. Playing it safe, I suppose he thought." I nodded at the logic of it. My brother mostly did play it safe, but that was a good thing in a general. Wasn't it? "Anyhow, they traveled a good ways, but the fallen trees slowed them down. They camped for the night alongside Cosby Creek, and at dawn the Fifteenth Pennsylvania hit them. There was a brief skirmish. A few men killed. The rest surrendered. Apparently they were able to capture my brother before he could put up a defense."

"Why didn't the other troops rejoin the General?"

"I don't know, but I intend to find out."

"What about an exchange of prisoners, Governor?"

I considered it. "It doesn't seem likely," I said. "Not unless we capture somebody equally important to them. I will do all I can." I had already learned how little that was.

In March of 1864, I was up for reelection as governor, and with things going as badly as they were in North Carolina—what with the blockades, the invasions, and the salt famine—you'd think I'd have been going door to door begging somebody to take the office off my hands, but I would have felt like a rat abandoning the ship of state at that point, and so I went on the hustings asking for the people's vote, and more importantly trying to keep their spirits up through the dark days of war. My opponent was W. W. Holden, the editor of *The Standard,* who favored making peace with the enemy, and for a while I was afraid that people might be so sick of war that they'd vote for him, but because few men can best me on the speaker's platform, I thought to put my case to the people in a round of orations, and finally I went to the soldiers themselves.

I took the train up to Virginia, and went around giving speeches to the Tarheel boys, as they are called these days, for it's said that they stick in battle as if they had tar on their heels. The soldiers' vote had put me in office in the first place, and I hoped I could count on them to see me through again. A pair of distinguished visitors turned up at several of my speeches, and nobody had to tell me who they were. The patrician countenance of

Robert E. Lee was familiar to everyone these days, and the red-bearded, barrel-chested fellow at his side, sporting a cape and thigh-high boots, and general's braid, was J. E. B. Stuart, two years my junior and already a renowned commander. General Stuart was kind enough to say that he enjoyed listening to me on the stump, and he wished me well. Of course, Lee and Stuart are both Virginians, like most of the top brass in the Confederacy, so they will not be able to vote for me, but I was honored that they came more than once to hear me all the same. I did not ask them how the war was going. I was afraid they'd tell me.

All my fulminations about my brother's capture did not succeed in getting anyone punished for the incident, nor did I secure his release, but as the war wore on and generals—Jeb Stuart and A. P. Hill and so many others—were killed in battle, I began to think that perhaps it was a blessing that he was a prisoner of war. At least he had a chance of living through it.

I was reelected governor. The wonder was that Holden would have been fool enough to take it. The ship of state was a sieve now. The eastern part of the state was under Federal occupation, General Sherman's troops were fulminating along the border in the south, and east Tennessee was in Union hands, which meant that raids into the mountain counties would soon become more frequent and more terrible. And I was sitting in the middle of it, in the governor's palace on Fayetteville Street, knowing that sooner or later it would all come down on my head.

I scarcely had time to know or care what blow would befall us next, but by January 1865 we lost the coastal battle at Fort Fisher, and thus the port of Wilmington fell, severing our last link with the supply lines from Europe. We were bottled up now with only our own resources to see us through. I knew that the railroads would be the next target. The previous month, an army out of east Tennessee under General George Stoneman had attacked southwest Virginia, raiding Saltville—another blow to our supplies—and his troops had torn up the railroad line between Wytheville and Bristol, further cutting supply lines. And also lines of retreat, for if the Army of Northern Virginia ever lost its hold on Richmond, Lee would be pulling his troops back south, and the railroad from Danville to Greensboro would be his best means of evacuation. The blow to it would come soon.

It was as if they were going room by room through a great house and blowing out the lamps one by one. Soon we would be left in darkness.

In February of '65 Sherman finally invaded North Carolina. He sacked Columbia, South Carolina, and marched north, apparently headed for Charlotte, as Cornwallis had done before him in the Revolution, but in Fairfield County, he changed his tack and went instead northeast to Fayetteville. His army proceeded north in two great divisions, traveling a day's march apart, in order to inflict the greatest possible destruction and devastation on the surrounding countryside. The reports preceded him, and I'm sure I did not hear of every outrage perpetrated by that army on hapless civilians, but I heard enough to sicken me. Houses burned, stock shot in the fields and left to rot, rings snatched from young girls' fingers, and household goods carried off by a legion of uniformed thieves.

I flung the stack of dispatches down on my desk. "Well, no doubt the necessity of robbery and torture gives pain to those who have to inflict them, but the Union must be restored, and how can that be done whilst a felonious gold watch or a treasonable spoon is suffered to remain in the land, giving aid and comfort to rebellion?"

"Well, such is war, I suppose," said Richard, who was as used to my rages as he was to hearing of Sherman's atrocities.

"Such is war, indeed! Remember that eighty-four years ago the army of Lord Cornwallis marched over that same ground, also determined to put down a rebellion. His men were shot at by the local citizenry and treated to every show of hatred and bitterness, so that they might have had every reason to reply in kind. But have you read the order book of Lord Cornwallis? The historical society has it, and I got it and read it." I pulled a hastily scribbled sheet of notes from my coat pocket and read aloud, *"February 2, 1781 . . . Lord Cornwallis is highly displeased that several houses have been set on fire today during the march—a disgrace to the army— and he will punish with the utmost severity any person or persons who shall be found guilty of committing so disgraceful an outrage. His Lordship requests the commanding officers of the corps will endeavor to find the persons who set fire to the houses today."*

"Well," said Richard, "Perhaps it—"

"Or this one . . . *Smith's Plantation, March 1781 . . . A woman having been robbed of a watch, a black silk handkerchief, a gallon of peach brandy, and a shirt, and as by the description, by a soldier of the guards, the camp and every man's kit is to be immediately searched for the same, by the officer of the brigade . . .* —That was eighty-four years ago. But last week in Fayetteville, Sherman's men hung four citizens up by the neck until they were nearly dead to force them to disclose where their valuables were hidden. Then they shot one of the men to death. And you tell me: Such is war!"

Richard said, "It is regrettable, but . . ."

I rummaged through my desk and retrieved another paper. "All right, listen to this one, Richard: *The commanding General considers that no greater disgrace could befall the army, and through it our whole people,*

*than the perpetration of barbarous outrages upon the un-
armed and defenceless, and the wanton destruction of
private property . . . It will be remembered that we make
war only upon armed men."*

"Well, sir, the British had very chivalrous ideas about
warfare."

"Perhaps they did," I said, "but that last order I read
came from Robert E. Lee—just before Gettysburg."

Fayetteville was sacked in February 1865. The great
blow to the mountains came in March. A swarm of
Union cavalry under General Stoneman swept into
western North Carolina with very little to stand in their
way except the old men and little boys who made up the
Home Guard—everyone else being dispatched to hold
off Sherman in the east.

They were planning to pillage their way southeast to
Salisbury, where there was more railroad to destroy, and
also the stockpile of such supplies as we had left to be
held in readiness for Johnston, or if he should be forced
to retreat south, for Lee himself. Watauga was the first
county between the Tennessee line and the Yankees'
objective at Salisbury, and on March 28, some six thousand Union soldiers with the Twelfth Kentucky in the
vanguard descended on the little town of Boone.

We watched the drama unfold in a series of dispatches from the invaded territory, and although the
news was indeed alarming, I no longer had the urge to
take up arms and wade into the fray. Someone had to
stand back and see the whole of the map and decide
what was best for the entire state.

"There was a battle at Boone," Richard announced
when the day's news arrived. "The Home Guard engaged the Yankees on the outskirts of town."

My mouth dropped open. "The Watauga Home
Guard against six . . . thousand . . . Union . . . troops?"

"That's what it says, sir. Our informant believes that it was a mistake, though."

"I should say it was!"

"No, he means that the Home Guard—while brave and steadfast, I'm sure—did not quite realize that there were . . . um . . . six thousand enemy soldiers in the opposing force. It seems that the Twelfth Kentucky was somewhat ahead of the rest of the troops, and apparently the Home Guard attacked thinking that they were the whole of it."

I almost smiled. It is the sort of thing that would be humorous in a history book, if one were reading about Caesar's legions or Napoleon's army, but this was too close to home to be anything but tragic. "How bad was it?" I asked.

"Well, apparently they managed to shoot one Yankee with their initial volley, but just then they received a signal—a little boy up on the ridge flashing a mirror, I think—and his message was that more soldiers than John ever saw were heading up the road, and a few continued to fire anyhow, but most just melted into the woods after that. I can't say that I blame them."

"No. More power to them," I said. "So Boone was taken?"

"Yes. Civilians robbed and murdered. Prisoners taken. General Gillem did burn down the county jail to teach the town a lesson, it says here."

"I wonder what lesson that would be," I said with a sigh.

Rattler

The Harkryders have a tattered old Confederate flag hanging outside their trailer. Jeff McCullough says he shakes his head every time he goes past it. "All the Harkryders in these parts in 1862—the ancestors of this current bunch—they were Union sympathizers during the war," he said. "Not that they were ever much use to anybody, but that's where their allegiance was back then. Seems funny to think of them switching sides this late."

"They never did switch sides," I told him. "They're always on their own side, the one with nobody else. The thing is, they're every one of them Harkryders bone contrary. Never can stand to agree with folks, and if there's a side to be taken, they'll generally take the unpopular one. Now during the War, being Confederate around here meant siding with the state government and the local bigwigs, so they set dead against it. Nowadays, though, the Confederacy is the underdog, and the gentlefolk are mostly embarrassed by the mention of it, so now the Harkryders show the flag and mourn the Cause—now that it's good and lost. No, the Harkryders haven't changed sides. They're on the side of Contrary, same as always."

The long-ago past isn't a place any of us have ever been. It's just words, so when you change the words you change the past, seems like. So people forget what was, or they make words to commemorate a past that didn't happen, but the land remembers. You want to know about the past—the land knows. Take that locust tree out in the weeds behind my cabin. You get locust trees sprouting up if you don't mow your grass often enough. It's the first tree to turn brown toward the end of summer, and its wood isn't good for much except fence posts. Just an old weed with scraggly leaves and bark full of thorns, but it remembers better than we do.

The locust tree has sharp thorns along its bark to protect itself from grazing animals, because if the bark gets stripped away, the tree is wounded—open to insects and fungus. Now the thorns protecting a locust tree grow twenty feet up the trunk of that tree, but that's more protection than a locust tree needs these days. The main threat of the bark is deer, but a deer, even on her hind legs and stretching out her neck for all it's worth, can't reach up more than a dozen feet or so along the length of the tree trunk, but the thorns go up twenty feet. The locust tree remembers. It remembers a time ten thousand winters back when glaciers lay five hundred miles to the north, and this land was a frozen wilderness with ceaseless winds and no summers. A time without oaks and poplars and timothy grass, without deer or starlings, without people. But not empty. Far from empty. There were great birds of prey with wingspans of twenty-five feet, and saber-toothed tigers stalking the evergreen forests. And there were elephants here. Right here in these old mountains—big shaggy, curved-tusked beasts standing fifteen, twenty feet high at the shoulder, locust-eating beasts . . .

They're gone now. Died out ten thousand years ago, along with the tigers and the raptors and the American horses—maybe with some help from the ancestors of my tribe who arrived here right about then—those woolly mammoths are gone now. But that locust tree remembers.

The locust tree remembers . . . but it doesn't call the mammoths back into the world.

I wondered whether people were calling the soldiers back—or if we had just never let them go to begin with. And I didn't know what thorns we could have about us to protect ourselves from their return.

The Ravenmocker's warning laid heavy on my mind, and I knew I was bound to try to warn the sunshine soldiers what they were stirring up in these mountains. I sat around and studied about it for a couple of days, and at first I thought maybe I'd speak to Spencer Arrowood, but a sheriff has no jurisdiction in the Ravenmocker's lands, and besides he is too grounded in what he can see and touch. Has to be. Nature of his job. To believe me—and he would try to, being that we're old friends—he would have to disbelieve in too many things that put the world in order for him.

In the end I couldn't think of anything better to do than talk to McCullough about it. Being a newspaperman he has to listen to just about anybody, so the day after the *Hamelin Record* came out—which meant that its editor had a week before his next deadline—I took myself down to the newspaper office on Main Street with a paper sack of wild onions and field greens for McCullough. He's one of them earth-shoe people, is McCullough. He'll eat just about anything as long as it don't come from a grocery store.

"What brings you to town, Rattler?" he said, after he had thanked me for the weeds.

"Care to take a walk?" I said. I don't do my best thinking in little boxes.

He looked worried for an instant, but he must have remembered that I'm not the kind of person that constitutes a problem for a newspaperman. I don't want my picture in the paper and I don't want to argue about last week's editorial, 'cause I don't read 'em. So he glanced at his wristwatch, flipped the cardboard sign on the door to say CLOSED, and off we went. Hamelin is one of those towns where you can dial a wrong number and still talk, so it didn't take more than a hundred yards or so to get us off the pavement, and onto green grass. I was grateful. I couldn't say what I had to on tar and asphalt.

I figured I'd start out slow. "I've been thinking about the reenactors," I said. "They planning anything else anytime soon?"

McCullough smiled. "I'll see that you get an invitation," he said. "My stew must agree with you."

"Well, that's mighty nice of you, but I was thinking more along the lines of getting them to call it off."

He stopped and stared—hadn't seen that coming. "Call it off, Rattler? But I thought you liked the company."

"Oh, I don't mind, but there's other folks out there that might."

"I haven't heard any complaints," said McCullough. "Has anybody said anything to you?"

Well, that was a poser. If I said *yes*, then he'd say *who?*, and then I'd find myself trying to explain a Ravenmocker to somebody who doesn't even believe in dousing rods. I didn't see any percentage in having that conversation, because the only outcome would be to convince Jeff McCullough that I was soft in the head.

Finally I said, "My neighbor has been having bad dreams. Maggie Raincrow. You know her. I think seeing the soldiers is frightening her." *Well, that was true enough,* I thought.

"We'll try not to disturb anybody," said McCullough.

I tried again. "Look, it's dangerous to be running around in the woods with guns."

McCullough looked bewildered. "Rattler, this isn't

like you," he said. "Do you want to tell me what's really bothering you?"

"Look," I said. "The war isn't over. Not really. And if you go traipsing out there playing soldiers, you just might start the hostilities all over again."

He frowned. "Are you talking about the antisocial militia types who might mistake us for ATF agents?"

"Well, no, McCullough. I'm talking about ghosts."

He started laughing then, and punched me playfully on the arm. "You had me going there, Rattler," he said. "Now I've got a newspaper to put out. See you this weekend!"

Well, I had tried.

Malinda

They say that once a dog has killed a chicken, you might as well put him down, because there ain't no way you can ever trust him again. The only reason I didn't think that about Keith was because I knew he had seen some terrible things while he was piloting and working with Kirk's Legion over in Tennessee. I remembered the pale stone face of that boy sitting by the fire in the Pritchard cabin telling what happened at Shelton Laurel, and I knew that somebody else was calling this tune. Anyhow I wasn't going to be sent over to Carter County to sit out the war in a skirt, so I held my peace.

Not many days after William Coffey had been got out of the way, we had got tired of sleeping rough in huts in the snow, and we had gone to the house of Mr. Madison Estes on the Johns River to sleep warm and eat hot stew. I wanted to wash my socks and get the dirt out from under my fingernails. Keith was hoping Mr. Estes had some tanglefoot put by that would either keep him warm or make him too drunk to mind the cold.

Jim Hartley, who was a scout and a lieutenant in the Third North Carolina Mounted Infantry, was there al-

ready, on account of Mr. Estes's son Langston had
joined up with Hartley. They were taking some new recruits and Rebel deserters back over the mountain to
enlist in the mounted infantry. (Early on I asked Keith
what the difference was between "mounted infantry"
and "cavalry." He thought for a minute and said, "Cavalry stays mounted while they fight, but mounted infantry just rides horses to where the battle is and then
they fights a-foot.") They weren't mounted on this sortie, though. Horses were getting scarce. We had our men
bedded down in the barn or wherever in the house they
could stretch out without getting stepped on.

"What news?" Keith asked Hartley, when he had got
his boots off and settled in by the fire.

Jim Hartley was a lean, serious fellow in his thirties,
from the Carolina mountains same as we were, and he
had been piloting for much of the war, so we respected
his judgment. I thought he looked the worse for wear
that night. His eyes smoldered, and he looked so skinny
you'd have to throw a tent canvas over him to get a
shadow. Hartley started coughing, and he took a swig of
acorn coffee, which is boiled tree nuts and tastes like it,
from a tin mug to quiet his throat. "Well," he said when
he could talk again, "we hear tell that a couple hundred
Confederates have been sent out in your neck of the
woods. They're camped out on Carroll Moore's place.
They'll want to know about that in Tennessee."

"I want to know about that myself," said Keith.
"Moore's farm is in Globe. It's too close for comfort.
Which way are they supposed to be headed?"

"Toward the Union lines, they say."

"Well, good, let's just keep an eye on them until they
set off to march through the pass over the mountain,
and then we can ambush them and kill 'em all."

"They'll have scouts all around that column when
they're on the move," said Hartley. "I think catching
them by surprise in camp would be safer."

"But they outnumber us by—what?—four, five to one?"

Jim Hartley smiled for an instant, but then the chills hit him, and he stretched out his hands to feel the warmth of the fire. "Well, that ought to be about right, don't you think? We've got repeating rifles and they've got sorry muzzle-loaders that soot up half the time. I believe we can take them." He started coughing again. "Anyhow we don't know how many are there. Might be twenty or two hundred."

"I don't think you better go," said Keith.

Hartley took another swig of acorn coffee. "I reckon you're right. A night raid wouldn't help this fever any."

"Well, I was thinking more about that cough of yours giving the game away."

Keith saw the sense of a surprise raid on the encampment, and the two of them sat up until the fire burned low, talking about how they would set up the attack. We knew the Moore farm, living in Globe so close by like we did, so we sketched out a plan of the place, making x's for house, barns, and outbuildings.

An hour before daybreak, they roused a dozen of our best fighters and a couple of the Third NC's scouts, and told them to get ready to head out at sunup.

"Just steal me some horses," Jim Hartley told Keith. "We need all we can get. And good luck."

Keith said, "I'll see you both when we get back."

"I'm going, too," I told Keith.

Keith has about given up trying to argue with me. "Just keep back," he said. "Take all the shots you want from cover, but don't go charging into the thick of things."

"We'll see," I said.

We figured on taking the Rebel soldiers by surprise, sleeping under their blankets in the cold. There's a wooded ridge above Carroll Moore's house, thick with laurel bushes, and we headed for that, because if you're partway up the slope, you can see the rest of the farm spread out before you. The plan was that the best sharp-shooters would take up positions up there on the ridge, and Keith sent the rest to storm the house. "Might as well stir 'em up and get 'em moving," he said.

That put me in mind of how bee trackers steal honey from a hive of wild bees. Like them, we knew what was coming in general, but we got stung worse than we had expected.

It wasn't far to the Moores' place, and we wanted to keep quiet, so we walked there. The sky was just begin-ning to crack with light when we climbed out on the ridge. Everything below was white and quiet, with just the tail of smoke from the Moores' chimney moving in the wind.

"Hell, there ain't no army down there," said Keith. "Look at the horses. It's not more'n a dozen men, I'd say."

"It's probably just the family, then," I said. "Let's leave 'em be."

Keith shook his head. "They're enemies all the same. We attack."

"That'll help the Yankees win the war," I said.

Keith pretended he hadn't heard me.

"General Stoneman might be studying about captur-ing the supply warehouse in Salisbury or breaking up the railroad line that goes north to Virginia, but those are trifling matters compared to your plans, McKesson Blalock."

That nettled him. He pushed his hat back away from his eyes so I could see the meanness in them. "Well, *Sam*," he said. "Maybe if I had a regiment to command, and a unit of cavalry and six cannons or so, then maybe I might go after Camp Vance or even Morganton, but since it's just ten of us bushwhackers and one little mouthy *girl* a-doing the fighting, I believe I'll set my sights low, if it's all the same to you."

"But he's warned off now," I said. "When we went over there awhile back and plundered his house, when he warn't to home, that gave him notice that you was after him. I've heard tell he's got guards around him now."

Keith laughed. "Guards! Little boys!"

"Little boys that can shoot straight, and that know you on sight."

"You can go back to Estes's place if you're scared, Malinda. In fact, I'd feel easier about it if you did stay away."

"I'm as brave as you, McKesson Blalock. Now lead on."

"I'm going in for the kill." He motioned to a couple of the others, and they started down the slope toward the yard. "You stay up here and cover us. Sam Blalock, you, too!" He touched my cheek for an instant and gave me a little smile to show the fight was over, and then he was gone.

I stayed put. I don't like to talk back to Keith in front of the others, because he has to have respect to lead. And I do respect him, mostly. There's nobody braver, but sometimes he doesn't think far enough ahead.

The other half of the raiders, led by Hartley's man, name of Philyaw, had gone down the road to take their position opposite the house, but before they had got themselves situated, one of the Rebel guards spotted movement and came around to see what was happening. When he spotted Philyaw's men, he let out a yell to wake the rest, and then the fight was on.

I could see the whole thing from up on the ridge. There was the guard, his arms thrown wide, staring at Philyaw's men, and then turning and running for cover. Half a dozen horses were hitched up next to the house, and they were rearing and stamping at the sudden noises, kicking up snow.

On the other side of the house one of Carroll Moore's

boys was walking across the orchard with a Flintlock Kentucky Rifle resting on his shoulder and a mess of fresh-killed rabbits draped over his arm. What was he doing out hunting at daybreak, I thought, but I didn't have time to study on it, because a heartbeat later the boy, Jesse, heard the guard's cry, and pitched the rabbits into the snow just as Keith and his men tore out of the woods, heading straight at him. He took off running for the house, with bullets popping all around him and his possibles bag full of powder and shot flapping behind him as he ran, but he stopped before he got shut of the orchard, and hid there behind a tree trunk. I had him in my sights, but I shot me a good few bare apple trees there at first. There didn't seem to be any point in killing the boy. He wasn't shooting back. Maybe he had used up all his shot on the rabbits.

Then some of the boy's kinfolk burst out of the house, shooting off rounds as they ran, and they headed for the orchard, using the bigger trees for cover so they could shoot back. There were bullets buzzing all over that field—Moores in the house shooting Enfields out the windows; Moores in the orchard trying to pick off soldiers coming at them; us on the hill putting down cover fire for our men; and there's Keith in the middle of it, sashaying around like it's a rain shower he's walking through instead of a hail of bullets.

I was keeping an eye on him as much as I could, and I saw him take aim and pop one off at one of the older men. The feller fell down and his leg opened up red, making a patch on the snow around him. He was rolling around in the snow grabbing at his thigh, and I thought, *That's one down.*

Then I looked over past the pile of dead rabbits, and I saw that the boy Jesse had never made it to the house. He was still there in the orchard, too far from his kinfolk to reach them, and caught between them and Keith's men who were barreling straight at him. For just

an instant him and Keith must have been looking right
into one another's eyes.

Then I saw Keith break stride a moment and level the
barrel of his Spencer right at the boy, and at the same time
the boy swung his flintlock up to his shoulder and then
they both fired straight at one another at close range like
two dueling gentlemen, only they weren't using pistols,
and neither one of them missed, or aimed to.

They both went down. I saw the boy grabbing at his
boot and then I turned to look for Keith and saw that he
had dropped his weapon and had both hands covering
up his face. One of the men pulled him to his feet, and
in that instant I saw the side of his face—what was left
of it.

I shut my eyes just for a second. Just 'til I could take
a swallow of cold air deep into my chest, because things
were bad enough without me remembering my woman-
hood and bouncing screams off the mountains. I never
made a sound. When I opened my eyes again, I set to
with my rifle, giving cover fire to Keith and Joe Webb
who had run to fetch him. We kept the Moores nailed
down for the next minute or so while our people made
it back to the trees.

"Go find us a good, steady horse," I said to my cousin
Adolphus.

"We didn't bring none!" His face was the color of the
snow.

"No, but the Moores have hid out theirs. Find out
where. We're getting out of here."

Joe Webb half dragged Keith up the hill to where we
were waiting, and when he reached us he slid Keith on
the ground and said, "You tend to him. I'll round up the
horses." He took out his pistol and started back down
the hill toward the slave quarters.

After that I let the rest of them do the shooting and the
watching, and I knelt down in the snow and tended to
Keith. "It's bad," I told him. He wouldn't want me telling

lies to him. "There's not enough bleeding to kill you, I don't reckon, but your right eye is gone, McKesson."

"Is it?" He sounded half asleep. "It don't hurt much."

"It will, I expect."

He reached for my hand. "You won't leave me?"

"You never left me, did you?"

I got him some water out of a canteen, and I tried to staunch the wound with a wet rag while we waited for what seemed like hours 'til we saw Joe Webb and a couple of our men with him, trotting across the fields with a string of mules on a lead, and prancing right in there with them was the prettiest white pony you ever saw. It looked like it was made of ice, picking its dainty feet up out of the snow drifts. *That's some rich girl's best friend,* I thought. *There'll be tears tonight.*

"How'd you find 'em?" Adolphus asked Joe Webb.

He shrugged. "Put my pistol to a darky's head and said he could tell me where them horses were or get his head blown off."

Adolphus sighed. "I reckon he'll be delighted when us Yankees win the war."

"Needs must," said Webb. "They were hid out in a ravine past the fields. 'Cept for this fairy horse. She was eating oats in a stall. Had to fight to get her. How's Blalock?"

"He'll make it," I said.

We got Keith up on the white pony, for she was the smoothest gaited of the lot, and I slipped up behind him to hold him on while Joe and Adolphus rode bareback on the mules on either side of him, to make sure he didn't pitch off into the snow.

We got back to the Estes's place a little quicker than we had left, and Jim Hartley was pacing the yard a-waiting on us. When he saw us heading for the house, close enough for him to get a look at Keith's shattered face, he swore a little, and then he ran to help us get Keith down off that silver pony.

"Is he bad?" he asked me in a whisper.

"He'll do," I said. "But we ain't stopping long. Just to get water and clean bandages. Then we're going with you over into Tennessee, before the Home Guard can catch up to us. They should be along pretty soon now."

Joe Webb patted the pony's rump. "There's a pretty little girl back there at the Moores' place about to lose *her* eyes from crying over this animal," he told Jim. "I promised her I'd send this here pony on back to her if it was all right by you."

"Well, it ain't," said Jim Hartley. "This here animal is a conscript, and she's going with us to Tennessee, like it or not." Then he turned to Keith who was standing there in the yard, swaying like a bent sapling. "Keith, you have got yourself a mighty pretty piece of horse flesh to ride over the mountain on . . . I wish you could see her."

It was a sorry procession of weary soldiers that made their way through the gap that joins Carolina with Tennessee on that January day. We had put a saddle on the fairy horse, as Webb called the little white mare, and Keith did better at staying on, but he was still weak and swimmy-headed.

When we reached the Watauga River, Jim Hartley rode up alongside us, and said, "I think it's best if we stop here tonight. No point in going any further. The Carolina Home Guard won't come after us on this side of the mountain. They're too afraid of running into Stoneman. I know a safe house here on the river."

"Can we get a doctor?" I asked. "I think he's still carrying that bullet."

Hartley nodded. "There's one back in Shull's Mill we can trust. Tomorrow I'll send riders through the gap to fetch him."

I sat up that night with Keith, afraid that if I nodded off I'd wake up to find him cold beside me. He was feverish now, and he'd shake from chills, but he hung on to life.

We were still afraid that Major Bingham and the Home Guard was after us, so the next morning we decided to head back into Carolina and hole up at Lewis Banner's house. He was a man of substance in the county, and known to be strong for the Union, but nobody could ever explain to me why a man who owned seventeen slaves would be rooting for the Union in this war. Anyhow, we didn't think the Home Guard would go looking for us on Banner land, because there was always a fair number of Federal soldiers about the place. It wasn't any log cabin, either. The Banners had a proper wood frame house with a parlor and a room for the table and the dish cupboard, and a big hall that went all the way down the middle of the house, with a Turkey carpet, and a walnut staircase leading upstairs to the sleeping quarters.

As we were headed back into Carolina, sure enough, we met some of Kirk's men on their way back to headquarters in Tennessee. Jim Hartley, who had been getting more restless by the hour at the thought of playing nursemaid instead of soldier, said, "If you think you can manage your husband, ma'am, we'll leave you here and head back with my troops."

"We'll be all right," I said.

Joe Webb came over and patted Keith on the arm. "I'm going to go with them. Just wanted to wish you luck—and to ask a favor."

"What is it?" I said.

"Well, that fairy horse Keith's a-riding stands out like a sore thumb. You might be better off without her, and I'd sure like to take her back with me."

"Give us one of the mules, then, and we're quits," I said. "Are you taking that pony back to a pretty Moore girl, Webb?"

He shook his head. "That mare is ours now," he said. "You be careful on that trail now. The doctor will be waiting for you at Lewis Banner's."

We got Keith down off the white pony, and hoisted him up on one of Carroll Moore's mules. Then they all said their good-byes to Keith and wished us well, and then they headed west with Kirk's men, and I started for the Banner's farm with the reins in one hand and my rifle in the other. I could tell that Hartley and the others didn't think they'd see us again. They were all figuring on Keith to die, and I'd go back to being one of them pippin-faced widow women trying to keep body and soul together on a hardscrabble farm. I thought different.

It was still bone-chilling cold up in the pass, but the sun was bright, and the snow was beginning to melt a little. Keith was still as wobbly as a poleaxed steer, and he hardly said ten words the whole way, but I didn't mind, because I figured he needed to save his strength, and the longer he hung on, the better his chances were of pulling through.

The sun was low in the sky by the time Banner's house came in sight, and we had made it the whole way without passing anybody but Federals on the road. The Banners saw us coming, and folk hurried outside to help me get Keith into the house. They put him in the bedroom on a straw mattress. The old doctor was waiting in the parlor, sipping some of the Banners' whiskey, and warming his feet by the fire. He gave us time to get Keith settled into bed, and then he came in to inspect the damage.

"Well, he's a lucky man," the doctor said. "People have died from less. All he's lost is an eye. The side of his face is torn up. That'll scar badly, but if he doesn't get an infection, he will pull through." He leaned down close to Keith's ear, and said loudly, "How are you feeling, boy?"

Keith groaned and his good eyelid fluttered. "Room's spinning. Wanna sleep."

"Well, let me do a little cleaning up around the

wound, son, and then you can sleep the livelong day if you've a mind."

I waited until the doctor had finished cleaning the wound and changing the dressing, and then I drew him aside. "The bullet never came out," I said. "Can you get it?"

"I wouldn't care to try," he said. "I could do more brain injury poking in there to get the ball out than might be done by just leaving it where it is. You'll need to keep this swelling down, and clean the wound to keep him from getting gangrene. You must watch what I do here. How to clean that eye socket to keep it from getting infected. Mind you use clean rags to do it, too!"

"I will," I said. "Is he going to make it?"

"An infection would kill him," said the doctor after a moment, "but barring that I think he will recover." Then he looked down at Keith and smiled to himself. "It almost makes me believe in that old wives' tale—that nothing else can kill you if you're born to be hanged."

The Home Guard had a happy few weeks thinking Keith Blalock had perished, but we left Lewis Banner's house as soon as Keith was able, because we didn't want the Confederates to find out any different. We slipped back through the gap into Tennessee, and went to ground with my Pritchard kinfolks while Keith rested and got his strength back, and the war went on without us.

We should have known that the Rebels weren't going to let us have the last word in that war. On the fifth of February, while I was still over in Tennessee tending to Keith, Bingham's Home Guards and a battalion commanded by Major Avery paid a call on Coffeys Gap. We heard about it after it happened from just about every Union sympathizer in these parts, but the one who saw most of it happen was Keith's own mother.

When it was over, Lewis Banner saw to it that one of our boys got her over the mountain so she could find us and tell us what happened. When she come into the Pritchards' house she was already a walking shadow, but when she drew in by the fire and got a look at Keith's shattered face, she let out a scream and started to cry and beat her fists against the log walls. We got her quiet and made her take a slug of whiskey out of the jar we kept for Keith when the pain got too bad for him to bear. Finally she trailed off into silence, except for little snuffling sounds and mutton-tallow tears sliding down her cheeks.

"I swan," she said. "That's the first time I cried since it happened. I never thought I would feel nothing to move me again. How are you, son?" She looked old, all of a sudden. Her grizzled hair was sticking out every which way and her eyes were sunk in her face like gooseberries in biscuit dough.

"They tell me I'll live," said Keith. "I ain't blind. The other eye still works. I know who done it, though."

"Does it matter?" she said. "First one side kills somebody and then the other, and then the first one takes somebody else to come out ahead again, and it never ends. If you could bring one of ours back to life by killing one of theirs, why, I'd say do it and welcome, but to cause more dying. What will that change? Nothing."

She commenced to sob again, and Keith said loud, "What did they do, Momma?"

"Bingham's men and some regulars under Major Avery showed up last Sunday, near dusk, and surrounded the house. I'd heard noises outside, but before I could do anything, they was pounding on the door with their rifle butts and yelling for us to open up. I wonder if somebody had betrayed us, and I was standing there trying to think who knowed that we harbored Federal soldiers and who would have told it. The men poured in like ants, and started breaking chairs and smashing plates. I didn't say a word.

"Then they tore open the door to the root cellar, and two of them went down the ladder while the rest stood at the top with their guns trained on the hole. Then the two in the root cellar give a yell, we heard an almighty thumping and more yells, and then they shoved Thomas Wright up the ladder and threw him on the floor, where another man tied up his wrists with hemp rope."

"Where was Daddy Austin while this was going on?"

"Hid out at his brother's house. McCaleb's, that is. McCaleb had lit out after William was killed, and everybody knew it, so Austin figured no one would think to search there. And they wouldn't have, but for John Boyd. He rode up just as they were taking Thomas Wright out the door, and he yelled that Austin and some others had been seen at McCaleb's house, and for them to head over there."

Keith tried to stand up, but two of the Pritchards eased him back down into his chair. "You can't do nothing now," one of them told him. "It's over and done with."

"Yes," said Mary Coffey. "It's done with. I tried to stop it. I tried. When the Home Guard left on their horses, taking the road to McCaleb's, I ran through the woods and got there just ahead of them, yelling *Rebels coming!* at the top of my lungs. Then I ran to the trees and hid out in some laurels to see what would happen next.

"One of your men—that Alex Johnson—heard me in time, and he got away. He slipped out the back door and made for the woods. Some of Bingham's men caught sight of him on the run and took shots at him, but it was getting dark by then, and he made it into the woods. Some of the Guard chased after him, but they never got on his trail, and he got away.

"I stayed where I was, and I saw some of the regulars bringing Austin out of the house with his hands bound, and they slung him up on a horse. John Boyd and the

Home Guard rode away then, and the regular soldiers started toward Shull's Mill with Austin as their prisoner. I remember thinking that he was lucky to be with the real soldiers instead of Bingham's butchers. They'll put him in jail over to Camp Mast, I thought, and he can sit out the rest of this sorry war.

"I didn't hear nothing for a day or so after that, but then John Walker came tapping on the door a few nights later, looking like all hell was after him. He had been with Major Avery's battalion when they took Austin away."

"John Walker?" said Keith. "The John Walker I know ain't secesh!"

We used to laugh about John Walker's schemes to escape conscription. One time, he hit upon the idea that if he had a paper saying he had been captured and paroled by the Federals, he wouldn't be made to fight for six months at least. So he got some of the outliers to borrow some Union uniforms, and then he dressed up his womenfolk and some neighbors and they acted out a capture, hauling him out from his house while folks was watching, and taking him on horseback over the mountain. When he came back a week or so later, he had his forged paper, saying he was honor bound not to fight for either side for the term of his parole. It had worked on the Home Guard, but I reckon things were getting desperate in the Confederacy, and they weren't taking any more excuses from draft dodgers.

"He was made to join up," said Keith's mother. "His heart ain't in it, but he's soldiering for Captain Marlow's troops. He was with them that night. He told me what happened. He thought they were heading for Blowing Rock, but once they passed Shull's Mill, they stopped at Tom Henley's house. Most of the men camped outside, but Captain Marlow and some of his men went in, kindled a fire, and fried up supper. They even give some bacon to Austin, so John Walker figured it would be all right, and maybe Austin could escape once they reached Camp Mast. But then when things had settled down, and Austin curled up near the fire and dropped off to sleep, Captain Marlow told John Walker to shoot him."

Keith tried to get up again. "John Walker . . . *John Walker* . . ."

"He stood up to them, son," Keith's mother said. "He told the captain he wouldn't do it. So the captain turned to another man—Robert Glass—and gives him the same order. And he did it."

"Did they bring the body home?" I asked.

Mary Coffey shook her head. "We never heard another thing. But before John Walker ever come to see me to tell me what happened, I knowed Austin was dead. We went out hunting him, of course. I'd seen him taken by the Home Guard, and when he didn't come home, we went out a-hunting him. Me and the neighbors. Some of the men are trackers, and if Austin had managed to escape to hide out somewhere, we thought they could pick up his trail.

"At first they didn't find nothing, but later on, when they started looking around between Shull's Mill and Blowing Rock . . ." She stopped for a moment, closed her eyes, and took a big swallow of air. "One of the men saw a dog running around with something in its mouth. They chased it down, and when they rolled it over, they saw that the thing in its jaws was a hand. Just . . . a hand . . . Most of the flesh had been gnawed away . . ."

One of the Pritchard girls gave a little scream at that, and Keith swore, but Mary Coffey didn't flinch. She had lived with it too long to feel the pain of it any more, I thought.

"They let the dog go," she said. "And they tracked him back to a spot near the Henley place, and that's where they found it. Him. They found Austin. The Rebels had shot him in the head and thrown his carcass in a laurel thicket. The dogs had got at him bad by that time, but they brought back what they could, wrapped in a blanket, and we buried him proper."

Everyone fell silent then. I saw that my cousins were looking away, probably wishing we'd stop bringing these terrible stories to their hearth and home. Maybe wondering if the Rebels would come for them next.

Finally Keith said, "I'm sorry, Momma."

"They didn't ought to have done it," his mother said. "Austin fed Union soldiers, it's true, but he'd also take in Confederates. He'd give charity to anybody. They oughtn't to have killed him for that."

"No, they didn't ought to, Momma, and I'll make them sorry they did."

His mother had hidden her face in her shawl to hide her tears, but when he said that, she looked up at him. "McKesson, you haven't heard a word I said," she said. "What good will more killing do?"

"Well, don't worry," I said quickly. "The war ought to be over soon, and Keith is still a long way from being well enough to fight."

"Well, Palmer and Stoneman may quit fighting," said Keith, "but damned if I will."

Zebulon Vance—1865

I felt like the last man in Raleigh.

Indeed, I very nearly was in that week of early April 1865, for Sherman's army was steadily making its way toward the capital through the eastern part of the state, now at Fayetteville, now Goldsboro, with a force of more than a hundred thousand men. They were chivvied along the way by Confederate cavalry, and a smattering of battles took place ... Kinston ... Bentonville ... but our defenders were inexorably falling back, fading just beyond the reach of the superior Union force, and before many days had passed they would drift away from Raleigh and leave us in the path of the enemy.

Last year the daughter of Robert E. Lee had been in Raleigh, completing her education at St. Mary's, but mercifully she had gone now—one less potential tragedy. I did not think that even William Tecumseh Sherman would be so base as to capture a young girl, but I had worried about poor Mildred Childe anyhow until she departed our fair city.

The people of Raleigh fled in the wake of the army,

but before they left, they were determined that their long-hoarded provisions should not fall into Sherman's hands. So before they departed, the fair ladies of Raleigh lined Fayetteville Street with baskets of food, and handed out parcels to Johnston's soldiers as they marched by until all the food was gone.

Now was the lull—like the calm center that is the eye of a hurricane, when all the winds and noise cease for an hour or so, until the storm moves forward again, and the tempest engulfs you once more. It was eerily quiet. Not just the absence of guns, but of ordinary street noises as well. No horses clattered along Fayetteville Street, and there were no sounds of voices from outside.

I was very nearly alone in the Governor's Palace, for I had sent Harriett and our boys away when I saw that the end was coming. I did not want personal matters weighing on my mind when I had so many other troubles to contemplate. Rumors—as yet unconfirmed— had reached us that General Lee had surrendered his army somewhere in Virginia, and that President Davis and his cabinet had fled Richmond by train and were headed for Greensboro, hoping perhaps for protection from General Johnston's forces. I thought there was little chance of that. The Confederacy was falling to pieces and I was one of those left behind to sweep up.

I had sent my two old friends, the former governors Graham and Swain, away from Raleigh on a special train under a flag of truce with orders to proceed to the headquarters of General Sherman and to deliver a letter to him asking that the state capital be spared.

While I waited for some sign of the city's impending fate, I wandered around my office, tending to the hundred little matters that were my obligation—letters from citizens in distress, messages from old friends, and the endless slurry of official communiques from a government and an army who would soon cease to be. Whatever his other regrets, Mr. Seddon would no doubt be glad to be nearing the end of our official correspondence.

I heard the clatter of boots in the downstairs hall.

My thoughts went first to the pistol in my desk drawer, but if Sherman's men had come to take me, my weapon would be useless against their rifles and bayonets. I went outside to the landing and peered over the balustrade.

The intruders stared back up at me and I saw that their uniforms were not blue but a dirt-streaked butternut gray.

"Are you General Johnston's men?" I asked them, hurrying down the stairs to meet them.

They were delicate-looking boys, no more than seventeen I judged, and they were standing idly in the hall without evincing much interest in the furnishings or ornaments about them.

"Junior Reserves," one of the boys said.

"South Carolina born and bred," said his companion, with an accent testifying to the truth of his words.

"We want something to eat," the first one said.

I sighed. Of course they were hungry. All of Johnston's boy soldiers were short on shoe leather and rations, but I had troubles enough without having starving boys invading the Palace, and so with some impatience, I attempted to get rid of them. "Boys," I said, "there is certainly food to be had in Raleigh, for the army decamped without being able to take all the rations with them. If you will go to the quartermaster, I'm sure he will be able to—"

But I was speaking to an empty hallway. Without waiting to hear me out, the two young men had wandered into the dining room, and I found them seated at the long mahogany banquet table, looking up at me expectantly. They did not seem inclined to follow my instructions on military procedure.

"You need to go the army quartermaster," I said

again. "I am nearly alone here. My family and my staff have gone. The provisions are nearly exhausted, and I have but two servants left, and they are too overworked to take on the task of feeding you."

The two lads grinned up at me. "Well, sir," one of them said, "that's what we always told the soldiers when they came to our house, too, but it didn't do a bit of good. They always made sure they got something to eat before they left."

I paused for a moment, looking at those gaunt young faces with old eyes, and then I nodded. "Wait here, boys," I said. "I'll go and bring you up some dinner."

The end of the war came to everybody in a different way. Mostly it arrived by word of mouth, or in an official dispatch delivered to a field commander somewhere. Even when Lee surrendered at Appomattox, no one was entirely sure that the war was over. President Davis and his cabinet had fled south on the train. I met with them when the train stopped in Greensboro. General Johnston's troops stayed in the field awhile after the Army of Northern Virginia had dispersed, but his troops were melting away like snow in March, and so finally toward the beginning of May everybody agreed that the fighting was over. Not the hostilities, maybe, but at least the fighting. Some fools out in Texas—and I don't know what business it was of theirs—had a battle in late May, but the last one fought in any pertinent area was a skirmish in Waynesville, North Carolina, on May 6, killing only one soldier, a Yankee. Then it was over.

After the surrender became official and the Confederacy dissolved, General Sherman sent a message saying that I might go home. The Union had appointed a new governor of North Carolina—Holden, the newspaperman, the very man I had defeated in the last election. At last his harangues for surrender had availed him something. Sherman himself occupied the Governor's Palace, but he would find the accommodations spartan, for we had removed all the furniture and the state records before his army reached town.

I had received a safe conduct pass from General Schofield so that I might make my way west to Statesville to join Harriett and the boys in a rented house on West Main Street near the college. It was a far cry from the Governor's Palace, but with the weight of the war off my shoulders, it would be a far more pleasant place. I thought that I might resume the practice of law once things had quieted down and the state returned to the happy monotony of peacetime.

In preparation for my return to private life I gathered together all my remaining personal possessions—all I had accumulated in the four years of war: a saddle horse, a pair of old mules, and one wagon. I shipped them westward on a freight car, and with a few friends I took passage on that same conveyance myself. The railroad cars and the highways alike were all choked with disbanded soldiers heading home, and at every depot where we stopped, more people poured into the overcrowded train.

It was all I could do to keep from being shoved out of that freight car altogether, and several hours of being prodded and stepped on had not improved the sweetness of my disposition one iota. At one stopping place I looked up to find myself face-to-face with a boy who was attempting to climb through a hole in the side of the freight car—our only means of ventilation.

"Get back outside!" I shouted at the boy.

He ignored me and kept worming his way through the hole.

I shouted several more times for him to stop, and was still ignored, so at last in a fit of temper I pulled my navy repeater out of its holster and said, "If you don't go back, boy, I will shoot you on the spot!"

He ignored me as serenely as if I had been a barking cat, and completed his passage into the freight car, plopping down near me on the straw floor and brushing off his clothes. Then he looked up at me and said, "You didn't look like you'd shoot."

That might have been the end of my sojourn as a Confederate citizen, as it was for the soldiers in Johnston's army, who simply signed the oath of allegiance and went home, but a few days after Appomattox, President Lincoln had been killed by a deranged actor. The hole in the world made by that assassination sent out cracks in every direction. The new government, under Andrew Johnson of Tennessee, issued orders for the arrest of all the Southern governors. Perhaps the government feared that more insurrection was contemplated, or perhaps President Johnson was anxious to distance himself from the taint of his Southern heritage, and so he was harder on the conquered nation than his predecessor might have been. I do not know.

All I know is that early on the morning of May 13, 1865—I am not likely to forget that date—we found our little house surrounded by a squadron of cavalry under the command of General Kilpatrick. With my wife and children standing there, shocked and frightened by this intrusion, the officer informed me that he had an order for my arrest—signed by the secretary of war in Washington.

"Where am I to be detained?" I asked the soldier. I was still dazed by this turn of events.

"In Washington" was his curt reply.

"How are we to get there? The trains are not running in these parts."

"We will ride to Salisbury, and travel from there to Raleigh by rail."

I nodded. "Have you an extra mount for me?"

He scowled. "Only pack animals. I suppose you could walk, but that would delay us too much."

I hoped he wasn't going to go off and commandeer some poor citizen's horse on my account, for Harriett would be left behind to bear the resentment that would bring, but fortunately a kind gentlemen called Samuel Wittkowsky came to my aid with the offer to drive me in his buggy to the appointed place, and the Union commander agreed to this plan, giving me one more day at home to pack my belongings before we should set out.

It was my thirty-fifth birthday, and while we had no heart and less money for a celebration, I think the day might have passed with some joy and contentment had it not been for the weight of my impending arrest so suddenly sprung upon us. Harriett tried mightily to hide her tears, so as not to alarm our sons, but neither of us had much success in pretending that nothing was amiss. She had planned a birthday dinner with such food as we had, but I cannot remember eating a morsel of it. She packed most of it for me to take as a lunch when they came for me on the morrow.

The next morning around nine, Mr. Wittkowsky turned up in his buggy, and we set off under heavy guard, with four mounted soldiers on either side of the buggy and the rest of the squadron divided before and behind us. As we passed out of the town, I could not hold back my tears, knowing that I might have said farewell to my wife and sons for the last time. I confided to Sam Wittkowsky that it was not the thought of being hanged that troubled me so much as the knowledge that Harriett would be left without a cent of money to live on.

He cocked his head, and then leaned close so that the soldiers might not overhear him. "But you were the governor, Mr. Vance. Chances must have come your way. Surely you've got a bit put by?"

I shook my head. "I never did. I know that with ships running the blockade, I could have feathered my nest by shipping cotton to Europe and ordering the proceeds placed to my credit. Indeed, I was urged to do so, but I did not. My hands are clean, and I can face my people and say that I have not made money out of my position."

"Still, a little money would be helpful now," Sam Wittkowsky said with a shrug. "You know, in prison maybe they don't feed you so good."

We had by now all heard the terrible rumors about prison camps both North and South, with men starved into skeletons, and cholera epidemics sweeping them away by the score. I wondered if hanging would be an improvement over that fate. I realized, though, that nothing would be gained by lamenting my lot, and I set out to give every impression of a carefree man on an excursion, for I've noticed that people are often wont to treat you as you act.

After we had traveled about a dozen miles on that hot May morning, the commander halted the procession in a shady grove next to a stream, announcing that we would eat here before continuing the journey. I hadn't much appetite anyhow, what with all my forebodings, though I hid them well, and I insisted upon sharing my food with the officers, and while they ate I set myself to amusing the cavalry with tall tales and jokes, much as I would have done at a governor's dinner party.

After the meal was over, I announced that I needed some exercise to aid my digestion, so I put it to one of the officers that I would ride his horse, and that he should take my place in the buggy with Sam. With some good-natured prodding from his comrades, he fell in with my plan, and obligingly climbed aboard, while I rode alongside and kept up a running banter, which served to take my mind off my troubles. We changed back again about six miles on, and I resumed my place in the buggy, which soon clattered so far ahead of our mounted escort that they were out of sight, but I had no intention of attempting to escape. My training in the law had taught me that attempting to run before one has had one's day in court only makes matters worse, and I was satisfied that my best chance lay in facing my accusers in person.

Presently we reached the outskirts of town, and I asked Sam to stop the buggy so that the soldiers could catch up. When the commander cantered up level with the buggy, I said: "You are giving me a good opportunity to get away."

He smiled a little and said, "I know my man. In fact, Governor, if you will give me your word of honor that you will present yourself at the depot tomorrow in time to take the train, I will not subject you to the indignity of marching you through town under guard."

I readily gave him my pledge, and he waved us on. "Where to, Governor?" said Sam, hitching up the reins, in case I were to order him to make a run for it.

But I patted his arm, and said, "Take your time, Sam. I have all night, and just now I'd like to go to Colonel Shober's house, please." Charles Shober was a brother attorney who had served in the House of Commons before the war, and then he had seen action with the North Carolina Forty-fifth. I thought I might presume upon our old acquaintance for hospitality, and he did not disappoint me. I told him that I had been arrested by the new government under President Andrew Johnson, and that I was headed for prison without a cent to my name. Shober sympathized with me, saying that he must see what could be done to make my situation less dire.

Before long a number of friends and well-wishers had congregated at Colonel Shober's house, commiserating with me and vowing to do whatever they could to remedy the situation. The first thing they did was pass the hat, so that when Sam appeared again the next morning to drive me to the depot, I had $65 to see me through my captivity.

My Union cavalry friends greeted me like a long-lost brother, and we all crowded together into the train, bound for Raleigh, and then on a different train on to Washington, where on the twentieth of May, I was locked away in a cell in the Old Capitol Prison, which was situated on a hill northeast of the Capitol building. I had often ridden past it during my years in Congress, but I had never thought to see the inside of it under such circumstances as these.

I was allocated to a small cell on the first floor, containing two iron bedsteads and two straight chairs. As I entered my cellmate rose to greet me.

"Good afternoon, Mr. Vance," said the distinguished gentleman in his fifties. "I thought I might expect to find you here."

I recognized him at once. "Good day to you, Governor Letcher," I said, shaking his hand. "I see that they are putting all their governors in one basket. How is life in the Old Dominion?"

John Letcher sighed. "Things in Virginia cannot get much worse. Even if there were supplies to be had, nobody could afford them. But now that the war is over, I hope the situation may improve soon."

"Are they treating you well here?"

"Well, I think you will find the food tolerable but it is expensive. We must order our meals from a local restaurant—and pay the bill ourselves."

"Well, at least I trust the salt will be free," I said, and he laughed, for during the war our correspondence had largely been devoted to the problem of getting salt from the Virginia Blue Ridge to North Carolina.

"Salt is no longer a problem, but the enemy is pretty much the same," he replied.

"I don't see why we have been detained," I said, pacing up and down the cell. "On the fifteenth of April I was given a letter of safe conduct approved by General Sherman himself, and the Union army's permission to return home without further consequences. Three weeks later, a squadron of cavalry shows up at my little house in Statesville and hauls me away."

Governor Letcher nodded. "President Johnson's government apparently has a different view of Reconstruction from that of his predecessor. Being a Tennessean gives him all the more reason to deal harshly with Southern politicians—to distance himself from their disgrace."

"You don't think he'll hang us just to make himself look good, do you?"

Governor Letcher considered it. "What were you charged with, Vance?"

"Why nothing. My captor showed me an order that had been sent to General Schofield in Raleigh, telegraphed from Washington by Grant himself: *By order of the President you will at once arrest Zebulon B. Vance, late Rebel governor of North Carolina, and send him to Washington under close guard* . . . Not a word as to why it was so ordered."

"They're probably trying to think up a reason," Letcher told me. "What I think is this: The assassination of Mr. Lincoln has frightened them out of their wits. They think it was part of a continued plan of insurrection on the part of the Confederacy, and they are waiting for further developments."

"But there is no plan! Lincoln was shot by a madman—wasn't he?"

"I hope so, Vance. I hope so. Because if no further treasonous acts occur within the next few months, I anticipate our release."

The weeks passed in cordial monotony, as my distinguished cellmate and I passed the time swapping stories and reminiscing about our days as small-town newspaper editors and congressmen. Despite the two decades difference in our ages we had much in common, and in other circumstances I would have enjoyed his company.

We were allowed visitors from time to time, and I took advantage of the kindness of old friends to ascertain how things were going back home. One old comrade from North Carolina who had business in the capital stopped by to help me pass the time. He looked worried at my reduced circumstances.

"You don't look well, Governor," he said.

"Call me Zeb," I told him. "*Governor* is a common name around here."

"Well, I'm glad you're keeping your spirits up. I was afraid that you might have suffered harsh treatment. The people back home don't know what to think on account of all the rumors. General Kilpatrick is telling people that when you were taken prisoner they forced you to ride to Salisbury on a mule."

"Why, no," I said. "I surrendered to General Schofield at Greensboro on the second of May, and he sent me home. On the thirteenth of May Major Porter came to Statesville and fetched me, and I rode to Salisbury in a buggy. I saw no mule on the trip, yet I thought I saw an ass in General Kilpatrick's headquarters."

"That seems to have been confirmed," murmured my honorable cellmate from Virginia.

I smiled at my visitor. "So you see that we are leading a quiet life here, but we are not suffering unduly. I wish I could say the same of my family. I have had a letter from Harriett, and she tells me that a few days after I left, a squad of Federal soldiers came to our house in Statesville and carried off everything in the house. They said it was because we had some of the furniture from the Governor's Palace. Of course, we did! We were trying to protect it from looters. But Harriett tells me that they took everything—our own furniture and the Governor's Palace pieces alike."

"Perhaps you can retrieve your goods from Raleigh when you get home, sir."

I shook my head. "None of it was sent back to Raleigh—not the Governor's Palace furniture and not our personal belongings. None of it has been seen again. I suppose if you went house to house in New York and Pennsylvania, you might recover a good bit of it."

My visitor look distressed. "Where is Mrs. Vance now, Governor?"

"She is at home in Statesville. We are poor in material possessions, but rich in neighbors. She tells me that before nightfall a steady stream of Statesville citizens had come, bringing beds and chairs and linens, so that by morning the house was as full as before. God bless the people of Statesville. But tell me, how are things faring in Asheville. Have you heard?"

"Yes, sir," he said. "I have some news. In early April, the town was invaded. Union forces under Colonel Isaac Kirby followed the French Broad from Tennessee and—"

"That was before I left," I said. "I know they were beaten back by Martin's men near Camp Woodfin."

"Yes, and after that Colonel Clayton took a force of old men and little boys out and faced down Kirk's Legion. Made them pull back into Tennessee. Asheville finally fell on the twenty-sixth of April. After the surrender at Appomattox—yes, I know it was. But they weren't ready to stop fighting in the mountains. Anyhow, General Gillem's men finally overran the city."

"I am sorry to hear it," I said. "I thought the surrender might have spared them that ordeal. There's not much I can do about it from a Federal prison in Washington, but still I worry about my family and friends back in Buncombe County. Was there much destruction?"

"Well, you know how armies are. Chickens are scarce, and if you had coffee, you wouldn't have a spoon to stir it with. But one thing should relieve your mind: Your mother's house was completely untouched."

"I am relieved," I said. "Surely the Federal troops did not respect the family of a Rebel governor to that extent?"

"Well, sir, it was on account of you, all right, but not because of your position. It was personal. When the Yankees overran the town, one young soldier made it his business to find out which house belonged to Zeb Vance's mother. Somebody told him, and he hared off over there, and set himself up as a one-man guard detail. Wouldn't let any of the rest come near the place. They say he even slept on the porch."

"I am astonished," I said. "Has anybody got an idea why he would do such a thing? A *Federal* soldier, you say?"

"Oh, we know why," said my friend, smiling. "He told everybody that would listen. It seems that he was on a train with you sometime during the war, and you gave him your lunch. He was quite positive about it. Do you recall the incident?"

I nodded. "Remember what the Scripture says about bread on the waters? Well, I added apple brandy as well, so I reckon a miracle was in order."

"Well, it certainly boosted my faith, sir. It's the first thing I've heard that makes me think the country's wounds might heal."

The summer passed, hot and muggy, as it does in Washington, and Governor Letcher and I saw very little of it, but we passed our time in correspondence with friends and family and hoped for better times.

"Well, here's some news from Chapel Hill," I told my cellmate one day in early July, as I opened my stack of letters. "Do you remember Governor Swain? He's the president of the state university now, but he was governor the year I was born."

"I have heard you speak of him," the Virginia governor said. "Have you given that career path any thought yourself? College president, I mean."

"Lord, no!" I said without a moment's hesitation. "It would kill me in a few weeks to be obliged to behave as is required of a college president in order to furnish an example to the boys."

"Well, you're young yet," said Mr. Letcher. "But what news do you have from Chapel Hill?"

"Why, there's to be a wedding next month. It's an extraordinary thing. At the end of the war, Chapel Hill was occupied by Union troops, under the command of General Smith Atkins of Illinois. Well, it seems that the general took a shine to President Swain's daughter Eleanor. She's a lovely girl, and I've no doubt that she was more than a match for the conquering general. Swain says that the smitten young officer wrote Ella a love poem, and she made him rewrite it before she was satisfied with it!"

Governor Letcher smiled. "Why didn't we put her in charge of a battalion?"

"Well, she seems to have accepted the surrender of one Yankee anyhow. The two of them have made a match of it, I am invited to the wedding in Chapel Hill on August 21, if I am at liberty by that time." I continued to skim the letter. "There's more news . . . Governor Swain has been appointed one of the visitors at West Point. He seems to be recovering from the war without much difficulty. And . . . hmmm . . . here's a thing—It seems that General Sherman dropped in for a visit to Chapel Hill, and while he was there he gave President Swain the gift of a saddle horse."

"I wonder whose horse it was," said Governor Letcher.

We were still chuckling about that when the guard walked up to the door of our quarters. "Zebulon B. Vance," he said, standing to attention.

"Why, yes, Jim," I said. "It's me. Present and accounted for. Same as yesterday, and the day before that. Have you come to take our dinner orders?"

That snapped him out of his pose, "No, sir! I got orders here to turn you loose. Governor Letcher has one, too." He handed the paper through the bars so that we could see for ourselves.

The order was terse. It gave the details of my arrest and imprisonment, ending: *"Released by order General Augur, July 6th, 1865, on parole to go home and remain subject to President's order; charges, etc., for orders Secretary of War."* I looked up as the guard began unlocking the cell. "They are hedging their bets, Jim. They say I can leave, but they reserve the right to lock me up again if they feel like it. And they still don't say what I'm supposed to have done."

"You were a Rebel, sir."

"So was George Washington," I said, "but he had the good sense to win his war."

So they let me out of the Old Capitol Prison, and I left Washington—but I supposed one way or another I would be back someday. Later on we heard that the day before I was pardoned Governor Morehead of Kentucky, Governor Murrah of Texas, Henry Allen of Louisiana, and a host of other distinguished Confederate leaders had crossed over the river into Mexico intending to live in exile, but I was not tempted to join them. I had stood with North Carolina all my life, and I didn't mean to abandon her now. I was headed for the mountains.

Spencer Arrowood

When time permitted that summer, Spencer Arrowood haunted the East Tennessee State Library, reading accounts of the Civil War in the mountains and paging through the rosters of various regiments in search of the last soldier who died in the War, the one with a variant of his own last name.

In the course of a few weeks he had become a familiar visitor to the desk of Michael Baird, a research librarian and the staff expert on the regional aspects of the Civil War in the Southern mountains.

"How's it going?" Baird asked him one day, as he sat surrounded by books and microfilm printouts, trying to make sense of it all.

Spencer shook his head. "It's all tangled up," he said. "Not like the movies, where the good guys fight the bad guys."

"No, it wasn't that easy," said Michael. "Maybe war never is. What's bothering you this time?"

"Everything," said Spencer. "I started reading general accounts of the war for background, and the facts are a lot more tangled up than a mini-series would have you believe. Grant was the Union commander, but his family owned slaves. Stonewall Jackson fought for the Confederacy, but before the war he started a Sunday school for blacks in Lexington, Virginia, teaching the people to read and write. I believe it was illegal in Virginia to teach blacks to read and write, but he did it anyhow. The song 'Dixie' was written by a man from Ohio."

The librarian shrugged. "I've given up expecting people to make sense."

"And then in the war, there was an account of the raid on Morganton. The newly freed slaves sat on a fence rail and cheered the Union soldiers as they rode by. Then one of the soldiers—one of the *Union* soldiers—pulled his pistol out of his holster and started shooting the black men off the fence."

"That one doesn't surprise me, Sheriff. It's fashionable these days to paint the Federals as saints who fought to liberate black people, but that idea would have horrified most of the real soldiers. Rebels used to yell out *'Abolitionist'* in hopes of making a Yankee mad enough to poke his head up so they could shoot him. It worked, too."

"And everybody around here thinks their ancestors fought for the Confederacy, but from what I've found, I'll bet more than half of them are dead wrong. It isn't a simple story."

Baird smiled. "In regards to that, I'm fond of quoting a line from Oscar Wilde: *The good ended happily, and the bad unhappily: That's what fiction means.* Once you start dealing in facts, goodness has nothing to do with it. Are you any closer to finding that soldier you're looking for?"

"A little. The Battle of Waynesville was a skirmish between a part of Kirk's Second North Carolina Mounted Infantry commanded by Colonel William C. Bartlett—"

"Yeah. The Home Yankees that people have forgotten about."

"—And a regiment of Confederate sharpshooters led by Lieutenant Robert Conley." He had it off by heart now.

"So you've checked the roster of the Second North Carolina?"

Spencer nodded. "All the sources agree that the Second North Carolina force at Waynesville was commanded by Colonel William C. Bartlett, including the Flag and Staff Companies. However, the roster of the Second North Carolina lists only three Arwoods, but they were in Companies B and A, and according to the records they spelled their names Arrowood anyhow."

"It's pronounced the same, right? Spelling doesn't mean anything."

"I know. Not that far back it doesn't. There is an Arwood in the Third North Carolina, but since they weren't in the battle that doesn't count, I suppose." Spencer sighed. "It's a mare's nest, isn't it?"

Baird smiled. "I know some people who believe in the divine infallibility of the Bible, but I don't know anybody who's fool enough to believe that historical records are perfect. History is just what people write down, and sometimes they get it wrong. Does it really matter whether it was James Arrowood or Edmond Arrowood who died at Waynesville? He's still just a name on a roster."

"I thought I could work back from there. Census records."

"And find what? A young boy from a mountain farm, descended from a millennium of farmers, who—if he had survived the war—would have gone home, married a local girl, and farmed. That's who he was. It's who they *all* were."

"I just want to know, I guess. To feel that I've found him, whoever he was."

"Well, Sheriff, I think you've done all you can do here. Have you ever thought about going over to Waynesville? Maybe they know."

* * *

Nora Bonesteel could not have said why she was uneasy. Her bones told her that a storm was coming, but the leaves on the oaks had not turned up their undersides the way they did before a cloudburst, and the sky was still clear.

Something wasn't right, and it bothered her that she didn't know what it was, because she usually did know. She had that cold, tingling feeling along her arms, and she shivered even in the bright sunshine. She stood on her back steps looking out above the trees at the green valley stretching away into the distance. She searched for dark clouds on the horizon, but the afternoon sky was clear. It was hot, though, without a breath of air moving in the stillness. That oppressive heat often did work its way up to a thunderstorm before the day was out. She would wait until evening to water the tomato plants. No use putting water on them in the blazing sun.

Something was going to happen. Without taking her eyes off the sky, Nora Bonesteel ran through a list of problems that might arise among the people in the community—the Anderson baby's vaccination, the Johnsons' drive to Wrightsville Beach for vacation; Dick Fortnum's bypass surgery ... No, she didn't think so. When her thoughts touched upon those situations, she got no frisson of impending danger. She couldn't think of anything else likely to go wrong, but then that was the trouble with having the Sight: it was like trying to tune a radio at night, when your local stations might become pools of static or be drowned out by some far-off station. She was getting something in the way of a premonition, but for now it was more static than message.

"Give me a sign," she muttered, and then she knelt to weed the garden while she waited.

* * *

Spencer Arrowood had called ahead to the Haywood County Public Library at Waynesville, and told them that he wanted to see the battlefield. The patient soul on the other end of the phone, perhaps accustomed to such pilgrimages, offered to relay his request to the local historical society, and a day or two later, he had received a call telling him that a volunteer from the historical society would meet him at the library on Saturday and take him around.

He was fifty-six miles from Asheville, and Waynesville lay maybe an hour southwest of there. As he drove along the new four-lane road that had simplified the over-mountain travel since his childhood, Spencer thought back to the people who had crossed that way before. One of the books said that when Kirk's Legion had crossed into North Carolina to begin their raids on the mountain towns, the Union sympathizers had set fire to trees along the road to guide them over the mountain. He wondered if any part of that old trace was contiguous to the streamlined modern road on which he was now traveling.

Spencer Arrowood had come prepared for tramping across the battlefield. In deference to the thunderheads on the horizon he had brought his raincoat, and he wore his hiking boots and thick trousers in case of snakes. He had a camera, a notebook, and a pocket tape recorder so that he could preserve his findings. Just like going to a crime scene, he thought. Well, perhaps it was a crime scene, in a way. The battle took place after the surrender of the Confederacy, so technically it wasn't a war. He thought there must be some special bitterness attached to dying for a conflict that had already ended elsewhere. He had read about men killed a few hours after the armistice in World War I, and the futility of those deaths had always saddened him. Perhaps that's why he wanted to find this Arrowood, the last man to die in a war that everyone else had stopped fighting. The gener-

als would have been back home, perhaps enjoying a
brandy by the fireplace and reading a translation of Vic-
tor Hugo's new novel, jestingly called *Lee's Miserables*,
and here was poor young Arrowood, not fifty miles
from home, dying in the mud of Haywood County, all
for nothing.

The Waynesville library was a modern red-brick
building, easily found. He pulled into the parking lot a
few minutes early and assembled his gear, checking to
see that his pens worked and that the camera's flash was
functioning properly.

As he entered through the glass door, he saw a silver-
haired gentleman near the check-out counter being
talked at by a leather-faced woman with tinted blond hair.
"I think it's wonderful that you're going to do *Schindler's
List* in the book discussion group," the woman was saying,
"but I wonder what the rednecks will think of it?"

The man caught sight of Spencer in the doorway and
broke off the discussion with the apparent relief of one
who looks through a barrage of arrows to see the cavalry arrive.

"Sheriff Arrowood?" he said, only he pronounced it
"Arwood" as natives of the mountains always did. He
murmured an apology to the strident woman and has-
tened forward, hand outstretched. "Hello, Sheriff. I'm
Ken Collier. Historical society. I understand you're in
need of a guide? Let's go outside." In an undertone he
added, *"Now."*

He hurried out the door, and Spencer followed, re-
pressing a smile. He'd had his own share of persistent
old ladies to contend with. "It's very kind of you to take
the time to show me the battlefield," he said.

"No, I'm glad to do it. Especially at the moment. Why
don't we take my car then? It isn't far."

Spencer retrieved his notebook and camera and
climbed into the passenger seat of Ken Collier's Mercedes.
"You *are* from around here, aren't you, sir?" he asked.

"Now don't *you* start," said Collier. "The Floridians think they're the only people around here who don't ride mules." He made a face. "*What will the rednecks think of* Schindler's List? It was all I could do not to smack her."

Spencer smiled. "Well, I think I would have said, 'The *rednecks* just might think that the first step toward genocide is to start calling an entire group of people by a demeaning name.'"

Collier grunted. "I wish I thought Phyllis was smart enough to get that message. She has an IQ around room temperature, but I may try it on her anyhow."

"I have constituents like her," said Spencer. "Not as many as North Carolina does, but we get the overflow. When they start talking like that, I remind them that most of the locals they actually know have the same middle name—*the*."

"Oh, yes," said Collier. "Shirley *the* maid. Wayne *the* stone mason. Cloyd *the* carpenter."

He drove slowly along the side streets of Waynesville, passing well-kept brick houses and tree-lined streets. "To answer your question, yes, I'm a native of here. Left to go to college, serve in the army and all. But I moved back as soon as I could. I was a research chemist. Retired now. So I play a lot of golf and dabble in history. It's a good life."

"Pretty little town," said Spencer.

"Well, keep it to yourself. Tell folks we have outhouses, and Indian attacks, and toothless Neanderthals marrying their sisters. Otherwise we'll be overrun with people like Phyllis. I say, let them keep going to Oregon and leave us alone."

Spencer, who had been reading census records for weeks, said, "It's funny how many people from here moved to Oregon in the 1880s. New frontiers, I guess. Their descendants stop by my office every now and again, needing directions to the old home place. Names not on the map anymore. Shull's Mill is under a golf course now."

They hadn't come more than a mile from the library, and they had never left the residential area. Spencer had been waiting for the houses to end, looking for a sweep of open field ending in forest at the base of a mountain, but one row of houses gave way to another.

"Waynesville sits in a little bowl in the hollow of the mountains," Collier said. "You can see that. Now when Stoneman ordered Kirk and Bartlett to leave Asheville and search the surrounding mountains for partisan guerrilla forces, this is where they found them. Bartlett and the Second, anyhow. Kirk was off annoying people somewhere else."

Spencer nodded. "Yes, sir. I've read all the material on the skirmish. Just thought I'd see the terrain for myself."

Collier looked over at his passenger. His gaze lingered on the hiking boots, the raincoat, and the camera. "Oh, dear," he said.

Before the sheriff could ask what the matter was, Collier eased the car to the curbside, and parked in front of a one-story ranch house with a carport. Spencer wondered if Collier had decided to make a stop at his own home before going out to the battlefield.

Collier got out and gestured toward a brick outdoor grill beside the driveway, perhaps fifteen feet from the street. "This is it, Sheriff."

Spencer got out and looked around. The street consisted of an unbroken line of small, but well-kept houses on half-acre lots. The architecture of the brick ranches made him think of the early sixties, and the full-grown maples in the front yards confirmed his estimate of the age of the neighborhood. "This is . . . it?" he said.

Collier gave him a rueful smile. "I'm afraid it is. You see, forty years ago people weren't so mindful of local history. Everybody thought history was something that

happened somewhere else. Back then the term Civil
War battlefield meant *Gettysburg* or *Shiloh*. Not Way-
nesville. As battles go, this was pretty small potatoes.
Only one casualty."

Spencer dutifully took a picture of the brick barbecue
grill and looked around at the flower beds and tomato
plants in the meticulous side yard. "Yes. One casualty,"
said Spencer. "I came to find out about him."

"Oh, well, I can tell you all about him," said Collier,
looking relieved that the suburbanized battlefield had
not been too great a disappointment. "The fellow who
was killed was a Union soldier. And his name was Arrowood."

"I know," said Spencer. "Tell me the rest."

Ken Collier blinked. "Well . . . that's it."

"That's *it*? What was his first name? Where did he enlist? What rank did he hold? Who were his parents?"

"Well, we don't have any information on that. But if
you want to know about the Confederate side, it was
Thomas's Legion, you know. The Cherokees. Now
Colonel Thomas—"

"But you know nothing more about the soldier who
was killed?"

"Well, Sheriff. He was a *Union* soldier. Our historical
society is mainly interested in the Confederates. I can
get you a list of Thomas's troops, if you want it."

Spencer shook his head. "No thanks," he said. "I ap-
preciate your bringing me out here, but I have to be getting back now."

If he left right away, there would still be enough time
and daylight to visit Shelton Laurel on the way back
through Madison County. On the drive down, Spencer
had seen the historical marker commemorating the
massacre. The marker said that the execution of the
thirteen Union sympathizers had occurred a few miles
from the location of the sign. Spencer wondered if there
would be anything commemorating the site where the

killing took place. Something other than a barbecue grill, he added to himself.

They got back into the Mercedes and retraced the route to the library. "It's funny, isn't it?" said Collier.

"What's that?"

"Well, Will Thomas and his Cherokees *won* the Battle of Waynesville. The Confederates won the last battle. Bartlett sent out a flag of truce and went to a parlay with General Martin and Colonel Thomas, who were attended by tomahawk-toting Cherokees in war paint, feathers, and very little else. That must have been a sight." He scowled. "Phyllis is expecting them to show up in her kitchen any day now, I reckon."

Spencer thought about it. What do you do when you've won the battle but lost the war? "So Bartlett surrendered to the Confederates after the war was over?"

"Not exactly. After the commanders finished shouting at one another—and Thomas threatening to scalp some Yankees, I hear tell—they all agreed that it was futile to continue the hostilities. So they did some paperwork, made some concessions, and everybody went home. Not with a bang, but with a whimper."

Spencer nodded. "Well, except for Arrowood."

Ken Collier nodded. "Well, Sheriff, maybe it would help if you thought of it as the military equivalent of being killed by a drunk driver. Wrong place at the wrong time, a needless death, sure, but not at all unusual in the scheme of things. Just bad luck."

He pulled into the parking space next to Spencer's car. Spencer shook his hand again and thanked him for his time, and as he turned to leave, Collier said, "Drive safely now, Mr. Arrowood."

Nora Bonesteel had finished weeding her garden, and had made a pitcher of iced tea in case the sign, when it turned up, was thirsty. Now she was sweeping the front

porch, when a car pulled into the driveway, and Jane Arrowood—the only woman in Wake County who still
wore white gloves in the daytime—got out, waving as
she came up the path.

Nora set aside the broom and brushed off the already-
clean cushions of the wicker chairs. By the time she returned from the kitchen with the iced tea pitcher and
glasses on a tray, her visitor was sitting in the wicker
chair, fanning herself with the minutes of the Watauga
Pioneers' last meeting.

"You're a long way from that meeting," Nora said as
she set the tray down on the little wicker table. Ashe
Mountain was a lóng way from anywhere, and no one
dropped in on Nora Bonesteel by accident.

"I know," said Jane. "I was hoping I could persuade
you to come to the meeting this afternoon in case
there's a vote. Some of the men have gone off to fight
the war, and I'm afraid we'll be outnumbered."

Nora blinked. "Fight the war?"

"Oh, you know! Those play-acting soldiers! They
dress up in old uniforms and go fight the Civil War
again. I swear, girls play dress-up when they're little, but
boys wait 'til they're forty! That's not what I wanted to
talk to you about, though. It's this theme business for
the annual fund-raising dinner and silent auction."

Nora looked thoughtful, staring out at the mountain
in the distance, whose rock countenance called the
Hangman dominated the view from her front porch.

"There's considerable disagreement about the theme,
and the front-runner at the moment is Southwestern.
All turquoise and coral with coyotes, cactuses, and
Kokopelli. He's a flute-playing god of the Navajo or the
Zuni, or somebody. He's not Cherokee, I can tell you
that."

For a moment Nora's gaze wavered from the distant
mountain. "Navajo? But what does that have to do with
here?"

"Well, not a blessed thing," said Jane. "It's these silly new people who want to pretend that they live in Arizona with unlimited water and seasons. You know—the western mountains are fashionable. All the catalogues feature turquoise this and coral that, and cactuses and coyotes all over everything. And of course they don't have any roots here, so they're just going with what's trendy."

"They?"

Jane nodded. "I'm afraid it's going to be a showdown between the old people and the new people. I was hoping you'd come and give us moral support."

"I cannot go," said Nora. "If I were you I'd ask Dr. Banner to go. He can tell them some of the stories about this land. Don't be too hard on them, though, Jane. They'll settle in one of these days. Both sides ought to give a little." She thought about it for a moment. "Coyotes might be all right. We've got them nowadays."

Jane set down her iced tea glass. "I might have known you'd be all for sweet reason," she sighed.

The old woman smiled. "There's been enough fighting in these mountains," she said. "It's got to stop sometime."

"All right, but are you sure you won't come? It would do you good to get out."

"Thank you, Jane, but this is my day to tend an old grave."

Tom Gentry peered out at the trees across the clearing from his tent, but he could see no blackened limbs or charred trunks. No signs at all of the fire he had seen so clearly the night before. On the hillside opposite his hiding place one tall tree—some sort of evergreen; he didn't know much about tree species—had burned like a torch in the night, and Tom had thought about packing up his belongings and trying to distance himself from the conflagration, but he was too tired to make the effort. He slept a good deal now, and he scarcely stirred from the confines of his shelter. He had wondered at the time if the fire would spread to the surrounding forest, but only the one tree had flamed for hours through the night, and now that it was daytime and he could survey the landscape, he could find no evidence that there had ever been a fire.

He was forced to consider the possibility that he was hallucinating. As his body weaned itself from the physical bonds of life, he had expected to experience visions, but he had hoped for something more exalted than a burning tree on a dark hillside. An angel would have been gratifying, he thought. Or perhaps a visit from his old high school buddy Steve, who had died of a brain tumor at twenty-three. Tom supposed that a saint or a shaman might have been able to turn the flaming evergreen into a sign, but its meaning escaped him. Maybe he had just dreamed it, after all.

He had thought that the reenactors had started it with one of their campfires, but now he supposed that he couldn't blame them for something that had not happened. He wished they would go home, though, because he was afraid that they might stumble across him, despite the fact that he hid when he heard them coming. Still, sometimes it was interesting to peer out from the rhododendrons and watch them pass by. He found it odd that they were so varied in their attempts at authenticity. One stocky fellow who looked too old to be anything but a general strode past talking into a cell phone, and then a few hours later a blue-uniformed soldier strode past looking like he had walked straight out of a Matthew Brady photograph. Did they have some sort of dress code in the reenactment organization?

A few days earlier Tom might have contrived to stroll into their encampment and ask them, but now he could no longer risk being seen. He was bleary-eyed, unshaven, and unsteady on his feet. One look at him would send the soldiers into a panic, and the cell phone would be used to summon an ambulance.

He would just watch from the thicket, he decided. He wondered if there was going to be a battle. He didn't know much about the Civil War, because he came from a state too far removed from the fighting to dwell on the subject in its American history classes. The uniforms stirred no instinctive emotions in him. It was a pageant, that's all, like watching a foreign ceremony on the travel channel.

As long as both armies left him alone, Tom Gentry was indifferent to them.

Malinda

In April we got word that the war was over, and the Pritchards laughed and whooped, and then straight-away prayed their thanks to the Almighty, because they were safe now from the thieving no-accounts on both sides. They thought the war was over. I didn't. One look at Keith's scarred and stony face ought to have told them different.

When baby Columbus seen his daddy for the first time after the shooting, he screamed and hid his face against my dress. Keith just set his jaw and didn't say nothing to the child for a good while after that, and finally Columbus came around and let himself be dandled on his daddy's knee. Pretty soon I think he forgot there was anything different about Keith's face at all. Keith never forgot though. Even after he put a patch over that hollow eye socket, he took to sitting off by himself in the yard, not whittling, but just running his knife blade along the edge of a stick, skinning it, and then throwing it away and picking up another one. Once he said, "I will settle up with the man that killed Austin Coffey if it takes me forty years to do it."

It's easier to start a war than it is to stop one.

Some wars don't end when the generals shake hands and go home. Sometimes they just burn on down deep like a fire in a coal mine—giving no outward sign of trouble but flaming on in the darkness just the same.

The last battle was in May in Waynesville, but an army is like a runaway wagon, and takes a long time after you yell *whoa!* to stop it rolling forward. It was October before the Tenth Michigan let us turn in our gear, and then wrote up the paperwork so that Keith could go home. Captain Minihan allowed as how Keith was so shot up that he was entitled to a disability pension, and he explained that we would get a monthly check at the post office ever after on account of Keith being too sick to work. Keith took one of his first checks and bought himself a seven-shooting Spencer rifle, for we had given our government-issue ones back to the army.

We went back to our place in Globe in the winter of '66, and you might have thought we'd be hounded and shot at by our Rebel neighbors on account of what had happened over the past three years, but either they were tired of fighting or else they were mindful that we were on the side that won, because by and large folks left us alone. Of course, Keith took that rifle with him every time he left the house, so maybe they didn't fancy their chances, even with a one-eyed man.

Keith kept on brooding about Daddy Austin, though. If it was me, I'd a been spoiling for revenge against the Moores for that lost eye and the scarred face, but Keith seemed to think that he had been wounded in a fair fight and that he give as good as he got, so he called it quits with the Moore clan. Men are funny like that. They'll forgive a real injury that a woman would kill over, and then they'll choke on a little point of honor that makes no difference to anything.

"That John Boyd is no better than Judas," Keith kept saying. "He went over to McCaleb's house with the

Home Guard and he pointed out Daddy Austin for them, same as Judas did in the garden, and I will get him for it."

It wasn't no use to tell him that the war was over. I must have said that a dozen times, and now it had got to where I didn't believe it either.

He didn't wait long. In February 1866, just a few weeks after our boy had turned three, Keith went out with Tom Wright who had rode with us some of the time when we was bushwhacking. I don't know if it was happenstance or if they was hunting on purpose, but along about evening they was on a path in the Caldwell County end of the Globe Valley, and they heard somebody coming and hid in the brush. The two men come up closer, talking to one another, and then Keith could see it was John Boyd his own self, out walking with young Will Blair who was fixing to marry Boyd's daughter.

Boyd was hobbling along on a stick, for he had taken a bullet in the last days of the war, too. When Keith recognized his enemy, he stepped out of the bushes and said, "Is that you, Boyd?"

Boyd must have took fright at seeing Keith appear out of nowhere, with that eye patch on his torn-up face and a Spencer rifle in the crook of his arm. Boyd swatted at him hard with his walking stick, and caught Keith on the arm, making him stagger back a step or two, and then I reckon nothing in the world could have saved John Boyd.

Keith swung that rifle around and aimed it square at Boyd's chest, blowing a gourd-sized hole in him, spraying them all with blood and bits, and sending the man crashing to the ground, face down. Boyd's would-be son-in-law was backing away, but Keith gestured toward the body with his rifle, and said, "Do you turn him over, and let's see that he's dead."

So Blair knelt down and turned Boyd over, best he could, and when he didn't stir, they were satisfied that he was done for. Then Keith and Tom walked on down the track just leaving Blair there with the corpse. Directly they come to a house, and Keith knocked on the door and told the man, "I have just settled with John Boyd. I am going home now. You tell the provost marshal it's me he wants, and not Tom Wright here. Will Blair will tell you the same. He saw it all."

They came home then, and Tom told me most of what went on.

"Do you reckon they'll hang him?" I asked Tom, when Keith had gone outside to wash up.

He shook his head. "I don't know. They got a witness, that Blair. I told Keith he should have killed him, too."

"No," I said. "Keith is funny about settling scores. He didn't have no quarrel with Blair, even if he did fight for the Rebels, so to Keith's lights it would have been murder to shoot him. But Boyd was different. He had it coming."

"Well, I hope the jury gives him credit for his delicacy," said Tom.

I hoped so, too.

It was Federal soldiers that come for Keith, and I was glad to see them, for I thought he stood a better chance of making it to jail in one piece with them than with the local lawmen. They took him down to Morganton, which isn't too far from home, not that I would want him held any nearer. No jury in Watauga or Caldwell was likely to be open-minded about Keith Blalock. The provost marshal must have been to my way of thinking about that, for he set the trial to be held in Statesville—farther east still, but he said that Keith could do his waiting in the jail at Morganton so that his family wouldn't have to travel so far to visit him.

Major Frank Walcott was one of the military commissioners in charge of western North Carolina now, and when he heard how Keith was a veteran of the Tenth Michigan, with a pension to prove it, he went to see

Keith in the Morganton jail and asked him how he had come to shoot John Boyd. "The war is over now, Mr. Blalock," he said.

"Well, it is for some, and for some it isn't," said Keith.

"But the witness says you shot that man in cold blood."

So Keith told him how John Boyd had led the Home Guard to McCaleb's house and pointed out Daddy Austin for the soldiers. And how the dog had brought Daddy Austin's hand back from Shull's Mill, and how Daddy Austin's widow dreamed of it to this day and would wake up screaming.

"I owed him," said Keith. "And I paid him."

"But an unarmed man, sir!"

Keith scowled. "Who told you that? Boyd was toting a cane that could break your head wide open. He laid into me with that cane before I ever touched him, so I shot him."

Major Walcott chewed on that awhile. "Self-defense, then? And I suppose your neighbors are persecuting you on account of your allegiance to the Union cause?"

"They devil me night and day," said Keith, seeing the bolt-hole.

"Well, I think that's all I need to know about this case then, Mr. Blalock," said the major.

"Sir, do you think you could arrest those Home Guard men who killed Austin Coffey? I can give you their names," said Keith.

The major hesitated, and finally he said, "I think you know that a life for a life is a fair settlement. Why don't we leave it at that?"

So the major told Judge Mitchell that the shooting of John Boyd was as clear a case of self-defense as could be made out, and the upshot of it was that in March they said Keith was free to go, and we got the horses and headed west for home.

"That ought to show those Rebels a thing or two," said Keith, with a big smirk on his face.

I put my hand on his horse's rein and pulled. "It stops now, Keith," I said.

He tried to jerk the reins away, but I held fast. "Oh, come on, Malinda," he said. "You heard what the major said. There ain't no harm in shooting Rebels. They lost the war."

"You got lucky," I said. "After all the times the world has given us the short end of the stick, somebody finally bent over backwards to do you a favor, but don't make too much of it, Keith. The Union army wants peace in these mountains, if only to make things easier on themselves, and if you go around prolonging your own private war, they will string you up like a mad dog, and don't you think they won't."

I let go of the reins then, and we rode along in silence for a while, seeing the dark shapes of the mountains looming up ahead of us. Finally Keith said, "Will you miss the war, Malinda?"

"Yes," I said. "But it'll be a good miss."

Zebulon Vance

Attorney-at-Law—1866

I had been released from the Old Capitol Prison in Washington and told to go home to await further instructions, which I took to mean that the government could arrest me again any time they took a notion. I waited, but they never did come back for me. Since I had been a high-ranking Confederate official I was prohibited from holding office in the restored United States, so for the foreseeable future, I was barred from politics. That left the law, as I had never trained for any other profession. Well, I suppose I could have become an educator, but as I had told Governor Letcher, the ordeal of setting a good example would overwhelm me, whereas in the law I had only wrongdoers to outshine.

Harriett and I moved the family to Charlotte, and in March of 1866 I entered into a law practice with two distinguished old friends, Clement Dowd and R.D. Johnston.

Augustus Merrimon was a district judge. Sometimes I think that when I reach the Hereafter, I will find that Augustus Merrimon has got there first, and has got first pick of the harps—or the pitchforks.

I did my best for my legal clients, but my heart wasn't in the practice of law. I had no interest in wealth—and wasn't going to get any anyhow practicing law in North Carolina—and since the meddlesome Reconstruction government controlled most of the judgeships, and they were none too fond of me, I made up my mind to endure my servitude before the bar until the people of the state were permitted to elect me to something again.

In late September Nicholas Woodfin and his wife came to visit us in Charlotte. Eliza Grace Woodfin was a daughter of the McDowell family of Morganton in whose home my wife had spent her youth, and Harriett was delighted with the prospect of a visit. After dinner we left the ladies to their discussions of gardening and ladies' fashions, and Woodfin and I repaired to our covered front porch, for the weather was mild and pleasant for the season.

"How goes the law practice?" Woodfin asked me, when we had exhausted the topic of politics and exchanged information on our old friends and comrades. We did not speak of Woodfin's brother John, who had been killed at Warm Springs by Kirk's Legion, but he was by no means forgotten. I got my start in life under the Woodfins' tutelage, and I would always be grateful that when my Rough and Ready Guards left Asheville to go to war, Nicholas Woodfin's daughters had presented us with our first battle flag, sewn from scraps of their silk dresses. I felt that my life was entwined with the Woodfins as much as Harriett's was.

"My law practice?" I said, taking a sip of my apple brandy. "Well, it's tolerable. I have a devil of a case coming up in Wilkes County. A murder case. Well, it's set for trial in Wilkes, but I hope to have it transferred to Iredell County for the trial. Statesville."

Woodfin smiled. "Statesville has been getting its share of interesting trials lately. Were you there last spring when they tried that Union bushwhacker for shooting down an enemy a year after the war was over?"

"Blalock? I heard about it. They let him off, as I recall. His Union army friends claimed it was self-defense while the eyewitness said otherwise. I suppose it's now open season on Confederates, but I do what I can to obtain justice, anyhow."

"I wish you joy of it," said Woodfin.

"Well, my current case has nothing to do with politics, though the defendant is a veteran. I simply thought that Statesville would provide me with the change of venue I needed for a cool and rational jury."

"Judging from the results of the last election, they like you better in Iredell county than they do in Wilkes, anyhow. But a murder trial is a great responsibility, Zeb. Are you sure you're ready for such a burden so soon after resuming your practice of law?"

He seemed so concerned by the prospect of my taking the case that I said, "Why do you ask?"

"Such cases haunt a man," Woodfin said. "I only ever took one murder case in my entire career, and that was in my first year of practice. A young mountain woman—a Mrs. Silver—was accused of killing her husband and dismembering the body postmortem. Although I later came to believe that the poor woman had acted to preserve her own life, I did not succeed in saving her from the hangman's noose. David Swain was governor then, and it was he who refused to grant her a pardon."

This sidetracked us for a bit into a discussion of the University at Chapel Hill, and of Swain's new son-in-law, the Yankee general, but Woodfin could not be diverted from his memories of that old trial. "The case has haunted me ever since," he said, "and I never took another."

"Well, I doubt if I shall be much troubled by the poor fellow in this instance," I said. "His only saving grace is that he made a good soldier. He fought with the Forty-second North Carolina, but otherwise all accounts call him a terrible and desperate character."

"What has he done?"

"He murdered a young girl. Stabbed her to death. It is a sordid tale. The fellow—he is only twenty-two—was having"—I glanced around to see that no one was within earshot of the porch—"intimate relations with a married woman in the community, *and* with her visiting cousin from Tennessee, *and* with the young woman who was murdered. The prosecution contends that my client killed the girl because she had given him what he calls the pock."

"Good heavens!" said Woodfin. "How do you plan to defend this wretch?"

"Well, my client and his married paramour are both charged for the murder of Laura Foster. First I intend to petition to get them tried separately. The evidence in the case is circumstantial at best. Maybe the fellow did it. Maybe the married woman. The State doesn't have the evidence to prove it, either way. Still, I don't suppose I can save him. For all my efforts, I expect he will hang one of these days."

"What is the prisoner's name?" asked Woodfin.

I told him.

"Well," he said, "perhaps it isn't as troublesome a murder case as the one I had. Poor little Mrs. Silver's name will resound in legend, but a year from now no one is going to remember the sordid story of Tom Dooley."

"It's Dula," I said.

He smiled. "See? I've forgotten it already."

I was right about that. Tom Dula was found guilty of the murder of Laura Foster, and hanged from the back of a cart in Statesville in 1868. Perhaps the only noble thing he ever did in his life was near the end of it, when he

wrote out a paper confessing to the crime and saying
that his codefendant, Ann Melton, was guiltless in the
murder. I don't know that I believe him, but I defended
her, too, and that bit of paper saved her life. They say
that she died of syphilis a few years later, raving about
black cats and demons that had come for her soul—so
perhaps there is justice somewhere, after all.

I endured a few years of the practice of law, and then
I ran for the United States Senate in 1870. I won, and
those sorry rascals refused me admission to Congress,
claiming that I had not been "pardoned" for the crime
of losing the war. I tried to overcome this difficulty but
it was no use, so I gave it up, and ran again two years
later.

This time I was defeated in the election.

By Augustus Merrimon.

It was a peculiar sort of contest. I don't know that I'd
have believed it of old Merrimon who has a hymn book
for a soul. Merrimon and I were in a protracted wrangle
over the post of senator, and since neither of us were
making any headway against the obstinance of the
other, we both withdrew our names from consideration.
I went back to my law cases, and Merrimon had cases to
adjudicate from the bench and so we thought we were
quits. When he left, though, the Democrats nominated
me again. I suppose they thought they'd square it with
me later. The Republicans, not to be outdone went and
nominated Augustus Summerfield Merrimon as their
candidate—without his permission. He *says*.

Then the House met in a joint session to take a vote,
for that's how the senator was to be selected. It was Reconstruction still and things weren't entirely normal.
The Republican weasels all voted for Merrimon to confound the Democrats, and a few sincere Democrats who
had backed him anyhow voted for him as they had always intended to. And he won.

Then they sent a delegation to his courtroom to tell

him that he had been elected United States Senator from the state of North Carolina. They tell me he thought it over. Weighed the irregular circumstances behind his elevation to the post. Consulted Governor Graham and other distinguished political animals to tender advice. And then he jumped on the appointment like a duck on a June bug.

When I was four years old, the frontiersman Davy Crockett had been turned out of his seat in Congress by his Tennessee constituents, and he told them that they could go to hell and he would go to Texas, but I shall not follow his example. I never liked the idea of running away from anything.

I hope I behaved better about my loss than Merrimon did when I defeated him for our first lawyering job back in Asheville so many years ago. I hope I shook his paw and wished him well. But privately I resolved that his stay in Washington should be a short one if I had any say in the matter.

Terms of office are relatively brief, and my time will come again. I might like to try being governor again, too. I never had a chance to enjoy the office the first two times, what with the war and all. I mean to try it in peacetime for a change.

Rattler

Seeing the reenactors back and camped out in my neck of the woods did not surprise me one bit. I knew it wouldn't do any good to talk to McCullough and try to warn them off, not without telling them exactly what the trouble was, and I was afraid that Jeff had too much education to listen to reason on matters like that.

What did surprise me was that the moon and stars were out. I had been looking for a potentate of thunderstorms to blow in and shroud the valley in darkness well before sunset, bringing cutting winds and lightning like cannon fire to pierce the fog. I'd had a storm feeling all day—hairs on the back of my neck standing up, and the air smelling funny, the way it does. But I waited and waited, staying around close to home so as not to get caught in it, and by and by the sun set and the breeze cooled and a million stars came out like a cloth spread over the mountaintops.

"Well, this is as fine a summer night as a body could ask for," I said out loud. "I believe I'll go over and see what the sunshine soldiers are up to."

I found them camped out in that wide, flat meadow

about halfway down the mountain on the North Carolina side. People loved it up there. The rhododendrons on the edge of the field made it into a garden in June, and the view eastward looked out over miles of blue and purple ridges, rolling on toward the horizon like ripples on a lake. About all you could ever see of civilization from up there were the little dots of rich people's houses far down in the valley like little stars on a velvet quilt, stretching on toward Boone. Other than that it must have looked the same for a thousand years—except for the chestnut trees, which we lost, but don't get me started on that.

Jeff McCullough was stretched out on a quilt in front of his tent with his eyes closed, listening to a couple of fiddle players who were practicing tunes a dozen yards away.

"Evening," I said.

McCullough opened one eye, got me into focus and grinned. "Why, hello, Rattler! How did you find us?"

"Heard the music," I said, nodding toward the fiddlers.

"Forget your flashlight?"

"My eyes are still good in the dark, full moon and all."

"Well, you're a little late for supper, but if you'll give me a minute, I'll try to scare you up a plate."

I shook my head. "I'm not hungry, thanks all the same. I just came to see how you were doing."

He sat up and motioned for me to join him on the quilt. It was an old one—soft from many washings and so finely stitched that the pattern hardly made a bump under your hand. "This quilt has a nice feel to it," I said. "Of course I can't see much of the pattern in the dark."

"It's a double ring pattern," said McCullough. "My grandmother made it."

"I know the pattern," I said. "Interlocking circles."

"Right. It's only about sixty years old, but you find

the same design carved on stones all over Scotland and Ireland—the design must be four thousand years old. This quilt is quite an heirloom. My grandmother made it out of old feed sacks during the Depression. You know they used to print feed sacks with designs on them so that people could make clothes out of the empty sacks. This one had little four-leaf clovers. And feel the squares right here where the rings come together."

I slid my hand over the cloth. "Wool?"

"Green army uniform. My grandfather's."

"And you brought it on a camping trip?"

"You're thinking it belongs in a museum? It's too beat up for that. We've used it for as long as I can remember."

I sat down beside him on the quilt and looked up at the stars. "I was kind of hoping you'd talk the reenactors out of doing this," I said.

"Oh, don't worry," said McCullough. "We aren't staging a battle. We're just camping out, socializing."

I gave him a long look. "In Confederate uniforms?"

"Well, just for practice. We came out and did some target shooting—"

"With muzzle-loaders?"

"Well, sure." I could hear the bewilderment in his voice. "We didn't want to miss a chance to practice for the next event."

In the place, with the weapons of the time . . . I shuddered. "You seem a little short-handed out here tonight."

"Well, three of the guys went off to Johnson City to see that new war movie, and Wade Jessup swore it was going to rain, and he and two of his buddies went to bed down in that old church a mile or so away."

"So it's just you and the fiddlers, huh?" I said.

"That's right. The joke's on Jessup, I guess. It sure doesn't look like rain." He leaned back and looked up at the stars. "Aren't they beautiful? The same stars the real soldiers would have seen when they camped up. Just the same . . ."

I felt a breath of cold wind on my neck. "Just the same . . ."

"It's a feeling of connection, Rattler. I don't know why, but I—What's that? Forest fire?"

Jeff grabbed my arm and pointed to a spot on one of the nearby ridges, along about the gap where the old road led over into North Carolina.

I looked where he was pointing, and saw a tall tree in flames. Just the one tree, blazing like a torch in the darkness, but the fire wasn't spreading to anything else, and though the wind was blowing cold from that quarter, I didn't smell any smoke.

"I don't see nothing," I said.

"How can you miss it? It must be twenty feet high, burning like crazy."

But I wasn't looking at the tree anymore. I had turned away and was looking out in the darkness across the valley to the east. The mountains were still dark shapes meeting the starry sky, and it took me a minute to figure out what was wrong with what I was looking at, but finally I noticed.

The valley was dark.

I turned my head this way and that, trying to catch a glimpse of one of those new houses that usually glowed in the black hollow of the valley down there like lightning bugs in clover. But they were gone. *Well maybe they all went to the movies, too,* I thought, but I knew better. It was just like the Ravenmocker had said: A resonance had been set in motion, and things were starting to happen.

"Jeff, I said. "I want you to promise me something with the most solemn oath you have. Will you do that?"

"I guess, Rattler. What a strange . . . Well, what is it?"

"This quilt. I want your oath that no matter what happens—no matter what, McCullough!—you will not move one inch off this quilt of yours until I tell you to. Swear it."

"Okay." He sounded bewildered, but a little scared, too, because he could hear how serious I was, and he'd heard things about me. The Sight and all. "What's happening?"

"Don't you feel it?" I asked him. Because I did.

The wind had picked up, but the sky was still clear— same sky as 1864, I thought, when east Tennessee's Union loyalists had set that tree alight to guide Stoneman's raiders over the pass into North Carolina. But it was more than the wind and the vanishing lights of the houses in the valley. It was a feeling, as if a heavy weight was pressing down on my head, and a prickling sensation that means something is watching you.

The fiddlers had quit playing now, and the silence was sharp. One of them called out, "Is anything wrong, McCullough?"

"It's just Rattler stopping by," McCullough called out to them, trying to keep the strain out of his voice.

"Do y'all know any hymns?" I asked. "Something old?"

They got quiet for a minute, and then we heard the bow drawn across the strings and the first notes of "Abide With Me" cut through the stillness. "That might help some," I said.

"Rattler, what is going on?—Is there somebody watching us?"

"Or some thing. What are you doing? I told you to stay on that quilt!"

"I am, but my gun is in the tent . . . just a second . . . there! I've got it."

"Oh, wonderful," I said. "You've got a muzzle-loader and a cartridge box. Now we're safe. That's what started all this in the first place. You toy soldiers have been calling things up out of the past. I tried to tell you."

"Well, you didn't put it like that."

"Shhh! Let's not argue about it. I got a feeling that any more anger in the air will just make things worse."

"Well, what are we supposed to do?" McCullough was whispering now, and I knew that if it hadn't been for the lights and that burning tree, he'd have left long ago.

"We wait," I said. "Maybe they'll leave us be."

I didn't think so, though. The air thickened and through the suffocating stillness we could hear the tinny sounds of the fiddlers starting another tune.

"Why can't we run for it, Rattler?"

"Run where? They're all around us. You ought to be able to feel that."

"I feel something."

"I'll bet you do. Stay on the quilt."

"Why? Why on the quilt?"

"Because of the pattern mostly, though the love and the family connection will help, too. Your granddaddy's army uniform. That's powerful. But mostly it's the pattern. Don't you know about quilts?"

"What about them?"

"Well, they go back a long ways. Back to a time when people knew about what waited out there beyond the circle of light. And in those days when a woman made a coverlet to put over a loved one in the dark, she would fashion it with every symbol of protection that she could think of. To keep them safe through the night. People forgot what those old patterns meant, but they kept putting them on quilts anyhow. You said it yourself, Jeff: Those interlocking rings form a design that they once carved on rocks in Ireland. It's old magic."

"What's out there?"

"Soldiers. Or maybe something else. My kinfolks used to tell an old story about a wild hunt . . . the devil's hounds, maybe . . . Anyhow, it's evil. It can hurt us. And it's coming closer."

We hunkered down there, feeling the force of a storm that wasn't there, and I began to think I heard hoofbeats and voices, and then shots and the sound of shouting off in the distance, but drawing nearer.

Then I remembered that they had stopped for me once, and I was turning that fact over in my mind, wondering if the invitation was still open, and whether they might take me and leave the rest of them alone.

I noticed that I couldn't see out across the valley anymore. It looked like some low-slung clouds was hanging above it. The sounds of moving soldiers was louder, too. I got to my knees, getting ready to stand up and step off that quilt.

"You just stay put!" said a voice from the darkness.

We turned toward the copse of trees, and saw a shadowed figure coming toward us, emerging finally into the moonlight.

Nora Bonesteel.

She looked stern and terrible, but more fed up than afraid, as if we were a bunch of naughty schoolboys she had caught in her apple orchard. Seems to me like I remember that look from a long time ago. Her white hair shone in the moonlight, and she was wrapped in some kind of long knit shawl that made her look like some old priestess of yore. She looked at Jeff and me cowering on the quilt, and then over at the pair of fiddlers, whose playing had trailed off when she appeared.

"What is going on here?" she asked—only I wasn't sure who it was she was asking.

It was McCullough who answered her, though. "I think the world is coming to an end," he said.

And she gave a short little laugh that didn't mean she was amused at all. "Don't give me that, young man," she said. "It's only you young people who go around thinking that the world's going to end when things go wrong. Old people *know* it will. Ten years—twenty at most— and there's an end to it. Oh, it keeps on going for everybody else, but it'll end for us right enough." She was looking off toward the road that led back down the mountain. "Or at least it should end for you when you leave it. You're supposed to let go, do you hear!"

"They're back," said McCullough. "They're alive."

She rounded on him again. "Is that what you call living? 'Cause I don't. Skulking around on the edge of the world, still fighting the same old war. It isn't a forever that I want any part of. Anyhow, whatever it is, it stops now. The war is over now, and if it isn't, it should be. High time. Now go home. All of you."

The pressure seemed to ease a little, as if something that had drawn closer to us took a step back.

McCullough raised his head and peered at her in the darkness. "That's it? Just go home and forget about it?"

"No. You should remember. Remember what all this anger and hatred leads to, and what it feels like. Yes, you remember." She nodded her head toward the shadows. "It's them that has to forget."

She waited a moment, and the wind blew again, and the fog began to drift away from the valley, and the lights were back.

Gently now, Nora Bonesteel said to the darkness, "Go on now. There's nothing for you here."

She came over to the quilt and settled herself between us. "I reckon we'll wait here awhile until they've gone," she said. "Yes, we'll wait on this quilt you had sense enough to bring, young man, for they won't go away empty-handed."

The man sat in the opening of his makeshift tent watching the riders approach. He had wrapped a blanket around his shoulders, but he was still cold. He was cold all the time now. But not hungry. Not anymore. At first he thought the moving shapes were deer coming to graze in the moonlight, but as they drew nearer, out from the cover of the trees, he saw that the beasts were horses and that they carried riders.

These must be the soldiers he had glimpsed before in the distance. The ones he hid from. But he was not afraid of them now. He was past caring, past feeling much of anything except the spinning. He felt quite light-headed, as if he could float away were it not for the nylon covering of the tent keeping him earthbound.

The riders drew nearer.

Tom Gentry thought of getting up to go and greet them, but he found that his legs no longer wanted to take him anywhere, so instead he nodded to them and summoned a smile.

The man in the dark greatcoat touched his hat and nodded in return. "You a soldier?" he said.

"Well, I was . . ." He would have said more, told them about being stationed in San Diego, and how he didn't really like all those people he had to be around all the time, but he found that his throat hurt with the effort, and his voice sounded hoarse and unnatural.

He looked past the leader to the other figures on horseback waiting a short distance away. One of them was holding a white pony by a lead rein. An extra mount.

The dark man leaned forward and said softly, "Would you care to ride with us?"

"I can't ride," Tom said. "And I'm too far gone to walk anymore."

"If you want to go with us, you can," said the leader. "It won't hurt. Are you scared?"

Tom thought he might be, but he didn't want the dark man and the others to laugh at him. "I'll go," he said, and he felt another gust of cold wind rush past him. "Yes," he said. "I'll go. Is it far?"

One of them laughed, and the leader said, "We don't know. We ain't got there yet."

Tom Gentry struggled to his feet and took a few tottering steps toward the white pony gleaming in the moonlight.

Richard Battle—1900

They are unveiling a statue to Zebulon Vance today on Capitol Square in Raleigh, and I am to give the memorial address at the dedication. Dead these six years, and still the eulogies roll on.

I wonder if he would have got to be president if it had not been for the war. I never heard him say that he minded, though. I left off being the governor's assistant in '64, when he appointed me state auditor. After the war, I went back to the practice of law in Raleigh, joining my father and brother Kemp in a law firm. I dabbled in politics, but I had no wish for high office. Zebulon Vance had no wish for anything else.

He was elected to the senate again after Senator Merrimon's term ended. He got to be governor again in 1876, and from there he went back to the U.S. Senate, and there he stayed for the rest of his life. He grew stout and his health deteriorated over the years, and in 1891 he had to have his eye removed after a fall from a wagon on his North Carolina estate, but he kept working and seemed to have given no thought to retirement.

In November 1878 the frail Mrs. Harriett Espy Vance

died after a long illness, and when the Senator's year of mourning was over, he married a wealthy widow from Kentucky, Mrs. Florence Steele Martin. They don't talk about her much. I've read the biographies and the eulogies and the tributes to Vance, and Miss Harriett is praised loud and long, but you could go over those books with a divining rod and never find a word about Florence Martin. Now I wonder why that is.

Anyhow, after a long life of service to the people of North Carolina, Senator Vance died in office at his home in Washington a month shy of his sixty-fourth birthday. You would have thought that a star had fallen from the heavens the way people carried on. They had the first funeral in the Senate chamber in Washington on Monday the sixteenth, and then the senator's mortal remains were sent back from the capital on the Richmond & Danville Railroad, and mournful Tarheels lined the tracks for a glimpse of the train so that they could say their own farewells to "Zeb."

Many eulogies were given in his honor, in the State Capitol, where his body made a ceremonial stop for more obsequies, and then the train went on to make more memorial stops before weeping crowds at Greensboro, Salisbury, Morganton, and Hickory before it delivered him at last to Asheville. Old soldiers wept; the flags flew at half-staff; and when the funeral carriage reached its destination, a company of militia was needed to remove the floral tributes that Vance had garnered along the way. The funeral had to be held in the city's largest church to accommodate the crowds. I was there.

There is one story that people don't tell, though. I'll wager it doesn't make the history books, but I am old and garrulous now, and I knew the senator well enough to suppose that he wouldn't mind my telling this tale. He'd have told it himself if he could have.

In his final days, Senator Vance had expressed a wish

to be buried in Asheville. His son Charles was with him when he died. Not his new wife. His last words were *Charley, stay here, stay here.* Does that mean anything? I have wondered.

Anyhow, a delegation from the state of North Carolina asked that Vance be buried in Raleigh, but the widow Florence declined the honor, saying that she would grant his wish to be laid to rest in Asheville. And so he was, with a church full of dignitaries and all the pomp the state could muster. Schools and business closed for the occasion, and the procession to the cemetery comprised so many people that it's a wonder there was anybody left to watch it pass.

Zebulon Vance was buried in Riverside Cemetery in a plot purchased long ago for himself and Harriett, and he had left instructions that she should be disinterred from the Presbyterian Cemetery and laid to rest beside him. They held another memorial service the next day in Charlotte for the folks who couldn't gain admittance to the one in Asheville.

That, but for the mourning, should have been the end of Zeb Vance, but it is never wise to underestimate old Zeb.

A few weeks after the funeral, Charles N. Vance went back to Riverside to visit his father's grave, to leave a bunch of flowers perhaps. And instead of a mound of freshly turned earth, he found an empty hole. Well, there are people in the Carolina mountains who wouldn't be surprised to hear that Zeb Vance had got up after three days and gone back to work. There is a divine precedent for it, you know. But the wise and learned Charles N. Vance didn't think of resurrection for one moment. He marched up to the office of the cemetery keeper and demanded to know what had become of the earthly remains of Zebulon Baird Vance.

A stammering J. H. McConnell, grave digger, explained to the irate chief mourner that the senator had been moved to choicer accommodations.

"By whose order?" thundered Vance, evoking memories of his father in a temper.

"Why, the widow's," said McConnell.

"The widow. I see. And just where did you take him?"

"Just up the hill there, sir," the shaky finger pointed to the summit of a nearby hill, a promontory from which one could see for miles across the French Broad River to the valley beyond. "Mrs. Florence Vance bought that hilltop plot herself just last week. She said there would be a statue built to Mr. Vance, and that he ought to be in a more exclusive address where it could be seen. So we moved him. Is that all right with you, sir?"

Charley thought it over. "Provided that you move my mother's remains to that site, I shall not object," he said.

The grave digger shifted from one foot to the other. "Well, now Mr. Charles, I'd like to accommodate you, but the widow was most precise in her instructions. Senator Vance only. Not the first missus."

Charles Vance gave the poor man a look that could have melted sand. "Mr. McConnell," he said, "get your shovel. We're moving Daddy right back down the hill."

And they did. The story made the newspapers in June—a nine days wonder—with Miss Florence writing in her version of the story, and Mr. Charles as frosty as river ice holding his ground, so Zeb stayed put. At least I think he did. If the widow Florence was later discovered in Riverside Cemetery with a shovel and a lantern, I never heard tell of it.

Oh, dear me, even in death Zeb Vance cannot resist a jest. He outlived Augustus Merrimon by three years, and that is just as well. Merrimon was buried quietly, causing hardly a ripple in his lifelong home. He would have been appalled by the unseemly goings-on in the Riverside matter, but beyond that I think he would have minded that Zeb was so beloved that even in death, people fought over him. Judge Merrimon was a good and able man, but he never inspired the love and admiration that his rival took for granted.

Well, it is time to stop wool-gathering and give my speech. The dignitaries are waiting. Perhaps in my old friend's memory I will permit myself a small jest at the close of my oration. Perhaps I will say, "*Requiescat in pace.*"

Martha Jane Hollifield
Blalock—1913

Seventy-six years old, he was, and spry as ary grandson. If it hadn't been for the railroad, I expect the old devil would have lived forever. If being shot point blank in the face didn't kill him, and committing cold-blooded murder in front of an eyewitness didn't get him hanged, I reckon he could have outlived the French Broad River, but the railroad done him in. The war has been over for nigh on fifty years, and do you know there was still people in these hills who wouldn't speak his name above a whisper? They reckoned he was under the devil's protection.

Oh, he was a mean one all right. They say he'd as soon shoot you as look at you. Of course I didn't know him back then. I wasn't even born until long after, but sometimes when he was in his cups he'd get to talking about the war, and the tales he'd tell would curl your hair. People said the stories he told in his dotage won't nothing compared to how he had been when she was still alive.

Her. His first wife. Malinda Pritchard. She died a year or so before he married up with me, and she was close on seventy herself. My people said there won't no point in me being jealous of an old lady like that, but I knew better. He was like a lamp with the flame blowed out after she went.

In 1903, that was. She made it over the line into the new century before her heart give out. There'd been folks around here surprised to know she had one. Tough as a banty rooster, she always was, but beautiful—even old, she was beautiful, with good strong cheekbones and eyes that could bore right through you.

He was lost without her.

People said he only took up with me because he needed a nursemaid after she passed, him being so old and all. And they said I only married up with him on account of his army pension. When the baby son was born, it stopped a lot of tongues from wagging, but that don't mean there hadn't been any truth to it.

I was his wife right enough, but I never took her place. I wouldn't have it said, but I knowed it well enough.

I told myself that I wouldn't have wanted to, for I had heard the tales about her riding and shooting and dressing like a boy. Sleeping rough on the mountain with a bunch of soldiers, and stealing food from their neighbors at gunpoint during the war. I did not aspire to be that kind of a help-meet, and Old McKesson might put the blame on me for his life turning tame and tedious, but the truth was, he won't up to it no more his own self. He was old and tired. His head hurt, and his war wounds ached, and his strength was ebbing with age, but he never wanted to own up to that.

I won't the replacement for that Sarah M. Blalock, wife of, what is buried on a hill on the road to Newland, and I don't think she'd say I took her husband neither. She was married to a handsome young daredevil named Keith, who fought six counties out of sheer contrariness for what he believed in. He was her husband and her commanding officer. Fifty years on, I married a spiteful, ailing old devil called McKesson Blalock, who was older than my granddaddy. It won't the same. Wish I'd of knowed him back then, but he wouldn't have looked twice at me back then. Nor ever while she walked.

I don't know what he was doing out there on the railroad. He'd come and go without a by-your-leave to me. Them that found him said he had got hold of a handcar that the railroad had for the workmen to go up and down the tracks on. He had no business to be riding it, I do know that, but when did that ever stop him?

He probably wanted to get somewhere in a hurry, so he latched on to that handcar and went pumping along the tracks without a thought to the rights of it—or the danger. He had made it up the grade—on his good days he was stronger than some men are at twenty—and then when you'd think the hard part was over, and he had only to slide down the other side, disaster overtook him. The contraption got to going too fast and when it hit the curves, the tracks turned but the handcar kept going in a straight line, and he went over the side, crashing into the rocks and bushes down below, the machine on top of him.

So the railroad did what the Confederates did not. Stopped Keith Blalock in his tracks.

A lot of folks came to the burying. Some of them to make sure he was dead, I reckon. We laid him up on the hill next to her, and folks patted my hand and wished me well, and preacher said, "There, there, Martha Jane. You will see him in heaven, you know."

But I don't believe that.

He'll have gone off with her afore I ever get there.

Author's Note

During the Civil War in the Appalachian Mountains, the wrong side was to take a side. Everybody suffered, no matter which cause they supported. It was a tragic time in a wild and unforgiving place, and I have tried to capture that spirit in this novel. In Appalachia the war was farm-to-farm, neighbor-to-neighbor, up close and personal, and when your kinfolk were killed or your livestock stolen, you knew exactly who did it—by sight and by name. This made the conflict more like Bosnia and less like, say, World War II. When you know exactly which person to blame, it is hard to forgive and forget just because a peace treaty has been signed in some far-off place by people you've never seen. From this sectional guerrilla warfare came the feuds of the late nineteenth century, like the Hatfields and the McCoys, who were on opposite sides of the war and whose bitterness survived long after Appomattox. As Malinda Blalock says in the novel, "Wars are easier to start than they are to stop."

The history portion of this book is as true as I could make it, given all the wrangling about every single fact, but everyone agrees on the salient points: The mountain South was divided house-to-house in its allegiance, dividing communities and turning neighbors into enemies. The Shelton Laurel killings happened just as described, as did the activities of the Union bushwhackers.

I could not resist including photographs of the two principal characters in this novel. Zebulon Vance and Malinda Blalock were real people, and I have tried to render them as faithfully as I could in word and deed.

No one from North Carolina needs to be told that Zebulon Baird Vance was a real person. His legend still looms large after more than a century, and his charm makes itself felt even through the musty reference books through which I tracked him. Most of the anecdotes told about him in this novel were related by him in speeches during his lifetime. Zeb Vance was indeed the colonel who sent "Sam" Blalock home in 1862, and he was the lawyer who defended the legendary Tom Dooley in the murder trial.

Keith and Malinda Blalock are also depicted as accurately as I could manage at a remove of a hundred and fifty years, considering all the conflicting reports about them and their adventures. I have visited their graves on that hilltop on the road to Newland, and I can imagine how irate Keith would be to find that his headstone identifies him as a Confederate veteran. (A Confederate organization erected the monument.)

Now I realize that some people's greatest joy in reading is to try to find mistakes in the text and to argue with the author about it. My favorite so far has been the Texas gentleman who tried to tell me how they pronounce "Arrowood" in east Tennessee, unaware that "Arrowood" was the name of my east Tennessee grandparents. You can indulge in this pastime if it amuses you, but please leave me out of it. I checked every source I could find about everything and then I had a number of Civil War historians vet the manuscript. Your point of view on any given fact may be one that we considered and ultimately chose not to believe.

My thanks to Michael and Elizabeth Hardy, Jane Hicks, Charlotte Ross, Charles F. Price, Tom Perry, Rob Neufeld, and to all the librarians and booksellers who have helped me try to piece together this quilt of words.

A bibliography is appended at the end of this passage for those who want to read more about the Appalachian aspect of the war. One of the best and most concise histories of the mountain war is *Bushwhackers* by William Trotter (John F. Blair Press, Winston-Salem N.C.), a wonderful overview of the Civil War in the mountains. When other modern historians differed from Trotter's account of an incident, I generally decided to trust Trotter's version, and I recommend his book to anyone who wants more information on the subject. There are many contradictions in the records of the war in that remote region, where even the railroads did not go until the 1880s. I had to keep reminding myself that history is simply what people write down, and they may indeed be fallible or even mendacious, but I thought that it was worth reminding people that war sometimes seems to take on a life of its own and that hatred has a half-life.

Bibliography

Arthur, John P. *A History of Watauga County, North Carolina.* Boone, NC, privately printed 1915. Rpt: Johnson City, TN: The Overmountain Press, 1992.

Arthur, John P. *Western North Carolina: A History.* Rpt: Johnson City, TN: The Overmountain Press, 1996.

Bailey, Lloyd R., ed. *The Heritage of the Toe River Valley, Volume I.* Marceline, MO: Walsworth Publishing Co., 1994.

Bumgarner, Matthew. *Kirk's Raiders, a Notorious Band of Scoundrels and Thieves.* Shelby, NC: Westmoreland Printers, Inc., 2000.

Cannon, Elizabeth R. *My Beloved Zebulon: The Correspondence of Zebulon Baird Vance and Harriett Newell Espy.* Chapel Hill, NC: The University of North Carolina Press, 1971.

Crow, Vernon H. *Storm in the Mountains.* Cherokee, NC: Press of the Museum of the Cherokee Indian, 1982.

Dowd, Clement. *Life of Zebulon B. Vance.* Charlotte, NC: Observer Printing and Publishing House, 1897.

Dugger, Shepherd M. *The War Trails of the Blue Ridge.*

Banner Elk, Shepherd M. Dugger 1932. Rpt: Banner Elk NC: Puddingstone Press, 1974.

Ellis, Daniel. *Thrilling Adventures of Daniel Ellis.* Harper Brothers, 1867. Rpt: Johnson City, TN: The Overmountain Press, 1989.

Garrison, Webb. *A Treasury of Civil War Tales.* New York: Ballantine, 1988.

Inscoe, John G. and Gordon B. McKinney. *The Heart of Confederate Appalachia: Western North Carolina in the Civil War.* Chapel Hill, NC: The University of North Carolina Press, 2000.

Johnston, Frontis W., ed. *Zebulon B. Vance Letters.* Raleigh, NC: State Department of Archives and History, 1963.

Judd, Cameron. *The Bridge Burners: A True Adventure of East Tennessee's Underground Civil War.* Johnson City, TN: The Overmountain Press, 1995.

Killian, Ron V. *A History of the North Carolina Third Mounted Infantry Volunteers, USA, March 1864 to August 1865.* Bowie, MD: Heritage Books, Inc., 2000.

McWhiney, Grady and Perry Jamieson. *Attack and Die: Civil War Military Tactics and the Southern Heritage.* Tuscaloosa: University of Alabama Press, 1982.

Merrimon, Jas., ed. *Augustus Summerfield Merrimon, A Memoir.* Privately published.

Miller, Harvey L. *News From Pigeon Roost.* Greenmountain, NC: The Foxfire Press, 1974.

Mobley, Joe A., ed. *The Papers of Zebulon Vance, Volume Two 1863.* Raleigh, NC: Division of Archives and History, North Carolina Department of Cultural Resources, 1995.

van Noppen, Ina W. *Stoneman's Last Raid.* Raleigh, NC: North Carolina State University Print Shop, 1966.

Paludan, Phillip S. *Victims: A True Story of the Civil War.* Knoxville, TN: The University of Tennessee Press, 1981.

Robertson Jr., James I. *Soldiers Blue and Gray.* Columbia, SC: University of South Carolina Press, 1988.

Sakowski, Carolyn. *Touring the East Tennessee Back-roads.* Winston-Salem, NC: John F. Blair, Publisher, 1993.

Sakowski, Carolyn. *Touring the Western North Carolina Backroads.* Winston-Salem, NC: John F. Blair, Publisher, 1990.

Scott, Robert N., ed. *The War of the Rebellion: A Compilation of the Official Records of the Union and Confederate Armies, Series I, Volume XXX, Part III.* Washington, D.C.: Government Printing Office, 1890.

Scott, Robert N., ed. *The War of the Rebellion: A Compilation of the Official Records of the Union and Confederate Armies, Series I, Volume XXX, Part IV.* Washington, D.C.: Government Printing Office, 1890.

Spencer, Cornelia P. *The Last Ninety Days of the War in North Carolina.* New York: Watchman, 1866. Rpt: Wilmington, NC: Broadfoot Publishing Co., 1993.

Stevens, Peter F. *Rebels in Blue: The Story of Keith and Malinda Blalock.* Dallas, TX: Taylor Publishing Company, 2000.

Stoops, Martha. *The Heritage: The Education of Women at St. Mary's College, Raleigh, North Carolina 1842–1982.* Raleigh, NC: Saint Mary's Press, 1984.

Tatum, Georgia L. *Disloyalty in the Confederacy.* Lincoln, NB: University of Nebraska Press, 2000.

Temple, Oliver P. *East Tennessee and the Civil War.* Cincinnati, OH: The Robert Clarke Company, 1899.

Tessier, Mitzi S. *Asheville: A Pictorial History.* Virginia Beach, VA: The Donning Company/Publishers, 1982.

Triebert, Russell and Marjorie and Conyers Ervin. ed. *Burke County Heritage—North Carolina.* Morganton, NC: Burke County Historical Society, 1981.

Trotter, William R. *Bushwackers: The Civil War in the North Carolina Mountains.* Winston-Salem, NC: John F. Blair, Publisher, 1988.

West, John F. *Lift Up Your Head Tom Dooley.* Asheboro, NC: Down Home Press, 1993.

NOW AVAILABLE IN PAPERBACK

NEW YORK TIMES BESTSELLING AUTHOR

SHARYN McCRUMB

The Songcatcher

A Novel

SIGNET

New York Times
bestselling author
SHARYN McCRUMB

THE BALLAD OF FRANKIE SILVER   0-451-19739-9

A career lawman will bear witness to the final judgement, as a man he put away twenty years ago is about to be executed for the brutal slaying of two hikers. However, his conscience is no longer clear to the point of absolute certainty about the man's guilt. When he notices the parallels between this case and one from 100 years earlier, he finds himself in a race against and across time to see that history doesn't repeat itself.

"A NOVEL OF MESMERIZING BEAUTY AND POWER."

—RICHMOND TIMES-DISPATCH

THE ROSEWOOD CASKET   0-451-18471-8

A dying man's sons are gathering at his deathbed, but so is a local real estate developer hungering for the family farm. The old man's death will involve generations in a time-honored tradition and in a battle in which dark secrets of the past will unfold.

"SUSPENSEFUL...SPELLBINDING."   —WASHINGTON POST BOOK WORLD

SHE WALKS THESE HILLS   0-451-18472-6

Applying her psychic talents to two mysterious cases, police-woman Martha Ayers attempts to settle local superstitions about a two-hundred-year-old ghost while tracking down an escaped prisoner.

"LYRICALLY WRITTEN, EMOTIONALLY DISCHARGED."

—SAN DIEGO UNION-TRIBUNE

To order call: 1-800-788-6262

S440/McCrumb